THE SACRED CUT

DAVID HEWSON

This title first published in Great Britain in 2005 by Macmillan.

eBook edition published 2018 by
Severn House Publishers Ltd.

Trade paperback edition first published 2019
in Great Britain and the USA by
SEVERN HOUSE PUBLISHERS LTD
Eardley House, 4 Uxbridge Street, London W8 7SY

ISBN-13: 978-1-84751-952-8 (trade paper)
ISBN-13: 978-1-4483-0152-2 (e-book)

All Severn House titles are printed on acid-free paper.

Severn House Publishers support the Forest Stewardship Council™ [FSC™],
the leading international forest certification organisation.
All our titles that are printed on FSC certified paper carry the FSC logo.

Printed and bound in Great Britain by
TJ International, Padstow, Cornwall.

THE SACRED CUT

A Selection of Recent Titles by David Hewson

The Nic Costa Series

A SEASON FOR THE DEAD *
THE VILLA OF MYSTERIES *
THE SACRED CUT *
THE LIZARD'S BITE
THE SEVENTH SACRAMENT
THE GARDEN OF EVIL
DANTE'S NUMBERS
THE BLUE DEMON
THE FALLEN ANGEL
THE SAVAGE SHORE *

Other Novels

CARNIVAL OF DEATH
THE FLOOD *
JULIET AND ROMEO
DEVIL'S FJORD *

* *available from Severn House*

PROLOGUE

It was nine months now since she'd slipped out of Iraq, six hundred dollars in her pocket, knowing instinctively what she needed: men who owned boats and trucks, men who knew the way to places she'd only dimly heard of and who could take a little human contraband there for the right price. There'd been no work, no money at home, not since Saddam's soldiers came from Baghdad and took her father away, leaving them alone together in the damp, cold shack that passed as a farm, with its dying crops, wilting under the oil smoke of the fields outside Kirkuk.

She'd watched the dry, dusty lane that led to their home every day for hours, waiting for him to come back, wondering when she'd hear that strong, confident adult voice again, bringing hope and security into their lives. It never happened. Instead, her mother went slowly crazy as the hope ran out, wailing at the open door for hours on end, not cleaning anything, not even talking after a while.

No one liked crazy people. No one liked the decisions they forced on others. One day a distant relative came and took both of them away, drove them for hours in a cart behind an old, stumbling donkey, then left them with an old aunt on the other side of the plumes of smoke. Just another tin shack, no money, too many mouths to feed. Her mother was completely silent after that, spent hours with her arms wrapped around herself, rocking constantly. No one talked to them much either. They only took her to school every other day: there was too much work to be done trying to dig a living out of the desiccated fields. Then soldiers came and the school closed for good. She'd watched as boxes of shells got shifted into the classrooms and wondered how she was supposed to learn anything ever again.

Over all their lives now, bigger than the oil cloud and blacker too, hung the threat of war. The family men said there'd been one before, when she was tiny. But this war would be different. This one would end matters, once and for all, make the Kurds free forever in a new kind of Iraq. They told a lot of lies. Either that or they just got things wrong. Men were stupid sometimes, anyway.

It was February when the soldiers came to occupy the farm. They were Iraqis. They behaved the way Iraqi soldiers did around Kurds. When they wanted something to eat, they came into the house and took it. When they wanted other comforts, other services, they took them too. She was scared. She was full of an internal fury too real and violent to share. She wanted to escape from this place, go somewhere new, anywhere, so long as it was in the West, where life was easier. There was no point in staying. There'd been gossip when they'd tried to sell what little produce they had in the neighbouring village one morning. About how the Iraqis killed the Kurdish men they took, put them down like animals. These whispered tales of horror turned a key in her head. Her father was dead. She'd never hear the comforting boom of his voice again. She understood now why her mother had retreated to some inner hell where no one could reach her.

So throughout each long day, as it became more and more dangerous to travel, she sat in the corner of the squalid little shack and listened to the frightened talk around her. About death and war and uncertainty, and always, always, how more soldiers would come. Peshmurga. Americans. British. Men who would, she knew, look much the same as the Iraqis when she stared into their eyes. They would sound different, wear different uniforms, but they were just men, mortal men, bringing death and chaos along with them, invisible, ghostly comrades riding in the dun-coloured jeeps.

It happened on a cold, clear April day. The Iraqis had made themselves a position next to the dank waters of the dead fish pond, by the puny patch of feeble squash plants, blackened by oil smog, at the end of their lane. Five men and a big gun pointed at the sky. They were worse than most: vicious, foul-mouthed, dangerous. Scared men, too, and she knew why. They had just the one shell, nothing more. They were sitting there, wondering how to give themselves up before the Americans came and killed them.

In the middle of the afternoon she'd watched as an ugly dark plane circled the farm, like an old metal bird wondering where to lay down its feet. She'd felt nothing, not even fear for herself. She'd stood outside the shack, ignoring the screams from behind ordering her to hide, watching the fire streak from the black bird's belly, race through the beautiful blue sky and wrap itself around the upright cylinder of the gun before the Iraqis even had a chance to spit back their single shell.

It sent the soldiers screaming out of their sandbagged home, flames licking at their contorted bodies. She wanted to see more, wanted to make sure this memory stayed with her because it was important. So she walked closer, hid in the stinking outside toilet, looking on through the battered palm thatching as they danced and rolled on the ground.

Even now, nearly a year on, she remembered what she'd thought at that moment. The sight reminded her of the travelling troupe of clowns who used to come through the village from time to time, back when her father was alive. He always took her. One of her earliest memories was of being in his arms, watching them, almost hysterical with laughter. Even so, she was aware that there was something wrong when they returned again and again, something cruel in their humour, in the way it exaggerated the stupidity and pain of existence and invited their audience to be amused by it. She had thought about laughing at the soldiers trying to save themselves from the flames that fought to consume their bodies. There were plenty of reasons to. The Kurds hated the Iraqis. The Iraqis hated the Kurds. Everyone hated the Americans. It was a world defined by hatred and perhaps that was, in the end, why people laughed at all, because it made the pain go away, if only for a little while.

But she didn't have the time to stare at them, try to find some amusement in their throes. At that moment Laila was thinking of herself, sure that hatred was a luxury she'd have to save for later. Somewhere here there had to be the chance of escape. Of fleeing this dying, parched land where there was nothing left for her any more, no love and no hope.

When the flames died down she walked over to the men. They were dead, contorted husks now, partly charred by the fire that had spat at them from the sky. Except for one. He clung on doggedly, trying to breathe through cracked, ruined lips, each attempt coming with pained effort. She thought he wouldn't last much longer. So she slid her hand inside his jacket, staring all the time into his bright, frightened eyes. He mumbled something, a familiar insult, something about thieving Kurds. Then she found the envelope and he started to sob like a child.

This shocked her. She'd stared at him, affronted, and spoke in good Arabic, since she made a point of learning as many languages as possible in the old school which was now gone, books replaced by munitions boxes. 'You should go to God like a man. Not a child.'

Then she took everything she could from him, documents, coins, a pen, a watch, reasoning they would do a dead man no good anyway, and that a world in this condition could scarcely condemn a petty thief.

He must have been rich. Maybe a member of the party. He had close to $1,500 in mixed notes in an envelope. When she checked the other corpses, carefully prising away the burnt uniforms from the flesh beneath, she found more. Some were charred but they were dollars, the magical currency, and you could buy things just by waving the curled, brown sheets at someone. A man at a border post, say. Or the village elder – and there always was one – who knew the way out, the way West, where the rich people lived.

*

She was down to three hundred dollars by the time she got to Istanbul two weeks later. It was a strange and beautiful place, one that scared her because of the hard way people looked into her face whenever she begged in the street.

Most of the remaining money disappeared with the series of random trucks she took through Greece then along the Adriatic coast, through Albania, Montenegro and Croatia, past a shining spring sea, past lush green fields of vines and vegetables. And wrecked buildings slowly being brought back to life. She could speak a little Italian. It was the one European language the school had taught simply because it was the only one for which they had the books. She loved the sound, too, and the pictures on the pages, of a distant city where the streets and squares had beautiful names, beautiful buildings.

The locals on the coast knew Italian. It was a language from the West, worth understanding in the hope its good fortune might touch you one day. She talked to them a little, knew the signs, understood the looks in some of the old men's faces. There'd been a war here as well.

She gave the last hundred dollars to a burly German, who drove her over the border into Italy at Trieste, and left her, two days later, penniless, on the outskirts of Rome.

The money hadn't covered everything. Somewhere along the way – she wasn't sure of the day, it hadn't seemed important to keep track of the time – she'd turned thirteen. She knew about ways to keep men happy, and tried to tell herself it was easy when you lay there to think of something else: poppies waving in the yellow corn, bread baking over burning wood, pictures of the unknown city now a few kilometres away, with its lovely buildings, its wealth, its promise of safety and happiness. And the sound of her father's voice, singing in the fields. That was the warmest memory, one that she prayed would never disappear.

And when it was over, when he'd let her out of the cab on some grim housing estate in the suburbs, a place of dark, threatening streets, – nothing like the Rome she'd imagined – she'd made a decision. Stealing was better than this. Stealing allowed her a little personal dignity. It would keep her alive until . . . what?

Back on that warm day in early summer she hadn't known the answer. Now, in December, with the city shivering under a vicious and unexpected burst of snow, she was no closer to it. Each day was a new battle fought using the same weapons: keen eyes, agile hands. The charities had thrown her out for stealing. The street people rejected her because she wouldn't stoop to the tricks they used – selling themselves, selling dope. She was a world away from a home that no longer existed, alone in an empty piazza in the heart of Rome, looking at something that could only be a temple, one almost as old as some of those back in the place she now struggled to think of as home.

She'd followed the man all the way from the narrow street near the Spanish Steps, after she saw him leave a doorway next to a small store selling Gucci. He looked interesting somehow. The right type. So she'd followed him, and it wasn't easy. He kept ducking out of the way as if he was hiding too. Then she lost him again, turned the corner, found herself in the square. The temple was a kind of sanctuary, she thought.

The girl stared at the huge doors shut tightly against the freezing blast and wondered what the place was like inside.

A sanctuary could be warm. It could have something to steal.

She walked along to the side of the building, under the shadow of the gigantic pillars and the curious writing above them, down a low path towards the light in a narrow side entrance.

The door was just ajar. Snow was dancing around her like a wraith caught in the hushed breath of a newborn storm. She walked into a small, modern cubicle, which led into the dark, airy interior beyond, hearing voices. A man and a woman, foreign, American probably, were making sounds she didn't quite understand.

She was cold. She was curious. She slunk into the shadows, somewhat in awe of the building's size and majesty, slid behind a fluted column, then let her eyes adjust to the scene in the centre, lit by the moon falling through a giant, open disc at the focal point of the roof.

Close by, thrown on a bench, lay a man's coat and jacket. They looked good quality. There could be any amount of money in there, enough to see her through until the snow disappeared.

The two people inside were some distance away. The woman's clothes were strewn across the geometric stone pattern of the floor. She lay naked in the very centre of the hall. Quite still now, her arms and legs outstretched in an odd, artificial manner, as if each limb were pointing to an invisible angle somewhere in the circular building.

THE SACRED CUT

It was wrong to watch. Laila understood that, but her mind fought to interpret what was happening in front of her in the icy, airy heart of this strange, dead place. She thought she had seen everything the world had to offer back in Iraq. Then something caught the moonlight. Something sharp and silver and terrifying, a slender line of surgical metal, hovering over the figure on the floor. And she knew she was mistaken.

MERCOLEDÌ

The two plain clothes cops huddled in the doorway of a closed farmacia in Via del Corso, shivering, teeth chattering, watching Mauro Sandri, the fat little photographer from Milan, fumble with the two big Nikon SLRs dangling round his neck. It was five days before Christmas and for once Rome was enjoying snow, real snow, deep and crisp and even, the kind you normally only saw on the TV when some snap blizzard engulfed those poor miserable bastards living in the north.

It fell from the black sky as a perfect, silky cloud. Thick flakes curled around the gaudy coloured lights of the street decorations in a soft, white embrace. The pavements already owned a crunchy, shoe-deep covering in spite of the milling crowds who had pounded the Corso's black stones a few hours earlier, searching for last-minute presents in the stores.

Nic Costa and Gianni Peroni had read the met briefing before they went on duty that evening. They'd looked at the words 'severe weather warning' and tried to remember what that meant. Floods maybe. Gales that brought down some of the ancient tiles which sat so unsteadily on the rooftops of the centro storico, the warren of streets and alleys in the city's Renaissance quarter where they spent most of their working lives. But this was different. The met men said it would snow and snow and snow. Snow in a way it hadn't for almost twenty years, since the last big freeze in 1985. Only for longer this time, a week or more. And the temperatures would hit new lows too. Maybe it was global warming. Maybe it was just a trick throw of the meteorological dice. Whatever, the world was about to become seriously out of sync for a little while and that knowledge, shared among the two and a half million or more individuals who lived within the boundaries of the Comune di Roma, was both scary and tantalizing. The city was braced for its first white Christmas in living memory and already the consequences of this were beginning to seep into the Roman consciousness. People were preparing to bunk off work for any number of sound and incontrovertible reasons. They'd picked up the throat bug that was creeping through the city. They couldn't take the buses in from the suburbs because, even if they made it through the dangerous, icy streets, who knew if they'd get back in the evening? Life was, for once, just too perilous to do anything but stay at home, or maybe wander down to the local bar and talk about nothing except the weather.

And they were all, librarian and shop assistant, waiter and tour guide, priest and shivering cop, thinking secretly: *This is wonderful.* Because for once Christmas would be a holiday. For once the city would step off the constantly moving escalator of modern life, remember to take a deep breath, close its eyes and sleep a little, all under that gorgeous, ermine coverlet that kept falling in a constant white cloud, turning the black stones of the empty streets to the colour of icing sugar.

Peroni glanced at his partner, an expression Costa now recognized, one that said: *watch this*. Then the big cop from Tuscany walked over and threw an arm around Sandri, squeezing him hard.

'Hey, Mauro,' he growled, and crushed the photographer one more time before letting go. 'Your fingers are frozen stiff. It's pitch dark here with nothing to look at but snow. Why don't you quit taking photos for a while? You must've done a couple of hundred today already. Relax. We could go someplace warm. Come on. Even you clever guys could handle a caffè corretto on a night like this.'

The photographer's round, bulbous eyes blinked back at them suspiciously. He flexed his shoulders, maybe to shrug off the cold, maybe to get back some feeling after experiencing Peroni's muscular grip.

'This would be a duty break, right? I can still shoot if I want to?'

Nic Costa listened to Sandri's squeaky northern tones, sighed and put a restraining hand on his partner's arm, worried that Peroni's temper just might take a turn in the wrong direction. The photographer had been doing the rounds of the Questura all month. He was a nice enough guy, an arty type who'd been given some kind of government grant to create a documentary record of the station's work. He'd photographed all manner of people: traffic cops and forensic, the lunatics from the morgue, the paper-monkeys in clerical. Costa had seen some of his work already: a set of moody monochrome prints of the warders working the cells. They weren't half bad. And he had noted the man's steady progress around the station, understanding the greedy, interested gaze Sandri gave him and Peroni every time they crossed his path. Mauro was a photographer. He thought in visual terms, nothing much else in all probability. He must have looked at Nic Costa, small, slight, young, like an athlete who'd somehow quit the track, set him, in his mind, against the big, bulking frame of his partner, more than twenty years older and with an ugly, violently disfigured face no one ever forgot, and felt his shutter finger start to itch.

Gianni Peroni surely knew that too. He was used to sideways glances, for his looks and his history. He'd been inspector in vice for years until, almost a year before, he'd been busted down to the ranks for one simple slip-up, when he'd tasted the goods he was supposed to be investigating. All for a private, internalized reason he'd later shared with one person only, the partner who pounded the street alongside him. That didn't stop an intelligent man, one who could read an expression even on Peroni's battered features, seeing the two of them together and understanding there was a story there. It was inevitable that Sandri would pick them as his subject one day. Inevitable, too, that Gianni Peroni would see it as a challenge to ride the photographer a touch hard along the way.

'You can still shoot, Mauro,' Costa said and caught a glimpse of a resentful twinkle in Peroni's bright, beady eye.

He took his partner's arm again and whispered, 'They're just pictures, Gianni. You know the great thing about pictures?'

'Tell me, Professor,' Peroni murmured, watching

Sandri struggle to work another 35 mm cassette into his Nikon.

'They only show what's on the surface. The rest you make up. You write your own story. You imagine your own beginning and your own ending. They're fiction pretending to be truth.'

Peroni nodded. He wasn't his normal self just then, Costa thought. There were dark, complex thoughts rumbling around deep inside a head that temperamentally liked to avoid such places.

'Maybe. But does this particular fiction have a caffè corretto inside it?'

Costa coughed into a gloved hand and stamped his feet, thinking about the taste of a big slug of grappa hidden inside a double espresso and how little activity there could be on a night such as this, when even the most crooked Roman hoods would surely be thinking of nothing but a warm bed.

'I believe it does,' he answered, and scanned the deserted street, where just a single 62 bus was now struggling down the centreline at a snail's pace, trying to keep from slipping into the gutter.

Costa stepped out from the shelter of the doorway, pulling the collar of his thick black coat up into his neck, shielding his eyes from the blizzard with a frozen hand, then darted into an alley, towards the distant yellow light struggling from the tiny doorway of what he guessed just might be the last bar open in Rome.

There proved to be the only three customers in the tiny café down the alley beyond the Galleria Doria Pamphili, among the dark tangle of ancient streets that ran west towards the Pantheon and Piazza Navona. Now Costa stood with Gianni Peroni at one end of the counter, trying to calm down the big man before something untoward happened. Mauro Sandri was crouched on a stool a good distance away, concentrating hard on polishing the lenses on his damn cameras, not even touching the booze-rich caffè Peroni had bought him before war broke out.

The owner, a tall, skeletal man in his fifties, with a white nylon jacket, scrappy brown moustache and brushed-back greased grey hair, looked at the three of them in turn and declared very firmly, 'Were this up to me, I'd slap the guy around a little, Officer. I mean, you got to have limitations. There's public places and there's private places. If a man can't get a little peace and quiet when he wanders into the pisser and gets his cazzo out, what's this world coming to? That's what I want to know. That and when you people are getting the hell out of here. If you weren't police I'd be closed already. A man don't pay the mortgage selling three coffees in an hour, and I don't see anyone else showing up for this party either.'

He was right. Costa had seen just a couple of figures scurrying through the snow when they trudged to the bar. Now it was just solid white beyond the door. Anyone with sense was, surely, snug at home, swearing not to set foot outside until the blizzard ended and some sunlight turned up to disclose what Rome looked like after an extraordinary night like this.

Gianni Peroni had downed his coffee and added an extra grappa on top, which was unlike the man. He sat hunched on an ancient rickety stool, designed to be as uncomfortable as possible so no one lingered, staring mutely at the bottles behind the bar. It wasn't Sandri's stupid trick with the camera that had caused this. Costa knew that all along. Trying to get a picture of Peroni taking a piss – vérité was what Mauro had called it – was just the final straw that had pushed the big man over the edge.

They'd discussed this already earlier that evening when Costa had quietly asked if everything was OK. It all came out in a rush. What was really bugging Peroni was the fact he wouldn't see his kids this Christmas, for the first time ever.

'I'll get Mauro to apologize,' Costa said now. 'He didn't mean anything, Gianni. You had the measure of the guy straight away. He just does this, all the time. Taking pictures.'

Besides, Costa thought, it could have been quite something too. He could easily imagine a grainy black-and-white shot of Peroni's hulking form, shot from the back, shrinking into the corner of the bar's grubby urinal, looking like an out-take from some fifties shoot in Paris by Cartier-Bresson. Sandri had an eye for a picture. Costa half blamed himself. When Peroni dashed for the toilet door and Sandri's eyes lit up, he should surely have seen what was coming.

'I've bought all the presents, Nic,' Peroni moaned, those piggy eyes twinkling back at him, the scarred face full of guilt and pain. 'How the hell do I get them to Siena now with this shitty weather everywhere? What are they going to think of me, on top of everything else?'

'Phone them. They know what it's like here. They'll understand.'

'They will?' Peroni snapped. 'What the fuck do you know about kids, huh?'

Costa took his hand off Peroni's huge, hunched shoulder, shrugged and said nothing. Peroni had two children: a girl of thirteen, a boy of eleven. He never seemed to be able to think of them as anything but helpless infants. It was one of the traits Costa admired in his partner. To the world he looked like a bruised, scarred thug, the last kind of man anyone would want to meet on a dark night. And it was all an act. Underneath Peroni was just a straightforward, honest, old-fashioned family man, one who'd stepped out of line once and paid the heaviest price.

'Oh, crap.' Peroni sighed. 'I'm sorry. I didn't mean it. I don't want to lash out at you. I don't even want to lash out at Mauro over there.'

'That's good to know,' Costa replied, then added, 'if there's anything I can do . . .'

'Such as what?' Peroni asked.

'It's an expression, Gianni. It's a way a friend has of saying, "No, I haven't the first idea how I can help, and the truth is I probably can't do a thing. But if I could, I would." Understood?'

A low, croaking snort of semi-amusement escaped Peroni's throat. 'OK, OK. I am contrite. I repent my sins.' His scarred face screwed up with distaste aimed, it seemed to Costa, somewhere deep inside himself. 'Some more than others.'

Then he shot a vicious look at Sandri, huddled over the Nikons. 'I want that film, though. I'm not having my pecker pasted all over the notice board for everyone to see. They told the guy he could follow us around and take pictures. They didn't say he could walk straight after us into the pisser.'

'Mauro says there's really nothing there. People wouldn't even see it was you. And maybe it's a good picture, Gianni. Think of it.'

The battered face wrinkled into a set expression of scepticism. 'It's a picture of a man taking a piss. Not the *Mona Lisa*.'

Costa had tried to talk art to Peroni before. It didn't work. Peroni was irretrievably romantic at heart, still stuck on the idea of beauty. Truth came somewhere far behind. And it occurred to Costa too that maybe there was more to the big man's misery then the genuine distress he felt at being separated from his kids. There was also the matter of the relationship he had struck up with Teresa Lupo, the pathologist working at the police morgue. It was meant to be a secret, but secrets never really stayed hidden for long inside the Questura. Peroni was dating the likeable, wayward Teresa and it was common knowledge. When Costa found out, a couple of weeks before, he had thought long and hard about it and had come to the conclusion that they might, just, make a good couple. If Peroni could swallow down his guilt. If Teresa could keep her life straight for long enough to make things work once the initial flush of mad enthusiasm that came with any affair subsided into the routine of everyday existence.

'Gimme a cappuccino,' Costa said to the barman. 'It's going to be a long, cold night out there.'

There was a howl of protest from behind the counter. 'It's nearly twelve, for God's sake. What am I running here? A soup kitchen for cops?'

'Gimme one too,' Sandri said from the other end of

the bar, pushing away his cold corretto. 'Get one for all of us. I'm paying.'

Then the photographer walked over, looked Peroni in the eye and placed a 35 mm film cassette in his hand.

'I'm sorry,' he said. 'Really. I shouldn't have done it like that. It's just . . .'

Peroni waited for an explanation. When it didn't come, he asked, 'Just what?'

'I knew you'd have said no. I apologize, OK? I was wrong. But you have to understand this, Peroni. If a man like me had to ask every time he took a photograph, there'd hardly be any pictures in the world. All those ones you remember. All those ones you think are important. They came from some guy with a camera who pointed the stupid thing while no one was really taking any notice and went . . . pop. Improvisation. Speed. That's what this job's all about. Stealing other people's moments.'

Peroni looked him up and down and considered this.

'A little like your job, huh?' Sandri said.

The barman slid three coffees down the counter, spilling milk and foam everywhere.

'Listen, assholes, this is the last,' he snarled. 'Do you think you could possibly just pay for them then go steal a few moments some place else, huh? I'd like to go to bed and count the seven and a bit euros I earned tonight. And I got to open those doors at six thirty tomorrow morning, not that anyone's going to be walking through them.'

Costa had downed one mouthful of hot, milky coffee and foam when the radio went. Peroni was looking at him hungrily as he took the call. They had to get out of the bar, they had to find something to do. If they stayed any longer, they'd never leave.

'Burglar alarm,' Costa said when he'd listened to the message from the control room. 'The Pantheon. We're the closest.'

'Ooh,' Peroni cooed. 'A burglar alarm. Did you hear that, Mauro? Maybe we've got some wild action after all. Maybe all those bums who hang around there fleecing the tourists are breaking in, looking for somewhere warm to spend the night.'

'Damn stupid thing to do if they are,' Sandri said immediately, looking puzzled.

'In weather like this?' Peroni asked.

'It's got a hole in the roof the size of a swimming pool,' Sandri replied. 'The oculus. Remember? It's going to be as cold in there as it is outside. Colder even. Like a freezer. And nothing to steal either, not unless you can remove a few marble tombs without someone noticing.'

Peroni gave him a friendly slap on the shoulder. Not too hard this time. 'You know for a guy who talks art you're OK really, Mauro. You can take pictures of me all you want. Outside the crapper.' Then he gave Costa a querulous look. 'Are we calling the boss? He sounded desperate.'

Costa wondered about Leo Falcone. He had made a point of insisting he could be easily disturbed. 'For a burglar alarm?'

Peroni nodded. 'Leo doesn't say those things without a reason. He wants out of that place.'

'I guess so.' Costa pulled out his phone as they walked to the door and the white world beyond, feeling somewhat uneasy that Leo Falcone was so reluctant to spend a little leisure time with his superiors. And thinking all the while too about what Mauro Sandri had said.

There was no point in anyone breaking into the Pantheon. None at all.

Leo Falcone listened to the drone of men's voices echo around the private room in Al Pompiere, the stiff, old-fashioned first-floor restaurant in the ghetto where, by tradition, they met once a year just before Christmas. Then he looked at their heavy business coats, lined up on the hangers by the wall like black, dead-animal skins, and turned his head towards the window, wishing he was somewhere – anywhere – else.

The snow was now falling in a steady, persistent stream. Falcone took his mind off the dinner for a moment and wondered what the weather meant for the days to come. He liked to work Christmas. Most divorced men did. Those without kids anyway. He'd seen the quick, internal flash of disappointment on Gianni Peroni's face earlier in the week when the new rotas had been posted, and Peroni and Costa had realized they would both be on duty over the holiday. Peroni had hoped to go home to Tuscany for a brief reunion with his estranged family. Falcone had wondered, for a moment, whether he could arrange that. Then he'd checked himself. Peroni was just another cop now. He had to live with the hours just like everyone else. That's what duty was about. That and turning out for an annual dinner with a bunch of faceless grey men from SISDE, the civilian intelligence service, men who never really said what they meant or what, in truth, they wanted.

The seating arrangements were preordained: one cop, one spook, arranged in turn around the white starched cloth and the highly polished silverware. Falcone sat at the window end of the long banqueting table next to Filippo Viale, who now smoked a cigar and clutched a glass of old chardonnay grappa as clear as water, his second of the evening. Falcone had listened to Viale's quiet, insistent voice throughout the meal, picking at the food: a deep-fried artichoke to start, a plate of rigatoni con la pajata, pasta seated beneath calf's intestines sautéed with the mother's milk still inside, then, as secondo a serving of bony lamb scottadito served alongside a head of torsello chicory stuffed with anchovies. It was the kind of food Al Pompiere was known for, and, like his dinner companion, not to Falcone's more modern taste.

Viale had been his point man with the SISDE since Falcone made inspector ten years before. In theory that meant they liaised with one another on an equal basis from time to time, when the two services needed to share information. In reality Falcone couldn't remember a single occasion on which Viale or any other of the grey men, as he thought of them, were ever of real assistance. There'd been plenty of calls from Viale, fishing for information, asking for a favour. Usually Falcone had complied because he knew what the cost of reluctance would be: a call to an appointment upstairs and an icy interrogation from his superiors, asking what the problem was. Before he was promoted, he'd thought the grey men's power was on the wane. That was in the early nineties, when the Cold War was over and terrorism seemed a thing of the past. A time of optimism, as he saw it now, when a younger Falcone, still married, still with some sense of hope, was able to believe the world was becoming a smarter place, one that grew a little wiser, a little more safe, with every passing year.

Then the circle turned again. New enemies, faceless ones with no particular flag to identify them, emerged out of nowhere. While the police and the Carabinieri struggled to hold the fort against a rising swell tide of crime using increasingly meagre and conventional resources, the funding went to the grey men, filling their coffers for operations that never came under any public scrutiny. There was a shift in the moral fulcrum. For some in government the end came to justify the means. This was, Falcone knew, the state of the world he would probably have to work with, for the rest of his professional life. That knowledge didn't make it any easier to bear. Nor was he flattered by the grey men's apparent belief that they saw something in Leo Falcone they wanted.

'Leo,' Viale said quietly, 'I have to ask. I know we've been through this before. But still . . . it puzzles me.'

'I don't want another job.' Falcone sighed, hearing a note of testiness in his voice. 'Can't we just leave it at that?'

They'd been trying to recruit him off and on for a good four years or more. Falcone was never quite certain how genuine Viale's offer was. It was a standard SISDE trick to hold out lures to men in the conventional force. It flattered them, made them feel there could be a future somewhere else if life got too difficult in the Questura.

Viale downed the grappa and ordered another. The waiter, who was handing around a very old-fashioned sponge cake as dessert, took the glass and returned with it filled immediately. Viale was a regular here, Falcone guessed. Maybe he had booked the dinner. Maybe he was the boss. SISDE officers never said much about their rank. By rights Falcone was supposed to be matched against someone near his own position in the hierarchy. He didn't know Viale well. Like so many SISDE officers, the man was infuriatingly anonymous: a dark suit, a pale, nondescript face, a head of black hair, dyed in all probability, and a demeanour that embraced many smiles and not a touch of warmth or humour. Falcone couldn't even put a finger on his age. Viale wasn't the physical type. He was of medium height, slightly built, with a distinct paunch. Yet Falcone felt sure there was something more serious about the man than he allowed. Viale didn't sit behind the same kind of desk as he did, nor did he have to tackle the same, incessant trinity of problems: detection, intelligence and resources. Viale was, somehow, a man who made his own life and there, Leo Falcone thought, was something to envy.

Viale put a slight hand on Falcone's arm and looked directly into his face. There was northern blood in him, Falcone thought. It showed in the flat, emotionless landscape of his anonymous face, and those grey-blue eyes, cold, mirthless.

'No, we can't just leave it at that, Leo. Just say yes now and I can push through the paperwork straight away. You could be sitting behind a new desk before the end of January.'

Falcone laughed and watched the snow again. It made him feel good somehow. It reminded him of his parting words to every man he'd sent out into the city that night, ordering them, for once, to disturb his private time for the slightest reason.

'I'll think about it,' Falcone replied. 'Just like last time.'

Viale cast him a vile glance and muttered a low, obscene curse. He was, Falcone realized, more than a little drunk.

'Don't fuck with me, Leo,' Viale murmured. 'Don't play games.'

'It's always been one of my rules,' Falcone answered calmly, 'not to fuck with the grey men. It's bad for your career.'

Viale snorted, then casually stuffed a piece of sponge cake into his mouth, despatching crumbs and sugar down the front of his black jacket. 'You think you're above all this, don't you? Sitting there in your grubby little office. Sending out grubby little men to chase people you probably can't put in jail anyway, even if you catch them.'

'It's a job someone's got to do,' Falcone said, then looked at his watch. It was almost midnight. Perhaps it was late enough to make a polite exit without offending anyone except Viale, who was offended enough as it was.

'It's a job?' Viale snarled. 'Jesus Christ, Leo.'

The grey man cast his eyes around the room and shook his head. Falcone did the same. Most of the individuals there were getting stinking drunk. It was tradition. It was Christmas.

Viale barked at the waiter. The man came back with a flask of grappa. Viale clutched it and poured out a couple, just for them, as if no one else in the room existed.

'This is a hundred a bottle and I'm paying,' he muttered, then nodded at the tiny window, now blocked with snow. 'Even you need something warm inside on a night like this.'

Falcone took the glass, sipped at the fiery drink then put it on the table. Spirits had never been his thing.

Viale watched him. 'You don't like joining in, do you? You think you can get through all this shit on your own, so long as your luck holds and you keep getting good marks every time they come to check the statistics. What's a man like you messing around with that crap for?'

Targets, benchmarks, goals . . . Falcone didn't like the jargon of the modern police force any more than the rest of his colleagues. But unlike most he saw a point behind the paperwork. Everyone needed some kind of standard by which their efforts could be measured internally, and publicly if need be. It was anathema to people like Viale, who could screw up for years and never get found out unless a rare, scrupulous civil servant or politician got on their back. That thought jogged a memory from somewhere, but he couldn't nail it down.

Falcone looked at his watch then pushed the glass away. The raw smell of the spirit was overwhelming. 'Say what you want to say, Filippo. It's late. I want a good night's sleep. With this weather the Questura's going to be short of people tomorrow. Maybe we'll have to help out uniform or traffic. I don't know.'

'Traffic!' Viale snapped. 'Why the hell would you want to waste your time on that?'

'I believe it's something to do with being a public servant,' Falcone replied dryly.

Viale waved the glass of clear liquid at him. 'And I'm not, huh? How do you know?'

'I don't, Filippo. That's the point.' Falcone shifted awkwardly on his seat. He didn't want to upset this man any more than he had already. Viale had influence, power over him perhaps. But he didn't want to prolong this difficult interview either. 'Shouldn't we discuss this some other time? During the day. When we both feel –' he couldn't suppress a glance at the carafe of grappa – 'more ready to talk sense.'

Viale's immobile face flushed. 'I'm amazed you think you have the time.'

Falcone remained silent, waiting for the rest.

'Think about it, Leo. You're forty-eight. Has anyone asked you to sit the commissario interview recently?'

Falcone shrugged. He hadn't even considered promotion of late. Life had been too busy.

Viale provided the answer for him, which was interesting of itself. 'Not in three years. And you haven't even asked. That looks bad.'

'Promotion's not everything,' Falcone replied, knowing his answer sounded feeble. 'Some of the most important people we have are just plain street cops who'll never move up the ladder in their lives, or expect to. Where the hell would we be without them?'

Viale leaned along the table and breathed booze fumes in his face. 'We're not talking about them. We're talking about you. A man who looked like he was going far. And now he's treading water. Worse, he's making bad decisions. Backing the wrong people.'

Falcone bristled. He'd an idea now where this was leading. 'By which you mean . . . ?'

'Shit,' the grey man hissed. 'You know damn well.

You're getting sentimental in your dotage, Leo. You're looking out for people who don't deserve it. This Peroni idiot for one thing. If it wasn't for you he'd be out of the force now and without a pension. With good reason too. Why'd anyone with any sense stick up for a guy like that?'

Falcone thought carefully before answering. 'They asked my opinion. I gave it. Peroni's a good cop, whatever happened in the past. We can't afford to lose people of that calibre.'

'He's a disaster waiting to happen. Him and that partner of his. Now don't tell me you never stuck up for him. Hell, if it wasn't for you they wouldn't even be working together.'

None of this was SISDE's business. It infuriated Falcone that he was getting a lecture on personnel issues from someone outside the force. He'd be damned if he'd listen to it from anyone inside either. Costa and Peroni were on his team. It was his call who worked with whom.

'These are two lowly cops on the street, Filippo. My problem. Not yours.'

'No. They are two time bombs waiting to destroy what's left of your career. Peroni's going to go off the rails again before long. Mark my word. And the Costa kid . . .' Viale leaned forward and said this quietly, as if it were a confidence. 'Come on, Leo. You know who his old man was? That stinking commie who caused us no end of trouble when he was alive.'

Now Falcone recalled the memory that had been eluding him. Some fifteen years earlier Costa's father, an implacably incorrupt Communist politician, had exposed a series of financial misdeeds inside both the civilian and military security services. SISDE in particular came out badly. Heads had rolled as a result. A couple of fall guys even found themselves briefly in jail.

'What on earth has that got to do with the son?' he asked.

'There's trouble in the blood,' Viale muttered. 'People like that have got ideas above their station. Be honest with yourself. You know it as well as I do.'

'These are internal police matters,' Falcone replied sharply. 'You don't have to concern yourself with our business.'

'I'm concerned with you, Leo. People are taking note. They're starting to wonder. In this business you're either moving up or moving down. No one stands still. Which way do you think you're going right now? Huh?'

He leaned close, wreathed in grappa fumes, to make sure his last point went home. 'Where I am everyone moves up. You know why? This is our world. We own it. We have the money. We have the power. We don't need to go squeaking to a committee of bureaucrats so we can use it. We don't have to worry whether some asshole of an MP is going to start shooting his mouth off in parliament about what we do. Not any more. You're a man who wants results. That's what I like about you. We've got opportunities for someone like you. Ten years down the line you're still going to be employed too. Which, given how things stand . . .'

Viale paused and, with an unsteady hand, poured the remains of Falcone's glass into his.

'. . . isn't the case where you are now. Listen to a friend, Leo. These last few years I've been offering you a job. That's not what's on the table now. I'm throwing you a lifeline. One that could pull you out of all the crap you're swimming in. Before it's too late.'

Falcone's mobile rang. He excused himself, answered it, listening carefully to the familiar voice.

'I'm needed,' he said when the call ended.

Viale's face creased in a drunken sneer, one Falcone found faintly amusing. 'What is it? Some tourist got mugged again down the Colosseum? The Kosovans getting uppity about who rules the hooker trade?'

'Not exactly,' Falcone replied, smiling, getting to his feet, reaching for his camel-hair coat, wondering whether it really would keep out the cold on such a night. 'It's much more important than that. Excuse me.'

Viale raised his glass. 'Ciao, Leo. You have until the New Year. After that you're on your own.'

They left the car where it was, tyre deep in drifting snow in a blocked dead-end off the Corso, and walked to the Piazza della Minerva through a squally wind. The weather changed by the moment. Briefly, through a clear patch high overhead, a full moon illuminated billowing banks of heavy cloud scudding over the city. The stars shone, bright and brittle in the thin winter air, possessing a piercing clarity that was almost painful.

Then the blizzard returned, and the three men pulled their jackets around their faces and turned the corner into the small square, where the plain, brute cylinder of the Pantheon's rear wall loomed above them, luminous under the night's silver light. It was a sight Nic Costa had never expected to see. The vast hemisphere of the dome, the largest in the world until the twentieth century, so vast that Michelangelo had made the diameter of St Peter's dome half a metre smaller out of respect, was now swathed in snow, cutting an unmistakable semicircle out of the sky, like the meniscus of a gigantic new moon rising above the dark urban horizon.

Costa cast a glance at Bernini's famous elephant in front of the church. The creature was almost unrecognizable. A heavy drift had engulfed the statue and the foot of the diminutive Egyptian obelisk that sat on its midriff. A perfect, miniature mountain rose up from the ground to form a triangular peak, surmounted by the bare needle-like pinnacle of the column, etched with impenetrable hieroglyphs. Sandri fired off some more shots. Peroni watched and shook his head. Then they carried on, walking parallel with the eastern wall of the Pantheon, into the small, rectangular open space of the Piazza della Rotonda.

Costa felt he knew every inch of the piazza. He'd arrested pickpockets working the busy summer crowds who had flocked to see the impossible: an imperial Roman temple unchanged in its essential form over almost twenty centuries. And a sight that, just as important to many, was free, since Hadrian's original shrine to every last god in the heavens had in the seventh century been converted into the consecrated church it still remained. Once Costa had picked up a drunk who'd fallen asleep beneath the spouting mouths of the comical dolphins and fauns of the fountain opposite the temple's massive, colonnaded portico. But long before he became a cop, when he was just a school kid full of awe and passion for the history of his native city, he'd come here whenever he could, just to sit on the steps of the fountain and listen to water trickle from the dolphins' beaks like liquid laughter, just to stare at the way everything changed in the shifting light of the day and the season, feeling two thousand years of bustling history brush up against his face.

Tonight he scarcely recognized the place. The blustering northerly wind was funnelling down the narrow alleys facing the piazza, cascading new and fallen snow straight into the square and the mouth of the Pantheon's portico. Curious organically shaped drifts clung to the fountain. The streams of water from the dolphins' mouths and the fauns' were now frozen solid, like lumpen jewels gleaming in the moonlight.

Peroni was scanning the piazza for signs of life. Mauro had his camera out, changing films. Costa approved. This was a rare sight, he thought. It deserved to be recorded.

'Where the hell is everyone, Nic?' Peroni asked. 'I don't even see the bums.'

The poor were with you always. Particularly in a place like this.

'Maybe they're inside already,' Costa said. Or, even better, perhaps the city had discovered hidden reserve of compassion and found space to house them for the night.

'We've got company,' Peroni said, pointing to a figure emerging from behind the western wall of the building.

The man shivered inside a dark uniform, shielding his face against the snow, which seemed to have found some newly energized vigour. He stumbled through the blasts, stared at them hopefully, then asked, 'You the cops?'

Peroni waved his badge. Costa looked around the square again. More people should have been there. Falcone ought to arrive soon too.

'I'm not going inside on my own,' the caretaker said. 'Some of these scum use knives.'

Peroni nodded at the doors. 'Best open them up then.'

The man let loose a dry laugh then looked at Sandri, firing shots right, left and centre. 'Sure, Officer. That's all it takes. Is your man here going to shoot some pictures too? They say you see it just once in a lifetime. Snow coming down like that, straight through the eye.'

'So what are we waiting for?' Peroni asked.

Costa knew the problem. Behind the portico lay the largest pair of imperial Roman doors in existence. Worked bronze, almost as high as the porch itself, and more than a metre deep. Sometimes, before going on duty, he'd take a coffee in the square in the early morning, watching the Pantheon being prepared for another day's crowds. No one who worked in the building ever approached through the front, not to begin with. The doors opened inwards, their mass being drawn back slowly from behind.

'We need the tradesmen's entrance,' Costa said.

'Precisely.' The man sniffed, then drew back his collar to reveal a gnarled, florid face that looked as if half a bottle of grappa could be wrung out of it. 'All three of you coming?'

Costa looked at Peroni. 'I can handle a couple of street people. Stay here with Mauro. Wait for Falcone.'

'No,' Peroni said, striding towards the shelter of the portico. 'I stay here.'

Costa followed in the caretaker's swift footsteps, walking to the western flank, where they descended some stairs down to what must have been the original level of the city when the Pantheon was built. There was a locked iron gate, then further steps and a long, narrow path, in the shadow of the high modern wall of the adjoining street, to a small, secure door almost at the rear of the building.

'The tradesman's entrance,' the caretaker said icily, then turned a couple of locks and threw it open. Costa stepped into the alcove and waited as the man fumbled with some keys at a second door, which led, he guessed, to the great circular interior, wondering what kind of bum locked the doors behind him.

He listened to the metal tumblers turn.

'After you,' the caretaker said. 'I'll get the lights.'

Nic Costa walked into the darkness and felt the chill of fresh winter air on his face. The night breeze was circling in the vast hemisphere he knew lay before him. And there was another sound too. Of a human being moving: short, anxious steps in the blackness beyond.

He felt his jacket, wondered about the gun. Then the lights of the building burst into life, bringing a sudden harsh sun into the shadows of the vast, airy, artificial universe enclosed beneath the structure's huge dome.

Someone cried out with surprise. A young voice. The noise reverberated around the vast emptiness so quickly it seemed to come from everywhere.

'Will you look at that?' the caretaker said, not even thinking about the intruders any more.

Through the the giant open eye of the oculus came a steady, swirling stream of snow, pirouetting around itself with the perfect, precise symmetry of a strand of human DNA.

It fell in the dead centre of the room, where an inverted, icy funnel was growing, spreading out beyond the central marble ring and rising, at its peak, to a metre or more.

Costa heard movement to his right. A slight, small figure dashed through a brilliant yellow beam cast down by a spotlight near the main altar, then fled into the pool of shadows in a recess on the far side of the building.

'Scum,' the caretaker muttered. 'What are you going to do?'

Costa had been running the options through his mind. Chase some lone, cold, hungry bum through the darkness of Hadrian's holiest of holies? And all for what?

'Open the doors,' he said. 'The main ones.'

Costa was walking towards them already, anxious to enjoy the look of astonishment on the faces of Gianni Peroni and Mauro Sandri when those gigantic bronze shutters were pulled back to reveal this wonder to the world on the other side.

'What?' the caretaker asked, putting a hand on Costa's shoulder until something in the detective's eyes told him this was not a good idea.

'You heard!' Costa snapped, getting angry with the man, wondering what he thought he was protecting here.

There were more keys and some kind of electronic monitor needed attention. Costa got on the mobile and called his partner, just beyond the doors.

'I'm not playing hide and seek in here, Gianni,' he said. 'I think it's just a kid. If he runs, you can get some exercise. Otherwise . . . hell, it's almost Christmas.'

The big man's laugh came back as a double echo, from the phone and, fainter, from beyond the doors.

'You're itching to do Leo's clean-up statistics some good tonight.'

'Just stand back and watch when we open this place.' Then he thought about what Peroni had said. 'Is Falcone there?'

'Walking right across the square. And on the phone too. This isn't a conference call or something?'

Costa heard a low metallic groan and put the phone back in his jacket. The caretaker was heaving at the bronze behemoth on his right, tugging it back on a set of ancient hinges. Costa took hold of the second door and pulled hard at the handle. It moved surprisingly easily.

In the space of a few seconds they had them open. The night wind rolled straight up the portico and blew snow into their faces. Nic Costa brushed the stinging flakes out of his eyes. Gianni Peroni stood there, transfixed by what he saw. Sandri was a few steps behind him, tense, upright, firing off photos constantly. Falcone had arrived too and seemed to be barking angrily down the phone.

Costa turned round and took another look at the magical scene behind him, snow swirling down from the heavens, as if tethered to a magnetic, twisting beam of light.

The bum was moving in the Pantheon now. Nic Costa no longer cared. He stood back from the door to let the intruder run, break out from this tight, enclosed universe that was the dream of an emperor who had been dead for nearly two millennia.

Then he looked outside again and recognized a different shape – upright and stiff on the steps of the fountain – not quite able to believe what he was seeing, to reconcile it with this bewitching night.

A figure slipped past him, brushing against his jacket. Costa didn't even look. With fumbling fingers he unzipped his coat, felt for his gun in the holster.

'Get down,' he said, still trying to marshal his thoughts, letting the words slip from his mouth so softly he doubted the caretaker even heard. Then he took a deep breath and yelled, as loudly as he could, 'Gianni! Get down for Christ's sake!'

Automatically, without planning the move, he dashed out into the portico and felt the freezing wind bite at his face. Gianni Peroni was still staring into the interior of the Pantheon, face alight with joy, grinning like a kid. Falcone was getting close to him too, his stern, immobile features for once rapt, captured by the scene inside.

'Get down!' Costa screamed again, waving his hands, waving the small black revolver through the falling cloud of white flakes. '*Now!* The bastard's got a gun.'

He heard the first shot drown out the end of his words. Something small and deadly sang its way through the air. Sparks flew off the column close to the astonished faces of the two cops under the portico. Falcone's arm went out and pushed Peroni down to the stone pavement.

Costa was focused on the man on the steps now. The figure was on his own directly by the fountain, dressed in black from head to foot and wearing one of those idiotic tie-down hats with earpieces that made you look like Mickey Mouse caught in a storm. He was standing in a professional firing position, the Weaver stance, right hand on the trigger, left supporting the gun, feet apart, comfortable as hell in the sort of pose Costa sometimes saw at target-shooting events. The small pistol was aimed, very deliberately, in their direction. A tiny flame lit up the barrel as Costa watched and a muffled crack rolled their way.

Costa scanned the piazza, doing his best to check there was no one else in the vicinity, then unleashed two shots towards the figure in the snow. A stream of tiny fires lit up furiously in response, sending more sparks up from old stone that was, at least, some kind of protection for them. For those who were smart enough to take it.

Mauro Sandri was still standing. Maybe it was panic. Maybe it was just second nature. He was flapping around like a wild man, one hand still on the stupid camera, loosing off frames of anything, the Pantheon, the night, the three cops trying to squirm their way out of the firestorm coming at them from the square.

Then he turned, and Costa knew precisely what would happen next. Mauro spun round on his little heels, camera in hand, the motor drive of the Nikon clicking away like a clockwork robot, turned and faced the black figure still upright on the steps.

'Mauro,' Costa said quietly, knowing there was no point.

He was a stride away from the little photographer when the bullets hit. Two. He heard the reports as they left the barrel of the gun. He heard them hit the diminutive black figure on the steps, tear through the fabric of his winter jacket, bite like deadly insects deep into Sandri's body.

The little photographer flew into the air like a man

receiving an electric shock then fell in a disfigured heap onto the ground.

'See to him,' Costa yelled at Peroni and Falcone as they scrambled to their feet in the deep, consuming snow. 'This son of a bitch is mine.'

Knowing the idea was pointless, that no one could shoot that well, not even the dark-hearted bastard standing by the frozen dolphins and fauns, Costa let off a bullet all the same, then began to sprint, began to hit his speed, and thought: *At least I can run. Can you?*

The figure was folding on himself, turning, like a crow shrinking into a crouch before it half jumped, half fell off a fence. There was fear there as he fled down the steps on the far side of the dolphins and fauns. Costa knew it and the knowledge made him pump harder with his legs, not minding how slippery the centuries-old paving stones were beneath his feet.

He loosed off another shot. The man was fleeing into the corner of the square, trying to find sanctuary in the dark, tangled labyrinth of narrow streets and alleys that lay beyond, in every direction.

And, just as Costa was beginning to digest this thought, the weather joined in. A sudden vicious squall careered straight out of the north, a thick wad of snow deep in its gut. The cruel, cutting ice stung and blinded. His feet gave way. The rugby player in him surfaced from the long dead past, told him there was no option but to roll with the fall, to tumble into the soft, freezing blanket on the ground, because the alternative was to pitch gravity and momentum against the weakness of the human body and snap a tendon or a bone along the way.

It was dark and cold as he fell into the soft, fresh

snow, taking the hard stone beneath with his shoulder. For a brief moment the world was a sea of whirling white and sharp, violent pain. Then he was still, feeling himself, checking nothing was broken.

When he got his equilibrium back and forced himself to his feet, the figure in black was gone. Dense clouds of white were falling with an unforgiving force again, burying the man's footprints with every passing second, turning everything into a single, empty shade of nothingness. Costa strode to the corner of the street. He could have gone one of two ways, west down the Via Giustiniani, towards the church of San Luigi dei Francesi, with its Caravaggios and, for Nic Costa, some bitter memories. Or north, into the warren beyond Piazza della Maddalena.

Costa stared at the ground. It looked like a fresh bed sheet, scarcely crumpled, full of secrets, all of them unreachable.

Reluctantly, understanding what he would find, he retraced his steps to the portico. A siren was sounding somewhere in the wintry night. Costa wondered how long it would take the ambulance to make its way through the treacherous streets. Then he saw Gianni Peroni hunched on the flat stone of the portico next to Mauro Sandri's inert form, and knew it didn't really matter.

He walked over, determined to handle this well.

'Hey,' Costa said, placing a hand on his partner's shoulder, then crouching down to peer into those strangely emotional squinty eyes, which were now liquid with cold and a bright inner fury. 'We couldn't have known, Gianni.'

'I will remember to point this out when I break it to

his mamma, or his wife or boyfriend or whoever,' Peroni replied bitterly, trying to bite back his rage.

'He must have looked like one of us, I guess. It could have been you. Or me. Or anyone.'

'That's a comforting thought,' Peroni mumbled.

Costa glanced at the dead photographer. Blood, black under the moonlight, was caking in Sandri's open mouth. Two more patches, one on his upper chest, the second in the centre of his abdomen, shone on his jacket. Costa remembered that curious stance the gunman had held while firing at them. It contained some meaning. When they had started to swallow down the bitter bile of their shock, when the investigation proper began, this was a point to note, an item of interest to be pursued.

Peroni patted Sandri's still arm. 'I told him, Nic. I said, "Mauro, you're not going to die. I promise. You're just going to lie there and wait for the medics to come. Then one day you go back to photographing mugs like me, and this time round you can take snaps of my pecker as much as you want. This time round . . ." Oh shit.'

'We'll get the bastard, big man,' Costa said quietly. 'Where's Falcone?'

'Inside,' Peroni said with a slow, deliberate venom. 'Maybe he's enjoying the view.'

A blue flashing beacon began to paint the walls on the far side of the square. Then a second. The caterwauling of the sirens became so loud that lights came on in apartment windows in the neighbouring streets. Costa got up. There was no point in talking to Peroni when he was in this mood. He had to wait for the storm to pass.

Costa walked through the doors towards the stream of white that fell, still circling around itself, from the vast open eye of the oculus.

The caretaker was in his cabin by the entrance, florid face down into his chest, trying as hard as he could to stay out of everything. Leo Falcone stood by the inverted funnel, which kept growing as it was fed from the sky. Costa remembered studying the Pantheon at school in art class. Here, at the centre of the hall, lay the defining focal point of the building, the axis around which everything was arranged in a precise show of ancient symmetry, both the great hemisphere and the monumental brick cylinder which tethered this imaginary cosmos to the ground.

'The photographer's dead, sir,' Costa said, trying to allow a note of reproach to slip into his voice.

'I know,' Falcone replied without emotion. 'Scene of crime are on the way. And the rest. Do you have any idea where the man in the square went?'

'No.'

Falcone's stony face said everything.

'I'm sorry,' Costa added. 'We came here thinking it was a bunch of bums breaking in to keep warm. It was a burglar alarm, for God's sake.'

'I know,' the inspector said carefully. He walked to the head of the funnel, where it was close to the apse and the altar, pointing due south, directly opposite the portico entrance and the open bronze doors. Costa followed. There Falcone bent down and, with a gloved finger, pointed at the edge of the fresh snow.

Costa's breath caught as he began to understand. A thin line of pigment was running from inside the funnel, out to the edge of the crystals as they tried to turn to water on the marble and porphyry. The stain became paler and paler as it flowed towards the edge but there could be no mistake. Nic Costa knew the colour by now. It was blood.

'I've done this once already,' Falcone said, pulling out a handkerchief from his coat. 'Damn snow.'

Slowly, with the same care Costa had seen Teresa Lupo use in such situations, Falcone swept at the funnel with light, brushing strokes.

Costa stood back and watched, wishing he were somewhere else. The head of a woman was emerging from beneath the soft, white sheet of ice. An attractive woman with a large, sensual mouth, wide open dark green eyes, and a face which was neither young nor old, a full, frank, intelligent face that wore an expression of intense shock so vivid it seemed to border on outrage.

Falcone briefly touched her long jet black hair, then turned to watch the snow coming down and the way it was beginning to bury her anew.

'Don't lay a finger on a thing,' Falcone said. 'I shouldn't have done as much as I did.'

'No, sir,' Costa whispered, his head reeling.

'Well?' Falcone didn't even seem put out by this. It was as if everything was as normal, just another everyday event that the cold, distant inspector could take in his stride.

'Well what?' Costa snapped back.

'Well how about you sit down on that chair over there and write down every last thing you remember. You're a witness here, Costa. Interview yourself. And don't skip the awkward questions.'

GIOVEDÌ

Falcone played it by the book. He sealed the Pantheon and the immediate vicinity. He called in every officer he could lay his hands on and marshalled the best scene-of-crime team available. When the crew from the morgue arrived they were led, as he'd hoped, by Teresa Lupo, who'd been dragged out of bed and, when she saw the reason, glad of the fact. Then Falcone supervised an initial search of the Pantheon's interior, uncovering enough evidence to ascertain the identity of the dead woman, and set in train the sequence of events needed to inform the American embassy and Mauro Sandri's relatives. Finally, along with a string of more minor requests, he'd ordered the recovery of the tape of every last CCTV camera in the area, including several inside the Pantheon itself.

When Falcone was satisfied that the crime scene was effectively preserved in aspic, ready for a more thorough and searching examination in the light of day, he'd walked through the continuing blizzard to one of the empty squad cars parked next to the frozen fountain. There, exhausted, he had reclined the passenger seat all the way back and tried to get a little sleep. It would be a long day. He needed his rest and the energy to think. And even that was denied him because one thought kept running through Leo Falcone's mind. When he'd reached the portico of the Pantheon he had been about to climb the very steps where Mauro Sandri stood. All that had stopped him was the phone call, the nagging, drunken tirade from Filippo Viale, which had begun when he entered the square and went on, pointlessly running through the same question, over and over again.

Are you with us, Leo?

Falcone hadn't understood why Viale felt the need to come back to this tedious issue so quickly. He'd put it down to the drink and the SISDE officer's curious mood. The call was still in his head, every precise second of it. Viale's voice had become so shrill in his ear that he had paused just short of the portico, and in doing so had avoided walking into the space created by the two central pillars and outlined by the light from the interior, which formed the perfect frame for the gunman on the fountain steps.

Without Viale's call, he would have gone on to join the photographer. And perhaps he would now be the one lying in the black plastic body bag stored on a metal gurney, safe inside the Pantheon, parked like a piece of luggage in front of the one of the building's more hideous modern accretions, the gross and gleaming tomb of the first king of a post-Roman united Italy, Vittorio Emanuele.

Professionally, Leo Falcone met death and frustration frequently and never gave them any more consideration than the job required. On the rare occasions they had touched him personally, he found himself less confident of his response, and this lack of certitude became itself one more unfamiliar, unwelcome intruder into a life he tried to regard as sane, ordered and functional.

In the space of one evening an officer of the security services had given him a curious warning that his career had, at the very least, stalled and was, perhaps, already in decline. Then, in short order, almost in response to this very idea, the black veil of the grave had swept against his cheek, so closely he could feel how chill and empty a place it truly was.

Sleep, real sleep, was impossible in such circumstances. When Leo Falcone was woken by the rapping of a gloved hand on the window, just after sunrise at seven on that frozen Roman morning, he had no idea whether he'd slipped fully into unconsciousness at all during the preceding hours.

He wiped the condensation from the window and realized there was no time to worry about the loss. Distorted by the condensation on the glass, Bruno Moretti's stern, moustachioed face was staring at him from the white and chilly world outside. Falcone's immediate superior, the commissario to whom he reported on a daily basis, had found a reason to drag himself out of the office and visit a crime scene. It was a rare and unwanted event.

Falcone climbed out of the car, trying to fathom some reason for this departure from custom.

'This is a nice way to start the holiday season,' the commissario moaned immediately, glancing at the lines of uniformed men blocking off the Pantheon and most of the piazza. 'Just what we need, Falcone. The tourist people are screaming down the line at me already.

They've a lot of people on their books who thought they were coming here today.' He scanned the square, full of cops. 'Now this . . .'

'We have two deaths, sir,' Falcone replied patiently.

'That was more than six hours ago.'

Moretti was a bureaucrat. He'd worked his way up through traffic and intelligence, branches of the service that had their merits in Falcone's opinion, but left the man with little feeling for investigation.

Falcone glanced at the scene-of-crime officers and wondered if Moretti had any idea how important their work was, how easily it could be spoiled by a hurried search. 'I can't expect the SOCOs to make a serious effort in the dark. It's impossible. Particularly in a place like this.'

Moretti sighed and said nothing. That was, Falcone thought, the closest he was going to get to some sign of recognition there really was no other way to proceed.

'We have to do this very carefully, sir. It's the only chance we have. Once we're out of there the hordes are going to be climbing over everything. If we've missed one small piece of evidence, it's gone, for good probably.'

Moretti was glowering at the building, as if he wished it weren't there. The snow had stopped now but the sky was the colour of lead, pregnant with more. The great dome of the Pantheon wore a picturesque mantle. The rest of the square was a hideous sight, frozen slush churned to a grey mess by the constant movement of emergency vehicles and the tramp of feet.

'"Probably,"' the commissario snorted. 'When will you be out?'

'Mid-afternoon at the earliest.'

'Make it twelve. You've got the manpower. You managed to requisition half the Questura without my knowing last night. You could have called.'

Falcone nodded. He could have done that. But he chose not to. Nothing got past Moretti easily. There was too much explaining to be done and all for no reason. He'd worked for better bosses, and worse. With Moretti it was simpler for both of them if they stuck to their own particular skills. In Falcone's case, investigation. For Moretti, the behind-the-scenes management of internal and external relations, the marshalling of budgets and staff. *Politics.*

'I didn't want to disturb you. Not until we knew who she was.'

Moretti laughed. The sound shocked Falcone. There didn't even seem an edge inside it. 'She's an American. That's all. I find it a little insulting you think it's worth calling me over for her but not for that poor bastard who was taking the photos. He was at least Italian.'

'I don't make the rules,' Falcone murmured. 'Sir.'

It was a standing order these days. Verbal and physical attacks on Americans were rare and usually had nothing to do with nationality, but the previous October an American military historian had been badly beaten up in the centro storico. Had a couple of uniformed cops not stumbled on the scene the man could have died. The brutal assailant had escaped. No one had claimed responsibility. Initially it was assumed that the Red Brigades were behind the attack, and everyone waited for the customary anonymous phone call citing it as a blow against American imperialism. But it never came. No one – not the police, not SISDE, not even the military spooks as far as Falcone knew – had come up with a shred of evidence to suggest who was really responsible, or whether this was part of a concerted campaign against US citizens. Nevertheless, the order had come down from on high, in all probability from somewhere in the Quirinale Palace itself: all incidents involving Americans had to be reported to a senior level immediately.

'Just another tourist, huh?' Moretti said. 'Woman on her own? Well, I suppose I can guess what happened there. Probably met some complete stranger. Thought it was just a little romance. Throw a few coins in the fountain then walk here for a little fun. It's just another sex crime, right?'

Falcone checked his watch, then looked at the activity inside the building. 'You tell me,' he replied, and began walking towards the Pantheon door, knowing the commissario had no choice but to follow.

The lights of the Pantheon burned brightly, supplemented by a forest of police spots. Half a dozen SOCOs in white bunny suits were now scouring every last square millimetre of the patterned floor. A makeshift canvas tent had been erected over the corpse in the centre, with a set of lights tethered at the corners. Snow had continued to fall steadily through the night. Teresa Lupo and her team had built the contraption to keep the body from being buried ever more deeply by the continuous white stream that worked down through the oculus directly above them. From the moment Falcone saw the corpse emerging from the ice under Teresa Lupo's care, he understood the body was in good hands. She was a wonderful pathologist, the best, even if his relationship with her was often strained. She had seen immediately that it was important to preserve any shreds of evidence that might be hidden in the ice as it melted under the heat of the lights. There was another reason too. The body had been arranged, quite deliberately, on the circle which marked the exact mid-point of the building, arms and legs outstretched to their limits in an angular fashion Falcone recognized, though he was unable to remember from what. The pose of the body – there was no other way to describe it – possessed meaning. It was, somehow, a cryptic message from the woman's murderer and one they needed to try to understand as quickly as possible.

Carefully, Falcone wound his way through the clear area marked by tape which had been set up to allow safe access in and out of the building. Moretti followed on in silence. They reached the mouth of the tent. Falcone stopped and gestured towards the body. Lupo and her deputy, Silvio Di Capua, were on their knees moving gently around it, poring over the dead woman with painstaking, obsessive deliberation. He had watched them get to work in the early hours of the morning. Teresa Lupo ordered her people to erect the tent the moment she saw the scene, but it had proved a long and difficult job in the bitter cold of the Pantheon's interior under a constant whirling downfall of snow. It was almost an hour before they could crawl beneath the covering to examine the ice funnel, slowly sweeping away the snowflakes with tiny brushes, revealing the horror that lay beneath, millimetre by millimetre.

Moretti looked at the naked woman, then fired a disgusted expression somewhere into the dark corners of the building. 'Sex crime, Leo. As I said.'

'And the photographer?'

Moretti scowled. He didn't like being put on the spot like this. 'That's what you're supposed to find out.'

Falcone nodded. 'We will.'

'Make damn sure you do. The last thing this city needs is something that scares off tourists.'

Falcone reached into his pocket and took out the woman's passport. They'd found it in a bag in a corner of the building. It named her as Margaret Kearney, aged thirty-eight. The next-of-kin details weren't filled in. Her driving licence had been issued in New York City six months before.

'We don't actually know she was a tourist. All we have is a name.'

'This is going to be messy, isn't it?' Moretti grumbled. 'The Americans are asking questions already. They've got some resident FBI people up at the embassy who want to talk to you.'

'Of course,' Falcone murmured, trying to decode what Moretti had said. 'I don't understand. You're saying these are FBI people who are resident here in Rome?'

Moretti emitted a dry laugh. 'Well, isn't that wonderful? Something you don't know. Of course they've got FBI people here. Who the hell *knows* what they've got here. They're Americans, aren't they? They do what the hell they like.'

'What do I tell them?'

Moretti's dark eyes twinkled with delight. 'Welcome to the tightrope. You tell them just enough to keep them happy. And not a damn thing more. This is still Italy as far as I'm concerned. We police our own country, thank you. At least until someone tells me otherwise.'

Falcone glanced at Teresa Lupo. She'd broken off

from the work in the tent to speak, in low and guarded tones, to Gianni Peroni, who was standing by the altar looking exhausted. Nic Costa hung around just out of earshot.

'I understand,' he murmured.

'Good,' Moretti replied. 'You didn't say how the dinner went. I would have gone myself but, frankly, I don't think they feel I'm sufficiently . . . interesting. At least they never talk to me with quite the enthusiasm they seem to summon up for you.'

'It slipped my mind. It was . . . fine.'

'Really?' the commissario sniffed. 'That's not what that slippery bastard Viale said when he called this morning. He doesn't like hearing the word "no", Leo. You're either very brave or very foolish.'

Two people were walking into the building now, picking their way through the tape maze like professionals. A man and a woman who were complete strangers. He was about forty-five, thickset, with cropped grey hair, like that of a US marine, and a head that looked too small for his body. The woman was much younger, perhaps twenty-five, striking in a bright, scarlet coat. They were walking into a crime scene as if they owned the place and Leo Falcone already possessed a gloomy, interior conviction about who they were.

Moretti eyed the couple too, watched Costa and Peroni walk briskly over to intercept them, then shuffled his coat around him, getting ready to go back to the warmth of his office. He laughed. 'Tell your monkeys to be polite, Leo. We're all watching. Maybe Filippo Viale too. Brave or foolish? When this is over, I suspect we'll all know which.'

*

Costa saw them first, brushing past the uniforms on the door with a flash of an ID card and a cocky self-assurance that irked him immediately.

'Hey, Gianni,' he murmured, 'you know these people?'

Peroni looked washed out. Teresa had told them to use her place in Tritone when they got a break. There was no way Costa would make it home to the farm on the Appian Way. As for Peroni . . . Costa could only wonder when the big man had last slept in the small, functional rented apartment he'd found out in the suburbs on the other side of the river, beyond the Vatican. Peroni already had a set of keys to Teresa's place. Maybe he lived there most of the time anyway.

'No,' Peroni answered, perking up suddenly. He moved quickly to block their path, holding out his big arms wide, stretching from tape to tape.

The man with the crew cut glowered up at him in return, half a head shorter but just as big in the body.

'You don't mind if I ask –' Peroni said – 'this isn't exactly a public performance we're giving here.'

'FBI,' the American murmured in a low, grunty voice and kept on walking.

'Whoa!' Peroni yelled, and caught the man firmly by the arm, not minding the filthy look he was getting in return.

'Officer,' the female agent said, 'this woman is an American citizen.'

'Yeah,' Peroni replied, 'I know. But let's go through some niceties first. My name is Gianni Peroni. This is my partner, Nic Costa. We are policemen. This nice-looking gentlemen walking towards us is Inspector Falcone.

He's the boss around here. When he says you get to go further, you go further. Until then . . .'

Falcone arrived, looked the two FBI agents up and down and said, 'Over here we like people to call ahead and make appointments.'

The man withdrew an ID card from his pocket. The woman in the scarlet coat did the same. Costa leaned forward and stared at the photos, checking them, making sure the two Americans understood the point. There were rules here. There were procedures to be followed. She didn't look much like the photo on the ID card. According to the date it was two years old. She'd seemed much younger then.

'The IDs are fine,' Costa said politely. 'We have to check. You'd be amazed what the press will do over here just to get a picture.'

'Of course,' the woman answered. She was trying to look like a business executive: expensive, well-cut clothes, blonde hair tied back a little scrappily in a bun that seemed to want to work itself free and let her locks hang more freely around an attractive, almost girlishly innocent face. Something didn't match up and, just for a moment, he couldn't stop staring at her. She had razor-sharp, light blue eyes that were cutting into him now.

'I'm Agent Emily Deacon,' she said in perfect Italian. 'This –'

She pointed at her colleague without once looking at him and Costa thought, on the instant, she didn't like the man by her side.

'– is Agent Joel Leapman. We're here for a reason. If you let us through to see what you've got, we just might be able to help.'

Peroni tapped Leapman on the arm and gave him a broad grin. 'There. Now that's asking nicely.'

'So do we get through?' the American snapped.

Falcone nodded and led the way. Teresa Lupo had cleared the body of snow entirely now and indicated to them to wait as she quietly dictated some notes into a voice recorder. The dead woman lay on the geometric slabs, legs and arms splayed, her white, bloodless skin waxy under the artificial lights. When he'd had the chance between phone calls and working with the SOCOs, Costa had watched closely as the body had emerged from the ice. The positioning of the corpse on the central marble circle was quite deliberate. Her limbs were outstretched, directed at equidistant points in the vast, curving sphere of the Pantheon, as if making a statement. It was an image that jogged a memory and was, perhaps, designed to. He recalled it now. Leonardo da Vinci's sketch of an idealized figure, a naked man with a full head of hair, set inside first a square then a circle. His limbs described two positions: legs together, at the base of the circle, touching the central arm of the lower side of the square, then apart, on the circle alone; and arms outstretched first horizontally, touching the square alone, then raised, to both the circle and the square's upper corners.

The dead woman's stiff position on the shining, damp floor, one surely fixed by her murderer, matched the second of each of these poses perfectly. This was not simply a striking image. It had a meaning, a very specific one.

'The Vitruvian Man,' he said quietly, remembering a distant art lesson from school.

The American woman looked at him oddly. 'Excuse me?'

'She reminded me of something. From a long time ago.'

'You've got a memory, Mr Costa,' she conceded, half interested. 'What else do you recall?'

He tried to flesh out the hazy recollection his brain had dug up from somewhere. It *was* a long time ago. The idea itself was elusive and complicated too. 'That it's about dimensions and form.' He nodded at the huge spherical roof above them. 'Just like this place.'

'Just like this place,' she repeated and, for a moment, smiled. The change in expression was remarkable. It took years off her face. She looked like a student suddenly, fresh, unmarked.

It didn't last. Leapman was making impatient noises. He looked at Teresa Lupo, who was still chanting into the recorder. 'You're the pathologist, right?'

Teresa hit the pause button, blinked and gave him a hard stare. 'No, I'm the fucking copy typist. Just give me a moment and I'll take your letter next. Who the hell are you, by the way?'

The card got flipped out again as if it were some kind of magic amulet. 'FBI.' He nodded at his colleague. 'Both of us.'

'Really?' Teresa sighed and got back to talking into the machine.

Quietly, calmly, with a distinct effort designed to cool down the temperature of the conversation, Emily Deacon said, 'I think we can help.'

The pathologist hit the stop button. 'How?'

'She was strangled. With a piece of cord or something. Am I right?'

Teresa glanced at Falcone, searching for a sign. He looked as lost as Peroni and Costa.

'There's no sign of sexual assault,' the American woman continued. 'This isn't sexual at all, not in the common sense anyway. Which begs the question: why did he undress her? It happened here? You do have her clothes?'

'It happened here,' Costa conceded. 'Some indeterminate time between eight in the evening, when the staff closed the place, and midnight, when we turned up.'

Teresa Lupo was staring at the body again, trying to think. She didn't stay mad with people for long. Not if she thought they had something she wanted. 'We're not going to get much better than that. It was snowing all last night. All that ice is going to play havoc with everything I normally use for time of death. There are calculations I can use, but they're not going to be wonderfully accurate in the circumstances.'

The two FBI agents exchanged a glance. It was almost as if they'd seen enough already.

Falcone finally found his voice and Costa couldn't work out why he'd stayed silent for so long. 'I've been very generous around here. What do we get in return?'

'We'll let you know,' Leapman murmured.

The woman glanced at the pathologist. 'This is your call. I'm not trying to push you along. But do you think it would be possible to turn her? I need to see the back.'

Teresa glanced at her assistant Silvio Di Capua, who was putting away some of the equipment they'd been using. Di Capua shrugged.

'We can turn her,' she said, then held out a hand to stop Leapman, who was heading for the body without the slightest hesitation. 'I said, "we".'

The American held himself back reluctantly. Teresa

and Di Capua called on two morgue assistants to help. They positioned themselves around the right-hand side of the corpse and placed gloved fingers on her limbs and shoulders.

'Is this going to be nasty?' Peroni asked, worried. 'I like warnings about nasty stuff whenever possible.'

'Then don't look,' the Deacon woman said bluntly.

On Teresa's call, the team lifted the white corpse, rotated it on its own axis and gently placed the woman front first onto the marble floor, her head now tilted to one side against the shining stone. Peroni swore and went to stand in the corner. Costa stared at the woman's back and the strange shape carved there, an oddly symmetrical pattern of curves cut straight into the skin from above her waist to the shoulders, like a huge, cruel tattoo.

'What's it meant to be?' Costa asked. 'A cross?'

It was a diagonal shape, with four protruding curving arms.

Teresa stared at the body. 'I've never seen anything like it.'

'Consider yourself lucky.' Leapman moaned and bent down to take a closer look at the corpse. 'He used the cord. At least I don't see any other marks. She was dead when he got round to doing what he wanted to do.'

The pathologist was shaking her head, bemused. 'The pattern's so precise. How could you do it? Here?'

Emily Deacon didn't want to look at the shape on the woman's back. She knew it too well already, Costa guessed. 'To begin with you'd need a crayon, a ruler, possibly, and a scalpel,' she said softly. 'After a little while I guess you just need something that cuts and a very steady hand.'

Leapman took out a hankie and blew into it noisily. 'We've seen enough. We need a meeting in our office at the embassy. Five this evening. Bring who you want, but I'm going to trust you people with material I don't want to go any further than our front door. So make sure whoever you bring can keep their mouths shut, and listen good because I don't like repeating myself.'

Falcone shook his head in disbelief. 'This is Rome. This is a murder inquiry. We are the state police force and we do this our way. You will visit us when I say. And I'll ask you any damn thing I like.'

Leapman pulled an envelope out of his pocket and handed it over. 'This, Inspector, is a signed order from a guy in the Palazzo Chigi none of you people want to argue with. This is all agreed with your superior and with SISDE too. Take a look at the signatures. It gives me the right to take this body into our custody any moment I choose. Which happens to be now. So don't you go messing with anything before our people arrive.'

Teresa Lupo's pale face went florid with fury. She walked over to the American and stabbed him in the chest with a podgy forefinger. 'What were your names again? Burke and fucking Hare? The age of body-snatching is over, my American friend. I am the state pathologist here. I say where she goes and when.'

Falcone was glaring at the sheet of paper, livid. 'How long before your people get here?' he asked Leapman without even looking at him, ignoring Teresa Lupo's growing shrieks of complaint.

'Ten minutes. Fifteen.'

Falcone handed back the envelope. 'She's yours.

We'll see you at five. Until your people arrive, you can wait outside.'

Agent Leapman snorted then stamped off back to the door and the snow beyond.

Emily Deacon hesitated for a moment, some uncertainty, regret perhaps, in her sharp blue eyes.

'I'm sorry for the unpleasantness,' she said. 'It isn't intentional. It's just . . . his manner.'

'Of course,' Falcone replied flatly.

'Good.' She took one last look at the pathologist before leaving. 'Forget what he said. We won't have a vehicle here for thirty minutes or more in this weather. Why not make good use of the time?'

There was only so much that could be done when the bodies had gone, Mauro's into the white Questura morgue van, the American woman into the hearse the FBI had provided. At midday Falcone took one look at Costa and Peroni and ordered them to take a break. He wanted them both to attend the meeting at the embassy. They'd seen the man in the square. They were involved. Falcone said he needed them wide awake for the FBI.

So the two of them took their leave of the crime scene and walked the fifteen minutes to Teresa Lupo's apartment through an icy ermine Rome that was uncannily deserted under a brief break in the cloud that meant a bright winter sun spilled over everything.

Nic Costa had visited her home once before. It was on the first floor of a block in Via Crispi, the narrow street running down from the summit of the Via Veneto. There had been a thoroughfare down the hill here for the best part of two thousand years. In imperial times, it had linked the Porta Pinciana in the Aurelian Wall with the Campus Martius, the 'Field of Mars', which was dominated in part by the architectural might of the Pantheon. The street opposite Teresa's home, the Via degli Artisti, was named after the nineteenth-century Nazarene school of painters who had lived in the area. The walls of the neighbourhood seemed littered with plaques that bore witness to the famous names who had once lived there: Liszt and Piranesi, Hans Christian Andersen and Maxim Gorky. The snow had restored a little of its charm. Few cars now snarled up the narrow streets. No tourists walked wearily along the Via Sistina to the church of Trinità dei Monti, set at the summit of the Spanish Steps, with its panoramic view over the Renaissance city that had come to occupy the Campus Martius over the centuries.

As the two of them trudged in silence, dog-weary and cold, Costa thought about the body laid out stiffly on the geometric slabs and fought to remember the history lessons that had gripped him as a schoolboy. It was important, always, to remind himself: this is Rome. Everything interconnects. The inscription on the portico of the Pantheon read: **M·AGRIPPA·L·F·COS· TERTIUM· FECIT** – Marcus Agrippa, the son of Lucius, three times consul, made this. Yet, like so much else concerning the Pantheon, this was a deceit, a subtle sleight of hand performed for reasons now lost. Augustus's old friend and ally Agrippa had built a temple on the Campus Martius and called it the Pantheon, a dedication to 'all the gods', but that had burned down some time after his death. The building which replaced it some hundred and fifty years later, between AD 120 and 125, was the work of Hadrian. Some even thought the emperor had designed it personally. Circular monuments, ideas stolen from Greece and points further east, reworked for a new age, were his hallmark. Nic Costa's knowledge of architectural history was insufficient to give him reasons. But when he thought of Hadrian's legacy – the private villa in Tivoli, the ruins of the Temple of Venus and Rome in the Forum, with its huge, extant half sphere of a ceiling – it was easy to see this was a thread that ran throughout his thinking. Even to the end. The huge round mass of the Castel Sant' Angelo on the far bank of the Tiber had served many purposes over the years: fortress, jail, barracks and papal apartments. But the emperor built it as his personal mausoleum. The spiral ramp to his initial resting place still existed, just a ten-minute walk from the dome of St Peter's, which Michelangelo had created some fourteen hundred years later in the image of Hadrian's own Pantheon.

Costa watched Peroni fumbling with the key to the apartment block door. 'Gianni, are you OK?'

The big man looked wiped out. 'Yeah. I just need some sleep. Something to eat. Excuse my moods, Nic. It's not like me.'

'I know,' Costa said. 'You go inside. I've got something to do. Plus I'll bring you a little present.'

Peroni's eyes sparked with worry. 'Don't overdo the vegetables!'

'It's a promise.'

It was just before one. There was a store around the corner he knew. They did the kind of food Peroni liked: roast porchetta, complete with crisp skin, nestling inside a panino raked with salt and rosemary. He could pick up something for himself too. The place did more than meat.

But first he caught the photographic shop before it closed and half talked, half badgered the man behind the counter into running the seven cassettes from Mauro's cameras and his accessory bag straight through the Fuji developing machine. The prints would be ready before four. Costa could pick them up by ringing the private bell to the apartment above.

When he got back Peroni was sprawled out on Teresa's sofa, looking very at home and listening to the weather on the TV. He took the pork sandwich and started stuffing his face with it straight from the bag.

'Not bad,' he conceded. 'How come I never found this place?'

'You do much shopping when you're staying here?'

Peroni sniffed then said, 'The snow's locked in for days, Nic. No trains. No planes. Not much moving on the roads either. I guess that means our man's not going to find it easy to get out of Rome. If he wants to.'

'Why would he want to?' Costa asked. There was a message in the American woman's body. A problem demanding a solution. Why would a person set a riddle then walk away without seeing whether it was solved?

'I dunno,' Peroni grumbled, finishing the sandwich then struggling to his feet, brushing crumbs off his front. 'I don't know a damn thing any more. Except I need to sleep. Wake me at the right time.'

Then he hesitated, thinking. 'Why the hell did Leo give in to those Americans so easily? I mean, he could have put up a fight. I can't believe we're trooping round to their place like this when the poor bitch got killed on our territory. Her and Mauro too.'

That was one thing Costa did understand. Leo Falcone never fought battles he knew he couldn't win.

It was one of the things that made him stand out in the Questura. He was smarter than most. There was, perhaps, another reason too. A faceless figure from SISDE had turned up halfway through the morning – just in time to see the American woman loaded into the hearse – and had talked to Falcone in private. Costa had never seen him before. Peroni, who knew just about every cop and spook in town, civilian and military, had and swore bitterly under his breath at the sight.

'What was that guy's name? The one from SISDE?'

Peroni pulled a sour face. 'Viale. Don't ask me what he does. Or how big he is. Very, probably. I ran into him a couple of times on vice when we picked up people he wanted left alone. He's good at the pressure.'

Costa could feel he was treading on delicate ground. 'Good enough to squeeze you?'

'I could tell you, Nic,' Peroni said pleasantly, 'but the trouble is, afterwards, I'd have to cut out your tongue. I joke, but I'm not supposed to. The honest answer is men like him get what they want these days. You mess with them at your peril.'

Costa smiled, said nothing, and moved over to the sofa, stretching out for the first time in what seemed like twenty-four hours.

'Point taken,' Peroni said with a wave of his hand, then disappeared into the bedroom.

Monica Sawyer stood at the plain wooden counter of L'Angolo Divino and wished to God she'd learned to speak Italian. Someone at the rental agency had recommended the place and tried to explain the play on words, how 'divino' meant both 'divine' and 'about wine'. She kind of got the joke. It was a wine bar. Or, more than that, an enoteca, a place that sold a variety of wines, cheap and expensive, and some pretty pricey plates of pasta, cheese and cold meats too. At least, that was what she'd been told. Now she was in the bar, which was set on the corner of two narrow alleys off the Campo dei Fiori, she didn't have much of a clue about anything. One end of the L-shaped room looked like a library, with row upon row of expensive-looking bottles stretching up to the high ceiling. The rest of the bar was a plain narrow channel that could take three people deep, no more, with a wooden-plank floor, a few pine tables and some plates of very fragrant cheese in a glass cabinet. An old guy in a brown jacket, the kind people in hardware stores used to wear, was talking rapid Italian at her from behind the counter, and it might as well have been Urdu. There was only one other customer in the place, a man in a black suit who sat on a nearby bench reading an Italian paper and sipping at the biggest wine glass Monica Sawyer had ever seen, swilling around the splash of red liquid in the base from time to time before sniffing it, smiling and drinking the tiniest drop.

Monica came from San Francisco. She was familiar with bars. She ought to be able to handle this, she thought. So she said very distinctly, for the third time, '*Una copa de chardonnay, por favor*,' and felt like bursting into tears when the man just babbled on incomprehensibly and waved at the huge selection of bottles behind the counter.

'Oh crap,' she muttered. Things just went from bad to worse. The weather meant she was going to be alone in Rome for days with nothing to do, no one to talk to.

And not much chance of getting a decent drink when she wanted one, outside of hotel bars, where a lone American woman of forty-two who was, Monica Sawyer knew, still pretty good-looking, could not sit safely without the risk of constant harassment.

'Italian and Spanish are close relatives, but they are, I fear, hardly interchangeable,' said a warm Irish voice at her shoulder.

Monica Sawyer turned and saw that the man in the dark suit was now at her side. He'd got there without making a sound, which in normal circumstances would have been a touch creepy. But she didn't feel that way somehow. He was smiling at her, a pleasant smile, from a pleasant, intelligent face, somewhat lined and hewn, as if it had been through the wars, but becoming all the same. He was, perhaps, fifty and still had perfect, very white teeth. He wore wire-framed, rectangular spectacles, which were a little old-fashioned, and slightly tinted too, so she could only just make out what she believed to be grey, thoughtful eyes behind the glass. He had a good head of hair, salt and pepper locks, long and wavy, like an artist's.

They never leave you alone, she thought. But at least this one was Irish. Then she watched him unfold the scarf at his neck and felt deeply and childishly guilty.

'Father,' she said, staring at the slightly crumpled dog collar, feeling the blood rush to her cheeks. 'I'm sorry. I didn't realize.'

He was a handsome man. That was the problem. Given that Harvey probably wouldn't make it to Rome for days, possibly a week or more, she was, she had to admit, in need of a little company. Just the sound of a friendly voice speaking English made such a difference.

'And why should you?'

He was six feet tall and well built. And he was glancing at her fox-fur coat, wondering, perhaps, what kind of woman roamed around the empty, snow-blocked streets of Rome looking as if she'd dressed for the theatre.

'It's the warmest thing I've got,' she explained rapidly. 'Besides, I was wearing it for my husband. He was supposed to join me from New York today. Then they said the airport was closed. For God knows how long . . .' She cursed herself inwardly and knew she had to watch her mouth. Monica Sawyer had gone to a convent school in Palo Alto. She ought to be able to remember how to behave. Not that he seemed shocked. Priests were different these days.

He touched the coat just for a moment with two long, powerful fingers. 'You'll excuse me. I don't see this kind of thing very much in my line of work.' Then he held out his hand. 'Peter O'Malley. Since we are two strangers stranded in Rome by snow, I hope you won't mind if I introduce myself. I've been hanging around all day wondering what to do and, to be honest with you, it's a pleasure to hear the native tongue.'

'I was thinking exactly the same thing!' She took his hand, which gripped hers with a brief, muscular strength. 'Monica Sawyer.'

'Then that's out of the way.' He glanced at the old man behind the counter. 'You were wanting a drink, Monica?'

'Damn right,' she said automatically and found the heat rushing to her cheeks again.

'Then damn right you shall have one. But not

chardonnay, I beg you. It's a French grape, not a bad one either, but when in Rome—'

She felt like giggling. Here she was, alone in a strange, foreign city, and a priest, a rather good-looking one at that, was precious close to flirting with her.

'Recommend something, Peter,' she said firmly.

'If it's a white you're after it would be a crime to leave without tasting a Greco di Tufo.'

The old man behind the counter raised his heavy, grey eyebrows. It seemed a gesture of approval.

'A what?'

'It's from a grape which is, perhaps, the oldest in Italy. The Pelasgians brought it in from Thessaly way back before Christ. If my memory serves me right there are just a hundred or so small aziende – vineyards to you, Monica – east of Naples that still make it. When you drink a Greco you're drinking what Virgil did while he was writing the *Aeneid*, as near as dammit. If you go to Pompeii, as you must, there's a couple of lines of graffiti on the fresco there, two thousand years old if they're a day. They go something like, "You are truly cold, Bytis, made of ice, if last night not even Greco wine could warm you up."'

She wondered about this, watching as the barman, unbidden as far she could see, poured a glass of the white the priest had merely waved at with a long finger. 'Who the hell was Bytis?'

The Irishman shrugged. 'A lover? What else? One who seems to have shirked his duties, in spite of the wine. Or perhaps because of it. Remember Macbeth. "Lechery, sir, it provokes, and unprovokes; it provokes the desire, but it takes away the performance. Therefore much drink may be said to be an equivocator with lechery; it makes him, and it mars him; it sets him on, and it takes him off; it persuades him, and disheartens him; makes him stand to, and not stand to; in conclusion, equivocates him in a sleep, and, giving him the lie, leaves him."'

He cast a sudden, dark, regretful glance at the door. 'There, you see. Too much of my youth spent wasting away in the stalls of the Abbey Theatre. It leaves one with a quotation for every occasion. To wit—'

Suddenly, he was very close and whispering in her ear. 'Hamlet and the omens of change. "The graves stood tenantless, and the sheeted dead Did squeak and gibber in the Roman streets."'

It was a very hammy performance. She couldn't help but laugh. The wine – clear, dry and quite unlike anything she'd ever tried before – helped. 'You've done a lot of reading.'

'Not really. I'm merely a very ordinary priest who happened to have a lot of spare hours once upon a time,' he replied. 'Ordinary as they come. Ask my little flock of sisters in Orvieto. Though Lord knows when they'll see me again. To be frank I'm a little giddy at being released into the world like this. I've spent most of the day at the station trying to get a train. And the rest of it knocking on the doors of the few hostels I can afford trying to find accommodation. After which –' he raised his glass – 'the Irish in me will out.'

Monica Sawyer was surprised to discover she'd finished her white. It was a meagre measure anyway. The Greco was good: sharp, individual, unexpected. She wanted another. She wanted something to eat too.

'What's that?' she asked, pointing at the priest's balloon-like glass, which still had a smear of red running around the bottom, one he'd been sipping gingerly throughout their conversation as if he couldn't quite run to another. 'And why's the thing so goddamn big?'

Peter closed his eyes for a moment and his face suffused with delight. 'Amarone. A small pleasure I allow myself when in Rome. The stuff we have to drink at home—'

He wrinkled his nose and didn't need to say another word.

'And that thing you're drinking from?'

He swilled the smudge of red liquid around the base and held it in front of her face. She took the glass, accidentally brushing his warm fingers on the way, stuck her nose deep inside the rim and was amazed as an entire, enclosed universe of aromas rose through her nostrils and entered her head. It made her think of the flowery prose she read in *Decanter* magazine: a sudden rush of a warm, spicy, summer breeze rising up off the Mediterranean and sweeping over a scrubby brush of parched wild thyme. Or something.

'This is a fine establishment,' he said, glancing at the barman. 'Like any fine establishment, it will keep a selection of glasses according to the rank of wine. Amarone is in the pantheon and at nine euros a glass it bloody better be.'

'OK,' she said, slapping a hundred note on the counter. 'Is your Italian good enough for "Line 'em up buster, the rich are paying"? And food. I want food, Peter. Don't you?'

He hesitated and, for one short, worrying moment, she felt she had lost him.

He pulled out a small, rather feminine purse and stared mournfully at the contents. 'I'm still enough of an Irishman to feel uncomfortable about having a lady buy me drinks.'

She put her hand on the soft, black arm of his priestly jacket. 'Then consider it a tuition fee.'

'Done,' he said and rattled off some orders to the barman.

The wine came: Amarone, with a brief lecture about how the grapes were dried before being fermented, then something called Primitivo di Manduria, which, from what she gathered, was kind of the red equivalent of the Greco, an ancient grape still kept alive by a handful of small producers, this time in Puglia, the heel of Italy. And the food: paper-thin slices of mountain-dried wild boar; a selection of salumi, some spicy, some mild; pale, translucent parings of pork fat, lardo di colonna; slivers of ripe, fruity Parmesan and a salad of buffalo mozzarella served with pomodorini di Pachino, tiny red tomatoes as sweet as cherries.

They ate and they drank and outside day turned to night through a steady, continuous veil of falling snow.

She didn't know how much time she'd spent in the bar. She didn't care. She was alone in Rome. She didn't speak a word of the goddamn language. And Peter O'Malley was such good company. The single most charming man she could remember meeting in years. He listened and when he spoke afterwards it was about the very subject she'd been discussing. He could talk about anything. Architecture. Literature. Politics. The pleasures of the table. Almost everything, it occurred to her, except religion. Perhaps Peter O'Malley had enough of that, trapped in servitude to his sisters back in Orvieto. Perhaps he felt abruptly and briefly free in this strange, small world of cold, white impassable streets.

Monica Sawyer listened and she laughed, knowing she was getting more than a little drunk. She was used to the attention of men: tall, with a well-kempt head of long, chestnut hair, and a smart, articulated face, one people liked to look at. Back home, when Harvey was away, she didn't hesitate to indulge a little now and then. Finally she took his wrist, looked at his watch then looked at him, with an expression she was sure did not amount to an invitation. That would be wrong. Improper. It wasn't what she was feeling or planning. She simply wanted company and his was, at that moment, the best.

'Peter,' she said quietly, 'I have to go. I don't want this to sound wrong. Please believe that. I'm not in the habit of picking up men in strange bars. Certainly not ones with a dog collar. But we rented an apartment round the corner. For the next two weeks, would you believe. It's as empty as the grave with just me rattling around in it. The TV doesn't even have cable and I can't understand a damn word of those Italian stations. If you need somewhere to stay, you can take the sofa or the floor. It's up to you.'

He did something odd at that moment. He looked at their two glasses – his almost full with red, hers empty – and very carefully moved them so they were in a perfect line, parallel with the edge of the table. It was a touch obsessive, she thought. Or perhaps not. His pale, smart face had turned thoughtful. It really was his choice, she guessed.

'I don't know,' he murmured. 'I can find somewhere, I'm sure.'

'It's got a terrace,' she added. 'We're right on the top of the block. You can see the dome of St Peter's. You can see places I don't even know the names of.'

'A terrace?' he repeated.

'One of the best damn terraces in Rome. That's what the agent said and I can't imagine a Roman would lie, now would he?'

'Not for a moment,' he said and raised his glass to her.

Five minutes later they went outside. She was giggling, light-headed, and scarcely noticed the softly falling snow. A handful of office workers were struggling through the deep, crisp drifts in the street. Peter had just a small bag with him, a black polyester one stuffed to bursting, the way single men did.

He reached into his coat pockets, pulled something from the depths, stretched it out and looked ready to begin adjusting it over his finely sculpted grey head.

His quick, intelligent eyes caught hers. He was unsure about this for some reason.

'I'd look a fool now, wouldn't I?' he asked, abruptly stuffing it back into his pocket as if he'd just had second thoughts.

It was one of those stupid Disney-style hats that kids wore. Big Mickey Mouse ears you tied around your head.

'You'd look a fool,' she said, then took his arm when he offered it, leaning on him as they struggled through the snow, past a deserted Piazza Navona, on towards home.

Listening to Gianni Peroni cough his way through a series of bathroom ablutions, Nic Costa flicked through the prints that had come back from the photo shop and found himself bugged by the minutiae of the last sixteen hours. The focus of the investigation was now fixed understandably on the man in black, who stood on the steps of the fountain, locked in the Weaver stance next to the frozen dolphins, dispensing deadly fire from his outstretched hand. Trying to summon up a vision of that distant figure made it easy to forget there was one other unknown actor in the scene: the person who was trapped inside the Pantheon when they arrived, the individual who had brushed against Nic Costa as he fled the cavernous interior of the hall, with its macabre secret trapped beneath a growing mountain of ice and snow.

Costa knew it was important to gather information on the man in black, to find out where he stood in the story the FBI agents were about to share with them. But he couldn't forget the other player in events either, someone who seemed an interloper at the scene, one whose presence there – as accomplice or accidental spectator? – demanded an explanation.

He tried to remember his impressions of those hurried moments in the dark, tried to follow Falcone's sensible if caustic admonition: interview yourself, and don't leave out the tough questions. He'd scarcely seen the figure who dashed in and out of the murky corners of the airy, freezing hemisphere that night. Mauro's photos didn't help either. Costa had scanned through most of the two hundred prints, covering everything from their time in the bar to the last moments outside the Pantheon. In the crucial shots all Mauro had captured were vague, ghostly shadows, black smears on film. It was surely unreasonable to expect anything else. Once they returned to the Questura, he would pass the photos to a specialist in forensic, but his gut told him there was nothing there worth keeping.

Or worth killing for. Surely the man in black would have understood that too?

Interview yourself. Nic Costa knew he'd seen nothing but shadows. But there were other senses. He closed his eyes and tried to think. There was something there. He recalled the moment now, and it was surely the very oddness of the memory that had sent it to the back of his mind since it seemed so implausible.

When the fugitive had brushed past him two things had happened. A hand – small, quick, nimble – had flicked at his jacket, automatically searching, as if it did this always without thinking. And there was a fleeting fragrance – something musky and lingering, familiar too, a scent that was fixed to a single connection in his head.

He looked at the slight shadow slipping out from the corner of the illuminated portico in the last-but-one photograph Mauro Sandri took in his life.

The perfume was patchouli oil. He knew the kind of person who liked to wear the old hippie scent these days too. Street kids, the ones who'd worked their way in from the Balkans, Turkey and beyond, looking to find a welcoming paradise, discovering, instead, that for many the only way to stay alive was to develop, as quickly as possible, a talent for pickpocketing or worse.

Peroni walked into the room and stared over his shoulder, interested.

'Anything there?'

'No,' Costa replied, tapping his forehead. 'It was there. I should have known. Whoever was in the interior, it *was* a bum. Of a kind anyway. He tried to get something out of my pocket on the way out. He had that . . . kind of perfume you get on the street kids. Sweet. Almost like dope. Patchouli. You know the smell I mean?'

Peroni sat next to him on the sofa. He was fresh from the shower. Costa liked the way his partner looked now. Activity was good for both of them.

'Oh yes,' Peroni said with a nod.

'It's an eastern thing. You see them selling the stuff in the Campo a lot.'

'Around Termini too,' Peroni added. 'From what I recall you tend to find that stuff only on girls. Which means they're into dope. Or selling themselves. Or both. On very rare occasions, they can be remarkably conscious of their personal hygiene for kids who live on the streets.'

Costa thought about that light, fluting voice in the dark. 'It's a girl, then.'

Peroni frowned. 'Why'd she try to lift something from you? If I'd been running out of that place, you wouldn't have seen me for dust.'

'Maybe she's a pickpocket. Not what you say.'

'It's possible—'

'They're not all into dope and prostitution, Gianni. Just the ones you met. I've dealt with plenty of street muggings too. Some of these kids are professionals in their own way. They steal out of second nature.'

'I believe you.' Peroni didn't look convinced.

'So tell me again about the CCTV. In the Pantheon.'

'Nothing to tell.' Peroni grimaced. 'There were four cameras. He'd done something to each of them. The security guy I talked to didn't know what. He said it had to be in the control box or something. It wasn't just a matter of snipping the wires either. If he'd done that—'

Costa interrupted him. 'The alarm would have gone off.'

'Quite.' Peroni pulled on a tie and yanked it roughly around his bull-like neck. 'What are you getting at?'

Some small certainty was growing in Costa's mind. 'He somehow got into the place without triggering the alarm. Maybe he'd some keys, we don't know. He must have talked the woman inside somehow too. He couldn't risk attacking her in the square, even in weather like this. And he did what he wanted without triggering the alarm either. Otherwise he wouldn't have been out of the place by the time we arrived. It took us, what? Ten minutes, no more, to get from the bar to the Pantheon after we got the call. He had to kill the woman, undress her, make that mark on her back. That must have taken the best part of hour, possibly more.'

Peroni nodded, unsure where this was going. 'Maybe he stepped on an alarm or something after he'd killed her.'

'Could happen, I guess. But what if he got out of there clean too? What if he locked everything up carefully behind him and he was just walking away when the bell started ringing? So he thinks: *Why?* He's not in there. Nothing alive's in there, or at least that's what he thought. He's disabled the alarms in all the places he needs to. He knows where to walk without triggering anything. What he doesn't know is some immigrant kid is hiding inside too, maybe trying to get out of the cold, I don't know. And this kid saw everything he did. Everything.'

'Not good,' Peroni murmured darkly.

Costa was still flicking through the prints absent-mindedly, not really looking at them. He realized now they were out of order. The developer had processed them in a rush, mixing them up. Some didn't match the right envelopes.

'So what would he do?' Costa queried.

Peroni nodded. 'He'd wait outside till we opened the doors. Until whoever was inside tried to get away. And he'd kill the kid. Or try to. Except poor Mauro got in front of the bullets instead. And you started chasing the bastard before he could finish the job. Jesus—'

Costa's fingers skipped over the prints, stopped over one and pulled it out of the pack. The photo had slipped into the wrong bunch. It was stacked in the middle of the series in the bar. So easy to miss.

Mauro had wound up the zoom to go in close. It was probably the last real photo he ever took. The girl was almost as tall as Nic Costa, but slightly built, and wore a dark windcheater and jeans. She was slipping past the portico, just beginning to run. The shot was taken at an angle. Maybe Mauro was falling already, struck by the bullets, as he pressed the shutter button, spinning on his heels trying to avoid the deadly fire.

It was hard to gauge her age from this single shot, but that was often the case with kids working the streets. Physically she looked no more than thirteen or fourteen, with a waif's haircut rough cropped short into the head. But there was an adult, haunted look in her pretty, dark face. Her young mouth was stretched into what looked half yawn, half scream. A chilly mix of terror and determination stared out from her wide-open eyes, beyond Mauro, straight at the man on the steps standing by the frozen dolphins, trying to end her life.

Peroni looked closely at the photo. 'An immigrant kid. Turkish maybe. She won't have a home. She won't even have a real identity. She isn't going to come running to us.'

Costa looked at his watch. They had fifteen minutes till the appointment in the Via Veneto. They'd need to move quickly to get there on time.

'Someone's got to know her,' he said.

Gianni Peroni sucked through his teeth, still transfixed by the photo and the vulnerable face gazing back at them. He'd worked vice for years and understood the inevitable path some of these kids took from petty street crime to drugs and prostitution. He hated the idea of kids going astray too, probably even more now given his present delicate state.

The big man sighed and peered into Costa's face.

'I can call in some favours, Nic,' he said, sounding reluctant. 'But maybe we've got to go places Leo had best not hear about. That OK with you?'

Costa glanced at the photo again and the kid's dark, desperate eyes.

'Yeah,' he murmured. 'You bet it's OK.'

The American embassy stood on a steep bend on the Via Veneto, a stiff climb up from the Piazza Barberini. Here, behind well-guarded iron gates, a small army of diplomats, paper-pushers, military officers, immigration officials and, for all Costa knew, professional spooks populated the elegant nineteenth-century labyrinth of corridors of what had once been the Palazzo Margherita.

Leo Falcone met them in the waiting room, silent and serious in a grey business suit. To Costa's surprise, Teresa Lupo was with him, twiddling her nascent pony-tail, a touch scruffy in an old winter jacket and jeans, and not happy either.

'How are you, Gianni?' she asked Peroni as they all sat together, waiting.

'I'm doing just fine,' Peroni replied. 'No offence, but what the hell are you doing here?'

'Working,' she answered gruffly. 'If I'm allowed. Do you have a problem with that?'

He grunted something that sounded like an apology.

'She's here because I wanted her here,' Falcone explained. 'Whatever papers these people have, that body still has to be accounted for.'

'Told you,' Teresa added. 'Just the fucking copy typist.'

'If that's the way you see it,' Falcone murmured, watching a tall formal-looking man walk towards them, some papers in his hand. 'But let's keep these arguments to ourselves, please.'

The embassy official introduced himself as Thornton Fielding. He didn't look like a natural colleague for Agent Leapman. The man was diplomatic and articulate. He wanted their signatures on some non-disclosure papers too.

Falcone stared at the paperwork. 'This is Italy, Mr Fielding. I'm not in the habit of signing forms about what I will or won't do in my own country.'

Fielding didn't even blink. 'Technically, Inspector, this is the sovereign territory of the United States of

America. That's how embassies work, I'm afraid. Either you sign these forms or you don't get to see Agent Leapman.' He hesitated. 'Personally I'd find that a damn good reason for *not* signing, but the choice is yours.'

'You like him too, huh?' Peroni asked.

'He's just the most fun guy you're ever going to meet,' Fielding said quietly. 'Now are you putting your name to these or not?'

When they were done he made a call from the desk. They watched as Emily Deacon walked down the corridor towards them.

'Nice woman,' Fielding said. 'Don't judge her by the company she keeps.'

Then he disappeared down the corridor, leaving them to Emily Deacon. They followed her and watched as she swiped an ID card on the security door to what turned out to be a large, high-ceilinged office.

Agent Leapman was seated in a leather executive chair behind a polished walnut desk, squeezed into a tight white shirt with the sleeves rolled up to display beefy, powerful arms. Emily Deacon, surely the junior partner in this relationship, motioned them to a leather sofa, then perched on an office chair next to him, demure in plain brown slacks and a cream shirt. She held a notepad on her lap and could, Costa thought, have passed as a secretary, were it not for the intent way she kept shuffling through a pile of papers on the desk, looking as if she knew every last sheet.

'I appreciate you coming here.' Leapman spoke with no visible emotion as he played with a remote switch in his hand. The blinds on the window turned through ninety degrees to block out the security lights outside.

A small presentation screen came down from the ceiling.

'We had a choice?' Teresa asked.

'Not really,' Leapman replied, staring at her frankly. 'I know I said I wasn't laying down any orders about who could come to this meeting, Falcone, but I rather expected it would be police only.'

Falcone took a deep breath before answering. 'A piece of paper from the Palazzo Chigi doesn't change Italian law. Miss Lupo has to sign a death certificate for the woman. She's every right to be here. You can make a phone call to check if you want.'

Leapman allowed himself a brief glance towards Emily Deacon, one that said, 'See, I told you what they're like.'

'OK,' he grumbled. 'Just remember what the deal is here. This is for you people only. I don't want to read it in *Il Messaggero* tomorrow morning. Deacon . . .'

He passed over the remote and she hit the button. A photo came on the screen. It was a building Costa recognized from somewhere, then a series of shots of the same place, taken from different angles: a rose-coloured temple of some kind, shot in bright sun, near fountains and water, with a large rotunda dome supported by open columns.

'It looks like the Pantheon,' Peroni said immediately.

'It should do,' she said. 'It's the Palace of Fine Arts in San Francisco. Built for the 1915 International Exhibition. The architect, Maybeck, was trying to recreate something classically Roman, like an engraving by Piranesi of some half-ruined temple.'

'Nice,' Peroni answered. 'You got a body there too?'

She nodded, surprised perhaps that he got the point so quickly. 'Last May. It was the first, as far as we know.'

'Who?' Falcone asked immediately.

'A man,' she said. 'Just a tourist from Washington. In spite of what we saw today we don't think this is sexual. We could be wrong . . .'

Leapman rocked his seat to and fro in disapproval.

'We just don't know,' she continued. 'The place is near the Marina. Pretty safe most of the time, but San Francisco's a city with some tough parts nearby. The cops put it down to street crime. Just the one odd thing, though.'

She pressed the button and ran through a new series of photos. They were of the victim, face-down on the rose-coloured stone floor. He was naked from the waist up. The cord that had been used to strangle him still dug deep into the flesh at the back of his neck. A rough pattern was cut into his lower back in an approximation of the shape they'd seen in the Pantheon that morning.

Leapman cleared his throat, lit a cigarette and said, 'He was still practising then. It took a little while before he got it right. Next.'

More photos, this time of a stumpy circular tower with two galleries at the summit, pointing up into a clear blue sky.

'Coit Tower, also San Francisco,' she continued. 'Three weeks later they found this when they were opening up for the day. On the floor of the tower too. He's good with locks.'

It was another corpse. Totally naked this time. A man, face-down, with grey hair. He was running to fat. Perhaps fifty. The marks on his back were a little less ragged. The area of the pattern was larger, running out to the folds of flesh at his waist, and more distinct: a geometric dance of angles and curves that made a recognizable image.

'Who was he?' Falcone demanded.

'Tourist from New York,' Leapman replied. 'In town on his own. He'd been hanging out in gay bars, which kind of complicated things for a while.'

They could just about make out the withering glance Leapman was casting them across the room. 'That's the trouble with city cops,' he continued. 'Narrow minds. They like to jump to quick conclusions. The San Francisco guys just thought they had another local weirdo on their books. They didn't even call us in. We hadn't a clue any of this was starting to happen. Not for another month.'

He nodded at Emily Deacon. She cued up a shot of a classical building, with a white colonnaded portico and a rotunda dome, partly in brick. Only the stars and stripes flag fluttering from a pole told them this was not in Italy.

She took up the story. 'Monticello, Charlottesville, Virginia. End of June now. This was Thomas Jefferson's home in retirement, which may or may not be significant. Jefferson designed it himself. The neoclassical influence probably comes from his time as ambassador in Paris but you don't need to be an architect to see where the idea originated.'

'Dead tourist in the hall when they opened up,' Leapman interjected. The image of a body came up on the screen. 'Woman this time, local, from Virginia. You can imagine the picture.'

'Still nothing sexual?' Falcone asked.

Leapman shook his head.

'Can I see the autopsy reports for some of these people?' Teresa Lupo asked.

'No,' Leapman replied. 'We don't have copies to hand. Besides, I don't see the point.'

'Maybe—' she began.

'The answer's no. Next.'

It could almost have been the same building, except for the window in the portico, which had now changed shape.

'This is Jefferson too,' Emily Deacon added. 'The University of Virginia just round the corner. The Rotunda is effectively a half-size copy of the Pantheon. Just four days later. A man's body set in the centre of the hall, and this is pretty much what we saw today. He's got the pattern he wants now and he doesn't shift from it.'

She keyed up the corpse. The arms and legs were at the selfsame angle as those of the woman in the Pantheon. A second photo showed the cadaver turned onto its front.

'His scalpel work is improving,' Leapman said.

'Plus,' Deacon interjected, 'he's getting picky about the way he positions the body. The head faces due south. He kept to that afterwards. From now on too he alternates the position of the limbs. Sometimes angled like this. Sometimes with the feet together and the arms at ninety degrees to the torso.'

Leapman made an unhappy noise. This was a detail that failed to interest him.

'The point about facing south is particularly odd,' Emily continued, 'because in most of those buildings there was no obvious reason. They weren't aligned in any particular direction. We only picked up on this later.

In the Pantheon itself the entrance and the high altar do face north–south. You could see why he'd lay the body that way. All these ones before – it's as if he was planning for what happened last night. As if the Pantheon was some kind of final destination.'

'How hard is it?' Costa said.

'What?' Leapman asked.

'What he's doing to their back.'

Leapman looked at his colleague. He seemed out of his depth once he went beyond purely procedural matters.

'It's not simple and it's not that difficult either,' she said. 'I can give you the summary of the psychological profiling later. We're not done here yet.'

Another photo, a tiny circular building almost hidden in a wood, but still with an obvious ancestry. 'We were on the case by this time but he wasn't making it easy for us. There was another break now, until the middle of July. Perhaps he was worried he was chancing his arm. This is a classical folly in Chiswick, west London. Again, an American visitor. This time a woman.'

Now another Pantheon copy, this time set by a lake. 'Ten days later, Stourhead in Wiltshire, south-west England. By now he's stretching out the miles. Maybe he knows we've seen something. Maybe he *wants* us to see something.'

A familiar facade from Venice filled the wall. 'End of August. Il Redentore. By Palladio, which has clear echoes of the Pantheon. He's playing games and earning a lot of air miles. A man this time.'

'How many?' Falcone asked. 'In all?'

'Seven that we know of, excluding last night's

victim,' she said. 'There's nothing to suggest we have every one, though. This guy's clever. He hops countries. He kills at unpredictable intervals. It's only over the last few months that we've managed to collate the information to prove there's a pattern that goes beyond those first killings in the States. All we know for sure is that he's murdered five men and now three women. All American. All Caucasian. All middle class. All unexceptional. For all we know they were just picked at random to prove a point.'

'Which is?' Costa asked.

She played with the remote and pulled up a composite shot, seven scarred backs, each with the flesh marked in a similar fashion, then moved on to a graphic.

'This is the pattern from one of the later deaths. Probably the closest he got to what he was trying to achieve.'

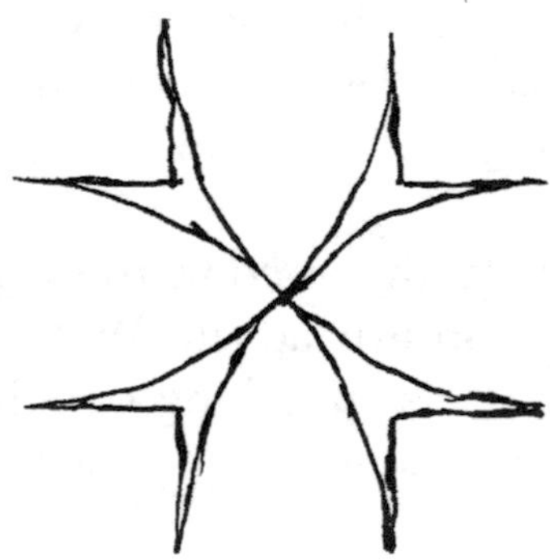

She turned on the room light, picked up a printout of the composite of the wounds, and placed it on Leapman's desk. Then she reached into a drawer and took out a thick, black pencil, a ruler and a compass and drew a square on the sheet, almost to the edges.

'The pattern's actually a subset of a more complicated idea.'

Very quickly, with the kind of skill Costa associated with an architect or an artist, she marked four straight lines inside the square, running from the point where the arms of the cross met the perimeter. Finally, she used the compass to join the points where both the curving lines and the straight ones met at the edge, describing a perfect circle.

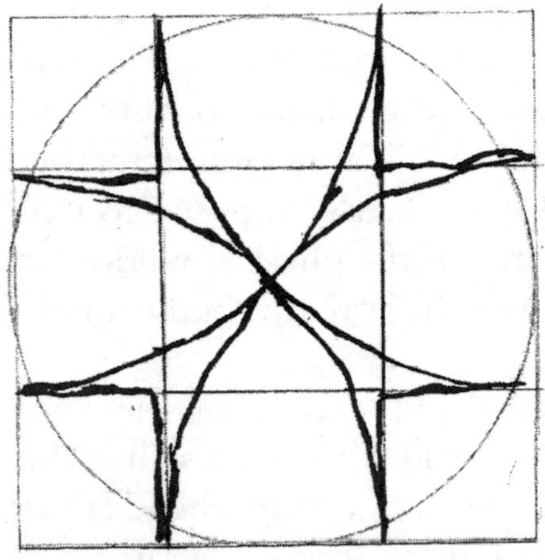

'This is what's called the sacred cut,' she said. 'With the first couple of victims you can even see the marks he used to align it properly.'

She pulled up two morgue shots, early versions of the shape. 'If you look closely, you can see he drew a couple of lines in felt tip to help him get the hang of things. The other pointer to suggest a link is the way he alternates the position of the limbs. This is a direct reference to the Vitruvian Man. A naked man, arms and legs outstretched, vertical and horizontal. Drawn within both a square and a circle. It's the same concept.'

She exchanged a brief glance with Costa. He understood the prompt.

'Like the body in the Pantheon,' he said. 'I get it.'

'Good for you,' Leapman muttered, making a point of looking at his watch. 'So, Agent Deacon. You're the architect here. What does it mean?'

'I just have a college degree in architecture,' she replied. 'It doesn't make me an expert.' She struggled to form the right answer, then looked at each of them in turn, as if to make sure they understood: she wasn't too sure of all this herself. 'On one level it's a construct used to explain the geometry behind ancient architecture. On another it's a metaphor for perfection, kind of a mystical symbol. It's supposed to represent a faultless union between the physical world and the spiritual one. Remember the way the body was laid out in the Pantheon?'

She sketched out a copy of the familiar da Vinci drawing, rapidly and with some skill. 'The Greeks were the first to set down in writing the idea that great buildings depended upon precise geometric proportions, though they probably stole it from Asia and the Middle East because you see the same theory in earlier buildings there. The Romans picked up the belief that those proportions came directly from the Gods through the shape of a human being. Vitruvius was a soldier under Julius Caesar before he became an architect. He wrote ten books that became the bible on the subject. They got lost for some centuries, until the Renaissance, when Vitruvius again became the primary source for most of the architects we respect today. Michelangelo drew Vitruvian bodies constantly, with limbs in both positions along the perimeter, trying to get inside the idea, and he wasn't alone.'

Emily Deacon placed both drawings side by side on the desk. 'Vitruvius used the human body, a holy vessel as far as he was concerned, as the starting point for the proportions needed to create the perfect building.'

Her slim fingers traced the outlines of the shapes. 'The Vitruvian Man squares the circle, just as the making of the sacred cut does. This had a religious importance. It symbolized the marriage of the earthly, the physical fact of the square, with the ineffable perfection of the celestial, the circle. It was about . . .' She looked across at Leapman, who was beginning to get restless with the detail. 'Finding some kind of truth, God even, inside a shape. The shape of a human body. The shape of a building. The proportions are the same. Look at these.'

She indicated the outlines of the sacred cut. 'You have just about every shape and proportion you are going to find in a great building there. Even the rectangles the cut creates fit a classically correct, arithmetic rule an architect calls the golden mean. It's the way things are meant to be.'

Costa tried to remember some of his old art lessons. They'd talked about the golden mean. It permeated everything: architecture, sculpture, painting, mathematics, even music.

She wasn't done. 'When this man, whoever he is, places a body in the centre of the Pantheon, or a place like it, what he's doing is making some kind of statement. Laying down a piece in a puzzle, looking to complete the picture. The Pantheon is simply a larger version of the geometric pattern he's describing with those dead limbs. A circle cut by a square. The woman lay where Hadrian must have once stood himself, looking out from the focus of an artificial cosmos, through the eye of the oculus, out to what he regarded as heaven. She was at the epicentre of this structured view of the universe he created. Equally, the real universe was looking back at her. Whoever this man is he knows all this. He's not just some . . . nut.'

'Really?' Leapman sighed. 'So where does this get us? Profiling has got us nowhere so far.'

'I don't know yet,' she half-snapped in reply. 'Maybe it makes him feel he's holy somehow. Maybe he's looking for something, trying to get order back into his world. But we've no data, so it's just guesswork. There's a missing piece here. This man is smart, educated and very, very capable. Something started him on this path. If we could find out what that is—'

'But we haven't,' Leapman interruped. 'And the odds are we won't. Why do we keep going over this? I don't want to understand the bastard. I want to catch him. This guy's killed at least eight people now, maybe more. All Americans. If we get the chance to ask him why once he's in jail, fine. But I'm not going to lose any sleep if he's just plain dead either. We're not going to nail down this animal by profiling or any other mumbo-jumbo. We get him through work.'

He gazed across the desk at Falcone. 'If we're lucky, we get him through you.'

A hint of a smile crossed the inspector's face. 'I'm not a great believer in luck, Agent Leapman. And by the way, that's nine people. We lost a photographer last night, if you recall. He was Italian, but all the same.'

Leapman cursed under his breath then glowered at the images of the dead, scarred backs.

'I do believe in detail, though,' Falcone continued. 'Why don't you just turn over everything you have and let us go through the material to see if there's anything you've missed?'

'We don't miss things,' Leapman snarled.

'Let me rephrase then,' Falcone said, correcting himself carefully. 'Perhaps there's a fact, an event in there that means something to us and nothing to you.'

To Costa's surprise, Leapman didn't throw the idea straight out of the window into the snow. 'It's got to work both ways,' he said eventually.

'Meaning?' Falcone wondered.

'Meaning a quid pro quo. Deacon works with you from now on. She reports back to me on what you find. In return you get some files and let her brief me on anything you discover.'

The woman looked up from the desk, her face suffused with sudden anger. 'Sir—'

Leapman interrupted, waving a dismissive hand in her direction. 'I can spare you. Saves me hearing all this shit about profiling and numbers and stuff.'

Falcone nodded and smiled at her. 'Agreed,' he said. 'Welcome on board.'

Leapman dragged the keyboard of his PC towards him. 'I'll email you some documents. Let me say this again. These are confidential. If you copy them outside the loop to anyone else, we'll know and I will personally drag your ass to the Palazzo Chigi for a serious kicking. It goes without saying that if I see them reported in the press you'll be writing parking tickets in Naples before the week's out.'

'You seem to have such influence,' Falcone said with a faint smile.

'If you like,' Leapman replied, 'you can test me.'

'No,' Falcone demurred. 'But you could tell me one more thing.'

'What's that?' Leapman answered without looking at him.

'How long you've been here in Rome, waiting for this man to turn up. How he sent you here in the first place. And—'

Falcone reached over and pushed the keyboard out of Leapman's reach, making sure the American had to look him in the face.

'Why the hell we had to wait for two people to die before you got around to telling us we had this kind of company on our streets.'

Leapman glowered at him. 'Deacon?'

She blinked, hesitating, then punched the remote. Costa could feel the hatred just rolling off her. A new photo came on the screen: an oriental temple, red walled with three roofs, set behind rows of white marble steps.

'The Temple of Heaven, Beijing,' she explained. 'A Chinese Pantheon if you like. The cosmology, the proportions, are virtually identical. It was a sacrificial altar once too.'

'Still is for the man out there,' Leapman said quietly, almost to himself.

Emily Deacon was struggling to keep her composure. 'This is the last we know of before Rome. In September a man of fifty-five was found there. You know the modus operandi by now. It took us a little while to get on the case. We never expected to see him outside North America or Europe. And –' she flicked the remote and pulled up some more tourist shots of the temple – 'there were other reasons.'

'Show the good people,' Leapman ordered.

She pulled up another shot and turned to stare at the wall. The man was on his back, naked, face contorted in death, a noose of cord biting cruelly into his neck.

'Excuse me,' she said and walked briskly out of the door.

Leapman sighed and picked up the remote, keying up the next picture: the victim turned face-down, with the now-familiar horned shape carved into his skin.

'After this,' Leapman continued, 'we had some intelligence. It pointed us to Rome.'

'Intelligence?' Falcone asked.

'Intelligence. Don't ask because I couldn't tell you even if I wanted. Just take my word for it. We had some idea that he was on his way here. So –' Leapman closed his eyes for a moment as if this were boring him. '– here I am, eating shit food, living in a service apartment, biding my time. Because my masters in Washington decide we should set up an office over here, wait around a little while and see what happens. Why didn't we tell you? Well, what do you think, Inspector? We didn't have any proof he was here. We didn't have a clue when or where he might do anything if he did turn up. What, exactly, would you have said if I'd walked in and placed this bunch of half-guesses and supposition on your desk?'

Leapman waited for an answer. It didn't come. 'I'll take that as a sign you see my point. We had to come. We had to wait. Now we know this animal's loose we've got to track him down once and for all. He's fucked around with us too much already. Besides . . .'

He keyed up some more shots of the corpse on the floor of the temple in Beijing.

'It wasn't some poor stupid tourist he killed this time. This guy was someone important. The military attaché at the US embassy in Beijing. Career diplomat. Talented guy. Stuffy background but you can't have everything. Came from one of those old New England families that put their offspring into public service just to prove what wonderful citizens they truly are, never once asking themselves whether it's the right job for the spoiled little brats in the first place.'

Leapman looked at the picture of the dead diplomat again and sighed. 'That's what class is about, don't you think? Being able to make choices?'

Then he pulled up another photo. It was the same man at a formal occasion, wearing a dinner jacket, shaking the hands of a smiling Chinese official. He was staring sourly at the camera, clutching at a full glass of booze as if it were a lifeline.

'His name was Dan Deacon,' Leapman explained. 'I don't see a family resemblance myself, but I guess it's there. Good old Dan fixed up his daughter with a fine career, huh? Not that I reckon he asked her once if it was what she wanted. One minute she's sitting back in Florence congratulating herself on getting an architectural degree. Next she's doing push-ups in boot camp because Daddy says so and, my, doesn't Daddy know how to glad-hand some of the people on the interview panels too. Still, it gives me an opportunity.'

He switched off the projector and rolled up the lights so they could see his face all the more clearly.

'You know what it's all about, folks?' Agent Leapman asked. 'Motivation. I'm giving you one motivated girl here. I picked her myself for that very reason. Use her well, won't you? And try to bring her back in one piece.'

Monica Sawyer's apartment was in a dark and narrow side street near the Palazzo Borghese, some way north of the Pantheon. The place was a square modern cabin built directly on top of the roof of a solid grey nineteenth-century block. It sat unnaturally on the summit of the building like a child's construction made of toy bricks. The estate agent boasted she had the best view in Rome. It was bullshit, but she had quite a view all the same, one so astonishing that she'd already booked another month at $3,500 a week, for May, when she and Harvey would be able to use to the full the terrace that stretched out on three sides of the ugly modern structure.

A perfect layer of snow, marked only by bird prints, now hid the warm terracotta tiles she'd seen when she arrived three days before. Monica walked carefully across the snow, which was close to ankle deep, listening to Peter O'Malley talk with wonder about what they could see. He had a soft, musical voice like that of an actor, one whose slightly metallic Irish tint reminded her how much the Hibernian accent had influenced American. The night was clear now, with a scattering of dark stratus high in a sky bright with a full moon. They had checked the TV when they arrived. Peter wanted to know what the weather would do and when he could return to Orvieto. She poured herself a Scotch while he listened to the impenetrable Italian on the box. There were pictures of cop cars around the Pantheon, shots of a police press conference with a tall, goatee-bearded inspector facing down the cameras and looking as if he wouldn't say a damn thing.

That wasn't what interested Peter, though. He wanted to know what the sky would bring. When the bulletin was done he told her. There would be more snow after midnight.

Now, on the terrace, still in her fur coat, she clutched the glass of Scotch and followed him round, listening. He'd stopped drinking. In truth, she thought, he hadn't consumed much at all in the enoteca. It was hard to tell.

Peter O'Malley was laughing now. They were standing on the northern side of the terrace, looking away from the river, up towards the rising lights of some hill.

His arm slipped through hers and squeezed gently.

'Symmetry,' he said. 'Can you see it?'

'Where?' she replied, feeling stupid.

'Everywhere. You just have to look.' He pointed to the twinkling street lamps on the distant hill. 'You know where that is?'

'No idea.'

'Trinità dei Monti. The church at the top of the Spanish Steps.'

She nodded. She'd walked there before the snow came and had been surprised to find there was a McDonald's near the foot of the twin staircases and an American-style Santa ringing a bell and yelling for money in Italian.

'Been there. So what?'

He led her round to the opposite wall of the apartment. The bright, white, wedding-cake building in the Piazza Venezia stood out like a sore thumb: in front of it the jumble of Renaissance rooftops, with the huge, half sphere of the dome she had come to recognize.

'That I do know,' she said, a little proud of herself. 'I went inside yesterday. It's beautiful. The Pantheon.'

'The home of all the gods,' he said. 'That's good.'

Then they went to the western wall, which had the larger part of the terrace, an expanse of open space a good ten yards deep, with flower pots, an old stone table, and a permanent, brick-built barbecue with a little sink by it. An awning had been built in front of the full-length windows. The shrivelled and leathery stems of a couple of meagre grapevines wound their way around the supporting pillars. A few blackened leaves still hung on the furled, wiry whips feeling their way through the trelliswork. Two tall gas heaters now whistled away, pumping out enough warmth to make it possible to sit outside, even on a night like this, to be alone in Rome, above everything, out of sight.

He was gesturing. She looked over the river, where a snow-clad circular building stood, brightly illuminated by a forest of spotlights.

'And that is?'

'I told you,' she objected. 'My first time here.'

'Castel Sant' Angelo. Think, Monica. Draw a line from Trinità dei Monti to the castle. Draw another line from the Pantheon, out to the Piazza del Popolo over there. What do you get?'

She looked out to the north, the direction he was pointing, out into the face of the icy breeze, then ducked beneath the trellis and fell into one of the hard, cold summer seats. She got what he was driving at. She wasn't stupid.

'A cross. A crucifix.'

'And we are?'

'Where the two arms meet? But so what, Peter? Don't get scary on me. It's just coincidence. It's just . . .'

She looked out over the city, shining under the icy, bright moon, and shivered. 'It's just how things are.'

He walked under the shelter of the awning, stole her glass from the table, took a sip of whisky from it.

'What if there are no coincidences? What if everything has form? A reason?'

He wasn't serious, she thought. It was just some game. 'In a place like this, you could come up with stuff like that anywhere,' she protested. 'I could say, look, here's the Colosseum. Or the Capitol. Or whatever. Look. It makes a circle. A square. An octagon. It's Rome, for God's sake. It's all here.'

'Quite,' he replied.

'You're sounding like a priest now,' she said softly, slurring the words a little. 'I'd forgotten for a while that's what you are.' She didn't know what to do. Whether to feel stupid for letting a stranger into her home, into her mind, like this. Or just to roll with it and see where everything went. He was a priest. There was nothing to be scared about.

'Must be hard doing what you do,' she said. 'Having to stay apart from other people.'

'There's nothing hard in that. It helps you think about what really matters.'

'You don't miss the comfort of another person?'

His smart eyes clouded over. 'You can't miss what you never knew.'

'I don't believe that, Peter. Not of you.'

Peter O'Malley was not a happy man. He was looking for something, all the time. Why? she wondered.

'Why are you a priest? It doesn't seem right. Whatever would make a man like you do this?'

'A man like me . . .' He laughed lightly, breaking the fragile spell that had begun to hover around them, something dark at its edges, and she felt relieved, lightheaded even. 'A man like me is just a fool looking for magic where none exists. And then . . .'

He waved a hand at the glorious night, the city slumbering under a jewelled sky.

'Then it just sneaks up on you and you realize it was there, in front of you, all along.'

It wasn't the face of a priest. That was the problem. It was the face of a man of the world, one who'd lived a full and active existence before retreating into this dark shell, the anonymous uniform of the calling.

'Magic,' she muttered, wondering if she would follow where she thought he was leading.

He looked at his watch. Her heart sank. 'And a city full of churches, Monica. I'd best find one to pray in, don't you think?'

An hour after they left the embassy, Emily Deacon arrived at the Questura. She'd dressed down for the night: black jacket, black jeans, blonde hair loose around her slim neck. She looked younger, like a student just out of college. And relieved too, Costa thought, to be out of the grip of Agent Leapman, even if being reassigned so abruptly had come as a shock.

She stood in the main office next to Costa's desk, scanning the room. The night shift were hard at work, making calls, sifting through records on computer screens, reading reports. Falcone had put virtually everyone he had on the job. Some fifty men and women had now begun the task of collating information, trawling through CCTV videos, interviewing the people who lived in the apartments over the shops and restaurants near the Pantheon.

'Are you getting anywhere?' she asked.

Peroni glanced at Costa. The two men had demanded a discussion with Falcone earlier, wanting to know exactly how much information they should share with the Americans. It had been inconclusive. Falcone had made a good point: it was ludicrous to labour the question until they found something worth sharing and that seemed some way off. They already knew the CCTV cameras in the Pantheon had nothing. Those in the streets nearby had captured little but the blizzard. Falcone had shrugged and left it at that, then closeted himself upstairs with Commissario Moretti for a private meeting.

'Early days,' Peroni answered hesitantly. 'Can I get you something? A coffee?'

The acute blue eyes looked him up and down. 'You don't trust me. It's understandable. I'd probably feel the same way if it was me. It's because I'm American, I guess.'

'No,' Costa told her. 'It's just . . . a little unusual.'

'You have difficulty dealing with the unusual?' she asked.

'Not at all. It's just that sometimes it takes a while to adapt. Police departments are like monasteries really.'

Peroni snorted. A smile flickered on Emily Deacon's face.

'Monasteries?' she asked, raising a slender fawn eyebrow.

'Really,' Costa protested. 'OK, we let in a few women for show. But these are institutions that keep themselves to themselves, rarely share their working practices with others and suspect all outsiders on principle. Big organizations work that way. The FBI's the same, surely.'

She thought about that. 'There *are* more women.'

'And the rest of it?' Peroni asked.

'Point taken.'

The two men looked at each other. Peroni kicked over a seat and beckoned to her to take it. Then he went off for some coffees.

She looked at the screen. 'What's this?'

'It's the database we keep on Balkan criminals,' Costa replied. 'It just gets bigger by the day.'

'He isn't Balkan, whatever that means these days.'

'You know that?'

'I know that. I saw the profiling reports. They had some data on where the man had stayed in the US. All phoney names, phoney credit cards. He did it well. We've interviewed people who spoke to him. They all gave different descriptions. He's good at disguise. He's good with accents. Sometimes American English. Sometimes UK. Australian. South African. He could handle them all.'

'You have a photo-fit?'

It was the obvious question. Her face said as much. 'How many do you want? Leapman has included them in the files he's sent to your boss. We've got them coming out of our ears. Every one different. I mean *completely* different. I told you. He's good.'

Peroni returned with the drinks. She looked at the stewed brew in the plastic cups and said, 'Do you call that coffee? There's a place near the Pantheon. Tazza d'Oro. If we have time we could go there. That's coffee.'

Peroni bristled and in very rapid, very colloquial Italian, the kind a couple of street cops would throw at each other in the heat of the moment, protested. 'Hey, kid. Don't throw your toys out of the pram. You're dealing with a couple of guys who live here. We know Tazza d'Oro. Since when did they start letting Yankees in?'

She didn't miss a syllable. 'Since they found out we tip properly. Where are you from in Tuscany?'

'Near Siena.'

'I can hear it.' She nodded at Costa. 'He's Roman. Middle class. Doesn't swear enough to be anything else.' Emily Deacon paused. 'Am I earning any trust here?'

'Kind of,' Costa conceded. 'You didn't learn that at language college.'

She nodded. 'Didn't need to. I lived here in Rome when I was a kid. Nice house on the Aventino. For almost a decade. My dad was based at the embassy for most of that time. Then I did an architecture degree in Florence. And you know what's funny?'

They didn't say a word. From her face they could tell this wasn't funny at all.

'Maybe it's from the last few years I spent in Washington, but sometimes I must still sound American. It just slips out. You can always tell. You always get someone on a bus or somewhere who gives you a nasty look. Or a little lecture about colonialism and how, being Roman, they just know this subject inside or out. Or maybe they just spit in your face. That happens from time to time too.'

' "Always"?' Peroni wondered, taking the argument back an important step.

She sipped at the coffee and pulled a sour face. 'No. That's an exaggeration. Just a lot more than when I was a kid. In fact . . .' She took her attention off them at that moment, began to conduct some inner conversation with herself. 'I don't ever remember it happening then. This was a happy place. I never wanted to leave.'

'The world's not so happy any more,' Costa said. 'For all of us.'

'Agreed.' She fidgeted on the hard office chair, uncomfortable at having revealed as much as she had. 'I'm still waiting for an answer, though. This guy isn't Serb or Kosovan or anything. So why are you going through all these records?'

Costa explained about the girl who'd escaped from them inside the Pantheon, and how some Balkan connection was probably the best way to find her, since they controlled the street people as much as anyone did. Then he pushed over the photo Mauro had taken. Emily looked at the young, frightened face.

'Poor kid,' she said quietly. 'Trying to pick your pocket when she must have been scared out of her tiny mind. Are they really that desperate?'

Costa hated simplistic explanations. 'Sometimes. It's what they do. I don't want to sound judgemental. There's plenty of people out there on the streets who'll scream "Zingari!" every time some petty crime happens. We've plenty of other crooks too. But the honest answer is: yes, they're that desperate. And it's an organized business. With its own structure. Its own rules.'

'Good,' she said. 'It should mean you can find her.'

That was Peroni's call. Costa watched him squirming.

'Maybe we can,' the big man conceded.

'Will she have family here? Can you track her down like that?'

'Most of them don't have family,' Peroni explained. 'Not what we'd regard as family anyway.'

She couldn't take her eyes off the photo. It seemed a good time to ask.

'When Leapman called you in for this assignment,' Costa began, 'you could have refused, surely. The fact this man killed your father means you want justice, sure. But it also means you're involved, beyond anything the likes of us would expect. You have . . . something personal invested here. That could worry me.'

Emily Deacon took one last look at the photo, then placed it on the desk. 'I could have said no when my dad laid a job with the Bureau straight in my lap. I'd got a good architecture degree. I could have gone on and done a master's. Here probably.'

She looked at him, trying to work out the right answer for herself too. 'You won't understand. We're Deacons, good Boston stock, going back a long way. We grow up with a sense of duty. There have been Deacons working for the government for the best part of a hundred years. In the Treasury. The State Department. The military. It's what we do. We don't ask why.'

He wondered how much of that she really believed. 'And when we find this man. What do you want then?'

'Justice,' she said with plain, flat certainty.

'Is that what Agent Leapman wants too?'

'Joel Leapman is a primitive organism driven by primitive desires.' She spoke with cold, aloof disdain. 'It's thanks to people like him that people like me get spat at on buses. Ask him what he's after. Not me.'

She thought for a moment then fixed them with her keen intelligent eyes. 'I know exactly what I want. I want to see this man standing up in court, getting convicted for every last human being he's killed. Every last life he's ruined. I want to see him go to jail forever and have those ghosts haunt him each and every day. I want to sleep better knowing that he can't, not for all those nightmares coming his way. Will that do?'

Peroni cast Costa a sideways glance. The one that said: why do we always get them?

Nic Costa knew what he meant. He was coming to understand a little about this woman and it didn't fill him with joy. She wasn't at the hard end of investigations with the FBI. Of that he was sure. Perhaps Leapman has called her in to the Rome inquiry because of her specialist architectural knowledge, much as he seemed to dismiss it. Or her perfect Italian. Perhaps it was even simpler than that. Her presence was down to who she was: the daughter of the last victim. The Deacons seemed to be an important family. Maybe he had no choice. Maybe Leo Falcone was in the same position. It would explain the uncharacteristic way the normally abrasive and individualist inspector had rolled over and allowed the Americans to walk straight into the case.

'You think this guy knows Rome?' Peroni asked.

'Like the back of his hand,' she said straight away. 'I'm certain of it.'

'Nah, he doesn't,' Peroni told her with some certainty. 'He thinks he knows it. He's like you. He goes to Tazza d'Oro and likes it because he feels it makes him Roman, not like some cheapskate tourist throwing coins into the Trevi fountain. Don't get me wrong. That's nice. That's good, because it means he's trying. You too. But it's not the real thing. Me and Nic are. This is our town. We drink coffee in places a million times better than Tazza d'Oro. Want some?'

Her delicate eyebrows rose in amusement. 'Now?'

Peroni scowled at the plastic cup. 'Yeah. Why not? This stuff is piss.'

'And you think it's going to be easy to find this kid?'

He nodded at the computer. 'Absolutely. But not sitting in front of the one-eyed monster there. This is a people business, Emily. Night people, if you get my meaning. I got a whole list of them in my head right now. You're going places in Rome you didn't even know existed.'

She considered this. 'Really. So if it's that easy, Officer Peroni—'

'Hey, hey! Gianni. Nic. Please . . .'

Emily Deacon smiled. 'If it's that easy, don't you think he might be doing it too? This girl must have seen what happened. She must know things we'd dearly love to hear. Why else would he want to kill her in the first place?'

Costa gave his partner a hard look. They should have thought of this themselves. They'd been distracted by the meeting at the embassy, and having an outsider attached to the investigation.

'I'll drive,' Costa said.

*

By the time Peroni was renewing his acquaintance with the first name on his long list of East European hoods, Teresa Lupo was dictating the preliminary autopsy results on Mauro Sandri, running through all the familiar terms she'd come to learn over the years when dealing with firearms deaths, still unable to push what she'd heard in the American embassy out of her head.

Silvio Di Capua was busy cleaning the stainless-steel table, watching her out of the corner of his beady eyes with the same guarded awe she'd come to expect, wondering, perhaps, what she saw in the big, old Tuscan cop who was now sharing her home. It was none of his business, even if it was a good question. Gianni Peroni was a good human being: honest, decent and kind, in spite of his tough outward appearance. She liked his company.

At least Silvio Di Capua's crush on her had waned a little since her assistant realized she was no longer available. He was by the door now, washing his hands and looking ready to grab his too-short black leather bomber jacket and head home for the night when Leo Falcone walked in. She watched with some dismay the way Silvio flinched at the sight of the inspector, like a mouse catching sight of a bird of prey. It occurred to her, not for the first time, that the analogy was appropriate. Falcone, as his surname suggested, had the beady eyes of a raptor and a bare, birdlike skull too. The sharp jut of his goatee only enhanced further the impression of a hunter. He was the kind of person someone like Silvio Di Capua feared the most. Not just for his acerbic tongue or the sudden, direct habit he had of tackling every issue head on. Worse, much worse sometimes, was the way he never let anything go. This irked Di Capua more than anyone because, when it came to morgue matters, he was the one Falcone chose as the weak point, the place to start poking at with a long, suspicious forefinger.

Teresa Lupo was apt not to play things by the book, if a few unorthodox methods suited her better, but she made a point of keeping those habits under her hat, most of the time, anyway. It was always Di Capua whom Falcone squeezed for proof, turning those bleak, suspicious eyes on him and asking all the questions the little man never wanted to hear. Then there'd be the recriminations and, worst of all, in the end Teresa would have to hear out Silvio's grovelling apology for blabbing, accompanied, as always, by an invitation to dinner.

She looked up from her notes, feigned a smile and said, 'Inspector. Good evening. And you've come alone too. Not with those nice new American friends of yours. How pleasant.'

'It wasn't my idea,' Falcone objected. 'You heard, didn't you?'

'Actually, no. I was trying to work out a few things in my head. Such as why a very odd corpse was stretched out on the floor of the Pantheon like that. Listening to cops bitch at one another is a secondary diversion at such times and I'm happy for it to stay that way.' She switched off the tape recorder and packed her notes back into a folder. 'So what can I do for you?'

Falcone came straight to the point as usual. 'You can tell me what you two found out when you had the woman to yourself. And don't tell me it's nothing because I won't believe you.'

She beamed at him. 'This is because of your great faith in our abilities?'

'If you like,' he conceded grudgingly. 'Or maybe I just know when you're not telling us something. There's an air of smugness around this place right now and I'd very much like to puncture it.'

'You don't want the report on that poor photographer?'

'I know what happened to the photographer.' He sighed. 'I was there. Remember?'

She looked into his miserable face and felt a twinge of guilt. Falcone wasn't happy about any of this. It wasn't fair to bitch. All the same, she did have something to bitch about.

'So you want me to offer some insights into a corpse which, with your full agreement, was snatched away from me right in front of my eyes, quite without reason, and completely contrary to Italian law, too, I might add?'

Falcone blinked back a rising inner tide of fury which, in what she recognized was a thoroughly childish fashion, made her feel they were now just about even.

'Don't start,' he said. 'I've just been upstairs listening to Bruno Moretti, among others, telling me how we need to keep the FBI sweet at every turn.'

Falcone went silent, thinking. It was an odd moment, Teresa thought. For once he looked as if he were racked by doubts.

Somewhere outside a car started with a sweet, certain rumble.

'Join me,' Falcone ordered and walked to the window. There he pointed to an expensive-looking Lancia travelling across the car park towards the exit, too fast for the treacherous conditions.

'Know who that is?' Falcone asked.

'What am I?' she snapped. 'Superwoman, perfect night vision through a car roof or something?'

'Filippo Viale. Top-rung spook from SISDE. I thought you might have bumped into him in the past.'

She didn't say a word. This was *so* unlike Falcone.

'He sat in on the entire conversation with Moretti. Truth is, *he*, not Moretti, was running things there.'

'Leo?' she asked. 'Are you all right?'

'I'm fine,' he grumbled. 'I'm just pissed off. I've got the Americans telling me I report to them about what we're doing. I've got Viale telling me I report to *him* about what the Americans are doing. And somewhere in the middle of all this I need to find out what happened to that woman and make sure it doesn't happen again.'

He was scared. No, that wasn't right. He was lacking in confidence, and in Leo Falcone that was almost the same thing.

'I'm sorry,' she replied. It was deeply out of character for Falcone to give away details like this, particularly the part about the SISDE officer. Those people moved in and out of the building like ghosts, unremarked, almost unseen. It was standard form that no one acknowledged their presence, let alone admitted to taking orders from them.

She reached for some papers in the folder in front of her.

'Since this is for you and you alone I'll make it short and sweet. Silvio? Get the camera.'

Silvio slunk off to the filing cabinet and came back with a large, semi-professional digital Canon.

Teresa Lupo looked at him. 'Lights, Silvio. Action.'

Hands shaking slightly, he fired up the screen. She took it and started flicking through the shots there.

'Do we know who she was, this tourist?' she asked.

'Not really,' Falcone answered. 'Just the name. Her hotel. Is it relevant? You heard what Leapman said. This man is supposed to select his victims at random. The only linking factor is that they're all American tourists.'

'I know that. But what did this woman do? What was her job?'

Falcone shook his head. 'I've no idea. I don't hold out much hope we're going to find out either. Leapman has put out a statement to the papers saying she was a divorcee from New York. No profession. No personal details. We're supposed to refer all media inquiries to him from now on, which is the one part of this piece I am quite happy with.'

'Illuminating.'

She pulled up a shot of the woman's torso and hit the magnification button. Falcone followed the direction of her finger. 'Of course, this would be so much easier if I had a body to work with, but I'll do my best. You see this?'

She was pointing to an obvious scar on the left-hand side of the woman's stomach.

'Appendix?' Falcone asked.

'Are you kidding me?' she gasped. 'What kind of surgeon leaves an appendix scar that size, with that much loss of flesh? If they did that in the States this poor bitch would have sued them for billions. She wouldn't be holidaying in Rome, she'd own the place.'

Di Capua was rocking backwards and forwards on his heels now, sweating a little, distinctly uncomfortable, as if he knew where this was going.

Falcone scowled at her. 'So—'

'So I don't have a damn body. I can't take a better look at this under proper lighting. I can't try and see what lies underneath the scar tissue. Thank you, thank you, thank you—'

'What is it?' Falcone interrupted.

'My guess? It's the scar from a bullet wound. Nasty one too. Judging by the size of the affected area, she got shot close up. She was probably lucky to live through it.'

Falcone's face screwed up in puzzlement. 'A bullet wound? How old?'

She traced her finger over the photo. 'Can't be exact. More than three years. It happened to her as an adult too. When she'd stopped growing. Beyond that I don't know. Of course it would be easy to clear this up if we could get the woman's medical history. What was she called?'

'Margaret Kearney,' he replied. 'We won't get any medical records out of them. You saw what they're like.'

'This happened in Rome, Leo!' Her voice had risen a couple of decibels. She couldn't stop it. 'Why the hell are we being pushed around as if we're disinterested bystanders or something?'

Falcone didn't look any more pleased with what was going on than she was. 'I don't know. Maybe because of who his last victim was. A diplomat. What's the point in asking? We just have to learn to live with what we have. You think I should walk back into Moretti's office and ask him to change things around? Do you really believe this kind of decision's coming from his desk?'

'I don't know.' Briefly she felt guilty for raising the

subject in the way she had, as if it were Falcone's fault. It was pointless taking her anger out on him.

'And that's all you've got?' he added. 'That she had a bullet wound? Even if it's true, so what? It doesn't mean a damn thing.'

'I guess not.'

She looked at Silvio Di Capua, who was quaking in his small, very clean Chelsea boots. 'Get the cord, Silvio. And the hair.'

He went away making a soft, squeaking noise of terror, and came back with a couple of sample bags.

Teresa Lupo picked up the first. 'In order to stop you screeching the place down, let me say I removed this entirely innocently from the woman's neck. They just said they wanted the body. I didn't think they'd miss it.'

The fabric lay coiled like a tiny serpent inside the evidence bag.

'That's the thing he used?' Falcone asked. 'It's a cord?'

'It *looks* like a cord,' Teresa replied, then took out the fabric and, with two sets of tweezers, carefully unrolled it. 'Until you take it apart a little.'

Falcone blinked at the object unfurling under her precise fingers. It was dark grey and green, an odd patchwork that had been tightly rolled into the ligature which had killed the woman.

Teresa pulled the fabric tightly to make her point.

'Recognize the shape?'

It was the Maltese cross pattern from Emily Deacon's sacred cut. As near as dammit.

'He cut it out of a piece of fabric and then used it to kill her?' Falcone asked, bemused.

'That's one explanation. This is very tough fabric, though, and it seems manufactured to me. I've asked forensic to take a look.'

Falcone scowled. 'I don't see where that gets us.'

'Patience, Leo. So what about this?'

Falcone looked at a familiar sight: a sample of hair in a transparent morgue bag.

'This is from Margaret Kearney's head,' she explained. 'Black as coal, as you can see.'

He nodded, not understanding the point.

'You're a gentleman, Leo. I'll say that for you. The poor cow was stone dead on the floor there and you didn't even take a good look down below, did you? This is not her natural hair colour. This –' she held up the second slide. A hank of light brown hair lay trapped between the pieces of glass – 'is what her head's supposed to look like. We took out the dye just to make sure. You can't rely on what the pubic zone tells you. This is a general observation that goes beyond the matter of body hair, by the way. I trust you and Silvio will take it to heart.'

Falcone sighed and glanced at the clock on the wall. It was now nearly nine. 'So you think she had a bullet wound. He killed her with some crazy piece of cloth. And you know she dyed her hair.'

'Oh, Leo, Leo,' she protested, 'you really know nothing about women, do you? Naturally, her hair was a pleasant brown. Personally, I would have been quite happy with it. See?'

She waved her own lank crop at him. 'What colour's this?'

'Black,' he replied.

'No, no, no! How can a man like you, someone

who's usually so observant, be so blind? It's really a very dark brown. Genuine black, the colour you have here –' she held up the second slide – 'that's quite rare naturally.'

He opened his hands in an expression of bafflement.

'Look,' she continued, 'a woman who had black hair to begin with and went grey might dye it black. The rest of us? Check out the statistics with the hair-dye manufacturers. I have. A lot of women dye their hair blonde because that's what gentlemen prefer, right? A good number like something chestnut or so too. Think about it. Have you ever met a woman with nice chestnut hair who had an urge to dye it jet black? OK. You're struggling to find the experience to answer that question. Let me do it for you. No. It doesn't happen. It's weird. It doesn't compute. Black, real black like this, is something you get handed down in the genes. You learn to live with it. Maybe you learn to get rid of it. What you don't do is make it happen if it wasn't there in the first place.'

'That's it?' he asked. 'Maybe a bullet wound? Maybe an inexplicable use of hair dye?'

Silvio groaned. They both knew what Falcone was doing. Daring her to come up with something else. However she happened to have acquired it.

'No. That isn't it. Silvio?'

'Oh, Jesus.' Di Capua walked towards the deep cabinet drawers where they stored everything that came attached to a death, however ordinary, however apparently meaningless. 'Jesus, sweet Jesus. Here comes the shit again, here come the written warnings. Why can I not work with normal people? Why can I not—'

'Shut up!' she yelled.

He picked out a green plastic box, brought it over and placed the thing on the table. The name 'Margaret Kearney' was handwritten on a label stuck to the front. Inside were a pile of neatly stashed clothing, a bag and several plastic folders full of personal belongings.

Falcone did a double take looking at it. Finally he said, 'The cord I can go along with. Now tell me this isn't what I think.'

'It's her stuff, Leo. Hell, if I can't have her, surely I can have her stuff, can't I?'

'I made it absolutely plain. Leapman had that piece of paper that gave him full authority—'

She was quick to interrupt. 'Just a minute. You weren't there when that team of dumbos he'd hired turned up with the hearse. "We're here for the body," they said. Well, that's what they got. I even let them take our own gurney. Do you have any idea what those things cost? I'll be billing the White House personally if we don't get it back.'

He put a hand on the green box. 'This . . .'

'This is something they never asked for. Will they? Sure, once someone realizes what a stupid mistake they made. And they can have it. I won't stand in their way. But tell me, Leo. What was I supposed to do? Run after them and say, "I think you forgot something"? Or leave it there in the Pantheon, for God's sake?'

Something extraordinary happened then. Leo Falcone's shoulders heaved an inch or two. Teresa Lupo realized she was witnessing him laugh, an event which was entirely new to her.

'I'm just a bystander in all this, aren't I?' he asked finally, then fixed her with a hungry stare. 'So?'

'So this.'

She pulled out Margaret Kearney's US passport and showed him the photo. 'Notice how very black her hair is there? How stiff the pose? She didn't get this done in some supermarket booth, now did she? I hate passport photos where people are actually thinking about what they look like. It's so unnatural.'

'And?'

She pointed to the picture. 'Note the glasses.' Then she picked up a plastic bag containing a pair of spectacles and began opening it. 'These. Don't worry. We've checked for prints. Nothing. No prints anywhere, as far as we can tell. Like the Americans said, this man is good. Here – try them. Tell me what you see.'

Falcone glowered at the spectacles in her hand. 'I don't wear glasses.'

'Try them, Leo!' she ordered.

He did as he was told and put on the plain black-plastic glasses.

'I don't see anything.'

'Not fuzzy? No different from normal?'

Falcone removed them and she could see he was starting to get interested now.

'Exactly.'

'No reason it should be. Those are plain glass. They're not corrective at all.'

And she wondered: would he run straight back to the Americans with this information? Or would he mull it over first? She couldn't take the risk, even if it did mean he just might go ballistic when he discovered what else she had done. There was an easy way to find out, too.

'One final thing,' she added. '"Margaret Kearney."

There's an address on her driver's licence. Leapman and his friends said they'd be contacting relatives, right?'

'They said that,' Falcone agreed.

'The Internet's a wonderful thing, you know. Tell him, Silvio.'

Di Capua stared at his shiny boots and said in a very low, timorous voice, 'There's no Margaret Kearney in the New York phone book.'

'What?' Falcone yelled.

'There's no phone number listed,' Di Capua continued. 'She could be ex-directory, of course. Except the residential address isn't an apartment either. It's just a forwarding service.'

'You've been looking up this woman on the Internet?' Falcone bellowed. 'This is a morgue. *We* get paid to do that kind of thing. What the hell gives you the right to interfere with our work like this? Again?'

Gingerly Teresa put a hand on his arm. 'But you didn't do it, Leo. They told you not to, remember? Nobody placed a gagging order like that on us. So, when I noticed the hair, when I looked at that passport, those glasses – please, don't blame Silvio, if you're going to blame anyone, blame me – I just kept looking at this woman and I couldn't stop thinking, "Something is wrong here." '

He didn't know whether to shout and scream or thank them, she guessed. It was hard being Leo Falcone much of the time.

'This doesn't go any further than here,' he said. 'Agreed?'

'Sure,' she said. 'And maybe now I should make a call to them explaining they left a few things behind.

What do you think? I don't want them to feel we're being uncooperative. I don't want them to get . . .'

She left it at that. The 'suspicious' word could have been pushing things a little too far.

'Do it,' he agreed.

'You see what this means, Leo? We don't know who Margaret Kearney is. But the hair, the glasses, that stupid fake passport photo, the phone number, the address . . . we sure as hell know who she isn't.'

Falcone scowled at the items in the green box, as if a set of inanimate objects could somehow be to blame.

'Still, I guess we don't need to tell Agent Leapman that,' she added. 'Do we?'

She watched him turn this information over in his head. Falcone was one smart man. He was surely there already. All the same, it had had to be said, just to lock the three of them together, deep in all this potential shit.

Stefan Rajacic didn't look like a pimp. He was about sixty years old, squat in an old tweed suit and brown overcoat, with a swarthy, expressive face and dark, miserable eyes. The moustache – heavy and greying, like that of an old walrus – gave him away. It belonged to a world that was gone, that of Eastern Europe before the end of the Cold War. The man could have been a portlier version of Stalin, trying to fade into old age with plenty of memories and what remained of his dignity. He was the seventh pimp they'd seen that night and the only one Gianni Peroni, who seemed to know every last man of his ilk in Rome, treated with a measure of respect.

Rajacic stared at the photograph of the girl through the fumes of his Turkish cigarette and shook his head. 'Officer Peroni,' he said in a heavily accented voice cracked by years of tobacco, 'what do you want of me? This girl is what? Thirteen? Fourteen? No more surely?'

'I don't know,' Peroni admitted.

The Serb waved his hand at the photo. 'What kind of a man do you think I am?' He looked at Emily Deacon. 'Has he told you I deal with children? Because, if he has, it's a lie. Judge me for what I am but I don't have to take that.'

'Officer Peroni said nothing of the sort, sir,' she replied. 'He told me you were a good man. You were last on our list. We'd hoped we'd never need to come this far. That tells you something, surely?'

'A good man,' Rajacic repeated. He stared at Peroni. 'You're a fool if you said that. And I don't think you're a fool.'

'I know what you are,' Peroni told him. 'There's a lot worse out there. That's all I said. And, yes, I know you wouldn't deal with a girl this age. I just thought maybe you'd heard something. Or could suggest who we might ask next.'

Rajacic downed his beer and ordered another. The barman wandered over with a bottle and placed it on the table with an undue amount of respect. He knew who Rajacic was. There were just two other customers in the place. Outside, the street was deep in filthy slush. Business went on as usual, though. Costa knew that, if he looked, there would be pushers sheltering in the doorways, and a handful of hopeful hookers too, hunting business with haunted, hungry eyes. There were places nearby that Costa counted among his favourites in Rome. Just a short walk away were Diocletian's baths and the church created by Michelangelo from the original frigidarium. In the Palazzo Massimo around the corner was an entire room from a private villa of Livia, the empress of Augustus, decorated to resemble a charming, rural garden, with songbirds, flowers and fruit trees. But they were rare oases of delight in an area that seemed to become more tawdry each year. Costa couldn't wait to be on the move again.

'We're struggling here, Mr Rajacic,' he said. 'We need to find this girl. She could be in danger. We know how the system works. They come here when they're young. If they're lucky, the welfare people pick them up, put them in a home. If they're not, they fall through the net and something else happens. First they learn to beg. Then they learn to steal. Then, when they're old enough, they become the goods themselves. And maybe sell some dope on the side. That's how it is. Somewhere along the way they must go to someone, a person like you, and see what the options are.'

'Not if she knows me,' Rajacic insisted, waving a big cracked open palm in their faces. 'Not if she asks. These people who deal in children . . . they're scum. I handle no one who isn't old enough to know what she's doing. And no drugs either.'

'I know,' Costa insisted. 'As I said, we're desperate.'

'Who isn't?' the Serb wondered. 'These are desperate times. You never noticed?'

He swigged some beer from the bottle, stubbed out the cigarette and looked at them. Maybe there was something there, Costa thought. Maybe . . .

'You know what?' Rajacic grumbled. 'When I came here fifteen years ago I used to have to call home and beg for girls. Most wouldn't even phone me back. They had dignity then. They didn't need the likes of me. Now? This is a world in motion, my friends. I got the United Nations working for me, and more women calling pleading for work than I can handle. Kosovans. Croats. Russians. Turks. Kurds. All those people who watched the Berlin Wall come tumbling down, the old world rolling over and dying, and they thought: "Now the good times begin, now everyone gets free and rich like all those big shots in the West promised." Some joke, huh? You guys never told them it didn't really work like that, did you? You left it to pimps like me. I'm the one who gets to say it to some pretty little seventeen-year-old straight off the boat, no papers, no money, nothing going for her except what she's got between her legs. And now you're coming asking for help—'

'We don't have time to apologize, Stefan,' Peroni grumbled.

'No.' The brown eyes flashed at him. 'You don't.' He picked up the photo and looked at it. 'What is she? Kosovan? Albanian?'

Peroni grimaced. 'We just don't know.'

'From the looks of her she could be anything. Turk or Kurd even. Jesus . . .'

'But she can't just walk into a city like this without knowing someone, surely?' Emily objected. 'She must have a name. A phone number. Something.'

'That's where you've been, isn't it?' Rajacic asked. 'Who?'

Peroni reeled off the names. The Serb scowled as he heard each one.

'My,' he said at the end. 'I wouldn't want to meet even one of them in a day. Six . . .'

'Can you think of someone else we should be talking to?' Emily asked.

The brown eyes blinked in disbelief. 'Do I look like I have a death wish?'

'Mr Rajacic,' she persisted, 'this girl's so young. She might not even be in the loop you're talking about now. We don't know where she is, but we know what she saw. She's got to be scared. And in danger too.'

He glowered back at them. 'What did she see?'

The two cops looked at each other. They were running out of options.

'A couple of murders,' Peroni said quietly. 'Don't go telling anyone, huh? The kid's got problems enough as it is.'

Rajacic finished the beer and clicked his fingers for another. 'Two?'

'It was on the TV,' Costa said. 'A woman was killed in the Pantheon. An Italian photographer was shot too. We know the kid was there. Inside. Probably just looking for shelter or something. There's no point in trying to guess. We know the guy who killed this woman realizes that too now.' He made sure Rajacic understood this last part. 'You see my point?'

The old man thought about this, then got up, went to the bar and, without saying a word to the man behind the counter, picked up the phone by the till and began talking rapidly in his native language.

'He acts like he owns the place,' Emily observed.

'He does,' Peroni said. 'Even a pimp needs an office. I don't suppose you understand any of that lingo?'

She shook her head. Rajacic was virtually yelling down the line now.

'He doesn't act like a pimp,' she said. 'Not really.'

Peroni watched Rajacic barking at the phone. 'It's not his chosen profession. He was a farmer in Bosnia. The Croats decided his land was theirs. He had the sense not to stay around and argue.'

Costa wondered about this. 'Big leap from Bosnian farmer to pimping here.'

'Yeah,' Peroni agreed. 'Like the man said, "A world in motion." I don't get it either. But who's asking? If every other pimp we had was like this guy – no drugs, no kids.'

Emily's blue eyes wandered over the pair of them, some bitter judgement there. 'He's still earning a living by selling women on the street.'

Peroni came back with the answer straight away. 'We've had people doing that here for the last couple of thousand years, Emily. Doubtless will for the next couple too. Do you think we can stamp it out somehow? We're cops. Not miracle workers.'

She stirred the empty cup of coffee. 'Sure. I just want to make sure we remember what he is.'

The big man leaned over to make sure she didn't miss the point. 'What he is, Emily, is maybe the only chance we've got to find this kid. These people lead separate lives. They talk to us on their terms, when they feel like it. No amount of screaming at them, no amount of time in a cell changes that. Trust me. I know. I've tried.' He nodded at Costa. 'We both have.'

'True,' Costa agreed, watching how Rajacic's attitude had changed while he was on the phone. He looked a little happier. He was getting what he wanted.

The Serb came back to the table and sat down. 'I don't know why I'm doing this,' he told them.

Peroni slapped him on the big, brown arm of his overcoat. 'Because you're a good guy, Stefan. Like I told my American friend here.'

'Or maybe just a damn fool. Don't go putting this around, Peroni. I don't want anyone getting the idea I make a habit of helping the cops. And maybe I'm not helping at all.'

A woman was coming out of the door at the back of the bar. She was about thirty, with long, black hair, a tanned gypsy face heavy with make-up, and a tight red dress cut low at the neck. Boredom and resentment shone out from her tired eyes. She must have been upstairs, taking the call on an internal line.

Rajacic pushed out a chair and beckoned her to sit down. 'This is Alexa,' he announced. 'My niece.'

Peroni looked her up and down. 'You mean this is a family business?'

'When he gets some business,' she snapped.

The Serb pointed to the window. 'Am I responsible for the weather now? Please. I've listened to enough shit for one evening. These people need your help, Alexa. You're getting paid anyway. You can go with them. Or you can clean up in the kitchen. Which is it going to be?'

'Some choice,' she grunted and took a seat. 'What do you want?'

Rajacic reached over and brushed his fingers against her fine, black hair. 'Hey, zingara. No tantrums. They just want a little advice.'

He looked at Peroni, who pushed the photo across the table. She picked it up.

'I don't know who the hell this is,' she complained. 'Why ask me?'

Rajacic smiled. 'A little gypsy blood crept into the family a while back,' he explained. 'Don't ask how. It's thick blood, huh, Alexa? Like this kid's maybe. My friends here are asking themselves, "Where would a girl like this hide out if she were scared and living off the street?" Can you tell them?'

Her black eyes didn't give away a thing. 'On the street? In weather like this?'

'Come on,' Rajacic wheedled. 'They don't all stay in hostels. They don't all have pimps looking after them. What if she's on her own? Where'd she go? What kind of choices have these kids got?'

'Not many,' she murmured, thinking all the same. 'What's in this for me?'

Rajacic leaned over, prodded her in the arm, hard. At that instant he looked the pimp he was.

'You make an old man very happy,' he murmured. 'Now get out of here. Before I think of something else.'

They'd borrowed a jeep from traffic. Costa sat behind the wheel, feeling out of practice, unused to the four-wheel drive which was the only way the treacherous roads were manageable at speed. Most of the narrow through routes in the centro storico had been closed. What little movement there was now funnelled down the main thoroughfares and the broad avenues which ran either side of the river. Alexa knew where to go. They'd checked out a series of sites – a derelict building north of the Pantheon, a squat in Testaccio, a grimy, freezing hostel in San Giovanni – and got the same result in each one, trying to talk to a bunch of surly adolescents shivering in cheap black clothes that couldn't keep out the cold. They'd look at the girl's picture and shake their heads. Then Alexa would yell at them in their own language, and still they'd say nothing.

Now the four of them were driving along the Lungotevere on the Trastevere side of the river, slowly checking the huddled bunches of people sheltering by the Tiber. The sluggish current was out of sight from the road here. The flat, broad shelf by its banks, reached by steps from street level, was a popular shelter for the homeless.

Alexa was in the front passenger seat blowing cigarette smoke out of the crack she'd opened up the window, not minding the freezing air it brought into the car, looking for where she wanted them to stop. The atmosphere in the car was bad. They all sensed failure.

'These kids won't talk to cops,' she said. 'Why should they?'

'Because this girl needs our help,' Emily muttered icily.

Alexa shook her head. 'They don't know that. They don't believe a word you say. They just think cops spell trouble. With good reason.'

'What do you suggest?' Costa asked.

'Leave it to me. Stay out of the way. I'll tell them you're family, looking for her. You got any money?'

Peroni reached over from the back seat and handed her some notes. She looked at them and whistled. 'Wow. You do have some money. You could buy a couple of tricks for that just now. Supply and demand. Lots of the former, none of the latter.'

'We need to find this kid,' Peroni insisted.

She stuffed the cash into the pocket of her bright red nylon anorak and pointed across the river. 'There. I know a couple of places. Besides, thinking about it, the wind's coming from the wrong direction for this side. These kids are destitute. They're not stupid. Not most of them anyway.'

The jeep moved into the right-hand lane and waited at the traffic lights at the next bridge.

'You're not his niece,' Emily stated with some certainty.

The woman turned and stared at her. 'Says who?'

'I just thought . . . It was a turn of speech.'

'You mean like "sex worker"?'

'N-n-o,' she stuttered. 'I'm sorry. I didn't mean to offend you.'

'I'm his niece. My mother is Stefan's sister. My old man was a gypsy who climbed in the window one night.' She paused for effect. '*That* was a turn of speech. They got married. Eventually. Then . . .'

The jeep moved forward onto the bridge. She looked down towards the river. 'Then things fell apart. Not just personal things, you understand. Life. The country. Everything. Pull in somewhere. I can see lights down there.'

Costa parked the vehicle on the deserted pavement. They got out of the car and stood in the snow, shivering. The night was bitterly cold, with a stiff wind whipping through the open channel cut through the city by the Tiber. They were close enough to the edge now to see the black, silky surface of the river and a silver moon reflecting back at them, a perfect shining circle. It was dark down there, but there were people around, huddled in the shelter beneath the bridge. Costa could see the tiny firefly embers of cigarettes and smell the bitter smoke of a makeshift brazier.

'Stay here,' Alexa said, 'until I call.'

She hesitated before heading for the steps. 'There's something you ought to know. Stefan is my uncle. When we lost the farm – his farm, our farm, everyone's – I just ran away here. I thought I could make everything right. I thought the streets were paved with gold. You know the funny thing?'

She stared at them, with those black, gypsy eyes, and didn't bother to hide the bitterness.

'Compared to what it's like back home now, they are. I sometimes have to remind myself of that when I've got some fat businessman wheezing into my face wondering if he's ever going to get there. I came here . . . and did what was easy. Stefan used what little money he had to find me, to try to get me to go back. We argued. I won. Which is as it should be because, in the circumstances, I was right. If you've got to have a pimp, best it's your uncle. Best it's an honest man, and Stefan is. Ask any of his girls.'

Emily looked her in the face and said, 'I'm sorry.'

The three of them waited while Alexa walked down the steps, shuffling their feet in the snow in a vain effort to keep warm. The night had the crisp, biting smell of a hard winter, one that wanted to hang around. The snow would surely resume soon. Peroni glanced down at the sound of voices below.

'What do we do when this doesn't work?' he asked.

'Keep looking,' Costa replied, 'until she runs out of places.' He turned to Emily Deacon. 'You don't need to stick with us. We're on night duty anyway. You're not.'

'I'm fine,' she answered.

'You could—'

'I'm fine.'

Peroni caught Costa's eye and shrugged. 'How many people has Leapman got working for him here?' he asked.

She scowled. 'I don't know.'

'Two? Three? Fifty?' Peroni insisted.

She hugged herself tight inside her jacket. 'Listen, until a couple of months ago I was a lowly intelligence officer working nine to five in a systems office in Washington. Then I got plucked out to come here. Why? Maybe because I know Rome. Or I speak good Italian. Maybe Leapman thinks I'm owed it because of my dad. But believe me when I say this. *I do not know.* He doesn't tell me. He doesn't listen to a damn word I say. As far as he's concerned we're just chasing some lunatic serial killer with a lot of air miles.'

'Maybe we are,' Peroni wondered.

'No!' she insisted angrily, 'that's just not possible. There's a logic here. A crazy, distorted logic but it's rational somehow too. We just have to see it.'

'I agree,' Costa said, and wondered how much that was worth. Leapman's focus might be awry but the man had a point. They all knew the way these cases went. Intelligence, forensics, careful investigation . . . all of these things were important. But the final act of closure usually came by accident. A mistake, a chance encounter. The man was active. With activity came risks. The point was to have people there, on the ground, when he slipped up. Falcone knew that as well as anyone. Both he and Leapman would surely have men on the street steadily building up a picture of the man from what little information they had, hoping that one day soon they would turn a corner and find him staring into their faces.

The reason they were chasing the girl was to save her and not, in all honesty, because they thought she'd lead them to his lair.

The voices from under the bridge began to grow in volume. They were heated too and it wasn't just Alexa shouting. Costa cast Peroni a concerned glance. They'd let the woman walk straight into the unknown, assuming she could handle herself. Then, to Costa's relief, they heard careful footsteps on the snow-covered stone steps. Alexa reappeared. She looked puzzled, a little scared maybe.

'We were getting worried,' Peroni said. 'They didn't sound too friendly down there.'

'They're just doped up to hell most of them. I've got a name for you. Laila. Kurdish. She was here tonight apparently. They don't know where she's gone. Or so they say.'

'And?' Costa asked.

'I don't know,' she answered hesitantly. 'They just took the money and came up with the story. It could be complete bullshit. Tell me, are you the only people looking for her?'

Peroni glimpsed at the American. 'As far as we know.'

'It's just that someone else has been asking. He didn't have a picture, but he knew what she looked like.'

'What did he say?' Costa demanded.

'He was a priest. He said she'd been staying at the hostel where he worked. There'd been an argument. He wanted to patch it up. Except . . .' She looked down at the faces by the river, from where some angry rumbles were coming. 'This girl, Laila. They say she doesn't stay in hostels much. She's a street kid, likes to be on her own. Kind of weird. Not dope. Just funny in the head. If they're telling the truth, it couldn't have been what this man said.'

'To hell with this,' Peroni grunted, heading for the steps already. 'We've got to talk to them.'

Alexa put a hand on his jacket. 'Be careful. There are some real assholes down there.'

'Yeah, right,' Peroni grumbled, and brushed past her.

He was there so quickly that Costa and the two women missed what he said to begin with. Then Costa listened and found himself remembering why he stuck with Peroni as a partner, why he never even thought of moving somewhere else. Peroni was speaking to a huddle of kids, perhaps fifteen of them, peering out of the darkness, young faces full of fear and resentment lit by a stinking brazier burning cardboard and damp wood. They knew they were talking to cops. They were waiting for all the trouble that meant. And Gianni Peroni was speaking to them in exactly the opposite way to the manner they expected: carefully, with conviction, and a quiet, forceful respect.

'You have to believe me,' he was saying. 'We know you want to protect this girl. We understand why you don't want to help the likes of us. But she's in trouble. We *have* to find her.'

Alexa barked something incomprehensible and pulled out some more of Peroni's notes. The gang of youths stood there, immobile, but restless too. Finally a skeletal kid as tall as Costa came out of the darkness and took the money.

'I show you,' he said, pointing up river, towards the Vatican. 'You come with me. Over there. Now. You come. You come.'

He was dragging Peroni's sleeve. It was all a game, Costa thought. Just a runaround for a few euros. He watched Peroni start to shuffle off, wondering at what stage they had to admit defeat. Then a sound made him turn his head. The huddle of bodies in the shadow of the bridge had changed. They were moving, making space for someone. Emily Deacon was walking straight into the middle of them, talking, in an accent which through fear betrayed her origins, asking, asking.

Seeing something too. A slim slight figure hiding at the back.

'Laila,' she yelled. 'Laila!'

Somebody murmured, '*Amerikane* . . .'

They were crowding round the FBI agent, pushing, hustling. Alexa was nowhere to be seen.

'Gianni!' Costa yelled, then saw something metallic flash in the light of the brazier.

Emily saw it too. She dodged the half-hearted lunge with the knife and kicked the youth behind it hard in the crotch. He went down, screaming, but there were a dozen more of them now, crowding round her, starting to yell.

And the slight figure was moving too. Edging out at the back, taking her opportunity.

Costa thought about the options, came to the conclusion there was just one. He fired off two shots into the empty sky, watching carefully to see that they understood what the deadly racket meant for them.

The girl was breaking into a sprint, moving quickly

towards the next set of steps. She was on her own now, clear in a retreating sea of dark, furious bodies.

'Oh great,' Emily Deacon barked at him. 'And I thought we were the ones who were supposed to be gun happy?'

'Just making sure I take you back to Mr Leapman in one piece like he asked,' Costa said. 'How good are you at running?'

'Damn good,' she replied.

He nodded at the bridge. 'Take these steps. See where she goes when she emerges. I'll go after her. Gianni, you stay with Emily.'

Peroni was heading for the stone stairway already.

A good twenty metres ahead of him, Nic Costa saw the kid tumble for a moment, slipping on the slushy pathway, then get up and continue to flee. He took a deep breath, broke out from under the bridge and set off in her tracks.

It was a minute before he reached the next set of steps. He raced up them, following her footprints in the snow, thinking all along it had been a mistake to loose off those shots, not quite knowing why.

Then he climbed back to the road level, checked Peroni and Emily waiting for his lead a couple of hundred metres down the Lungotevere, Alexa by their side, her cigarette sending a thin plume of smoke up into the icy night air.

Costa glanced across the street and saw the slim, young figure of the girl slip into the snarl of alleys adjoining Corso Vittorio Emanuele.

Watching her disappear, in the dun security lights of grocery store, was a tall, upright man dressed in black.

*

The heretical monk Giordano Bruno died at the stake in the Campo dei Fiori on a cold February day in 1600. Now his black, hooded statue stood on a pedestal in the centre of the square, dispassionately surveying the twenty-first century. The trash from the daily market – wooden boxes, limp vegetables, plastic bags – lay in the filthy slush, uncollected by market workers who'd pleaded the weather as an excuse for skipping work. Only a handful of late-night drinkers braved the snow to make the customary round of bars, the Americans heading for the Drunken Ship and Sloppy Sam's, the locals to the Vineria and the Taverna del Campo. And around the statue, huddling against the wind, wondering how to make money, a bunch of down-and-outs, permanent hangers-on in a part of the city that was never short of tourists to work.

Of the hundred or so people milling around the Campo that night Emily Deacon was one of the few who knew who Giordano Bruno was. She could, if she wanted, recall the reasons why an eccentric recluse, one who brought about his own death through sheer stubbornness towards a vengeful authority, became a founding father of modern humanist philosophy. She'd visited the square often as a teenager and, as her family gradually fell apart, come to wonder what Bruno, a man convinced the world of the future would be immeasurably better than the one he inhabited, would make of modern-day Rome. These ideas rolled around her consciousness now. She knew the city so well, the place brimmed with so many memories, good and bad, that it was hard to focus on what mattered. Leapman had brought her to Rome, surely, for her specialist knowledge. Maybe he was wrong. Maybe he'd be better off with someone who was fresh, untouched by the scars and connections of the past. And these thoughts themselves touched a raw nerve. They were unwanted, unnecessary. Emily knew she had a job to do, an important one. A job that could close this case for good because, when she'd left Peroni gasping for breath in the back streets near the bridge, when she'd realized Nic Costa had taken his own path and was now lost to her in the night, she'd found the girl herself, tracked her doggedly through the labyrinth of medieval alleys, over the broad main road of Corso Vittorio Emanuele, then past the Palazzo della Cancelleria, towards the Campo, noting, too, that they were not alone. Emily Deacon could run. She was as fast as the girl, faster probably. Whoever was following them was also fit, but older, a black figure flitting through the shadows, with one clear intent as he struggled to keep up with them.

She turned the corner into the Campo and knew what she'd see. The kid was predictable. She headed for crowds, particularly those she thought of as hers. Sure enough, the slight, young figure was slowing now, strolling into the knot of bodies by the statue, hoping to be anonymous again. Emily cast a worried glance behind her and saw nothing. Not a soul was moving down the narrow medieval thoroughfare of the Via del Pellegrino, and she tried to convince herself she'd lost the man.

'But he's good,' she muttered, and took out her issue revolver, put it snugly in the right-hand pocket of her jacket then placed the pair of regulation handcuffs she carried in her left, wishing all the time she'd paid more attention during the repetitive, noisy tedium of the firearms classes back in Virginia.

She put her head down, stared at the grubby snow, and began to cut a diagonal path across the square, marking out a decent distance from the statue, looking, she hoped, like any passer-by moving through the night.

Laila was cowering there, hiding herself in a crowd of youths. Emily didn't like what she saw. The girl looked odd.

Emily locked one cuff around her own left wrist, keeping the metal hidden from view. They could spend all night running around Rome after this girl. It was important to bring her to a halt here.

Then she doubled back to the statue quickly, silently slipped between two youths sharing a joint, stood beside the girl and placed a hand on her arm.

'Laila,' she said quietly, firmly, 'there's nothing to worry about. We're here to help.'

The kid turned, her pale face shining with pure terror.

'It's all right,' Emily said.

But Laila was ready to run again and there was no option. Emily Deacon found the classes came back to her when she needed them. She reached out, took Laila's slender right wrist, and locked the right handcuff around it, tight to the soft skin. The girl leapt away from her, as if touched by an electric shock. The others were aware of what was happening now and beginning to mill round the two them, not taking any notice when she kept on yelling, 'Police, police.'

Laila almost dragged her off the steps. Someone's hand tried to separate them, jerking hard on the cuff chain. It was the scene by the river all over again, and she thought of the options in front of her, thought about how carrying a knife was, in circles like these, just part of everyday life. Finally, she remembered what Nic Costa had done in similar circumstances. She needed help. She needed to make a point.

Emily Deacon took the gun out of her right-hand pocket, held it high in the air and, for the second time that night two shots burst towards the luminous disc of the moon.

'Nic!' she yelled. 'Peroni!'

The youths got the message. They were moving back, looking scared, ready to run, to get as far away from trouble as possible. There were faces at the windows of the Campo bars but no sign of movement. The shot had won her time. Now she needed assistance.

'Nic!' she screamed again and pushed the girl hard into the stone pedestal of the statue to stop her trying to drag herself away.

'Just wait . . .' she was saying, until something got in the way. A fist, hard as stone, coming from somewhere behind her right shoulder, catching her on the jaw, making her shaky grip of the gun loosen so much that it slipped, with a steady, inevitable momentum, right out of her fingers and flew rattling across the ancient, slushy cobblestones.

She half stumbled against the plinth, tasting blood in her mouth, trying to think straight. Then a figure bent over her, the face hidden in the shadows, and he was laughing, a normal, natural laugh, calm, controlled, one that made her spine go so stiff she wondered if it might snap.

'You ask for men,' he murmured in a flat, north American voice. Something black and cold and familiar pressed against her cheek, sending the stink of gun oil straight into her head. 'They send you children.'

Her eyes dodged the weapon, raking the square anxiously, wondering where the hell Costa and Peroni were. They'd surely heard the shot. Then he dragged her upright, stared into her eyes. He was about fifty, with a chiselled anonymous face and lifeless grey eyes. A stupid thought came to her: *She knew this man somehow.*

He yanked the chain of the cuffs high in the air, dragging the two of them together. With her left hand, unseen, she fumbled in her pocket, searching desperately for a solution.

'You cuffed her well,' he said. 'I watched. But you have to think about consequences. Always. Was it the right thing to do? What happens next?'

The gun moved from the girl's terrified head to hers.

'Decisions,' he said wearily. 'Sometimes there's no avoiding them. You American? Or Italian?'

'Guess,' she hissed at him.

She pushed in front of the kid, tugging against his strong grip on the chain and covered Laila's slight body, wondering all the time if it were really possible to escape from such a situation, to try to find a refuge in the scattering handful of people retreating from the violence of this scene.

Then some clarity entered her mind and it said: *Best not to fool yourself.*

She drew herself back and spat full into the pale, emotionless face then said, in a quiet, controlled voice, 'You killed my father, you bastard. I hope you rot in hell.'

The grey eyes blinked. Something went through his head at that moment and in a strange, unexpected way it changed things. Not that there was time to consider what he might be thinking just then. Her fingers had found what she wanted: the key.

This man recognized her. There could be no mistake. He was staring at her, partly bemused, partly lost, troubled, struggling to come to terms with something she couldn't fathom.

His hand reached out, jerked her blonde hair close to his mouth.

'Emily Deacon,' he murmured. 'Little Em. Following in Daddy's footsteps. Such a waste . . .'

He relaxed his grip a little, let her head move back from his face. The gun brushed her lips. Out of sight, she twisted the key in the lock on her wrist and, with one deft twist, released the clasp, cast the shortest of glances at the kid, squeezing her hand to let her know she was free, then held onto her gently, waiting for the moment.

'Civilians,' he whispered and there was doubt in his voice now, something holding him back. 'Don't you hate it when they get in the way? Huh, Little Em . . .'

'Don't call me that, you murdering bastard,' she hissed at him and lunged hard with her free hand, punching straight into the throat with the side of her hand, the way they'd taught her, not connecting well, just enough to see him fall back into the snow.

'Go, go, go!' she yelled at Laila, pushing the kid out from under Giordano Bruno's shadow, out into the square, beneath a sky that was beautiful with stars but starting to cloud over with the filmy promise of snow.

Someone was shouting. A familiar voice. Nic Costa's.

The figure on the floor pulled himself upright. She

wouldn't run. This man was good. He could bring her down any time she wanted.

He still held the gun loosely at his side, like a professional.

'Get it done with, asshole,' she hissed at him. 'No time for your scalpel, though, is there? No chance to leave your mark.'

'Steely Dan Deacon's girl,' he said quietly, casting a cautious eye at the two figures racing across the square now. 'Didn't she grow up smart and pretty? And don't the Deacons fuck you up just when you least expect it?'

He was on her in an instant, strong hand at the neck of her jacket, index finger and thumb pushing into her sinews, forcing his face into hers, looking cold again, deliberate.

'Don't get in my way again, Little Em,' the monotone whispered. 'I don't have time for distractions.'

He was so close she saw his breath clouding in front of her eyes. A kind of tic occupied one of his cheeks, made it stand out too prominently, marred the fake handsomeness of his features.

'Who are you?' she asked, trying to focus her attention on the angular face and the voice, to work out what part of him was familiar, locked hidden somewhere in her head.

He thought about the question. Something about it entertained him.

'Kaspar the Unfriendly Ghost,' he answered, distracted for a moment, as if an idea was coming to him. 'Go figure, Little Em. We've both got work to do.'

Then he relaxed his grip, took one last look at her and started running, away from the shadow of the hooded monk, fleeing into the darkness of a side street, gone for now, she thought, not forever.

She leaned back against the pedestal and found her mind racing. She'd touched the beast. She knew the beast, even if he didn't at that moment have a name that was anything but a riddle. And it came to her that what she'd felt instinctively about the error of Leapman's approach was true. The man wasn't born this way. Something had created him, and he was acutely aware of that fact himself, probably resented it with all his soul. Like the philosopher turned to stone above her, he didn't fear judgement. Perhaps, in a sense, he sought it.

Little Em.

No one had called her that since she'd turned twelve and started to grow. It was a name used by her family, and those close to them, during those warm, sunny days in Rome, back when the world was whole and human and new, back when a string of strange men came through their apartment in Aventino, leaving her presents, making her feel special, dancing with her in the bright, white living room to any damn music they felt like.

Little Em.

Someone approached. It was Nic Costa. The young Italian cop walked up, his interesting, intelligent face full of concern. He retrieved her gun from the slush, looked at her, then pulled out a handkerchief from his pocket.

'Here,' he said.

She remembered the pain now, and ran her tongue over her bruised lower lip, grateful it didn't feel too bad.

'Thanks. Where the hell were you?'

'Looking. It's a big dark place out there.'

She nodded. 'I wouldn't argue with that.'

There'd never been an experience like this in her life, ever. Nothing in the Bureau had prepared her for it.

'I lost the kid, Nic. Sorry. I didn't have a choice.'

He didn't say a thing. He didn't seem too bothered.

Gianni Peroni arrived, a little out of breath, plenty of obvious pleasure on his face too at seeing she was safe. She liked these men. A lot. Her head felt funny. Her balance wasn't what it ought to be. For a split second she thought she was going to cry.

By Peroni's side was Laila. The girl came straight up to her, looked in her eyes with something that resembled gratitude and held up the lone cuff dangling from her wrist, wanting to be released.

'Sure,' Emily Deacon said. 'After . . .'

After we've talked, she wanted to say. After I've done the FBI agent thing, all confidence and bluster, pretending everything's OK now, everything's just dandy, if only you'll answer a few questions, listen to what the cold, tough automaton from the Bureau has to say.

After . . .

The lights went out. She was only just aware that it was Nic Costa's arms that stopped her head from splitting open on the Campo's freezing cobblestones.

It was quiet in the cabin high over the side street close to the Palazzo Borghese. Monica Sawyer twitched and writhed under the heavy sheets, shadows moving through her head, unseen figures dancing to events that had an interior logic they didn't care to share with her. These were disturbing dreams, enticing dreams, ones she wasn't used to, dreams that made her roll and turn and moan from time to time, out of fear, out of anticipation. Made her sweat too, struggling inside the scarlet silk slip Harvey had bought her once, on a brief holiday to Maui, thinking he could inject life back into the marriage.

Harvey.

His name just popped into her mind, like a sour discordant note that had sounded in a piece of glorious, fiery, scary music.

Scarlet was her colour, or so Harvey said. Scarlet made her look slutty too. He liked that.

'Harvey, Harvey,' she whispered, not knowing whether she wanted to summon him there or not, wishing she hadn't drunk so much, hadn't let all those strange old grapes from Virgil's day get deep inside her head.

'Look at me now. Look at . . .'

With a sudden physical shock, a jerk that made her body go rigid, she was awake, mind racing with sudden activity, one awkward fact ringing in her head. It wasn't Harvey she was trying to summon into her dream, like an incubus invited in by some deep dark part of her imagination. It was Peter O'Malley.

Who was out looking for churches.

Except he wasn't. Now, with a half-hungover clarity, she could see something that was hidden from her when he was around. Peter O'Malley was just plain *wrong*. Priests didn't hang around bars like that, slyly working their way into the confidence of stray women. They didn't know about wine and food. They couldn't turn on the charm, steal their way into someone's head with such a sly degree of determined stealth. And they didn't stay out all night either. Monica knew she'd have woken up if he had returned. Even when she'd been drinking, she was a light, nervous sleeper.

Nothing in his story added up. He wasn't the kind of man to tend a flock of nuns in Orvieto, or anywhere else. Peter O'Malley was a loner wandering the streets of Rome, homeless for some reason, with just a small black bag for company. If it hadn't been for the dog collar she wouldn't have countenanced inviting him into the apartment. That thought made her feel foolish. And resentful too.

'He's a fraud,' she said quietly to herself and wondered why she didn't feel more scared.

Because you're kind of hoping he comes back and . . .

'No,' she said, and remembered. He'd taken the one set of keys. This was, the more she came to consider matters, deeply, deeply stupid. She was in a foreign city, unable to speak a word of the language, unable to pick up the phone and call for help if she needed it. She glanced at her watch, thought about what the time was in San Francisco, where Harvey might be during that part of the late afternoon.

And what would he say if she called?

There was this priest, Harvey. He didn't have anywhere to sleep. We put down some drinks and one thing almost led to another. *Correction.* I put down some drinks. And now I know he's not a priest at all, though what he really is still beats me.

This wasn't getting better. Maybe he was just a harmless bum looking for somewhere to sleep. Now she thought of it, he'd had an opportunity to take things further. If he'd pushed a little more after they'd talked on the roof . . .

Monica Sawyer considered that moment and knew

the truth of it. If he'd pushed a little more she'd have fallen into bed with him and thought: *To hell with Harvey, let's see what a little of God's glory can do.*

But he didn't. He went out.

Looking for churches.

Quite.

She got up, pulling on a nightgown because it was damn cold in this tiny, artificial box. Monica knew what she had to do, which was to find something, anything, that would make her suspicions concrete, give her reason to call the cops and scream down the phone until someone, somewhere listened.

'The bag,' Monica said to herself.

She opened the bedroom door. The living room was empty. The bag was by the French windows, which were just ajar, bringing a cold draught into the room. Monica cursed herself. It was a night for getting careless. Outside, the two gas heaters still burned, hissing quietly, like vents in the side of a small volcano sitting on a rooftop in the middle of the city.

She went and checked the single front door. It had this incredible lock – multiple bolts, the kind you'd expect on a miniature domestic Fort Knox. All of them still thrown from the outside as he left. She couldn't open it however hard she tried. But there was an old-fashioned manual bolt on the inside too. She threw it and felt a little better. Maybe she couldn't get out, but Peter was now unable to get back in unless she allowed him.

'Let's get this done with,' Monica whispered to herself. She went back to the sofa and picked up the black bag, finding it unexpectedly heavy, placed it on the table and blinked, trying to see better. The interior lights were terrible. Insignificant, tiny yellow bulbs that barely penetrated the shadows of the cabin. She glanced at the terrace, with its hissing heaters. Two big fluorescent spots threw a bright semi-circle under the awning there. It would be so much easier. She went outside and laid the bag on the plastic picnic table under the awning.

The night was extraordinary: starlit, perfectly still, beautiful, like a painting on one of those pretty picture Christmas cards old people sent each other.

You'll be old one day, the little voice inside her said.

'Yeah,' Monica agreed. 'But you won't find me sending out crap like that.'

Even though the bolt was closed on the main door she closed the French windows behind her. It seemed like a good idea.

She started to open the zip then shut her eyes. Was this really such a good idea? Going through a stranger's things, looking to find proof he wasn't what he claimed? She could stay where she was, safe from anyone getting in, wait until morning, call the cops and tell them she'd lost her keys.

Unless she met him on the stairs on the way out. Unless . . .

Too many possibilities started to crowd into her head. Monica pulled the zip all the way back and was dismayed to find staring out at her exactly what she would, in ordinary circumstances, have expected. Peter O'Malley's modest, inexpensive bag revealed a black woollen jumper, just the kind a priest would wear. Neatly folded, the way an organized man, one who lived inside an institution, would have learned over the years.

She hesitated and looked behind her into the cabin. The living room was still empty. It was now the small hours. Maybe he was gone for good, out doing whatever he really did for a living.

Which was probably nothing exciting at all.

She pulled out the sweater and placed it carefully on the terrace table, which, being well protected against the weather by the awning, was still relatively dry and clean. Monica was determined everything would go back in as it came out, in exactly the same condition, exactly the same order. As much as possible anyway.

One more sweater. Some underwear. Socks. All very clean. And a pair of light shoes, not the kind you'd normally wear in winter.

It was all so ordinary.

Then two shirts, folded so they creased as little as possible. Peter O'Malley, or whoever he was, surely knew how to pack.

The last shirt was different. Kind of khaki, woollen. Almost military issue, although maybe the Church made priests wear this kind of thing too, just to remind them who they truly were.

'You're prying, Monica,' she said to herself. 'You're a stupid, nosy bitch who's just got the night terrors through drinking too much. Who . . .'

She removed the khaki shirt, placed it in order alongside the rest of his belongings and felt her lungs freeze, go still, in unison with the breathless quiet of the night.

There was a gun there. A small, black, deadly looking gun.

She took it out, held it in her hand, where it fitted neatly, wondered how you made a weapon like this work if you needed one, then put it in the correct position on the table.

Next to the gun was a selection of things she couldn't quite comprehend. A radio, with a little ear-phone. A bunch of silver tubes the size of cigarillos, with wires sticking out of one end, emerging from what looked like a wad of wax. A few notes: euros, dollars, all small denominations. And finally something that really was beyond her.

Monica Sawyer took the stuff out of the bottom of the bag and held it up to the sky. It was a carefully rolled-up hank of material of some kind. When she unravelled a little she saw it was cut into a repeating geometric pattern, a series of slashes that were clearly part of the design. She stretched it with her fingers and watched the way the precise slashes in the fabric stretched and pulled, keeping shape, seeming to have some odd, internal strength that came as much from the material's pattern and its precise arrangement of tears as from the textile itself.

'It's rude to look,' said a voice from somewhere beyond her vision.

Monica Sawyer tried to speak but all that came out was a kind of clack-clack-clack. She was scared. Of the shapes in the fabric. Of this place. Of this cold, cold night.

But more than anything she was scared of this voice, which kept on speaking, using words her head blocked her from hearing, kept on changing accent, changing tone, all coming from a shape that must have been perched somewhere on the roof all the time, looking at a frozen Rome perfect beneath a frozen sky.

VENERDÌ

Nic Costa looked out of the living-room window, out at the bright morning and a garden that was a perfect sheet of white, broken only by the bent, old-men backs of olive trees sagging under the weight of snow. The farmhouse off the Appian Way couldn't cope with the weather. It was still cold, in spite of two log fires roaring away at either end of the big, airy room. This was home, though, a good place to be. Since his father died and Costa had embarked on a lengthy, solitary recuperation from a near-fatal shooting, the house had rarely echoed to anything but his own footsteps. That was a shame. It was a place that needed people to make it live again.

He glanced at last summer's logs crackling and sputtering in the ancient fireplaces, still damp from the snow, and remembered what his father had looked like during those final days, wrapped in a blanket in his wheelchair, slipping away gradually, fighting the disease every inch of the way. Then he heard the deep, rough sound of Gianni Peroni's guffaw roll out of the kitchen, followed, a little more hesitantly, by light young laughter.

Teresa Lupo walked out, shaking her head, and eyed

the tray in his hands. 'Are you going to take it up to her, Nic? Or shall I? That coffee's going cold and there's nothing Americans hate more than cold coffee.'

'I'll do it. How is he?'

'Gianni?' Her eyes were shining, as if she'd been close to tears. She looked exhausted, but happy too. Costa had called her after the incident in the Campo. It was her decision to drive there straight away, then on to the farmhouse. Costa wondered how they would have coped without her.

'He's fine.' She sighed. 'For an idiot. She's a messed-up immigrant kid, Nic. I talked to the social people on the phone when you were asleep. They'll have to take her into care. You can't just –' she formed the words very deliberately – 'transfer the way you feel about your own kids to someone else. However much you need to. Gianni just wants to be home with his own family. I know that. I don't blame him.'

Costa wondered if it was really so simple. 'The girl looks happy, Teresa. Maybe it works both ways. She's seeing a little of her own father in him. Besides, he's doing his job too. She didn't say a damn word until he began clowning around.'

'It's not the girl I'm worried about,' she said with sudden severity. 'He's not the big, invulnerable hulk he looks, or haven't you noticed?'

'I know.'

'Good. Now you take that coffee to your guest.'

He did as he was told and was unable to suppress some slight nervousness when he knocked on the door of the guest room. It was now just before eight. Emily Deacon had slept solidly from the moment they took her back to the farmhouse and probably remembered little about the confused hour or so after she fainted in the Campo. She was going to wake up with plenty of questions. Costa took a deep breath, then, when there was no response, walked in.

This had been his sister's room before she went to Milan to work. It had an uninterrupted view back to the old Appian Way. The outline of the tomb of Cecilia Metella sat, a drum-like shape, on the horizon. He placed the tray on the bedside table, coughed loudly and waited as the American woman stirred slowly into consciousness, watching, with no little fascination, the way she was transformed from slumbering innocence back to the taut, alert FBI agent of the day before.

She looked around the room and frowned.

'Where the hell am I?' she demanded, then gulped at the glass of fresh orange juice.

'My house. With the girl. She's downstairs with Peroni right now. You remember our pathologist?'

'I remember.'

'We got her to take a look at you after you fainted. We were worried you might have been concussed. You banged your head when you went down like that. You were . . . mumbling.'

'A pathologist? Thanks.'

'She used to be a doctor,' he said.

She felt her head. 'You could have taken me home.'

'We didn't know where home was. Your friend Leapman wasn't exactly helpful when we spoke to him. He seemed more interested in the man.'

'As was I,' she grumbled.

'I'm sorry. We just didn't know what else to do. We wanted Laila somewhere safe. It seemed to make sense.'

She swore quietly under her breath. 'My, won't I be

in his good books now?' Then she looked at him and Costa could see she was remembering something afresh from the previous night. Something she didn't care to explain just then.

'I need to go into the office. Can you drive me?'

'Of course. The bathroom's through that door. When you're done, come downstairs. Peroni's cooking breakfast. You might find it interesting. Also . . .'

He wanted to laugh. She was looking at herself, still in last night's clothes, wrapped in the bed sheets, trying to clear her head.

'This is like being a student again,' she complained. '"Also" what?'

'You might be able to forget about the bad books.'

Monica Sawyer lay still on the floor, arms hugging the coverlet he'd placed around her the previous night, the cord tight in her flesh, chestnut hair strewn around her face. She looked like a shattered doll dressed in a gaudy nightgown, mouth open, blank eyes staring at the ceiling. Purple thumb marks had turned livid on her neck. A line of dried blood stood on her lower lip.

It wasn't a dream. In truth, he'd known that all along. Kaspar looked at her and felt something approaching regret. It hadn't been planned. He'd lost control and that was bad. He fetched the bag and automatically, without a conscious thought, turned her over, sliced the scalpel down the back of the nightgown, then the scarlet slip and stared at her back. Not bad for a woman in her forties. Smooth skin, barely blemished.

He wondered what he would have done if he'd got the chance to lead a life of dissolution. If there'd been the space inside the last thirteen years to do anything but think of survival, a way of getting through the meagre day, then getting even.

'You'd be as fat as a pig, Kaspar.' It was another voice inside him. They just kept getting noisier all the time, all the more so since this last, unexpected misadventure. This was the guy from Alabama, whose name was lost to him now through the mist.

'You'd be wearing pinstripes, working in a bank, screwing a little wife once a week just to keep her happy.' Uptight New England WASP, speaking through the back of the nose. There'd been many an officer like that, he thought. Or maybe it was just a movie. Or Steely Dan Deacon himself. He'd got it. That was *his* New England whine, brought back from the dead by seeing his girl the night before. And letting her live . . .

'I'd be me,' he murmured, and that was a voice he only distantly recognized, one that had no accent at all because it *was* him. As close as it got these days.

'I'd be me, Monica,' he said again, stroking the side of her dead cheek with a single finger. 'And you know something? You wouldn't like me. Because I'm not like Peter O'Malley. Or Harvey. Or anyone you know. I'm just a piece of dry shit blowing on the wind. A part of the elements, like rain or snow, looking for the right place to fall.'

He straddled her buttocks, took the back of her scalp and turned her dead head around.

'*You hear me, bitch?*'

It was the guy from Alabama again. Maybe this one would hang around a lot today. He'd been a vicious bastard. He could be useful too. Black as hell, muscles like steel, a vocabulary that rarely strayed from A-class obscene.

Monroe. That was the name. Monroe had been the first to catch a bullet when they'd run from the Humvee, got pinned down with no option but to try to make a break to the most obvious place of safety. The shard of burning metal came clean through the man's head, tore off most of his lower jaw, left him running round with half his face off till a second shell came and finished the job. The guy was a moron too. Thought he was immortal, could just bark his way through anything, catch a piece of red-hot iron with his fist and fling it to the ground.

Sometimes, when the memories came back, he wanted to cry, to hold his face in his hands and bawl like a baby. Mostly, though, he could keep that away these days. He'd done enough bawling for one lifetime. He could keep it at bay by thinking of the pattern, the magic pattern in his little black bag, carved into the living, waiting to be complete.

'See, Monica,' he said, back in the old voice, the *real* one. 'They never read Shelley, my dear. Can you believe that?'

My name is Ozymandias, king of kings

He did a good Englishman – *posh* if you please.

Look on my works, ye Mighty, and despair!

He laid the scalpel on her back, got comfy on her plump ass, and called into his head the sacred cut and its magical subset, that shape burned on his consciousness, so set there now he could carve it out of anything without the pattern he had needed to begin with.

Shapes made sense of things, shapes told you there was sanity and truth somewhere in the universe. So he carved the first line, quickly, easily, and it didn't feel right.

'Look on my works, ye Mighty, and despair!' he whispered, but it was still the old voice. He couldn't quite find the tone.

Because it didn't work this time. There were tears in his eyes. He couldn't just run through the same procedure again. She wasn't right. She was like Little Emily Deacon, only not so lucky. She didn't belong there, not at all.

Screeching quietly to himself, the way he'd done when the guards used to come through the door and drag him back to the room with the electric poles and whips, he rocked from side to side, wildly slashing the scalpel across her waxy flesh, back and forth, back and forth, making marks that looked like the talons of a giant, crazy bird.

This went on for a while. How long he didn't know. He was looking for those voices in him: Dan Deacon, Monroe, the big black sergeant with half a jaw, one of the women even. Anyone, anyone, it didn't matter who, so long as it didn't sound like him, the old him.

They wouldn't come and he knew why. He'd offended them. They kept whispering something in his ear, Dan Deacon loudest of all. He'd been a fool. The list was incomplete. One final set of skin remained to be added to the pattern, the most important one, from someone he couldn't begin to guess at. And what did he do when he was supposed to be looking? Get distracted by some horny California gal who couldn't keep her hands out of his private belongings.

Thinking of rutting when you shoulda been cutting, forgetting who you truly are.

'Bitch,' he murmured, and found the scalpel flying in his hand again.

Also, he thought, she stood in the way. He could be here for days if he wanted. She could start to stink and he hated that stink. It carried so many black memories with it.

Haul her onto the terrace, boy! It's like an icehouse out there. You won't smell a thing.

Smart, Alabama boy. They had helicopters hovering overhead all the time, cameras on rooftops, mikes in the walls, people spying everywhere these days, listening to the words you whispered in your sleep. They had to do that because they knew he was among them, knew he was close to finishing the job.

Then KISS my ass, remember?

Keep it simple, stupid. The black guy said that all the time. Sometimes he had a point.

This was a place with a kitchen you could film a cookery show in: big knives, little knives, meat saws, cleavers. Monica Sawyer had brought two large, expensive-looking suitcases with her. They still sat in the living room with Delta's business class stickers on the side. It would be a crime to let them go to waste.

The Via del Babuino ran from the Spanish Steps to the Piazza del Popolo, a narrow, cobbled medieval lane in permanent shadow from the high buildings on either side. The shutters were still on the designer stores and the newspaper vendor next to the Greek church had only just opened his bundles that bright sunny morning as the three-car team rolled past.

The Fiat saloons squirmed on the slippery cobblestones, scattering a flock of black-coated nuns like fleeing crows, hurrying across the snow towards the outline of the familiar twin staircase winding down from Trinità dei Monti. Leo Falcone sat in the back of the first car with Joel Leapman by his side, and wished the sound of the sirens could drown out his growing misgivings. What Teresa Lupo had revealed the previous night continued to bug him, all the more because he'd decided to keep the information to himself and to defy Filippo Viale, at least for the moment. It was hard enough dealing with his own grey men without a bunch of FBI agents thrown into the mix. Falcone had tried to discuss this with Moretti earlier that morning, only to find the grim-faced commissario already sharing his office with Leapman and Viale. The spooks had the smug look of people in charge. It was a pointless meeting, relieved only by Costa's phone call with a possible address for them to search. Not that they were under any illusions. The idea that the man would stick around at the apartment seemed ludicrous in the circumstances.

Leapman wriggled in his black winter coat as the car approached the address Costa had given them. He shook his scalped head, gave Falcone a disapproving glance and laughed.

'Something wrong?' Falcone wondered.

'You guys kill me. It's all so damn *casual.* What if he didn't wise up? What if he's still in there? You gonna knock on the door and ask him to come out for a talk?'

'Maybe.' Falcone knew this area well. The houses

were identical: terraced properties that fetched a fortune in spite of the constant roar of traffic from Spagna to Popolo. They were apartments now, all with a single shared door at the front. There was just one way out. At this time of day it was easy, too, to gain entrance to any place like this in the city.

The car pulled up. Falcone got out, walked to the intercom, pressed a couple of buttons simultaneously and waited for the electronic lock to buzz. When it did, he held open the green wooden door and let his team of six walk into the narrow communal passage.

Leapman couldn't believe his eyes.

'It's what we do to let the trash man in,' Falcone explained, nodding at the pile of black plastic bags behind the front door.

'Jesus,' Leapman groaned. He pulled out a black revolver, checked it, then, under Falcone's fierce gaze, placed the weapon back in its leather shoulder holster.

'No guns,' Falcone ordered. 'Not unless I say so.'

One of the detectives was grilling a woman who'd come out of the first ground-floor apartment. He nodded upstairs.

'Third floor, Number Nine,' he said. 'Foreigner, rented apartment. Been here two weeks or so. She hasn't seen him since the night before last. She's got a key.'

Falcone sent the entry team ahead. Leapman stayed with him downstairs. The American seemed bored. Falcone took a look at his own pistol, just in case, then quickly put it away.

'You ever used that?' Leapman asked.

'Lots of times,' Falcone answered. 'Just never had to fire it, that's all.'

Leapman was laughing again. 'This is the European thing, isn't it?' he asked.

'You've lost me.'

'The idea that there's some kind of middle way we could take if only we were civilized enough to see it. The idea you can just walk down the centre of the road and then everything will be just fine, all the crap will never come and touch you.'

'I think sometimes . . .' Falcone tried to decide. 'Perhaps it's best not to judge situations too quickly. I don't believe that's a European thing or any other kind of thing either. It's just how some of us work.'

Leapman grimaced. 'Until you wise up. That's what separates us. See, we don't wait for the nasty surprises to prove what we know already. This guy's a lunatic, right? You treat him like one or you expect pain.'

'Possibly.' Falcone wondered how many men Leapman had in Rome, where they were, what they were doing. 'I thought you might have asked Agent Deacon along,' he said. 'Or someone.'

'Why? Is she supposed to give an art lesson here too?'

'She got us this far. With my men, of course.'

Peroni had called in at one a.m. with a brief report after the incident in the Campo. It had been shared with Leapman, at Moretti's insistence. Falcone had then called Viale, partly because he liked the idea of getting him out of bed. The SISDE man had listened, grunted, then put down the phone.

'She did,' Leapman murmured sourly. 'She saw the guy too and look what happened. He walks. She blacks out. It's a crying shame. That kid just can't cut it.'

Falcone wasn't going to argue. Emily Deacon

looked all wrong in the job Leapman had given her, though he had no intention of saying so. 'In that case why did you bring her here?'

Leapman resented the question. Falcone would have felt the same way in his position. These were operational decisions. You left them to the officer in charge, until they went wrong.

'It seemed a good idea at the time,' the American said after a while. 'She speaks Italian like one of you. She knows this place. And like I said yesterday, she's got one hell of an incentive to see this guy go down. Is that good enough? Can we get on with taking a look around now?'

Falcone went up the stone steps and walked into the room, where his team were making a slow and professional job of checking out what was there. It was a typical short-term rented place: a large studio with an old sofa, a tiny table with grubby chairs, a small, cheap colour TV. There was an uncomfortable-looking single bed in the corner, unmade, with the sheets strewn on the floor. Falcone walked into the cramped bathroom. At first glance there was nothing there he could work with for DNA: no toothbrush, no spent tissues. The main room looked just as bare.

'The guy came back and cleared everything,' Leapman said. 'Smart thing to do in the circumstances. He was probably in and out of here before you people finished dealing with the medics.'

But medics were important, Falcone thought. You had to work out your priorities.

'How'd this kid know he was from here?' Leapman wondered. 'Was she working a trick for him or something?'

'No.' They'd got some background on the girl already. One of the charities had worked with her for a few months with little success. It was a psychological problem, one that wouldn't go away. A form of kleptomania, constant, even when she knew she'd be caught. 'She follows people she thinks are interesting. Then she steals something from them. He just came out of this place and she saw him in the street, followed him to the Pantheon. She remembered a green door and the Gucci shop.'

Leapman looked interested. 'The kid saw him meet up with the woman?'

'No. She lost him for a little while. The couple were already inside the Pantheon when she went in. Which is interesting in itself. Perhaps they already knew each other.'

'That's ridiculous,' Leapman stated. 'I'd like to hear it from this street brat myself.'

'No,' Falcone said firmly. 'You can have the transcript of the interview but I'm not putting a child up for interrogation. We wouldn't allow that with one of our own. It's against the law. I'm sorry.'

The FBI agent sighed, but at least he didn't seem ready to argue. 'The law. I won't go to the barricades over this one, Falcone. But don't you try standing in my way when it comes to something important. I won't take that.'

'I imagine not.' Falcone sighed, 'What do you want of me, Agent Leapman?'

'Some action wouldn't go amiss.'

'Action?' That was, it seemed to Falcone, the last thing they needed. This man moved carefully, thought ahead. He wasn't going to be caught by some random, blanket operation. He'd disappear the moment he heard anyone coming down the street.

'We have almost fifty officers working on this case already. I think that counts as action.'

Leapman picked up a sweater one of the detectives had found in a cupboard. It was the only item the man hadn't taken. Maybe it didn't even belong to him. Leapman didn't look as if he cared. Falcone had to remind himself about the kind of officer he was dealing with here. Leapman wasn't a cop. He was part of an agency, a rigid, bureaucratic apparatus that worked by the book. He was accustomed to thinking that 'action' – constant investigation, the sledgehammer of detection that vast amounts of manpower allowed – brought results. It was one way of looking at things. Sometimes, Falcone thought, it made sense. But not always. You had to be flexible. You had to think round problems. You couldn't just follow a set of procedures laid out on the page of a handbook.

The American's cell phone trilled. He walked over to the corner so that no one could hear. Falcone turned to Ciccone, one of the team he'd brought along, and asked, 'Whose apartment is this? Who'd he rent from?'

The owner was, as Falcone hoped, the woman who had given them the keys.

Leapman finished the call and announced, 'I'm gone. I want an update when you hear something, Falcone.'

'I'll do my very best,' the inspector replied, smiling. 'Let me see you out.'

They walked back downstairs. Falcone held open the door. There was a flurry of snow outside. Maybe it was that which made Leapman hesitate. He gave Falcone a sharp glance.

'They think you're something, you know. That SISDE guy told me. My, isn't he a cryptic piece of work?'

'I really don't know. I work for the police, not SISDE, though I'm flattered all the same.'

'Or maybe I'm just getting some prime Italian bull-shit. "We got our best man on the case." Huh.'

Falcone had reached a decision on how to handle Leapman. Gently. Politely. From a distance. Just the way the American least wanted.

'I'll keep you posted,' he replied.

He walked to the door of the first apartment. It was ajar. The woman, middle-aged, frumpy in a white blouse and black skirt, peered back at him from behind the security chain. She had prematurely grey hair, too long for her. She looked worried.

'Signora?'

He waited for her to unhook the chain then walked in. The living room was overflowing with expensive antique furniture. The contrast with the hovel above could scarcely be more vivid.

'What's he done?' she asked.

'Perhaps nothing. Was he known to you personally?'

'He answered the ad. He paid a month's rent and I never saw him again. He went out at night mainly. Don't ask me why.'

'And his line of work was?'

She lit a cigarette with a shaking hand. 'He was a tourist. How should I know?'

Falcone nodded, thinking. 'How much does an apartment like that cost these days?'

'Four thousand for the month,' she answered.

'So much money?'

She wanted him out of there. He could feel there was something wrong.

'By law all property owners must keep a note of a foreigner's passport,' he said. 'You did that, of course.'

She walked over to a small, highly polished bureau and took out a sheet of paper. 'I know the rules.'

Falcone stared at the page. It was a photocopy of the main ID page of an EU passport.

'Thank you,' he said. 'And the receipt? By law you have to give him a receipt and keep a copy. For the tax authorities.'

The woman stared at the carpet. Falcone knew: this was what she was hiding.

'You don't have a receipt, do you? He paid in cash, I imagine.'

'Stupid paperwork,' she hissed. 'I'm a widow. Do you think I've got nothing better to do than keep receipts?'

'It's the law,' he said sternly. 'Without receipts who's to know that you're declaring this income on your tax return? Who's to say the money just doesn't go straight into a shoebox under your bed?'

Along with a lot else besides, he guessed. She probably hadn't declared any income from the apartment for years.

'I have a suggestion,' he said.

She looked into his eyes, hoping. He folded the photocopy of the passport and placed it in his jacket pocket.

'You don't tell anyone else about this if someone should come calling,' he said. 'I won't call the tax people. Is that a deal?'

She didn't even look grateful. She just said, 'And you wonder why people hate the police.'

Falcone thought about that proposition and felt a small red flicker of anger begin to burn at the back of his head. 'Actually, I do. After all, we're just doing what we suppose you want. It's not easy, you know. A woman like you. Middle class. Thinking of herself as decent. If something happened out there in the street you'd be the first to get on the phone and start yelling at us. Yet in private you're a little criminal too, except you don't quite see it that way. So what are we here for? Just to pick on the people you happen to hate?'

The woman didn't answer that. She knew when she'd gone too far. Falcone was damn close to changing his mind.

Then something happened: the sound of a siren in the street, voices and, far off, the soft *paff* of an explosion, a noise he now knew well, one that sent a cold chill of dread straight through his mind.

Before he consciously knew it, Leo Falcone was through the door and running, back towards the Spanish Steps and a visible plume of black smoke rising above the white, white street.

Emily Deacon showered, climbed back into the same clothes, then came downstairs into the farmhouse living room and found herself almost blinded by the bright winter light streaming through the windows.

Costa was waiting for her at the foot of the stairs. He looked sickeningly fresh and awake. She envied him. Her head hurt and it felt wrong to be in this beautiful solitary house, not knowing the aftermath of the previous evening's encounter with the man called Kaspar.

'Where the hell *am* I, Nic? I need to be back in Rome.'

'Leapman knows where you are. He's not screaming for you. This is my place. On a day like this it's twenty minutes, thirty at the most, to the Via Veneto. The Porta San Sebastiano is exactly one kilometre over there,' he said, pointing at the end wall with its blazing fire.

'Great. I have time for breakfast. And you could tell me what the hell's going on too, if that's OK with you?'

He walked her through the large living room into the bright, square kitchen. Gianni Peroni and the girl were busy around a huge hob, happily throwing food into a couple of gigantic pans.

Peroni gave her a mock-sinister leer. 'Soon you eat. My new friend Laila and I are cooking Kurdish. Which isn't that far from Tuscan, just a little less fashionable.'

'Good!' the girl protested. 'It's good.'

Emily walked over, as close as the sputtering fat from the pans allowed, and stared at a banquet of frying food: eggs swimming in olive oil, chunks of bread turning crisp and golden in a mess of whole cloves of garlic, sliced onions and a tangle of half-burnt peppers.

'I don't suppose you have toast?' she asked. 'Yogurt?'

Teresa arrived with a cup of coffee and gave it to her. 'This is a bachelor pad, in case you hadn't noticed. That means the bread's all stale and the yogurt . . . ooh. I have to warn you, Nic. Some of those things in your fridge are so past their sell-by date they wouldn't count as vegetarian any more.'

'I've been busy,' Costa protested.

'Of course you have,' Teresa said in a deeply patronizing fashion. 'How long, Gianni?'

'Come back in five.'

'Done,' Costa said and ushered the two women back into the main room, out of earshot.

Emily Deacon sat down and came right to the point. 'OK. What happened with the girl? What did she tell you?'

'Don't worry,' Costa replied. 'We've passed it all on to Leapman. She gave us an address. The place she first saw him. Probably where he lived. The chances of him being there now . . .'

'That's it? You didn't get any more?'

The two Italians exchanged glances. 'Emily,' the woman said, 'this is one seriously screwed-up kid. Even before what happened last night. The charities gave up on her, she was so unreliable, so disruptive. She's not – if you will excuse a non-medical phrase – right in the head. You can't just sit down, ask her questions then take notes. Try if you want.'

'Maybe I will. She doesn't look that way now.'

'She met the man,' Costa said. 'This is Peroni's patch. Give him a starving kid and a couple of pans. Don't ask me how he does it. I doubt I'll ever understand. He knew she was hungry, I guess. No, it's more than that.'

Teresa Lupo cast a backwards glance at the kitchen and sighed. Emily Deacon understood then: there was something going on between her and Costa's partner.

'He's being like a parent, for God's sake,' she sighed. 'We just did all the cop things. Threw questions at her. Kept on and on. Gianni waited a while, sat not saying much, then started listening. Like Nic said. Don't ask. It's a gift.'

Emily thought about Gianni Peroni and realized she understood that last point. There was something extraordinarily warm behind that pugilistic facade. All the same . . .

'We need to know what happened in the Pantheon,' she insisted. 'What she saw.'

'Now *that*,' Costa answered, 'is a place even Gianni can't go just yet. The shutters come straight down. Give him some time. We've got that, you know. This man, presumably, is on the run now. Maybe on the street himself. He knows we're looking for him. He's not leaving Rome in a hurry. There's not a train going out of Termini. No buses. No planes. Not much traffic.'

She thought about the way the man had looked at her the previous night, the conscious decision he'd had to make. 'He doesn't want to leave Rome. He's got unfinished business here.'

'Then we'll work on finding out what it is,' Costa insisted.

'This is crazy. Why am I here? Why are you keeping a material witness in a private house? The *only* murder witness we've got?'

'Why not?' Costa asked. 'Where else would she go? She doesn't have a home. She doesn't have parents, not here anyway. None of the charities want her because all she does is steal stuff in front of their eyes.'

'I don't care!' Emily yelled, hearing her voice rise a couple of decibels. 'This is all so *wrong*. You can't run a criminal investigation like this.'

The pathologist rolled her eyes up at the ceiling and said nothing.

'So what do you think we should do?' Costa asked.

'Talk to her some more. *Now.* Get Leapman down here.'

'She'd like Agent Leapman,' Teresa said quietly. 'She'd just love a man like that. I bet she wouldn't stop talking.' She looked Emily directly in the face, daring her to argue. 'Well?'

'OK,' Emily agreed. 'Maybe that's not such a great idea.'

'So what do you think we should do?' Costa repeated.

The girl put her head round the door of the kitchen. Emily could see the doubt in her face. The kid had heard her yelling, could sense the tension in the room. Perhaps she was like that: over-sensitized to everything.

Emily Deacon made herself smile.

'Let's eat,' she said under her breath, then added more loudly, 'Laila. You made us breakfast. That's nice.'

'Ready!' The girl gestured into the kitchen.

They walked in and sat around an ancient wooden table. Peroni and Laila handed out dinner plates of food: potatoes, onions and peppers, with a couple of fried eggs perched on top of each, everything swimming in olive oil, with bread on the side. Emily Deacon looked at hers and wondered when she'd ever eaten anything like this before for breakfast, lunch or dinner.

'Good country food,' Peroni said, stabbing a finger at the plate. 'In a normal house –' he cast a deprecatory glance at his partner – 'there'd have been some ham or sausage or something.'

'It's lovely as it is.' Emily sighed, watching Teresa Lupo retrieve an old bottle of ketchup from a cupboard, stare at the use-by date, shrug her shoulders and place the container on the table. The girl grabbed it straight away, deposited a pool on her food and started to eat manically, as if she'd been starving for half her life. Which, Emily reflected, just might be the case.

Then Laila looked up at them, amazed they weren't touching their food.

'Eat!' she ordered. '*Eat!*'

Emily Deacon tried a corner of crisp, almost burnt, egg, delicious in a way, and, suddenly, out of nowhere, found herself laughing, a self-conscious, half-hysterical laugh, one that stemmed in part, she thought, from her amazement at being among these odd strangers, being touched by the intimate ordinariness of the scene.

Somewhere out there a man was carving magical shapes on of the backs of dead people. He was waiting in the frozen city. And he had a name. Kaspar. It came to her now. A distant, returning memory from childhood, ten, twelve years ago, maybe more. She was in the study of their old apartment on the Aventine hill, stopping her practice on at the upright piano for a moment, overhearing a remark from one of her father's rare discussions of his work with her mother.

Bill Kaspar. What a guy.

'What a guy . . .' she murmured.

Peroni was peering at her. 'Who me?'

She smiled at the crude, makeshift feast on the table, and Laila, who'd just about cleared her plate and was eyeing Peroni, wondering if, like Oliver Twist, she could really ask for more.

'Sure, Gianni,' Emily agreed. 'You.'

*

It was just a car. Some lunatic with an ancient Renault, probably stolen, who didn't give a shit what happened once he'd had his fun. Falcone quickly picked up the story from the two uniformed men on the scene. The moron had torched the vehicle outside the church at the top of the steps then, watched by a couple of goggle-eyed street hawkers, pushed it over the edge. The vehicle had rolled and tumbled down the hill, settling in front of the fountain in the Piazza di Spagna, where the fuel tank had exploded with the soft roar Falcone had heard from down the road. Now a puzzled-looking fire crew were hosing down the damn thing in front of a small crowd of puzzled onlookers.

It was an odd and disturbing scene in a part of the city that never quite worked for Leo Falcone. The mix of tourists and McDonald's rubbing shoulders in the shadow of the house where Keats died puzzled him at the best of times.

Falcone strolled back down the Via del Babuino and ordered the uniformed men to return to the Questura, then he called intelligence to check the name on the passport. After they had run a swift search he set off on the drive out to Costa's house, taking the time alone to think, more than anything, about that morning's meeting with Joel Leapman, Bruno Moretti and Filippo Viale, the grey man from SISDE, and the way they just sat there, silent, as if this were all some kind of game.

The streets were treacherous: half snow, half slush. Even in the abnormally light traffic he had to be on his guard every moment. The average Roman had never driven on snow. What passed as the normal rules of the road in Rome were gone. Cars were careering around crazily, from right to left and back again. Drivers were arguing with each other over minor collisions. The city was, briefly, beyond control, beyond order. He thought about the old Renault tumbling down the Spanish Steps, bursting into flames at the foot of the staircase, and how amazing it was no one had got hurt. Rome, like any big city, had its share of vandalism. Still, there were always places that were somehow exempt, almost sacrosanct. People didn't mess with sights like that. It would be like spray painting graffiti on St Peter's.

Until now.

Falcone turned the car into the narrow lane that was the Via Appia Antica and couldn't stop himself laughing. The city streets were a mess. The authorities just didn't have the right equipment to clear up after the constant blizzards. Here, at the municipal boundary, the Via Appia became clear and safe, still showing cobblestones that were, in places, a good two thousand years old.

'Farmers,' Falcone said to himself. The tractors had been out, unbidden, without payment in all probability, ploughing aside the drifts. This was where the city ended and a different kind of Italy started. He made a note to remind himself of that the next time he wondered why Nic Costa lived where he did.

The drive to Costa's farmhouse was different, though: deep in snow so thick that Falcone just kept his foot lightly on the pedal all the way, and was grateful the car didn't grind to a halt. He made one call back to the Questura then stood on the doorstep, stamping his shoes to get rid of the packed ice, sniffing the air, trying to work out if the smell of the countryside, fresh and wholesome, really suited him.

Costa looked him up and down when he opened the door. 'Problems?'

'A few,' Falcone replied. 'Is she still here?'

'The girl? Of course.'

'No. I meant Emily Deacon.'

Costa nodded.

'Sure. I'm going to drive her to the embassy soon.'

'Has she told you anything?'

Costa looked baffled. 'About what? I wasn't aware we were interrogating her.'

'Maybe we should be.' Falcone stayed by the door, not wanting this conversation to go inside. 'About this Leapman character for a start. What the hell's he up to?'

Costa shuffled on his feet, uncomfortable. 'I'm not sure she's got anything to tell, to be honest. She's just as much in the dark as we are.'

'Maybe. Maybe not,' Falcone murmured then stamped his smart city shoes on the doorstep one last time and walked in, throwing his coat onto a chair and following Costa into the kitchen.

Peroni was clearing away a huge dinner plate still bearing a few eggs and fried potatoes. 'Hey, Leo. Want some?'

'I think I'll pass,' Falcone replied, staring at the group around the table: Emily Deacon, Teresa Lupo, the Kurdish girl. 'Am I interrupting something?'

Peroni shrugged. 'Just breakfast. Out here in the big wide world people tend to take it together, you know.'

'Cut the lecture,' Falcone snapped. 'You do have coffee?'

Teresa Lupo pushed the filter pot over to him. He stared mutely at the thing.

'This is a home, Leo,' she insisted. 'A bachelor's at that. Not a café. This is how coffee comes.'

Falcone looked at the girl and held out a hand. 'I gather you're Laila. My name's Leo Falcone. I have the –' this was for their benefit, not hers – 'dubious distinction of being their boss.'

The girl took his hand for a brief moment and stiffened. She didn't like authority. No one could miss that.

'How old are you?'

'Th-thirteen,' she stuttered.

'I'm sure they've asked you this, but let me ask again to make sure. Is there *anyone* in Rome you want us to contact? Your mother. Your father. Do you know where they are?'

'My father's dead. My mother's in Iraq. Somewhere.'

She said it in that flat, neutral tone of acceptance Falcone knew only too well. The kid really did have no one.

He took a ten euro note out of his wallet. 'Fine. You know what I liked to do when I was thirteen and the weather was like this?'

Teresa Lupo gasped. 'You were thirteen once, Leo? Now that's a hard one to swallow.'

'When I was thirteen,' Falcone continued, 'I just *loved* to build snowmen.'

'Snowmen?' the girl asked wide-eyed.

'Absolutely.' He waved the note. 'This is for you.'

Her hand reached out gingerly for the money. Falcone placed the note half under a spare dinner plate.

'Once you've built me the best snowman I've ever seen. And here's the best part.' He smiled briefly at

Teresa Lupo. 'Our friendly doctor here is going to help you.'

'*I am*?' the pathologist snarled.

Falcone leaned over and whispered to the kid, loud enough so they all could hear.

'She's good. I promise.'

Then he waited until the two of them had left the room, Teresa Lupo grumbling under her breath, waited until he heard their voices outside in the snow, ringing in that odd way they do in the extreme cold. Only then did he turn to Emily Deacon, take out a sheet of paper from his jacket and unfold it in front of her on the table.

'I have an ID for the man we're all looking for, Agent Deacon. Your friend Leapman doesn't know about this. You can give it to him when you go into your office if you like.'

Costa and Peroni crowded round to look at the imprint of the passport. It was issued in the name of Roger Houseman, with a contact address for a wife in London as next of kin, and a photo of an anonymous-looking man wearing thick, black-rimmed glasses.

'Is this who you saw last night?' Costa asked.

She shook her head. 'No. I mean . . . possibly. It's a fake passport, surely.'

'It's a fake,' Falcone agreed. 'I phoned to check just now. We seem to be having a run on fake passports.'

'Excuse me?' she said.

Falcone repeated himself. 'I said we seem to be having a run on them. The woman who was killed in the Pantheon. She had a false passport too. But I guess you must know that. After all, you were the people who were contacting her relatives.'

'What?' She seemed genuinely amazed, Falcone

thought. And Costa was already bristling on her behalf too, which was worth noting. 'What the hell are you talking about?'

'Margaret Kearney. Thirty-eight. From New York. No such woman. No such home address. We checked. I know we're not supposed to. We're supposed to swallow every last piece of bullshit you and Leapman push our way. But just this once we didn't. Margaret Kearney doesn't exist. So who is she, Agent Deacon? Whose relatives are you comforting exactly?'

'I don't know!' She was struggling to make sense of it. It didn't look like an act, Falcone thought, then reminded himself too of what she was. The FBI spent years training their officers. Maybe lying was top of the curriculum. 'I didn't deal with that side of things. I thought it was all handled by the usual people.'

'"The usual people." Are these the usual people?'

Falcone pulled out another piece of paper from his pocket and placed it on the table. 'This came to me this morning from the Palazzo Chigi. It's a list of five men. All FBI agents I'm given to understand. Do you know them?'

She peered at the names, shaking her head. 'I've no idea who these people are.'

'Really. Do you think they're armed? I guess so. Are they looking for Roger Houseman or whoever this man is? I guess so too. I've worked in the Questura all my adult life, Agent Deacon, and I've never seen a piece of paper like this before. It says you have five men here doing God knows what and all I know is, if I happen upon them, whatever's going on, I just look in the other direction, walk away and pretend they don't exist.'

He took a swig of the coffee and pulled a sour face.

'So you tell me. What's happening?'

'I don't know! I'd no idea anyone else was working on the case. What are they supposed to be doing?'

'You tell me . . .'

'*I don't have the first idea!*'

'You know who this man is . . .' Falcone began.

'*No!*' she yelled. 'Believe me. I am not part of this.'

Costa was going a little red in the face now. Peroni, sensibly, was keeping quiet. They both knew how Falcone worked. They'd seen this tactic often enough. You push and push and see how far you get. Emily Deacon was, it seemed to him, telling the truth. But he had to make sure.

'Sir,' Costa interjected, 'Agent Deacon helped us a lot last night at no small risk to herself. Without her we wouldn't know anything right now.'

'Thank you, Nic,' she said under her breath. 'I can't believe I'm getting interrogated like this. Not after . . .'

She didn't go on. Falcone finished the sentence for her. 'After Roger Houseman, or whoever, nearly killed you. Or, to be more precise, chose not to kill you. Why was that?'

It was such a small thing. A flicker of hesitation in her face. But unmistakable.

'I can't begin to guess. Perhaps it didn't fit his plan. Laila had escaped. Perhaps he doesn't just kill for the hell of it. In fact everything we know about him suggests that's the last thing he does. He's too careful. Too obsessed by detail.'

'I agree with the last part,' Falcone said. 'Still . . . if he was faced with an officer of the law. One who was determined to apprehend him.'

'He was too smart for me. And too strong. He . . .'

She thought about this carefully before saying it. 'He knows how we work. He actually *complimented* me on how I'd cuffed the girl. As if he was an instructor or something. Can you believe that? *As if he knew I'd done a good job.*'

'You didn't mention that, Emily,' Peroni said quietly, a faint note of distrust in his voice.

'It only just came back to me.'

'Of course,' Falcone said. 'It must have been very shocking. You should try to remember more.'

'I will,' she sighed.

'Can we get to hear it too?' Peroni asked.

'That's the deal,' she said icily. 'Isn't it?'

Falcone managed to work up half a smile. 'I'm sorry, Agent Deacon. This has been very stressful for you. I didn't mean to offend. Or interrogate you. It's just that I've spent rather a lot of time in the company of your colleague today and I have to say that man gets to me.'

She wasn't rising to the bait.

'But you see my problem?' Falcone added.

She didn't answer for a moment. Then she looked at Costa. 'Nic. I need to be in the office. I promised.'

'You should see it. This is your problem too,' Falcone persisted. 'If Leapman is lying to you as much as he's lying to us there has to be a reason. Can you guess what that might be?'

She didn't know which way to turn. 'I don't know how you work, Inspector. But when we have problems we raise them with our own people. Not strangers from another force. Another country.'

'Is that what we are?' Falcone queried. 'Just a bunch of curious foreigners who happen to be in the way?'

'No. You're the resident police force here. You've

got every right to know what we know. That's what we agreed. I'll try to honour it as much as I can.'

'I'll hold you to that.' Falcone passed the paper with the passport details over to her. 'You can give him this, for what it's worth. I don't believe you'll find he's interested. Agent Leapman is one step ahead of us. Of you, too, and I think you know that. You ought to consider what that means.'

She was getting up rapidly from the table, anxious to be out of there. Falcone stood up and placed his hand on her arm.

'In times like these, Emily,' he said, 'it's best we work together. When you need us . . .'

She just stared at his hand until he withdrew it. Emily Deacon was no pushover, however uncertain she felt about the position in which Leapman had placed her.

'I'll bear that in mind, Inspector. Nic. Can we go now?'

Peroni watched the two of them walk out of the door.

'More coffee, Leo?' he asked.

Falcone grimaced at the mug. 'Is this really the best Nic can do?'

'Like Teresa said, he's on his own. What kind of man goes to a lot of trouble to make good coffee just for himself?'

The look on Falcone's face told Peroni the answer.

'OK,' he replied. 'I guess you've got your own espresso machine or something. But just grin and bear it.' He filled the kettle and turned it on.

Falcone felt troubled by his talk with Emily Deacon. He'd got most of what he wanted, but he couldn't shake off the impression she was withholding something too. The faint expression on her face when he mentioned the incident in the Campo . . .

'You've got to remember to call me by my rank in these situations, Peroni. This relationship's getting too damn casual.'

'Sorry.' Peroni smiled wanly at the surroundings. 'It was this place. It's a home, Leo. Ooh . . . sorry again, *sir*. At least it *was* a home. For me it's starting to feel like one of those old tombs out by the road right now. What am I supposed to do about my partner?'

'He keeps asking me that about you.'

'Jumped-up kids . . .'

Peroni stared out of the window. Teresa Lupo and the girl were steadily building a snowman there. It was a good metre tall. Not bad for the short time they'd had.

'That's worth ten euros of your money,' he suggested. 'Don't you think?'

Falcone watched them working on the cold white figure and remembered how that felt as a child, when he'd spend hours building the same thing alone in the weekend house his father kept in the mountains close to the Swiss border. 'It is.'

'Where the hell did that idea come from anyway?'

'I loved building snowmen when I was a kid. Is that so odd?'

'No,' Peroni stuttered. 'Not exactly. It's just . . . ah, forget it.'

Falcone took the note out from under the plate and passed it over. 'You give it to her. You're better with kids than me. And after that you start talking to her. Hard. You and your friend.'

Peroni blinked. 'Hard?'

'Moretti's pushing me for progress. More than usual. Don't ask me what's going on here, but I need to come up with something and that kid's got to have it. There's a lot more we need to know. What really happened in the Pantheon?'

Peroni felt his blood begin to rise. 'We know what happened!'

'Not the details. She saw it.'

'She's a thirteen-year-old kid! You want me to drag that out of her just by yelling or something?'

'Yes,' Falcone barked back. 'If that's what it takes. It's what you're paid for. Remember?'

Peroni kept quiet. He was a good cop. One of the best, Falcone reminded himself.

'And here's something else,' Falcone continued. 'Why exactly did this creature want the kid dead, which he surely did? Just because of what she saw? It doesn't make sense. Not on the basis of what we know. All it would gain him was some more time where he was staying, and sure as hell he'd be out of there soon anyway. I don't get it.'

The kettle came to the boil and switched itself off. Falcone looked at his watch.

'Forget about the coffee,' he said. 'I don't have the time. Get that kid in here when I'm gone. Make her talk.'

Peroni couldn't distance himself from the girl. That was the problem. Maybe that would provide the solution too.

'I don't care how we get this out of her,' Falcone insisted. 'Cruel or kind. I just want to know.'

Peroni was getting mad. 'Listen to yourself just for

once, will you? You're starting to sound like that damn American. Is that what you want?'

'I'm your boss, Peroni. I don't care how you think I sound.'

'Really? Well, I'm your friend, dammit. I've known you for twenty years. I could be ordering you around by now if things had worked out differently.'

Falcone just stared back at him, lacking the heart to say it. Peroni didn't need to hear the words. They were there somewhere inside him, always. *Things didn't work out differently. Something, some hidden inner flaw, surfaced and sent a well-ordered life tumbling down the wrong turning.*

'Fine.' Peroni sighed. 'But let this humble minion offer you some advice. I know what you're thinking. You can run this all your own way, let Moretti and the rest of them stew in their own juices, work the old Falcone magic. And let me tell you something. This time it won't work. That ugly American has got the pen-pushers on his side. All those nice men in suits with titles that never really make much sense. If you screw with them . . .'

'This isn't the Wild West,' Falcone spat back. 'I've got the law. That's bigger than any damn piece of paper from the Palazzo Chigi.'

Peroni shook his big ugly head. 'The law? Don't you get a flavour of what's going on these days, Leo? Haven't you noticed the only people who care much about the law any more are idiots like us? These are pick-and-choose times, my friend. Wear the coat that suits you. Forget the one that doesn't. Start squawking about the law to the people you're dealing with now and they'll laugh straight in your face.'

He paused to make sure this hit home. 'Let me tell you something, Leo. I do believe that is the dumbest thing I have ever heard you say. And you are not, by nature, a dumb person.'

Falcone couldn't take his eyes off the two figures beyond the window: Teresa Lupo watching the girl work steadily on the snowman. He could smell the mountains. He could hear the dead voices of his parents. Single kids were like that. Those solitary years followed them around like ghosts all their lives.

'Is that so?' he asked.

Sweet, sweet, sweet, Billy Kaspar. You're doing OK for a white kid.

He'd watched the car roll down the Spanish Steps (straight on the line that led past the Pantheon, across the river, on to the Vatican, perfect in its flaming, smoking trajectory), still hearing the voices, baffled by why they refused to leave him, why they'd taunted him all night long, ever since he'd killed the woman. They played a part in that, too, Kaspar thought, not that he was trying to evade any of the responsibility. Something was wrong. The last piece of the jigsaw should have fallen into place. All of Steely Dan Deacon's team were dead now. The Scarlet Beast had died when he killed Deacon himself back in China. He'd been sure of that. He'd worked out the story, pieced it together in jail. There were pieces to be cleaned up. A couple of minor scores to be settled and now some property, important property, precious, sacred memories, to be recovered.

But the voices . . .

You can hear me, Kaspar. Loud and clear. What did Dan the man say that time?

The voices wouldn't go away. They sat on his shoulder, whispering, like cartoon demons.

What'd he say, boy?

The same thing, Kaspar recalled. Twice. Thirteen years apart. When they were working on the Babylon Sisters, he'd established a routine with Deacon. They'd meet in the Pantheon, sit together in a quiet corner. No one could eavesdrop on them in a place like that. And just once Deacon had let slip some doubts.

Say it.

Kaspar spoke the words out loud, 'Did you meet the man from the Piazza Mattei?'

It was November 1990. A month before they were due to go in. Kaspar hadn't understood a damn word. He'd said so. There wasn't time to bring anyone else in on the act. It was dumb. Insecure. And a part of him had, at the time, had to quell some rumbling suspicion, some little whisper inside that said Deacon seemed to be checking him out on something.

Then the conversation went awkward, went dead. For thirteen long years, until Kaspar had his cord round Dan Deacon's scrawny throat in Beijing, trying to strangle some last, cathartic confession out of him.

It never came. Dan Deacon just shook his head and said . . .

What?

'You should have met the man from the Piazza Mattei.'

And he'd tried to. Later, when he'd got free, though it all went wrong, damn near got him caught.

There were two ways to find a secret. You could look

for it out in the plain light of day. Or you could keep chipping away at what you didn't know, waiting for the truth to emerge from the lies. One would work. A certainty about that was growing inside his head, solid, reliable, like the patterns on the floor of the ziggurat all those years ago. It had to. Otherwise the voices would never go away.

How long we got to wait, Billy K?

'I don't know,' he whispered between gritted teeth.

The old black voice kept rising up to bait him. He didn't like remembering things. Remembering got in the way. There were more important matters to consider. Money, for one thing. Without it he was impotent. All the crucial tasks . . . buying airline tickets, finding fake passports, weapons, tools, information. Without money they just didn't happen, and he was running out, fast.

Since coming back into the world, fleeing that burning jail outside Baghdad, he'd salted away $35,000 in seven different bank accounts in the UK, France, Italy and the Bahamas. Small sums always, originating from some equally small crime, then turned into cash and paid in through a street money changer. It was more than enough for his needs, if only he had easy access to it. That wasn't simple. After 9/11 the American and European authorities had started to change the rules about foreign exchange movements. When the first transaction rang alarm bells and he'd been forced to leave San Francisco in a hurry he'd used the Net, the news groups in particular, to pick up information about how the new world order of money control worked. They watched cash movements as much as they could. They tried to heavy-hand information out of the small foreign banks that allowed just about anyone to open an account. Even with legitimate institutions, quite modest movements of money now attracted attention. It was a constant challenge to transfer a few hundred dollars around here and there, always to another ghost account to hide the trail if someone latched on to what he was doing. The result: only a trickle of cash came safely into his hands each week and he needed another source of income to cover sudden, unexpected expenses.

Like equipment. Three bugs and a receiver alone had cost him two thousand euros, almost all the ready money he had, from some crook out in Testaccio. With the block placed on his funds by the bureaucratic banks that left him virtually broke.

He'd used the grubby Internet café in the Piazza Barberini before. It was big enough for him to be anonymous. All he need do was pay for a few hours online, type in a fake Hotmail address to validate it, then access his accounts, try to shift a little cash around, do some research, read the news, from CNN to *La Stampa*, keep ahead of the pack. The place was perfect. You could sit on a PC all day doing anything. No one asked a damn thing. When he was done he just hit the reboot button and the machine wiped out every last keystroke, every place he'd been. It was more anonymous than a phone, more secure than a personal meeting, a place that seemed designed for what he wanted. Once he'd even picked up a woman there, a Lebanese housewife emailing back home, and stolen her handbag as she waited for him to emerge from the bathroom of one of the fancy Via Veneto cafés across the road.

Today the place was almost empty, the piazza close to deserted. Snow continued to paralyse the city. He'd read on the Net about the problems the authorities faced: a lack of ploughs since none had been needed for twenty years, an unwillingness by municipal workers to tackle jobs they'd never had to face before. The bus lines were running a quarter of their normal schedule and at a tenth of their usual capacity. The subway was largely unaffected, but in Rome that went mainly to the places people didn't work anyway. It was as if a cold white coverlet of torpor had fallen from the sky and now sat on the city, daring it to move.

There were opportunities here, surely. If only he could understand how best to use them.

He'd found some hair dye in Monica Sawyer's bathroom, washed it in before leaving her cabin, waited, washed it out, used her dryer, looked at himself in the mirror and liked what he saw: grey turning chestnut. Just to make certain, when he went out he bought a tube of fake tan and a pair of cheap sunglasses from a shop in Tritone. Change was good. It helped keep him on his toes, made him work to fit inside a new skin, forget who – what – he really was.

Now he stood in the toilet of the Net café working the tan into his face. It was a little exaggerated, a little too dark. That was good. It meant people didn't look at him too hard. The glasses fitted only loosely. He peered at himself in Monica Sawyer's hand mirror, hunching up his shoulders like a punk. This was better than the hair dye alone, much better. Now he could pass as an idiotic hustler, the kind of man who hung around outside tourist restaurants trying to coax the unwary inside with a menu and the promise of a warm, Roman welcome. The kind of man most people would want to avoid.

Then he went back into the deserted main room, sat

at a dusty PC out of sight of the moron at the counter, who just might be smart enough to register the change in his appearance, and started wasting time until his head cleared.

How long?

The damn question and the old black voice wouldn't go away and now he knew he couldn't stop himself looking, couldn't help himself when it came to punching the keys, trying out the combinations. All this was new when he first got out. It was amazing how much the world had changed in little over a decade. And it was useful too. A stored global memory you could log into anywhere, provided someone sold the key.

He pulled up Google and typed in 'Desert Storm'.

So much stuff, so much of it wrong, just the hindsight you got from the media and the old, old lies. But the dates were there and the deadline: 15 January 1991.

Get your sorry Arab ass out of Kuwait by then or we come kicking.

Yeah. That happened. Except you didn't wait for January to come, did you? War was about planning, preparation. You placed a few markers to make sure the bets fell your way. The good side of Christmas you slung two camouflaged Humvees underneath a couple of Black Hawks, loaded up two teams of 'specialists' who'd been locked in training in a secluded villa out beyond Orvieto for weeks. Then you dropped the vehicles and the crew somewhere in the desert outside Babylon, pointed them to where the friendlies were supposed to be waiting and never said – *never* – that good and bad were relative in the desert, depended on which way the sun was shining, how many dollars you had stashed alongside the M16s, the rocket-propelled grenades, and the radios that could bring those same Black Hawks storming back to save you any time you wanted.

Remembering. He hated remembering. So he hit the other Google button, the one marked groups, the one that took you straight into crazy territory, all those anonymous Usenet pits where anyone was anyone, could say what they liked and always be out of reach, untraceable, faceless, nameless, flaming each other night and day all around the world, just wishing there was something you could put in a mail message that would harm the other person – physically, permanently – like a demon biting its way out of the screen.

He liked these places more than anything. You could say your mind and no one ever got payback. You could type in 'Desert Storm Babylon Bill Kaspar' and see . . . what?

A list of episodes from some dumb science-fiction series spawned out of *Star Trek*. He'd tried it a million times when he first got free. It was always the same. Until this September in Beijing. Something had happened then. Something that had set him on his present path.

Nothing ever got erased on the Net. The message, the solitary first in a thread marked 'Babylon Sisters' was still there.

> The Scarlet Beast was a generous beast. Honor his memory. Fuck China. Fuck the ziggurat. Let's get together again back in the old places folks. Reunion time for the class of '91. Just one spare place at the table. You coming or not?

It was signed: *WillFK@whitehouse.gov* and, seeing it

again, remembering the way it first goaded him in the Internet café on the other side of the world, Bill Kaspar thought he might go crazy, just pick up the fucking screen there and then and throw it across the empty room, stomp on it till there was nothing left but shattered plastic and glass.

The Scarlet Beast was a generous beast. Honor his memory.

They were saying he was dead now, that he'd been Dan Deacon too. They lied, always, and maybe that was one good reason the voices wouldn't go away.

He closed his eyes, squeezed hard, tried to think, tried to remember, calm himself. He hadn't risen to the bait in Beijing. He'd been too shocked to see it there. Now, increasingly, there was nothing to lose.

He'd read Revelation during all that time in the wilderness, stuck in the stinking jail in Baghdad. The Bible was the only book they allowed him. It was a new experience. When he'd first got his orders, first seen that crazy codename for the unseen figure who created and bankrolled their little project, he hadn't got the reference. Revelation provided it. *The Scarlet Beast, the Whore of Babylon. She held a golden cup in her hand, filled with abominable things and the filth of her adulteries.*

Nine bodies in the ground now and the voices kept screaming at Bill Kaspar, telling him he still didn't have a face he could believe in, a real name, anything.

Thought you knew the guy, white boy? Or did you screw up there too?

'Like fuck I did!' Kaspar yelled out loud, and stomped a big fist on the grimy desk, sending the

Japanese teenager two seats along scurrying into the corner to find another machine.

Unable to stop himself, he typed in a reply and knew immediately that this was what they wanted. He was sitting in the biggest Net café in Rome, writing live down the fibre, while some spook just up the road or in Washington somewhere, some stupid little geek masquerading as the FBI, sat gawping at a screen, waiting for a fish to wriggle on the line.

'Lying fuckhead, treasonable, cowardly scum,' he wrote. 'I've waited long enough now. "Bill Kaspar" my ass. This is the real item, dweeb boy. Fear not. There will be a reunion. And soon. Pray we don't meet.'

You hunt. You get hunted. You wave to each other from across the canyon, wondering who gets to taste whose blood first. And when.

A part of him cursing his own impetuosity, he logged off, set the PC to reboot, ran a comb through his hair and took one last furtive look at himself in the reflection of the PC screen. Then he walked out through the side door, avoiding the front desk, out into the freezing street, thinking about distances, measuring the space between this tacky office block and the big building in the Via Veneto, spanning the icy air between them in discrete units in his head.

The bug worked for half a kilometre, maybe more. It was made almost entirely from plastic, which was supposed to let it through any standard scanning system. The little battery was designed to keep it running for a week. By his reckoning the embassy ought to be just in range. To make sure, he went outside, crossed the empty road, watched a bus struggling over the slush, then walked a couple of hundred metres up the hill, before taking out the earphone of the receiver and popping it in so that it looked as if he were listening to football on a little radio.

He cast one short glance back towards Barberini, just to satisfy himself. A couple of guys in dark coats were going into the Net café. Not the usual clientele.

Morons. It was like playing with amateurs. Like playing with little Emily Deacon, who wasn't that much changed, in some ways, from when she'd been a girl, shaking her long blonde hair to rock music in Steely Dan Deacon's parlour a lifetime before, a little kid wondering why two grown men full of beer found her so funny.

There was a café on the corner of a side street: standard coffee, an automatic door that worked only intermittently, two uncomfortable wooden seats by the window, just one customer, an old man spooning stained sugar into his mouth out of an empty cup. Bill Kaspar ordered an overpriced cappuccino and sat by the smeary glass, damp with condensation, looking out into the cold world beyond, listening. Bugs were unreliable. They'd never work from inside the embassy. There were devices to prevent that, networks of transmitters that sent out a constant blur of electronic noise to deafen anyone trying to intrude.

But he was fishing too. In truth he was starting to get desperate. He'd tried every other avenue he could think of. The idea had occurred to him the previous night, just when he was beginning to realize who Emily Deacon was as she struggled against his iron grip, just as he was struggling against the voices, trying to convince them there was something better he could do with the girl than take her life.

The bug was the size of a one cent coin. As he'd wrestled her into submission under Giordano Bruno's watching statue, he'd pushed the Velcro back into the underside of the collar on her thick black jacket, on the off chance, not knowing how he could use this opportunity or whether she'd be smart enough to pick it up anyway. It was worth a try.

The earphone crackled. There was just static, the unintelligible rustling of a digital infinity, maybe one the embassy was putting out itself. It could be two thousand euros, the last real money he had, straight down the drain.

Then, after thirty minutes, just when the man behind the counter was beginning to stare at his empty cup wondering when he'd buy another, something else, the unmistakable sound of traffic heard from inside a car. Muffled horns, a car engine, the guttural echo of a bus rumbling up the Via Veneto.

He signalled to the barman for another. And in his ear there came two voices: Emily Deacon and a man, a native Italian, so clear, so young and determined he could almost picture a face emerging out of the hissing, fizzing jingle jangle of sound.

'You can pull in here, Nic. I need to go home and pick up a few things first.'

She indicated an apartment block just up from the embassy. A fancy address. From her expression – Emily Deacon didn't miss much – Costa was aware a look of surprise had crossed his face.

'It's a government apartment,' she said, amused.

'No, I couldn't afford a place in the Via Veneto myself. Not on an FBI salary.'

She hesitated for a moment then scribbled a number down on a notepad, ripped off the page and handed it to him. 'If you want, call direct. On my mobile. It can be difficult getting through to the office. The apartment is the one with Clinton on the bell. Someone's idea of a joke I guess.'

He watched a bus work gingerly past the car, navigating the soft, grey slush, then made a U-turn and parked a little way up from the embassy, just outside the block she'd pointed out.

'You should get some sleep,' he suggested. 'It was a long night.'

'I did sleep. Remember?'

'Ah, right.' It was easy to forget. She looked exhausted, troubled too. She'd listened intently to Falcone's brusque interrogation. She was tough enough to take it, Costa didn't doubt that. But something was bothering her and he had a feeling it wasn't just a grilling from a pushy Italian cop.

'What do you do next?' he asked.

'Get some fresh clothes, take a shower and go into the office. What else is there?'

Not much, he thought. For either of them. All the same it was worth making the protest. 'Why? You can't work all the time. There's nothing new, is there? You saw the expression on Falcone's face. He's like a barometer. When things look up so does he.'

She was silent.

'Sorry,' he said, cursing himself. 'What I meant to say was, there's nothing new as far as we're aware. Maybe your friend in there is better informed.'

She smiled and he saw it again: the years just fell off her. Being a pseudo-cop didn't fit Emily Deacon. It was a dead weight on her slender shoulders, one she wouldn't shirk, even though he didn't doubt it had never been part of her plan.

'Maybe he is,' she answered. 'Maybe not. How many times do I need to explain this, Nic? Do you really think I'm going to find out?'

'I don't know.'

The light blue eyes didn't leave him for a moment. It was a kind of reproach. 'You don't?'

'No. All I know is we're getting bounced around like junior partners or something. And this is *our* town, Emily. You should remind the man in there of that some time.'

'I'm sure he'd listen.'

'Someone has to,' he said firmly.

She shook her head and ran a couple of fingers through her blonde locks.

'Are you asking what I think you're asking?'

'I'm asking for some trust.'

'I don't know you.' It came out as a flat, plain statement. It was true too. 'Do you go around trusting people you don't know?'

'All the time,' he replied. 'It's one of my many weaknesses.'

'Then you're a fool, Nic. Best I go now.'

He peered out of the jeep window, which was clouding over with condensation in spite of the air conditioning running full blast. She'd picked up her bag and was about to reach for the door.

Costa leaned over and put his hand on her arm. He needed to make this point. It was a straw worth clutching at. 'Leapman refused to tell us why he knew it was worth coming to Rome before anything happened. Did he tell you?'

'We've been through this,' she said with a weary sigh. 'I've no idea. I just know what he wants me to know.'

'Emily. We told you about Margaret Kearney being a fake. We gave you that passport photo. Seems to me that's a hell of a lot more than anyone in there –' he nodded towards the big grey building – 'has been prepared to give us. And another thing.'

What was the phrase the English used? In for a penny, in for a pound.

'I can't help coming back to this. What are you doing here? Don't you ever ask yourself that? Why you? A . . .'

He didn't even know what she was back in America.

'Junior systems analyst.' She came up with the answer for him.

'Exactly. Whatever the hell that means. It doesn't sound like ideal training for chasing a serial killer around Rome.'

'Look. I ask myself this all the time, Nic, and I don't hear any answers. What am I supposed to do? Shout and scream at Leapman until he cracks? You're not the only ones in the dark here. Leapman is his own man in that building. Half the embassy staff don't know who he is and those that do daren't talk to him.'

'Well, that's just wonderful . . .'

'*Yes, it is!*'

'OK,' he said, trying to bring down the temperature just a little. 'Let me make a suggestion. Maybe this is nothing, Emily. Maybe not.'

He waited. She had to ask.

'Well?' The blue eyes wouldn't let go.

'It's just this. We've been on a kind of alert over attacks on Americans since October. A man called Henry Anderton was attacked in the ghetto. Badly beaten up. He lived, but he was lucky. There were a couple of uniform cops in the area who got involved. Whoever the guy was ran off. If our men hadn't been there . . .'

'I didn't know that.' She was interested. He'd caught her attention. 'What did he do?'

Costa pulled out his notebook and riffled through the pages. 'I checked during the night. He was some kind of academic working over here on a project. A military historian. Does the name mean anything?'

She shook her head. 'Should it?'

'I don't know. I made a few more inquiries after that. I can't find an academic anywhere called Henry Anderton. He was out of hospital after two days, gone to some private clinic, no one knows where.'

'Keeps on happening.'

'Quite.'

He didn't want to come right out and ask it. He wasn't sure he was close enough to her yet. All the same . . .

'Someone in there will know, Emily. It could help. Both of us.'

She sighed, folded her arms, stared down into the foot well. 'This isn't about my father, Nic. Don't try and use that. I want this guy caught for all of them. More than anything I want him caught because that's my job now. It's what I'm supposed to do, like it or not.'

He shrugged. 'Sorry.'

She didn't move.

'Will you think about it?'

A flash of fury again. 'What? Smuggling information out of the confidential files of the US embassy? They fire you for that, I believe.'

'Would that be so bad?'

'You mean because I'm lousy at this anyway?'

Delicate territory. 'I meant because . . . I don't think you enjoy this kind of work.'

'Perhaps I don't. But they send you to jail too. I don't imagine I'd enjoy that either.'

He couldn't stifle a brief laugh.

'What's so funny?' she demanded.

'I had that kind of conflict myself once. Did all the wrong things. Which were, in my view, all the right things.'

'What happened?'

'Long story. You can hear it sometime if you want. I'm here, aren't I?'

'Oh yes,' she murmured, peering straight into his face. 'You're here. You and that partner of yours. No one's going to miss either of you.'

It hung on a knife edge. He could so easily ruin things.

'Henry Anderton,' she repeated.

'I can write it down,' he said, reaching for the pad.

She snatched it away. 'That would be really smart. Are you at home this evening? Six or seven onwards?'

'Could be.'

She started scribbling something else on the notepad. 'Do me a favour too. Look up this name. Everywhere you can find. Tonight we can compare notes. And . . . damn.'

There was a shape by the car. Costa felt his spine stiffen automatically, saw images from the previous two nights flash through his head, and felt for his gun.

The jeep door opened. Agent Leapman was there on the other side, staring in at them, looking even more pissed off than usual.

'What is this? The kindergarten run?' Leapman demanded. 'You should've been at your desk an hour ago, Deacon.'

Behind her back, Emily's hand, small, firm and warm, thrust itself briefly into Costa's, pushing the screwed-up page from the pad into his palm. Surprised, he took a moment to get the paper out of her grasp. Their fingers entwined, just briefly.

Leapman didn't see a thing. He was too busy making an impression.

'Go sit in there and look busy, will you?' the FBI man moaned. 'I got things to do.'

She pulled her hand free, reclaimed her bag and started to get out of the car.

'Can't I come along?'

'What's the point?' His back was turned to her already, he wasn't even bothering to watch. 'Go write a report. File something. Defrag a hard drive. Whatever . . .'

Costa watched them go their separate ways. She didn't look back. A part of him resented that. Another knew better. Falcone had said it. Perhaps he'd seen this coming all along.

'Dangerous games,' Nic Costa murmured to himself,

then opened the piece of paper and read the name: *Bill Kaspar.*

From across the road, seated on a hard wooden chair in a tiny café, someone else watched them too, watched Emily Deacon flash a card at the gate then walk past the security guard, straight through the door, into a sea of bright, unintelligible noise.

Gianni Peroni was good with the girl. No, Teresa Lupo corrected herself, he was amazing. He built a bond with her in a way Teresa couldn't hope to comprehend, able to communicate an emotion – sympathy, disappointment, expectation – with just a look, able to see too that Laila had a need for what he could provide. Reassurance. And sometimes just attention. It wasn't easy. It wasn't all plain sailing. When Laila got tired Peroni backed off. He knew just when to stop pushing.

And the kid wanted to be on her own a lot. Or at least that's what she pretended. It was an act, though. After a while – ten, fifteen minutes – she'd drift back to Peroni, nudge him with an elbow, ask some pointless question. Her Italian was heavily accented but much better than they'd first thought. She was quick-witted too. Teresa could see a glint of keen intelligence in her dark eyes, though much of the time it was marred by the stain of suspicion every street kid seemed to own. They were never quite happy, even in their own company. Something, some cataclysm, hunger, disaster, an encounter with the cops, was always waiting around the corner.

Laila couldn't stop stealing either, even in the house. Peroni had patiently removed all manner of stuff – cutlery, food, family photographs, even an old, stained ashtray – from the multitude of pockets in the grubby black jacket she wore all the time. God knows what she'd stashed in the room Nic had given her upstairs, where she retreated from time to time for some peace.

The three of them now sat in front of the bigger of the two fires, Laila sprawled out teenage-fashion on an old sofa, trying to read a comic book Nic had dug up from somewhere. Peroni was slumped in the chair next to her, eyes closed, snoring lightly. It was getting on for noon. Teresa had already called the office and checked with Silvio Di Capua that there was nothing new to deal with. The autopsy on Mauro Sandri was done, the report filed safely in the cabinet marked 'boring', the one that said people who die from gunshot wounds and knives were rarely deserving of further attention. Agent Leapman and his friends had made sure she couldn't get her hands on the one body that did interest her, that of the so-called Margaret Kearney.

Silvio sounded as if he was coping. He needed to be left on his own more, she thought, needed to understand he was capable of this.

Then the sequence of events of the previous day raced through her mind.

'Shit,' she hissed abruptly to herself. Gianni Peroni didn't even stir. He was sound asleep.

When she phoned, Teresa had meant to tell Silvio to take the dead American woman's belongings round to the embassy. It had just slipped her memory. *You're getting old*, she thought. *This is Alzheimer's kicking in, a world record.*

And it doubtless meant another argument soon, maybe more trouble for Leo Falcone from those faceless men above him. She'd heard whispers going round the

Questura the previous night. Falcone was not in good odour. The career escalator was stuck. Maybe soon it would start to go the other way.

Yeah, she thought to herself. These were the tricks men played when they wanted something. Don't take a person to one side and say, what's the problem? Just bring out the whips and the shackles and start talking demotion. Maybe worse.

On the other hand . . .

It meant there was the opportunity for another look. Once they'd achieved something here. Not that she expected to find anything. She didn't fool herself about that for one moment. It would just feel right to be trying. She'd been no use to Peroni and Nic with the girl. They might as well have invited in an alien.

Or Leo Falcone, she suddenly thought.

'Laila,' she whispered, catching the kid's attention. There was a hint of a suspicious smile in return. Teresa nodded at the sleeping Peroni, making the obvious gesture with her two palms pressed to the side of her head.

Then she pointed to the kitchen and got up. The girl, as she'd hoped, followed her.

There was just enough juice left for a couple of small glasses. Men and shopping, she thought. Venus and Mars.

'We made a good snowman. You must have done that before.'

The girl made a puzzled face. 'No.'

The squat figure sat in the garden, staring back at them through the frosted glass, an old man's hat found in a cupboard somewhere perched lopsidedly on his white head.

'We treat you like a kid. And you're not. Not really, are you?'

She squirmed. Teresa wished she could get the hang of this awkward challenge in communication. Peroni had a family of his own. It gave him a head start with a recalcitrant kid like this.

'It doesn't matter. When I go to town, is there something you need? Someone you'd like me to contact?'

The dark eyes clouded over. All that suspicion again. Maybe Peroni would have been graced with a real answer. Not her. 'No . . .'

Teresa touched the old, grubby jacket. 'How about some new clothes?'

'I get my own clothes.'

'It was just an offer. You're such a pretty kid. Slim too. It would be a pleasure to buy something. I was never slim. At your age . . .'

She tried to remember herself then, to put the image she had in her own head against what she saw in Laila now. 'I was a fat, bad-tempered little monster. Not much changes.'

The girl laughed, a little nervously.

'What's so funny?' Teresa asked. 'Don't you believe me?'

'No!'

There was a divide you couldn't cross and if she knew more about kids, as much as Peroni did, she'd have understood that already. A kid could never see an adult and imagine them when they were young, never envisage them as anything but what they were: part of another world, in Laila's case a threatening one, fixed, run by other people, with their arguments and hidden possibilities. Peroni had worked on that assumption from the moment he started talking to her. He didn't pretend to be anything he wasn't. He simply set out his position – *I will be your friend, you can trust me, just keep listening and you'll see* – and let her find a way to get close to him, like a moth attracted to a distant flickering flame. It established a connection, almost straight away. It created room for hurt too. She and the kid had both heard the tail end of the heated conversation with Falcone. Peroni even told her a little of what that was about. Teresa, the grown-up rational adult, was able to dismiss this level of bickering as the way things were. Laila was different. She heard the sound of men yelling at each other and shrank into herself, as if fearing the worst. That was part of the back story that, one day perhaps, she might share with them.

You could still try, though, Teresa reasoned to herself.

'So what do you think I was like when I was your age?'

Laila thought about it. 'Normal.'

'Hah! How wrong can you get? I'm not normal now, kid. You want to know what they call me? In the Questura?'

'What?'

'"Crazy Teresa." The lunatic pathologist. Mad as they come.'

Laila shook her head, refusing to accept a word of it. This seemed, to Teresa Lupo, dreadfully unfair.

'It's true,' she asserted, 'whether you believe it or not. And I *am* crazy. Crazy enough to buy you some stuff just because I want to. Just because all that black gear drives me nuts. Why be pretty and hide it?'

Laila didn't understand the argument. She didn't

think of herself as pretty. Pretty didn't exist in her world. She probably didn't think of herself at all. A flicker of anxiety crossed her face. 'When will they make me go?'

'Nobody's making you do anything, Laila.'

She didn't believe that either. Teresa couldn't blame her. It was a particularly vague answer, one full of holes even a thirteen-year-old street kid could see.

'Gianni stays with me?'

'Sure. For a while. But he's a cop. He's got work to do. Lots of work. You're not his . . .'

She checked herself, horrified at the words running through her head: *You're not his kid, he's got two of them and he thinks he's failed them already. You're just filling in the spaces without even knowing it.*

'It's not his job, Laila. We'll work something out. But Gianni and Nic are paid to find bad people and put them in prison. They have to find that man you saw. They need you to help them.'

The girl threw her skinny arms around herself, staring at the floor.

'I didn't see anything,' she mumbled. 'I just . . .'

You didn't threaten in a situation like this. That couldn't work. Yet they'd spent hours trying to pull out the facts of what happened, piece by piece, from Laila's head, and it was all so . . . meagre. The address had come easily. The rest was a jumble. She'd followed the man because he looked 'interesting'.

Really. *How, Laila?* She didn't explain. She just shrugged. This was what she did. Follow people. Maybe, Teresa thought, offer them something – she didn't want to think what – then take their money and their wallet too.

They'd got Laila to talk as far as she wanted to. Then she had clammed up, however subtly Peroni tried to find a way past her defences. Every understated question just walked straight into a brick wall.

Teresa Lupo tried to imagine what it was like for her that night. You sneaked into an old temple because someone left the door open. So what were you thinking?

It's warm in there.

OK. And what do you think when you get there and see two people, a man and a woman, close up to each other, something going on?

They're going to make out and I can watch.

OK too. She knew she'd have done that at thirteen.

You can steal stuff. God knows what.

And that was OK as well, except nothing had gone the way it was supposed to. The two didn't make out. Probably not, anyway, from what Teresa had seen of the body. But this was something different.

The man strangled her with his special piece of cord, the one he kept for such occasions. Then he took off all her clothes, got out a scalpel, looked around the room, flipped her over so that her dead face bit into all that ancient stone, did his work (which he'd know by heart by now, without the need for templates, because he'd done it – how many? – eight times before already), then flipped the poor mutilated bitch back and let her blank, unseeing eyes stare at the oculus, pulled out her arms like that, cold fingers pointing out at some hidden magical points in space.

Teresa looked at Laila and a hidden inner voice provided the answer, persuaded her she knew what had happened, so surely she didn't need to keep asking this poor kid over and over again.

Laila did what any sane person would have done in the circumstances. She hid in the shadows, just where she was when Nic came into the place, cowering, shivering, stifling the scream in her throat, refusing to look because seeing would make those noises she was hearing take on another dimension, let them climb straight into her head and stay there forever.

She put a hand on the girl's shoulder and smiled. 'Just tell me the truth, Laila. Then we'll leave it. You really didn't see anything, did you? It was just too . . . bad. Too scary to look. It's nothing to be ashamed of. We'd all have done the same.'

'I told you,' the girl said with a pout.

No you didn't, she wanted to say. Even Gianni Peroni had missed that, maybe because it needed a woman to understand how a teenage girl would react to that particular fear. Men had a curiosity they couldn't quell. They had to watch. It was compulsive. A woman had somewhere else to go, somewhere inside herself where she could believe the world was still warm and kind and ultimately good.

She wished to God Peroni had been awake and standing there then. Because Teresa Lupo knew this kid was telling the truth, and knew, too, she was hiding something. No amount of street life, no big, black prehistory, could explain the shifty expression in her eyes just then. There was a secret there. Maybe it was too personal – thirteen-year-olds could do things for a man too. Maybe . . .

You haven't a clue, she told herself. *Quit guessing. Either she tells or she doesn't.*

Teresa thought about Falcone and how he would have handled an interview like this. He and Peroni were so different, used such dissimilar tactics to reach the same end. Temperamentally she was closer to Falcone. She didn't like fishing, walking around a problem, looking for its weaknesses. You went in, asked the right questions, then stood there, arms crossed, tapping your feet loudly on the floor until the answers came. It was one reason she liked Peroni so much. Loved him even, though she wasn't quite sure exactly what that meant. Gianni added some charity into the day-to-day routine of investigation. He got what he wanted by exploiting an innate belief that in just about everyone there existed some small spark of humanity, if only you could find it. She was in no doubt this was a weird way for a cop to proceed. Even Costa, who was once a pushover, had started to toughen up his act of late. The job did that to most of them. Why twenty years of dealing with vice made Gianni Peroni the man he was, more sensitive, not less, was beyond her.

But Peroni had gone as far as he could. It was time to lean on Falcone's tactics a little. Besides, all she was doing was telling Laila the truth, juiced up a little.

'Do you know what it means to get fired?' Teresa asked sotto voce, casting an eye into the living room, making sure Peroni was still asleep.

Some emotion flickered in Laila's eyes. 'I'm not stupid.'

'I know that. I just wanted to make sure you understood.'

'Understood what?'

Teresa hesitated, as if she'd overstepped the mark. 'It's nothing. It's about Gianni. It doesn't concern you.'

Laila was curious. That was enough.

'I know what being fired means,' she repeated.

'When that other man came, the inspector,' Teresa continued, 'he asked us to go outside. Remember?'

Laila took Falcone's banknote out of her pocket, rolled it in her fingers and almost smiled.

'Quite,' Teresa said without emotion. 'You heard them arguing. Did Gianni tell you what he said?'

'No,' she replied, puzzled.

'Typical.' It would have been too. 'I don't know why I'm telling you this, Laila. I shouldn't but you two seem to get along so maybe you ought to know. Gianni's in trouble. Things haven't been going so well recently.'

She let it sink in, waited for the moment, hoped she wouldn't come to hate herself too much along the way.

'He came to tell Gianni that it's make-or-break time. Either he gets you to tell him what you know or he's fired. No job. No money, Laila. Nothing. He's got kids too. One about your age.'

The girl shivered and stared at the table. 'It's not true.'

Teresa shrugged. 'If that's what you want to think. It doesn't matter. Why should you worry about him anyway? You don't even know him.'

She reached forward, touched the kid's lank hair, and hoped to God Peroni never found out about this. 'I'm sorry. I shouldn't have bothered you with this. It's none of your business. I've got to go soon. I'll be upstairs for a little while. Please don't tell him I told you.'

Laila's eyes were glassy. There was a moment approaching. The kid was scanning the room and the rest of the house. It must have seemed like a palace to the girl.

Teresa went up the old stone steps and found a spare bedroom. There was nothing for her there. She just wanted them to be together. She could imagine Peroni waking up, finding the girl staring at him, ready to talk. It could work. She'd seen that extraordinary bond grow between them that morning. It *had* to work. The kid wouldn't talk to anyone else.

So she lay on the cover of the bed in the dusty, musky-smelling room, closed her eyes and dreamed a pleasant dream, a stupid, childlike fantasy set in a bright world of pastel colours where the sun always shone, where families, young and old, stayed together always, sharing the years, growing closer all the time. It was the kind of dream place you never wanted to leave, a warm, embracing neverland just beyond reach.

A noise intruded into this welcome reverie: the sound of the downstairs door.

Nic, she thought. He knew as much about family as Peroni in a way. It was all wrapped up in a tight bundle inside this old, cold farmhouse buried beneath the snow off the old Appian Way. Where you could just sleep forever with a musty, ancient coverlet keeping out the freezing cold.

Except . . .

The door went again after a while and that didn't add up, that could only be part of this half dream.

Maybe.

Cursing herself, Teresa Lupo threw off the stupor, forced herself awake and, with growing trepidation, went downstairs.

Peroni still slumbered in front of the fire. Nic was going through the place, room by room.

'Where's Laila?' he asked. 'Upstairs with you?'

'I don't think so,' she answered.

Teresa Lupo went to the front window. The snow was piling down again, a thick blanket of gigantic soft flakes. Through them she could just make out a couple of fresh tracks zigzagging towards the gate, fast disappearing in the blizzard.

'Shit,' she sighed to herself. 'Shit, shit and double shit. The kid's only thirteen for Christ's sake. How the hell am I supposed to know she's an escapologist? Didn't you see someone on a bike when you came here?'

He stuck a hand towards the blizzard beyond the window. 'In that weather?'

She went back to the living room. Her handbag was open, her purse too, the money all gone.

A big, familiar figure came and stood by her. She could sense his puzzlement without even looking at him. Peroni had some silent, unseen way of communicating his emotions.

'Where is she?' Costa asked again.

'You've got a bike here?'

He nodded.

'Not any more. She must have taken it. I'm sorry, I fell asleep.'

'For Christ's sake . . .' Peroni muttered under his breath.

'Excuse me! You were sleeping too. And you were the cop here, remember?'

Costa was juggling the keys to the jeep already. He looked wiped out.

'I was trying to help,' she yelled, watching them head for the door, not bothering to look back. 'I was trying . . .'

Then they were gone.

'Shit,' she said to no one.

She didn't even have time to tell them it was her fault. Or to wonder: *Why?*

A swirl of fatigue swam around her head. Then something made her jump: the phone trilling like a wild beast, the volume turned up to max the way a solitary man would in a big house like this.

'Yeah?' she yelled into the thing.

It was Silvio Di Capua, screaming hysterically from his mobile, wondering why she hadn't answered hers, not understanding it was in another room, dead to the world while she slept elsewhere. She listened, ruefully grateful that some work had appeared to thrust aside the doubts and guilt lurking inside her head. Silvio had danced this frantic little dance in tantrum land all too often, but this time round it sounded as if he had a good few reasons.

'It's a body, Silvio,' she said, when she had a chance to interrupt the babbling sea of details and questions. 'Just remember that and follow procedures.'

'Oh, wonderful!' he yelled. 'Procedures, procedures. Tell me that when you get here. It's a slaughterhouse and right near McDonald's too.'

'Well, in that case it's somewhat appropriate, don't you think?'

'This is *not* a time for jokes, Teresa. Falcone's livid you weren't answering your phone.'

'What am I?' she screamed back at him. 'Instant fucking pathologist? Just add water and I crawl out of the bottle?'

Besides, she thought, Falcone was going to have plenty more reasons to go berserk soon. His solitary witness had gone walkabout after that little lecture of hers and she didn't need to wonder about who'd catch the blame on that one.

Think about work. It's what they pay you for.

'One thing, Silvio. You say the woman's been cut about.'

'Oh yes.'

'Good. Now calm down and think about this because what I'm about to ask is important. Are there any signs someone's used a scalpel?'

The voice on the line paused for breath.

'That and the rest,' Di Capua panted. 'You've got to get here, Teresa. It's . . . scary.'

She picked her car keys out of the bag. At least the kid hadn't taken them.

'Twenty minutes,' she said. 'And make mine a quarter pounder with cheese.'

Emily Deacon sat in her small embassy apartment eyeing the phone, wondering what she could say. It had been a month since she'd spoken to her mother, a week since they'd exchanged emails. The relationship was close but had boundaries. They'd never really had the right conversation about her father's death. Even now she was uncertain how her mother felt about what had happened. Saddened, obviously. But shocked? A part of Emily said, unconsciously, that wasn't the case. And there was only one way to find out.

She called home, went through the niceties, heard the conversation fade into its customary silences.

'What do you really want, Emily?' her mother said after a while.

'I want to bury Dad,' she answered immediately. 'I don't feel I've done that yet. Do you?'

There was a pause on the line. 'We were divorced, honey. It wasn't pretty. By the time he died he wasn't a part of my life any more. It's different for you, I know. That's only to be expected.'

'But you loved him!'

' "Loved." '

Her mother could be tough. She knew that. Maybe it was all part of being married to her dad.

'And you hated him? After?'

'No . . .' Yet there was no emotion in her voice. In a way, Dan Deacon had vacated both their lives long before his last breath in a temple in Beijing. 'I can't have this discussion over the phone. Let it wait till you get home.'

'I can't wait. I'm in Rome. I've got memories. I've got things happening here . . .'

She had to hang on so long for an answer she wondered if the line had gone dead. 'Things?'

'Maybe they're not connected. I don't know. It's just . . .'

Connected or not, there was a larger point.

'Until I know what really happened,' she continued, 'until I really know who he was, what he did, why it ended this way . . . I don't think he's quite dead. Not in my head.'

'He got killed by a lunatic, Emily!' her mother yelled. 'What more is there to know?'

'Who he was. What he did.'

That pause again. And then the cruellest thing. An act she'd never have expected, not in the harshest, most difficult of times during the divorce.

'I'm not in the mood for this,' her mother snapped. Then the line really did go dead and Emily Deacon understood. She was the only one keeping Dan Deacon's memory from the grave.

Thornton Fielding was one of the embassy good guys, a longserving member of the embassy staff who'd gone native over the two decades he'd spent in Rome. She could remember Fielding from her childhood. He was now fifty-five or so, still as slim, as elegant as ever, today in a dark, fine-wool suit, perfectly ironed white shirt and red silk tie. He'd just lost the big, bushy head of dark hair, a feature which, she recalled, even back then seemed a little outré for the job. Now he was back to a conservative, short, scholarly clip, turning salt and pepper grey. This plain admission of age somehow made his intelligent, constantly beaming face even more likeable.

As a kid she'd had a crush on him, even though she understood he was, in some way she couldn't quite work out, different. Then, when she finally came back to the Via Veneto under Leapman's wing, she'd understood. Fielding stayed in Rome for two reasons. He loved the place so much it was now home. Just as importantly, Rome didn't judge him. His sexuality wasn't an issue here. Professionally, it clouded his career, kept him out of the constant circle of foreign postings that meant promotion in the diplomatic world. Privately – and Fielding was a very private man she now understood – the city let him breathe, let him be what he was. He'd never have got that in most places, and certainly not at home, amid all the backroom fighting and bitching of Washington.

Leapman just referred to him as 'the faggot', sometimes within his hearing. Maybe that was because Leapman realized she knew and liked him already. Or perhaps she was just being paranoid. Either way, the two men kept out of each other's company as much as possible. It was for the best, though Fielding's remit covered the maintenance of security systems. As far as she understood it, he was the Bureau's point man within the embassy, the one they came to when things need fixing or they had to liaise on relations with other agencies. It was inconceivable they'd be able to avoid each other all the time.

She had typed the two names she had – Henry Anderton and Bill Kaspar – into the network and got nothing. She needed more clearance so, after thinking this through, realizing there were so few options, she walked round to Thornton Fielding's office, waited for one of the assistants to finish talking to him and then went in, taking care to close the door behind her.

Fielding was a smart man. He watched her push the glass shut, then said, 'I'm just guessing here, but if you're about to complain about your boss, Emily, let me save you some time. First, I don't handle human resources issues for the FBI. Second, even if I did, there's nothing I or anyone here can do to help you. Leapman is his own man. We just provide you guys with floor space, heating and free coffee. What you do with them is your business.'

It was amusing, almost. Fielding automatically assumed she couldn't cope with a man like Leapman. He couldn't yet separate her from the kid he'd known more than a decade before.

'Why should I want to complain about him?'

'Are you joking? If I had to work with the pig I'd be complaining. Mightily.'

Which wasn't true at all. Fielding had too much of the diplomat in his blood for that. He'd have found some way around the problem. 'He's not employed for his manners, Thornton. He's there because he's good at his job. He is, isn't he?'

Fielding's eyes immediately went to the glass door. There was no one there. He held his long, slender arms out wide in a gesture of bafflement. 'I guess so. Do you know what that job is exactly?'

The question threw her. She'd never met Leapman before this assignment. He came out of nowhere, throwing so many demands and orders in her direction that she'd never thought about his background.

'You don't, do you? He's just a grade, one several rungs higher than you. That right?'

'I guess so,' she admitted.

'Well, let me tell you one thing, Emily. I recognize that kind of guy. If you could pull out his FBI records – and that's a big if, I doubt even I have clearance to get that far – I'd put good money on the fact he started life elsewhere. Military maybe. I don't know. Don't care either. I can live with the FBI, most of the time. You're just a bunch of people with a job to do. Leapman. He's something else. Something private's bugging that bastard. Don't know what it is. Don't care. But if it's not him burning you up, tell me what is.'

She pulled up a chair and sat next to his desk. 'I'm here to ask a favour. I want you to tell me about my father.'

'Right now?' he asked. 'This sounds like social. I like

social. Just not on company time. Couldn't we have dinner some time? After the holiday?'

'Yes, we could. But I'd like to start the ball rolling. Being here . . . it brings back memories.'

He looked baffled, reluctant to go along with this. 'I don't understand the urgency.'

'Let's say I have a sudden curiosity. I wondered what you felt about him. I was wondering what he did while he was in Rome. I was so young. And he wasn't exactly forthcoming about things.'

Dan Deacon was the military attaché. Strictly speaking that meant his role was to liaise with his counterparts in the country where he was stationed. But it could be one of those catch-all jobs too. She'd learned enough about that from scanning the newspaper files after he died. There was nothing specific about him. But there were stories everywhere, in reputable journals around the world, which made it plain the job could be a cover for something else.

'I didn't work alongside Dan,' Fielding said cautiously. 'We just knew one another. I guess he spent a lot of time with the military people here. Really, Emily, I'm the wrong guy. Ask your mom.'

'They divorced ten years ago. Not long after we left Rome. It all got . . . difficult around then. He was kind of cranky a lot of the time. Didn't you know?'

'I'd heard,' he said shiftily. 'All the same you could ask her.'

'I have. Either she doesn't know or she doesn't want to say.'

Fielding's good-natured expression dropped for a moment and, for the first time, she felt the distance in years between them. Thornton Fielding had always had something boyish about him. Now it was an effort to keep up the act. 'Maybe she's got her reasons.'

'Maybe she has. But if that's the case don't I have the right to know too?'

'Jesus,' Fielding murmured, then got up and stood with his back to her, staring out of the window, out at the torrent of snow.

She came to join him. It was an extraordinary sight: a cloud of soft white flakes pouring from the sky, creating a world that was cold and bereft of colour.

'Will you look at that?' Fielding murmured. 'I've not seen anything like it in twenty years. I doubt I'll see it again either.'

'Why not? It's just weird weather. It happens from time to time.'

He glanced at her. 'All kinds of weird things happen from time to time, Emily. You just have to sit back, do your best, watch and learn, then put the whole damn circus behind you when it's over.'

'Meaning?' she wondered.

'Meaning your father was a good, brave man who served his country. It's a tragedy he's dead. I'm sorry.'

It wasn't enough. She wouldn't leave it at that.

'Everyone's sorry, Thornton, but sympathy doesn't help. I'm trying to understand something here. You can help me.'

His fine eyebrows rose in doubt. 'You're sure of that?'

'Absolutely! You were here. You knew him. It wasn't just a casual acquaintance. I was a kid back then. I remember you coming round. There was music. We laughed. I think . . .'

It was a distant memory, one so odd it stuck out.

'We used to dance.'

He laughed. 'The beer used to flow in the Deacon household, Emily. Dancing was just a part of it.'

'I know. I wasn't blind, deaf and dumb. I remember things, not the exact detail but the feeling, the atmosphere.'

He wasn't taking the bait.

'I remember how bad that atmosphere got in 1991,' she continued. 'So bad it was what led them to divorce a few years later I think. So what was it? I know he went away sometime. I remember. It was my birthday. He wasn't there. That kind of thing never happened. He always came back for my birthday. He used to say . . .'

The memory was so sharp, so real, it almost brought tears to her eyes.

' "When you've only got the one kid spoil 'em rotten." He said it all the time. You must have heard it.'

'Must I?'

He cast an uncharacteristic look, one that just might have been fear, and returned to the desk. She joined him there, in the chair by his.

'Have you asked Leapman about any of this?'

'No. What's the point?'

'He's your boss, isn't he? This is business, Emily. There are rules.'

Fielding assumed she knew something. Maybe that was only to be expected.

'Thornton, I don't think you understand. Before I came here I was a trainee geek in systems. They put me there because I was so lousy out in the field. I'm in the Bureau because it's what I was supposed to do. Dad fixed it for me. I don't pretend I'm good at it. Then, all of a sudden, I'm on a plane to Rome with Joel Leapman in the next seat, staring hard at his copy of *The New Republic*, not saying a damn word about anything. Maybe I'm here because of my Italian. Maybe because I did that degree and I know a little of the background to this pattern he keeps obsessing about.'

The pattern. That magic weave of curves and angles. She couldn't get it out of her head. That was the idea, naturally.

'What pattern?' he wondered.

'This.'

She picked up a pen and started sketching a sacred cut on his notepad, outlining the part that made the shape of the beast. The man, Bill Kaspar, couldn't have done it more quickly, more fluently, she thought.

'I don't know anything about some damn pattern,' he complained, waving a hand at her. 'This is your business, Emily, not mine.'

Her voice rose. 'Yes! It *is* my business. But believe me. *I don't know what the hell's going on.*'

He thought about that, trying to measure if it were true or not.

'Are you kidding me?'

'No!'

Fielding rubbed his hand across his mouth, thinking. 'OK. Let's say I believe you. Here's the first piece of advice. Don't ask him any of these questions. You're right. You won't get an answer. And it may just make things worse between you.'

'Fine,' she persisted. 'So let me ask you. Again. What happened in 1991?'

An uncharacteristic sourness crossed Thornton Fielding's face. 'You've got books, haven't you, Emily? You *know* what happened in 1991. Desert Storm. A bunch of allies getting together to kick the Iraqis out of Kuwait.'

It seemed inconceivable. She'd no memory of the campaign ever being mentioned at home, only the vaguest recollection of news bulletins on the TV.

'My dad was involved in *that*?'

'He was the military attaché. What did you expect him to do? Stay here counting paper clips?'

So that part of her memory was accurate. He had gone away, and for some time.

'You mean he *went* there?'

Fielding shifted uncomfortably by the desk. 'I don't know the details. It's a million miles from my job and I don't *want* to know the details. Let me just say this. Rome's a great place for putting together certain kinds of project. Particularly ones that have to do with the Middle East. You've got the communication. You're near the action. You don't have the security issues you hit somewhere like Greece. There are facilities, too, out of town. That's as much as I know.'

'He was in Iraq?' she pressed.

'Maybe. Probably. Hell, I don't know and I'm not about to start asking. There was a whole bunch of spooky people around at the time. I kept clear. I didn't like what was going on. We had a casus belli there anyway – Saddam had invaded another country, for God's sake. But we hadn't thought it through. Which was kind of the opposite second time round, in my opinion. With that we'd done the war games over and over again and never quite found the reason to use them. Not in all truth. I very nearly resigned over that one.'

She was shocked. The idea of Thornton Fielding

walking out of the embassy after twenty years there seemed incredible.

'You thought about quitting?'

'Sure.' Her bafflement seemed to offend him. 'Is that so odd? Do you think we just sit here taking orders, never questioning them? I wasn't the only one. Some guy in the visa department just left his desk the day the first bombs fell, went outside and joined the crowds. Guess he's making coffee in a bar or something right now. Stupid idea. I can't believe I nearly joined him.'

His eyes moved to the closed door again. Suddenly she felt guilty for putting this decent man in such an awkward position.

'It's not always easy to do what's right, Emily. You have to marry up your conscience with your duty. Sometimes they don't match too well. One has to make way for the other. Either that or you just start all over again at something new and I'm too old for that. Hell, I'm too *good* for that. You can walk away or you can wait for another day to fight your corner. I chose the latter.'

She tried to think back to the blur that was her childhood.

'He was gone a long time, I think. I remember it was odd. My mom cried at night. She was worried.'

'He was gone for almost three months,' Fielding said immediately. 'But he came back, Emily. At least you got that. It wasn't a foregone conclusion. They didn't all make it.'

'And now he's dead. This creep killed him anyway. In a temple in Beijing. Killed him, then carved this crazy pattern out of his back, just like all these others.'

The connection hovered just out of reach . . . Fielding was waving a hand in front of his face. 'I thought I told you. No details. Don't give me any details . . .'

'Without details I'm lost, Thornton. And I can't get a single piece of useful information out of the damn system because it's blocked off to underlings like me. The moment I get near anything I hit the same barrier: no security clearance. I can't talk to Leapman. All I've got is you and some local cops who maybe know more than they're letting on.'

'I haven't got any more, Emily,' he said with resolution. 'I shouldn't have said what I did. Forget it. You want my advice? Go home. Get sick. Lay a complaint against Leapman or something. You won't have a problem making them believe that. Get back to Washington, find yourself a comfy desk somewhere and get on with your life. Just leave Rome and all this shit behind because there are graves around here you don't want to start digging up.'

'That's not possible.'

He looked into her face and there was no mistaking his expression. Thornton Fielding was begging her to be gone.

'Why not?'

'Because I met him last night, Thornton, and I can't just walk away from this now. He could have killed me, but he didn't. Why? I don't know. I *have* to know. Because of who I am. Because . . . shit. He's smart. Maybe he thought that's why I was here in the first place? To lure him out. And he just didn't want to play someone else's game.'

He put his hands together and asked very slowly, 'You met who?'

'Bill Kaspar.'

Fielding's handsome face drained of expression.

'Jesus Christ, Em. Where the hell did you get a name like that?'

'From the guy last night,' she lied. He'd only given her a surname. Her early memories provided the rest. 'He called me that too. "Little Em . . ."'

Bill Kaspar. What a guy.

They'd all said that of this man once upon a time. She didn't know how she remembered that or why. Just that it was true. Her father thought that. Perhaps Thornton Fielding did once too.

'"Little Em . . ."' she repeated. 'But I'm not little any more, Thornton.'

'I can see that,' he murmured. 'We've all grown up a lot over the last few years.'

'So tell me. What the hell's going on around here?'

'Can't,' he sighed, shaking his head. 'I'm not even sure I know myself. I just know this. *You steer clear of this shit.* Otherwise it just eats you up, like it did . . .'

He fell silent and looked at the door. It was different now. He *wanted* someone to intervene.

'Like it did my father? And these other people too?'

'Emily . . .'

She was making Thornton Fielding squirm and it felt awful.

'You know what I think, Thornton? Leapman brought me here as bait of some kind. I'm my father in disguise just to remind this man of something, to throw him off his guard. Joel Leapman thinks I'll bring out this . . . monster. Make him crawl out of the woodwork. Is that what Bill Kaspar was like all along? And if he was . . .'

He was staring at some papers on the desk, pretending she wasn't there.

She leaned over to hammer home the point.

'Dammit, Thornton! You were my dad's friend. Are you going to help me find out what happened to him or not?'

He didn't say a thing. It was all a waste of time. Maybe he was so scared he'd report it all back to Leapman the moment she was gone anyway.

'And you're the guy who nearly resigned over a principle, huh? You expect me to believe that?'

It didn't make her feel any better. Thornton Fielding was part of the good Rome she remembered, and here she was beating up on him for no real reason at all.

'I can't help what you believe, Emily. But please. Listen to me. Drop this. For your own sake. Just leave the whole thing alone.'

She stormed through the door and slammed it behind her. Fielding watched her go, miserable, hurt, she guessed, and with good reason. Then he turned round at his desk and started typing, very slowly, very deliberately into his PC.

Emily Deacon walked back to her seat in Leapman's office. The place was empty. Leapman hadn't even left a message.

You don't leave messages for bait.

So what she was supposed to do? Where she was supposed to be? It was an act. Everything was, and there wasn't a single thing she could do to change matters.

The icon on her email inbox blinked. She opened the message.

> I am sorry for the problems you have been experiencing with the embassy network. We are currently carrying out some urgent maintenance in order to rectify this. I have set up a temporary network identity which you can use in the meantime. This will expire permanently at 14.00.
>
> Username: WillFK.
>
> Password: BabylonSisters.
>
> Regards, TF

Breathless, she typed in the details, logged straight on. Then she looked at her watch. It was now 13.05. Fielding wasn't being generous but maybe this was about as much as he could risk.

Emily Deacon entered keywords she'd tried before, the ones that brought down the security block.

Then she sat back in her seat and watched the screen begin to fill with text.

Two uniform men had found Monica Sawyer. They'd taken a crowbar to the boot of the half-burnt-out Renault at the foot of the Spanish Steps, peered inside, wondered about the smell and the dark liquid leaking from the couple of suitcases in there, then popped the locks on them.

One was still in the emergency department of San Giovanni puking up diminishing returns from his breakfast. The second, a raw young recruit who looked no more than twenty, now sat between Costa and Peroni in the jeep, leaning back in the rear seat, eyes closed, face the colour of the grey, wan sky still dumping snowflakes down on the city.

Costa and Peroni had listened in silence to his story. They'd been called in by Falcone as they vainly combed the riverfront for Laila, Peroni complaining loudly that there had to be other cops in town who could handle the call.

Costa had pointed the car towards the Piazza di Spagna as soon as Falcone called. Peroni openly begged down the phone for more time to look for the girl. It didn't cut any ice. Falcone wanted them there for some reason of his own, and both men had begun to guess what that was. He was feeling cornered, outnumbered, scared even. Big players were gathering around him, people he refused to trust. Costa and Peroni seemed to be at the top of this very short list of confidants just now.

Peroni was right, though. There were plenty of other cops around, all of them on the job already. Falcone had assembled the biggest team of plain clothes officers and SOCOs he could muster. They milled around the wrecked vehicle, a tide of white bunny suits and dark winter coats. There were men and women working the nearby shops and offices too. This was a big operation. Falcone wouldn't commit this kind of resource without good reason. Either he felt things were coming to a head. Or they were falling apart.

'Best you go home,' Peroni said to the uniform. The man's face was utterly bloodless. He'd be round the counselling department before long.

'I go off shift at five,' the officer said curtly. 'That's when I go home.'

Peroni nodded. 'What's your name, son?'

'Sacco.'

'I'll remember that. You look a sound guy. This your first?'

Sacco closed his eyes in a childish, sarcastic grimace. 'The first time I found a body in a suitcase?'

'No,' Peroni replied patiently, 'the first murder?'

'Yeah.' He couldn't keep the cockiness up long.

'OK.' Peroni slapped his shoulder and started climbing out of the car. 'Take care.'

The two of them walked towards the crime scene, Peroni shaking his head.

'Rookies,' he muttered. 'What is it with this macho thing?'

'He's just doing what he thinks is expected of him, Gianni.'

'Aren't we all? And what about Laila?'

Peroni's insistence on treating everyone under the age of twenty-five as somehow not quite fully formed never ceased to astonish Costa.

'Laila's been living on the streets for months, Gianni. She's as tough as they come. Didn't you notice? Whatever you think of the rights and wrongs of the situation, I don't think there's any doubt about her coping.'

Peroni favoured him with an icy stare.

'Coping. That's what life's about, is it?'

'Sometimes,' Costa offered lamely. 'It's what you do in between working out what you really want to do with your time. I seem to recall getting this lecture from you once.'

He had, and he'd been grateful for it.

'OK, smart guy,' Peroni conceded. 'Throw my own bullshit back at me if you like.'

'Look. When we've got the opportunity I'll help you find her.'

His partner nodded at the wrecked Renault. 'If he doesn't get there first.'

That sparked something in Costa's head. 'He's got bigger things on his plate, don't you think? Besides . . .'

There was something else. He wished there was more time to mull over what they knew and less spent chasing phantoms.

'He could have killed her last night if he'd wanted, surely? Emily's not that great a deterrent. But he didn't. Have you worked that one out yet?'

Peroni looked at him. It was obvious this bothered his partner too.

'No,' Peroni confessed. 'Unless the Deacon woman broke his stride somehow. Not that *that* makes much sense. What the hell. Let's put it to one side for now.'

He walked towards the back of the car. A lone idiot in a Santa Claus uniform stood on the corner forlornly shaking a bell. The city never had this particular American import until recently. This Christmas they seemed to be springing up everywhere.

The fake Santa shook his bell, held out a candy stick, looked Peroni in the eye and nodded at the silver-foil bucket that stood between them on the snow.

'Have you been a good boy, Officer?' the man asked.

'Define "good",' Peroni snapped and brushed past him.

Nic Costa looked at the sign round the man's neck: a charity for foreign kids. He threw a couple of notes in the bucket then shook his head at the candy stick.

'Give it to your friend,' Santa said. 'Might sweeten him up a bit.'

'I doubt that somehow,' Costa murmured and joined the team by the car.

Falcone was off to one side, just outside the deserted McDonald's, talking solemnly with a couple of plain clothes cops, watched by the bored-looking Joel Leapman. Teresa Lupo and Silvio Di Capua were working steadily on something in the boot of the car, half-concealed by badly placed screens, one of which Peroni was moving to get access to the vehicle.

Peroni took one glance at the mess in the boot, one at Teresa Lupo, then turned away and asked sharply, 'Anything we should know?'

The pathologist moved her head out from under the shadow of the car, nodded at Di Capua to keep going and walked over to them. 'Did you find her?'

'Not yet,' Costa said quickly. 'We got called here instead. She didn't say anything . . . ?'

'No,' Teresa began. 'I'm sorry, Gianni . . .'

'Me too,' Peroni mumbled. 'It's just so . . . inadequate.'

There were tears starting to work their way into Teresa Lupo's eyes, something Nic Costa realized he'd never witnessed before.

Peroni spotted them, put his hand on her arm, briefly kissed her cheek and mouthed, 'It's OK.' Then the two of them turned away and cast vicious glances at the buzzards leering at them from behind the barrier tape: photographers, reporters and a whole bunch of spectators with nothing better to do.

'I guess you've been asked this a million times,' Peroni said when she'd got her act together again, 'but how'd this one die?'

Teresa shrugged, regaining her old self. 'This is all preliminary, understood? I'm just telling you what I told your boss, with the same reservations. I don't want to leap to conclusions, not out here. Also, unless someone tells me otherwise, I get to take this lady home. That American bastard isn't playing bodysnatchers this time around. Even if she is one of his, there's no way of knowing yet.'

'How?' Peroni asked again.

'Still working on the method. Let me put this delicately. She's not exactly *complete*.'

There was something she didn't want to say, probably for Peroni's sake. 'She's naked. Not a scrap of clothing on her. The tags have been taken off the cases. I'll hand them over to forensic once we're done here. They don't look like a common make to me. Expensive too. Maybe . . .'

They looked at each other and knew what each of them was thinking. Work of that nature took a long, long time.

'You haven't asked me yet,' she said. '*That* question.'

'He'd marked the skin?' Costa asked.

'Kind of,' she shrugged. 'It's the same man. But it's not like the others, though. If you want to look, I can . . .'

Both men had their hands up before she'd finished the sentence.

'Understood,' she continued. 'The honest answer is I don't know if they are by the same instrument. Ask me when I've cleaned her up a little back in the morgue. There are a lot of cuts on this woman. But there are marks on her back that aren't just . . . practical, if I can put it that way. They could be by a scalpel. Maybe.'

Costa thought of Emily Deacon drawing the pattern, so easily, so naturally, in the American embassy the previous day. 'And the shape?'

'I wouldn't put money on it,' she admitted. 'I'm sorry. But if you want something concrete, look at this.'

She reached round into the depths of the boot and came back with a hank of blood-stained material encased inside an evidence bag like a dead insect.

'It's the cord,' she said. 'He'd removed it from the neck this time. It was in one of the cases. He had his reasons. Make no mistake. This is the same material that he used on the woman in the Pantheon. Not a scintilla of doubt.'

Costa didn't know what to make of the thing. 'But it's not a cord.'

Teresa frowned. 'Leo didn't tell you, huh? We had a little chat about this last night. I guess he's had other things on his mind. No, it isn't a cord. It's a piece of very tough fabric cut in that exact same shape we all know so well then wrapped tightly to make a cord. At first I thought he must have done it himself, though it would have taken a hell of a long time. Still, he's a gentleman with an obsession, no?'

Peroni was getting interested. 'But?'

She handed the bag to Costa, then picked up her briefcase and shuffled through the mess of papers in it until she found what she wanted.

'Keep that for a moment, Nic. Silvio had this report waiting for me from forensic when I got here. Fastest piece of work those people have ever done.'

Costa took the single page. Peroni joined him and read it simultaneously.

'Has Falcone seen this?'

'Oh yes,' Teresa continued. 'I didn't dare hold back on that one, not that he seems to know what to do with it right now. Your American friend over there doesn't have a clue, though. Or an inkling even that I still have the original cord from that poor cow in the Pantheon. In fact, from what I've heard of his bullshit already, if you were to talk to him over there at this moment you would find he doesn't think this is part of the same game at all. Not directly, anyway. He's got a theory.'

The two men kept scanning the report, trying to work out what it all meant. Teresa was right. This didn't just put their man in the frame for both deaths. It said something about who he was too.

Peroni blinked, bewildered. 'A *theory*?'

'Oh yes,' she added. 'And guess what? It's one that lays all the crap at our door.'

The two men thought about that for a moment.

'Our door?' Costa repeated.

'You bet,' she said with a smile. 'Now would you boys like to borrow that report for a little while? Maybe you can give Leo some ideas.'

'Yes,' Gianni Peroni replied, and began walking towards Leo Falcone and Joel Leapman with a look of pure fury on his face that Costa hadn't seen in a very long time.

There was too little time and too much information. It was like being lost in a forest of unreadable signs and signals. She'd typed in the name Nic had mentioned, 'Henry Anderton', and got a short, uninformative report on the attack that had triggered the alert over security for American visitors. It seemed routine, unconnected to the present case. The man was simply an academic who'd been the victim of unprovoked street violence in a small square in the ghetto, the Piazza Mattei. The name rang a bell. It had a tortoise fountain in the centre. Her father had shown it to her a couple of times, taken her picture next to it on one of their many walks around Rome. However, nothing connected that assault with the current investigation. The man had been badly beaten. According to the records, he'd been flown back to America by his health insurer and hospitalized in Boston. A short search on the Internet proved that Costa's suspicions were unfounded. Henry Anderton was an established academic, now retired. There was only one item of minor interest in what she could glean of his background from the Net. One academic paper he'd published, on the structure and funding of Islamic terrorist groups, acknowledged the assistance of several FBI officers in the provision of advice and information. It was a tenuous link, but hardly earth-shattering.

Then she tried 'Bill Kaspar' and got nothing, not a damn thing, which was surely odd. Grateful as she was for Fielding's covert help, she understood it had its limitations. He hadn't taken her into the very heart of the FBI's internal network, its mother lode of precious intelligence, brought up to date each minute of every day, collated from around the world by systems that never went anywhere close to a piece of public cable. She guessed he'd set some parameters himself, a cut-off date of some fifteen years earlier judging by the dates on the material her searches found. Others had been set for him. There was another raft of security clearances still above her that brought down the shutters the moment she went near them. That made sense. Fielding was senior, but still an embassy official working in the field. There were many doors he couldn't open.

Yet there was a mine of precious intelligence here, if only she could find the right way to track down what she wanted. That required hitting the correct keywords – the terms that would take her straight to the relevant material. Without them it was impossible to hope to read more than a fraction of what lay on the network. Instead, she had to prioritize. And if she did find anything there was the problem, too, of what to do with it. Ordinarily she could have marked the documents she wanted and set them up as a set of reference points for future retrieval. Ordinarily, though, she wouldn't be using a phoney identity to hack the Bureau's database in a way that doubtless broke the terms of her contract and probably put her in jeopardy of criminal action to boot.

It was impossible to print a thing without leaving a record. She couldn't email material out of the system either. There were bars in place to prevent that. She couldn't even cut and paste items into another document and get them out that way, or, because the hardware prevented it, copy a thing to a floppy or pen drive. It was simply too dangerous to take notes, written or dictated. All she could hope to do was track down some key documents and, as best she could, memorize as much of the broad content as possible. Or . . . take a bigger risk.

'Find something first,' she reminded herself, and typed another phrase.

Babylon Sisters.

Thornton had surely given her the password for a reason. The words meant something too. It was another memory from childhood, more voices from the airy, bright apartment on the Aventine hill. Of some old rock number getting played over and over again by a band her father and his friends all adored.

The band was Steely Dan. 'Babylon Sisters' was the long, jazzy number he loved so much that someone – but who? – had called him 'Steely Dan Deacon' once and it stuck.

With good reason too. It wasn't just that, back in Rome before the sourness and the divorce consumed him, he loved that certain kind of music: cool, jazz-tinged rock, stuff she could never quite pin down, with weird, only half-comprehensible lyrics. It was because he was a tough guy too, and she'd known that all along but had kept the idea hidden until it was impossible to avoid any longer. The last few years he'd been alive he was so damn tough she scarcely dared go near him. Something else too.

She glanced at her watch – just fifteen minutes left on the system and nothing to show so far – and cursed herself, racked her brain for more of the numbers he and his beer buddies loved, listening to them over and over on the neat Bose hi-fi in the living room. They still sat in her head, dim stains on her consciousness from a time when music, for her, meant weekly piano lessons struggling with Hindemith under the sour gaze a some stuck-up old woman smelling of lavender in an apartment in the neighbouring block.

Such a contrast to the rolling, unpredictable keyboards, stabs of lyrical guitar and the weird, weird lyrics her dad loved.

'Babylon Sisters' most of all, with the throwaway line that came straight after the title, sung so rapidly you had to strain to catch the phrase.

Shake it.

She could picture her dad – Steely Dan Deacon – just a touch drunk with a couple of guys from work, singing along to the track, dancing, half swaying the way men did in that condition, yelling those words out loud in unison.

'You are so goddamn awful at this job, Emily Deacon,' she whispered to herself. 'Any moment now Joel Leapman is going to walk in, see what you're doing, and put you on the first plane home.'

And then she would never find out what had happened, never get to the bottom of the sacred cut.

The network had one of those freeform text-searching systems, a kind of internal SuperGoogle reserved for the spooks. You could throw any number of different terms at it – 'purple Transylvanian banana fetish igloo' – and it would trawl all the zillions of words it kept in its maw, try and put two and two together to make four, then shoot a few answers straight back at you within seconds.

It was clever for a machine, which meant it had the combined IQ of a million worker ants if you were lucky enough to hit the right buttons.

She typed in 'Bill Kaspar Dan Deacon Iraq'.

The same old stuff as before shot up on the screen – page upon page of documents, no particular order, no particular sense. Days of work. Weeks maybe.

She looked at her watch again. The minutes were just flying by now. Soon the shutters would come down for good. Thornton Fielding was risking a lot here. His career. Maybe more. She owed it to him to get better at this.

'Sacred Cut Bill Kaspar Iraq.'

It just got worse. There was all manner of crap

creeping in now and she knew why. 'Sacred cut' meant nothing to the system. Wherever that came from happened *after*.

'Think of the song, stupid,' she said to herself. 'Think of Bill Kaspar. Think of what Thornton was trying to tell you.'

The password wasn't BillK. It was WillFK.

Some people liked to shorten their names in conversation and keep it formal on paper. Some people had middle names. The FBI was an institution. The higher up the ladder you got, the more likely you were to gain a few affectations along the way.

She typed in 'William F. Kaspar Steely Dan Deacon' and said a little prayer to whatever silicon god lived behind that screen, asking it to cut her a little slack, serve up a soupcon of mercy for a change, pick the right team of worker ants for this problem because, in all truth, she needed them right now.

The system chugged. A document came up with a date from 1990. Then the message: *Access denied.*

'Shit,' she muttered and watched it chug through six other files blocked by the same rule. 'Shit, shit, shit . . .'

The network was running with all the speed of an octogenarian athlete. It was hopeless. It was dumb. It was typical of her career in the FBI.

Then Emily Deacon, more out of desperation than anything, typed in 'William F. Kaspar Steely Dan Babylon Sisters Shake It' sat back and wondered what she'd do next. Go see the good-looking Italian cop at his gorgeous farmhouse out there in the snowy wilds, open her hands and say, 'Got nothing. How about some wine? Why don't we forget about everything for a while and just talk because I like talking to you? I wish we could do it a lot more.'

Nic Costa hadn't even come close to making a pass. It was odd. It was so un-Italian because she had a feeling he'd like to, really.

'Ask me, Nic, because I'm going crazy staring at this stupid computer,' she whispered.

Somewhere – in Miami or Washington, Seattle or on a server just down the hall – a hard drive flipped into life and popped a single, unrestricted document on the screen.

It was just a memo. A *scanned* memo too, not a whole chunk of real, readable text, which may have been why it slipped through the security cracks. She checked the keywords some dumb underling had assigned to it. Just two: Shake It.

Ha, ha.

She was breathless. She felt stupidly alive. This was the only chance. Take it or leave it, because this never comes again.

So . . .

Emily Deacon cast a quick look at the door, saw no one beyond it, then took the tiny digital camera out of her purse, the one she kept for road accidents and shots of buildings, sights that interested her out of the blue. Then, trying not to tremble, she snapped the screen, and the next one, and the one after that.

FROM: WILLIAM F. KASPAR
TO: STEELY DAN B. ET AL
DATE: 1991, NEAR AS DAMMIT
SUBJECT: BABYLON SISTERS
STATUS: YOU HAVE TO ASK?

Let it be known that I, William F. Kaspar, the Lizard King, the Holy Owl, Grand Master of the Universe, etcetera, etcetera, shall be attending the court of the Scarlet Beast presently, accompanied by my royal harem, and I demand - DEMAND you hear me - fealty from you lazy, good-for-nothing, pasta-sucking ingrates.

There is a purpose, acolytes. A great one: mayhem.

The Scarlet Beast - where do they get these names, Danboy? This one of yours or what? - has charged us with creating such. We possess a God-given duty to deliver and it is a mighty relief to old Bill K this faceless bastard has volunteered you already. Though I cannot help but wonder, dear friend, whether you didn't understand that all along. NTK, huh?

I read the cast list. A few men I know. A few are new but I guess we're gonna love 'em all the same. Plus I'm bringing a couple of ladies of my own too, since we live in emancipated days and they can do things with radios and computers and stuff that beat the living shit out of me. Though I cannot help but wonder, dear friend, whether you didn't know that all along. NTK, huh?

Practicalities.

1. The Scarlet Beast is a generous Beast, though I guess you know that already! Those figures you sent me are enough to keep us going for six months in the desert if some spine-deficient pen-pusher in the Pentagon starts to get cold feet and wonder whether we shouldn't just pick up the phone, call Saddam and say: please, pretty please, mister, just take up your tanks and your soldiers and walk all the way home to Baghdad.

2. We got immunity. Hell, we got more immunity than a fifties Klansman in Alabama. We can do what we like, when we like, and no one's ever going to care. (Am I telling you something you don't know here or what, boy?)

3. We got deep cover. We're the Babylon Sisters, buddy. And no one knows our name. This is a cash-only, love 'em and leave 'em operation entirely in the hands of a bunch of ghosts. So don't expect no medals. Knowing what little I do of our anonymous master don't expect no thanks either. Duty is its own reward.

4. This Scarlet Beast guy may not have told you yet but you got extra work to do. I looked at your record,

brother. Hell, Danboy! You ain't fired a weapon in anger since Nicaragua! What happened to old Steely? You all logistics and money these days? I am the military guy here, so listen to me when I say this. When we hit the sand there we start running. This thing happens on army time. Two hours' sleep a day if we're lucky and more work, more action, in between than you've ever seen in your little life. We're pre-empting stuff here, laying down the groundwork for what comes after. And that means the shit just happens constantly, sometimes when old Bill here won't expect it to. I don't have room for passengers. So tell me this. Are you going soft now you got that lovely little rugrat running round your feet? If that's the case let me illuminate you a little. FORGET THE LITTLE CRITTER TILL THIS IS DONE. Kids are great, Dan. When I came visiting and bounced that little darling up and down on my knee last spring I thought you were the luckiest SOB on the planet. But you know something? You're not. You just got a whole load of new responsibilities to add to the old ones.

5. We got to toughen you up, we got to work on those desert skills.

You need to learn what goes inside a military Humvee in the magical nineties (and these ladies the Marines sent me are putting toys on board those two iron beauties you just won't believe, toys that can shoot and burn and kill, then talk you straight out to safety even if it's pitch dark and spitting fire out there). Plus I got two Black Hawks waiting in Saudi ready to sling those babies under their guts and deliver us out into no-man's-land. This is serious shit, Steely. We're all coming home afterwards. That I promise you (and this Scarlet Beast guy too, so you may as well pass it on - snuck, snuck). Also: I'll kill any damn man who gets in the way. Anyone who don't understand the meaning of the word 'mission' had better look it up in the dictionary 'cos there's no time for bookwork on the road.

6. We got friends. You know how many Iraqis it takes to change a president? Just a couple, provided you got the dough. We've been buying buddies on the ground there for years, making the down payments, preparing the way. They're waiting on us to make a courtesy call and close the deal. That check's just burning a

hole in someone's back pocket right now.

7. We got a home. A nice home too, picked it myself. No canvas for us, boy. No running hot water and mints on the pillow at bedtime either. But this place has got class. I'm a history man, Steely, got campaigns going back to Mesopotamia locked in these old cells. You should never forget that. This place is like you, it's got breeding. Also, it's real nice and peaceful, a little oasis in the desert where the Republican Guard got no reason to visit at all. Here's a word to think about, Steely. Ziggurat.

Your old friend Billy K. bids farewell now. Eat this paper after reading. Wipe your ass with it if you like. Or even - no, I mean this, this is the best of all!!! - file the damn thing somewhere among all those big metal cabinets you people in the Via Veneto love so much. Put away a little piece of my ramblings for history. It doesn't matter a damn.

I am William F. Kaspar which means, as you understand well, I don't exist.

And you know the good news, Steely?

```
For the next few months, neither do
you.
  We are the Babylon Sisters. Shake
it.
```

'I *am* calm,' Peroni protested, storming towards Falcone and the American, his face a deep shade of red.

The big man stopped and Costa felt the full force of his frank and intelligent stare.

'Nic,' Peroni said, 'Falcone has half the Questura here. He doesn't need me. That runaway kid does. I know what I'm doing. Trust me. Leo will love this one.'

'Oh great,' Costa replied ruefully. He knew it was no damn good arguing anyway. In this mood Peroni was unstoppable.

They marched over to the big black saloon, where Falcone and Leapman stood smoking, watching the SOCOs and Teresa Lupo's team at work, not exchanging a word.

'Sir,' Peroni said briskly into Falcone's face.

Leapman looked him up and down. The inspector cast him a puzzled glance. 'Officer?'

'I came to hear the theory,' Peroni demanded.

'The theory?' Falcone repeated.

'Yeah. There's some lunatic out there with a scalpel. This woman's been cut with one too. Seems obvious to me what's going on, but I gather our friend here's got a theory. I was wondering what it was.'

Falcone nodded at the American. 'Agent Leapman seems to think it's coincidence. And we're not absolutely sure about the scalpel, Peroni. Let's not jump to conclusions.'

Peroni pulled a face at Falcone. The two men

exchanged a brief knowing look that made Costa think something interesting was on the cards. Then Peroni gave his partner that 'Can you believe this?' expression and glowered at the FBI man. 'Coincidence? You're kidding me?'

Leapman blinked slowly, as if to show he was dealing with very stupid people. 'His word not mine. No, it's not coincidence. It's just sloppy police work. You people have been so goddamn lax with the news management half of Rome knows what this guy does to get his kicks. It's in all the papers. They're sitting around the breakfast table out there reading every last detail and guess what? Someone's starting to think maybe he'd like to get in on the act too. Chances are this is just copycat stuff, that's all. Maybe some guy was going to kill the woman anyway and thought he'd mess around with the scalpel just so's we'd think it was our man all along. Who knows? Not you, that's for sure.'

Costa couldn't believe his ears. 'Copycat? What the hell does that mean?'

'Read the stuff I send you,' Leapman barked. 'Think about it. This guy's a perfectionist. He kills these people in a specific way. He lays them out in a specific place, cuts pieces into their backs like he's a surgeon or something. He doesn't slash them around then chop 'em into pieces and stuff them into suitcases. This is just run-of-the-mill stuff. It's out of his class. Beneath him. Besides . . .'

Leapman stopped himself, as if he were about to go too far. Costa saw the moment and thought about what Emily Deacon had been saying. He knew too that Falcone would seize on it.

'Besides what, Agent Leapman?' the inspector asked.

'Besides . . . nothing. This is *not* our man. I've been working on this longer than you. I've got a feel for this guy.'

Falcone was quiet for a moment, thinking, watching the path team work at the car. 'I didn't think that was the way you people worked. Feelings.'

'Yeah, yeah,' Leapman grumbled. 'Come up with the smart stuff. Get it off your chest.'

'Perhaps something went wrong,' Costa suggested. 'He's losing his self-control. This wasn't someone he intended to kill.'

Leapman screwed up his face in disbelief. 'Don't you people understand a criminal profile when you see it? Don't you have a word for modus operandi in Italian?'

Falcone's eyebrows rose in amusement.

'I'll check,' he said dryly. 'Where's the girl, Peroni? I thought she was in your care.'

The big man grimaced. 'I don't know. I thought I'd got her trust. I didn't realize we needed to keep her under lock and key. I'll happily go looking if you want.'

'What's the point?' Leapman snarled. 'Immigrant kid like that. She could run rings round you guys. Not that it seems hard. I mean . . . letting a material witness go.'

The expression on Peroni's face cut him short. Nic Costa had to hand it to his partner sometimes. He surely knew how to scare the daylights out of people.

Peroni prodded Leapman in the chest and muttered, 'I wasn't aware I was talking to you. Sir.'

Leapman bridled and eyed Falcone. 'You got a discipline problem here too, Leo?'

Peroni breathed deeply, gave the American a stony stare, then turned round and walked inside the empty

McDonald's. The three of them watched as he marched to the deserted counter, jabbed a finger at something on the rack then returned with a burger, which he unwrapped steadily on the way, tossing the paper into the street with the casual nonchalance that drove Nic Costa crazy.

He rejoined them, with the burger now steaming in his hand.

Costa heard Leapman's whiny voice and knew what was coming next, couldn't believe the guy could be that crass.

'Whoa!' the FBI man yelled as loud as he could manage, so loud even Teresa Lupo turned to listen from the wrecked Renault. 'Do you people own some weird work practices or what? I mean, you've got a dead woman here carved up in suitcases. You got uniform men wandering round throwing up like brats at a prom. And the best this guy can do is go feed his ugly face. I mean what the fu—'

Peroni walked forward, took Leapman by the collar of his winter coat then crammed the burger full into the man's gaping mouth, pushing damn hard so that the bun, the mayo, the vegetables and the grey, greasy meat splattered all over his face, down to his bright white cotton shirt and expensive block wool coat.

Leapman reeled back, spluttering, hands waving, food falling down his front, eyes fixed on Peroni, scared of what the big man would do next.

'Ah, ah,' Peroni warned, waving a finger in his face. 'The next burger goes up your ass and that *won't* be pretty.'

'Morons!' Leapman yelled, beside himself with fury.

'Utter fucking morons! They'll get to hear about this, Falcone. I'm warning you.'

'About what?' Falcone wondered.

'About *him!*' Leapman screamed, pointing a finger at Peroni.

Falcone folded his arms over his camel-hair coat. 'Oh, *him.*'

He exchanged a single, sly glance with Peroni.

'Officer,' Falcone said in a flat monotone, 'that was quite unacceptable behaviour. Do you have an explanation?'

Peroni pulled Teresa's report out of his pocket. 'Yeah. This.'

Leapman stared at the sheet of paper, puzzled, suddenly a little worried. 'What the hell's that? I don't read Italian too well.'

'Forensic,' Costa said. 'When we looked at the cord he used to kill the woman in the Pantheon we found it wasn't a cord at all. It was a piece of material, cut into those shapes he likes, then rolled up tight like rope.'

Leapman blinked. He couldn't decide whether to be defensive or furious.

'You were supposed to hand over everything you had to us,' he said. 'I gave you that goddamn order.'

The three Italians surrounded him now. Agent Leapman wasn't going anywhere easily.

Falcone sniffed and stared at Leapman. 'Your men left the item behind when they came to collect the body. What were we supposed to do? Chase after them? You can send someone round for it whenever you like.'

'Dammit, Falcone . . .' Leapman muttered, then went quiet.

Peroni began to read the report. 'The fabric in question is all one-inch by three-quarter-inch textile webbing. Desert brown and green 483, mildew resistant, type X, class 2B, made in accordance with MIL-W-5665K, whatever the hell that is. Maybe the shape it's got. The shape all American military webbing's got. You know that shape, Agent Leapman?'

'It's just how it is,' the American replied.

'Is that the best you can do?' Peroni demanded. 'This is the shape of US military webbing. He's killing them with it. He's cutting it into their backs when they're dead. And this is US military army issue. No one else uses it. It never gets near to being sold to the public in any way.'

'Hey!' Leapman yelled. 'What the fuck do you guys know about the US military? Stuff leaks out of the army like candy from a store. Everything's for sale if you want it.'

'I'll take your word on that,' Falcone intervened. 'The problem we have, Joel, is this. Forensic is very clear. It's not just that the only people who use this material are your military. It's a new fabric too. It was produced for desert warfare. It only went into production a year ago. From what we can gather the only place it's been deployed in the field is covert operations in Iraq.'

Leapman glowered at him. 'You knew about this all along, Falcone. This is just some stupid set-up.'

Costa pulled out Teresa's evidence bag, with the latest cord noose inside it. 'This came from the car here. We never knew about the cord until a few hours ago. It certainly never found its way into the press. So you see, Agent Leapman, this *is* the same man. It has to be. And we were wondering, is this what you found with the others too? And, if it is, why didn't you tell us? Because surely this man's been near some US military facility. Recently too.'

The FBI man was lost, shaking his head.

'Maybe,' he murmured. 'But who the hell *is* the woman here? It doesn't make any sense. It doesn't . . .'

He clammed up, as if he'd said too much already.

Peroni brushed some of the burger off the front of Leapman's coat.

'You know I'm sorry about that,' he added. 'I sort of lost my temper. It's such a shame, Leapman. We could all get along really well.'

'Really.'

'Yeah. If it weren't for one thing.'

Leapman waited.

Peroni bent forward and removed a piece of gherkin off the American's collar.

'You've got to start telling us the truth,' he said. 'Maybe not me. Maybe not my partner. But Inspector Falcone here. He's a good guy. A reliable guy. He deserves your trust, don't you think?'

Leapman just glared back at him, glassy-eyed.

'That has to happen,' Peroni continued, 'because if it doesn't we're just going to keep going round and round in circles, not getting anywhere at all. With this person of yours – of *yours* – still out there.'

The FBI man sniffed, then looked down the street and signalled for his driver.

'I don't have the slightest idea what you are talking about,' he said and pushed his way between Costa and Falcone, taking the easy route, the one that didn't go near Gianni Peroni, stomping off down the street towards his car, not bothering to look back.

Peroni frowned and looked at Falcone. Costa knew what the gesture said: *I tried.*

'Am I helping around here?' Peroni enquired.

Falcone scowled, not at them, at the chaos around all of them. 'Ask me later.'

'I'd like to go after the girl, sir,' Peroni said quietly. 'Just me. You can spare one man. This isn't a personal thing. I still think she's got something to tell us.'

'Do it,' Falcone murmured. 'And, Peroni, it was a nice try.'

'Thanks,' the big man murmured.

Costa followed his partner back to the jeep and handed over the keys.

'Where are you going to look, Gianni?'

'Same places as we did before. I don't know.'

He had to ask – Peroni got wrapped up in himself sometimes. 'What if this guy's still after her too?'

'Then I guess we might meet. If it happens I'll call. Besides, I don't think you're going to bump into him with Agent Leapman around. Do you?'

'Not really.' All the same the difficult relationship with the FBI agent had surely been fractured beyond repair now. Was that what they wanted?

'When did Leo put you up to this little act?'

Peroni's face registered mock shock. 'Put me up to what?'

'You know damn well.'

He laughed. It was a good sound, one Costa had missed of late. 'Look, Leo and I know each other of old. Sometimes you don't have to put things in words. You just improvise a little. He's as sick of that asshole as we are. And what I said was true. It's time for the guy to level with us. Sooner or later he's going to realize that himself. We're supposed to be on the same side, aren't we?'

Leapman had been shaken by the forensic they'd got on the cord, Costa thought. But there was something else bugging the American too: the latest death. Somehow he still found it difficult to believe it really was the same man.

Peroni's face was serious again. 'Forget Agent Leapman for a moment, Nic. Tell me this. Why did Laila run away? I don't get it. I thought we were doing really well and normally I don't read those situations the wrong way.'

Costa shrugged. 'Who knows with a kid like that? Maybe it's *because* you were doing so well. Maybe the idea of closeness scares her.'

'Nah,' Peroni murmured and gave him a friendly slap on the shoulder. 'I don't buy that any more than I buy Leapman coming the innocent with me. You don't know the first thing about kids, do you?'

'As you constantly remind me.'

He watched Peroni fit his big bulk behind the wheel.

'Call me if you need me, Gianni,' he said.

'Yeah,' the big man laughed and gently began to ease the jeep out into the street.

Nic Costa hated instincts. They played tricks with your imagination. They lied constantly. He reminded himself of that as Gianni Peroni disappeared down what was once a narrow, medieval lane, now a line of upscale fashion shops running all the way down to the Corso. Some stupid, pointless instinct was nagging at him then, raking over the dregs of his memory to find the long-dead face of another partner, Luca Rossi, one who'd wandered off without him in much the same way and never come back.

Instincts intruded into real life, disturbed what really mattered. Besides, something was happening now. Falcone was listening to the squawk of a voice coming out of the car radio. He had a look of intense concentration on his face, one Costa recognized. One he liked.

The tall inspector finished the conversation and scanned the square. Then he caught Costa's eye, clicked his fingers and pointed, with some urgency, to the car.

Joel Leapman came back to the embassy looking uncharacteristically dishevelled, shambling through the door like a bull looking for somewhere to pick a fight. He was in a foul, unpredictable mood.

'Sir?' Emily asked.

'What have you been doing all day? Don't I get the courtesy of a call from you, girl?'

'I thought . . .'

She glanced at the computer screen, now back to her customary log-on with its round of low-level information. The camera was still in her purse. That was dumb. She should have taken it back to the apartment, got the evidence out of the building.

'You thought what?'

'I thought you wanted me to wait until you had something for me to do.'

'Jesus . . .'

Leapman seemed seriously out of sorts. Food spattered his front.

'Is there something wrong?' she asked.

'Wrong question.'

'What's the right one?'

'Is there something right?' he complained.

Leapman looked like someone with doubts and that wasn't a position he liked or understood very much at all.

'These cops,' he said, 'Falcone. The other guys. Why'd they hate us so much?'

'I don't think they do,' she answered promptly. 'Not for one moment.'

'Really? I just had that big ugly bastard stuff a burger into my mouth. What was that all about?'

She thought about Gianni Peroni. It didn't add up. 'You tell me.'

'None of your business,' Leapman barked back at her.

Emily Deacon was getting deeply sick of this man. Maybe Thornton Fielding was right. She should just file a complaint and get out of his presence.

'Then why ask?'

'Because, because . . .' he grumbled. 'You don't need to know the reasons. Sometimes events just run away with you, Agent Deacon, and there's not a damn thing you can do about it.'

Was that some kind of excuse, she wondered.

'If that's an apology, you should direct it at them.'

Leapman had pissed them all off. He'd been working on it from the moment they walked into the Pantheon. It was deliberate, determined. Part of the project.

'So they're the good guys, huh? I should go running to them?'

'I think they're doing their best in difficult circumstances.'

His voice rose. 'It's difficult for all of us, girl!'

Enough was enough. 'It's more difficult for them, Leapman. They think they're being kept in the dark. They're right. And one more thing.' She pointed a slender finger at his chest. 'Don't call me "girl". Not ever again.'

Or Little Em.

He laughed and Emily Deacon was surprised to find herself thinking that this was, perhaps, what he wanted to hear.

'So you can answer back,' Leapman said after a while. 'Who'd have believed it?'

He leaned over to his PC, keyed in a few words then turned the screen to face her. It was the RAI news website. The lead story was about another murder in the city, with a photo of a burnt-out car by the Spanish Steps.

'We're losing this, Emily,' he said in a flat, miserable tone of voice. 'And I just do not know why. He's killed someone else and I've got to tell you that's the last thing I expected. This isn't part of any pattern I can read. It's just some poor, helpless bitch who got in the way somehow. I never . . .'

Leapman fell silent and stared at the monitor.

'You never what?'

'I never thought he'd stoop to that.'

He picked up the phone and hit a speed-dial button.

'Viale?' he asked, and there was a different tone to his voice now, a resigned, almost scared resonance she scarcely recognized. 'We've got to talk . . . Just a minute.'

Leapman cupped the mouthpiece and stared at her.

'I'd like a coffee, Agent Deacon,' he said. 'Cappuccino.

The good stuff, from that place over the road. Take your time now. A man's got work to do.'

Nic Costa took a deep breath and found it amazing that, only an hour earlier, he'd been worried about Gianni Peroni. Wherever the big man was in the white, frozen world that was Rome it had to be better than this: clinging to a narrow, icy, fire-escape ladder a dizzying height above the cobbled streets in the labyrinthine quarter north of the Pantheon, trying to peer through the billowing blizzard that was sweeping all around him.

Another time, in different weather, when the wind wasn't trying to peel him off the roof and dash him to the ground below, it would have been quite a view. The Palazzo Borghese should have been somewhere ahead. On a good day the great dome of St Peter's would have shone from across the river. Now all he could see was a blinding cloud of ice swirling painfully around his face, threatening to confuse his senses.

Falcone had made it plain: it was his choice. The sly old bastard knew all along what Costa would say too. He was the youngest there and the most suited for the job. He'd done some mountaineering once, solitary trips into the Dolomites and the Alps as a teenager. They could have waited until a specialist was brought in, but that meant time, in this weather perhaps a long time. The problem was simple. A woman in the block had reported that an American tourist living on the top floor had, unusually, been absent all day. The previous evening she'd been seen entering the building with a stranger. The same stranger had walked out that morning carrying a couple of big, expensive-looking suitcases. They'd got a description of the man that morning. It could be the same person Costa and Peroni had seen twice now, outside the Pantheon and by the Tiber the previous night.

So should they pile through the door with an entry team, blundering into the place, hoping he was still hiding there? Or did they check it out first to see whether it was occupied or not? And if it was empty, wait a while outside to see if anyone happened to call back?

For Costa the decision was clear-cut. The man was human, not a monster. It was important not to let go of that fact. He needed somewhere warm and private to retreat to in weather like this. This could be the first real chance they had of trapping him.

Ordinarily there were easier ways to find out if someone was inside. They could spy from neighbouring blocks. They could use listening equipment through the walls. Not this time. The place was a tiny, probably illegal, cabin perched high above street level like a giant toy box thrown onto the big, flat roof of the nineteenth-century apartment block. The windows were higher than any of the buildings around. In any case it was so crowded in the neighbourhood that the adjoining blocks gave on to nothing but brick. This must be the only home in the area with a scenic outlook, which also meant it was impregnable, impossible to watch. The only way to find out what lay inside was to try to get close somehow, and not through the front door either, which lay up a narrow covered staircase leading from the top floor proper, giving no visual access into the cabin whatsoever. The fire escape was the only option. If the man was at home, Costa would, the plan said, see as much through the outside window and call in the forced entry team. If the place was empty, he'd just take a quick look around, get the hell out of there, then wait with the rest of them until someone came home.

Plans.

Costa shivered on the shaky ladder and wondered what they were worth now. He hadn't thought too hard about the weather after he'd talked to the woman who first made the call. He'd just cleared his ideas with Falcone then walked up three flights of stairs of floors in the building, found the ancient fire escape and started climbing through the swirling cloud of snowflakes. He hadn't thought much about the odd geography of the building either. Falcone and his men were parked discreetly outside, sufficiently close to stop anyone getting away, anonymous enough not to be noticed by someone walking in through the large, communal door. Or so they hoped.

Still, it didn't give Costa much room for manoeuvre. They'd agreed it was too risky to post a second person outside the apartment, even one posing as a cleaner or a delivery man. The individual they were after seemed too smart for tricks like that. Any intruder would stick out like a sore thumb if the man came back in the meantime. So if something went wrong Falcone and his team would have to make an entrance from outside.

Now he'd climbed those steep, steep stairs Costa appreciated how long that would take. He'd no intuition to tell him whether someone was at home, but if that was the case it was going to be vital not to alert him.

On this side of the cabin was a blind, narrow ledge just a metre wide, pointing back towards the hill where

Trinità dei Monti now lay hidden by the blizzard. Around the corner was a private terrace made for another climate. A couple of small palm trees cut incongruous shapes in their giant terracotta pots there, ice fringing their dead leaves, making them look like fantastic Christmas trees. The snow was so deep he could only guess at what occupied the other areas of the roof from the rounded white outlines they made: a barbecue, an outside sink with a single, swan-necked tap, a collection of brushes and brooms carelessly left to rot in the open air.

He took one final, careful step up the treacherous ladder, reached the wall and pulled himself upright onto the constricted concrete strip of the ledge, teeth chattering, shivering uncontrollably, feet almost off the edge of the building.

Falcone had ordered him to keep the ring tone on his phone turned off until they knew the state of the cabin. No one wanted the risk of an unwanted call. But in the freezing cold Costa found it difficult to think straight. His head felt numb. Had he remembered to turn it off or not? And if so when?

With numb fingers he struggled to pull the handset out of his pocket, fumbling it in his hands. The thing was off. He still couldn't remember doing that. Then he tried to put the phone away, found it slipping in his frozen fingers, knew what would happen next, how the ineluctable laws of gravity and stupidity could collide at times like this.

The handset turned in his dead, icy grip, revolved slowly through the snow-flecked air, bounced off the ledge and tumbled down into the street below.

Costa closed his eyes, felt the flakes begin to fall on

them instantly and cursed his luck. He couldn't go back down the ladder. He was too weary, too cold. The icy rungs were perilous enough when he was climbing, with the odds and gravity in his favour. Nothing could persuade him to risk a descent.

He took out his gun, checked the safety was on, the magazine loaded. He was a lousy shot at the best of times. Now, with unsteady fingers and a head that felt like a block of ice, he'd be as much of a danger to himself as anyone else.

Trying to clear an open space in his mind, he pushed the weapon into the side pocket of his jacket and hoped some warmth and blood would come back to his hand, with them some semblance of control.

Costa edged carefully along the narrow ledge, spent one dizzying, terrifying moment negotiating the corner, then rolled onto the deep snow of the terrace proper, glad finally that he had some railings between him and the precipice down to the street. When he got back his breath, when his head told him to keep moving or he'd just curl up in a tight, shivering ball, freeze and die on the spot, he stood up, clung to the wall and edged along it. There was just one small window here. A bedroom in all probability. He got close to the glass. The curtain was closed. There was no light inside, not a sign of life.

Keep it that way, he prayed and stumbled on towards the river side of the building.

A memory came from his mountaineering days. *Wind speed increases with altitude.*

A sudden, gusting blast roared round the apex of the cabin, full of vicious energy, dashing hard, stinging ice into his face. He huddled into himself, drawing his arms around his head, fighting to keep upright, vainly trying to wish away the blank numbness growing in his mind. Then the blizzard paused for breath. After a moment in which Costa doubted his ability to go on, he struggled towards the corner of the building, hugged the drain-pipe there, steeled himself against another battering from the storm.

Sometimes there were no other choices. Whatever the situation inside the cabin, he'd have to break in. It was simply too dangerous to do anything else. He turned the corner, clinging to the brickwork. Most of this side of the building was given over to a French window, almost opaque under a glazing of ice, with just a small gap kept clear by an updraught from the heating inside.

He crept forward and peered through the glass. From this angle he could see a table lamp glowing in the corner of the small, cluttered room. Costa tried to imagine what that meant. Then the wind abated briefly and his heart sank like a frozen stone.

There was a TV on inside. He could hear it. When he stretched his head further beyond the edge of the French door he could see it: a distant, small colour set playing a Western in the corner of the room. Rousing music, a horse whinnying and gunshots. He glanced at the screen and knew the scene instantly; it was one of those iconic Hollywood moments you never forgot.

John Wayne with an eyepatch turning his horse to face the bad guys at the end of *True Grit*. Costa almost wept at the irony.

Fill your hand, you son of a bitch.

It's so easy in the movies. You put the reins between your teeth and ride.

He tried to convince himself he was feeling braver.

Then he saw the man.

People watch TV, stupid, his distant brain reminded him.

He was where you'd expect someone to be while glued to the box. Upright in a chair on the other side of the little room, with his back to Costa and the window, just the top of his head visible, a good crop of brown hair now, not the stupid Mickey Mouse hat Costa had seen on two occasions.

Costa put his back to the wall, slid his body down to sit in the snow, head against the brickwork, eyes closed, desperately trying to think.

There was no alternative. The damn phone was gone. Falcone would wait in the street. Not forever. But maybe long enough for him to freeze to death in the vicious gale that gripped this cruelly exposed Roman rooftop.

Fill your hand, you son of a bitch.

You put the reins between your teeth and ride.

He glanced at the French windows. At least they didn't look much. No one expected burglars at this level. Then he took another look inside. The man was engrossed in the TV. He wouldn't, surely, be sitting in an armchair with a weapon on his lap.

Never assume.

Someone who carved shapes out of his victims' backs was impossible to read. All Costa could do was take every precaution in the book, and add a few of his own.

He got up, quickly stood foursquare to the windows and kicked as hard as he could. The doors flew open, glass crashed to the tiled floor inside. The volume of the TV set seemed abnormally loud.

'Police!' Costa yelled, and followed up that meaningless comment with all the other orders that were supposed to make sense on these occasions.

The man didn't budge. That much seemed good, anyway.

Costa moved purposefully towards the chair, wishing the damn TV would stop screaming like that, wishing the room wasn't so stuffily hot and filled with a strong physical smell, aware, too, that there was something deeply strange here, that the walls were covered with a familiar pattern, repeating over and over, painted in a colour he didn't want to think about too closely.

And the man didn't shift an inch, which made Costa feel foolish as he watched the back of his head and the full brown hair, waiting for a response, saying, more than once, 'Don't move.'

There was a noise: voices, the sound of wood smashing, the racket of an entry team on the other side of the door.

Focus.

'Don't,' he said, accidentally nudging the chair, and watched in shock as a woman's head, ripped from her body, red gore blackening around her throat, rolled sideways over the arm, fell on his foot, finished upright on the carpet, long brown hair flowing back from a pale dead face, mouth open, fixed in a scream, glassy eyes staring back at him, seeing nothing.

'Shit,' he gasped, and lurched over to the smashed French windows, turned his back on this crazy scene, breathed in as much of the freezing, snow-filled air as he could get into his lungs, hoping it would get the noxious smell of meat out of him somehow.

They were inside now. He could hear their voices

behind him, hear the shock and someone starting to retch.

And it was as if someone had turned a key, opened the door to a little enlightenment. The unnatural heat and the stench had stirred something the frozen rooftop had put into cold storage. Pieces started to fall into place. Teresa Lupo had, in a sense, warned him, if only he'd pursued the point far enough to get the detail.

She's not exactly complete.

The cord was in one of the cases, not around her neck, because it couldn't have been . . .

Nic Costa got a grip on his feelings, turned round and looked at the room. The geometric pattern covered half of the side wall and would probably have extended further had not the source run out. It was a running fresco carried out in what could only be the woman's blood. And a message too, in English. One word in big, bold, dark red letters, underneath the scrawls: WHO?

The SOCOs would have a field day here. The place had to be crawling with promising material and that, in itself, was strange. Costa had read the files, had understood what had happened in the Pantheon. Ordinarily the man was meticulous about cleaning up afterwards. Here he seemed to be leaving a deliberate sign.

I am nearly done. Help me.

Falcone walked through the room, stared at the item on the floor and sniffed.

'Neat,' he said. 'You just prop the poor bitch's head up on a couple of cushions, turn on the TV and all you see is someone working on a couch-potato habit. Some operator.'

Then he came up to Costa, something in his hand.

'You dropped this, that's why we came up,' the

inspector said, and gave him the mobile phone that, just a couple of minutes earlier, had tumbled all the way from the windy rooftop down into the drifts in the street. 'Nothing personal, Nic. But I think it's time you went home and got some sleep. Don't you?'

By four it was dark. By five the city was a treacherous warren of icy alleys, deserted under a blinding moon. But at least the blizzard was over. Gianni Peroni had taken the jeep everywhere he could think of. Back to the Serbian's café next to Termini. Down to the dark corners by the river where she'd lurked the night before. It was futile. The Serbians knew nothing. In the streets there were plenty of kids: dark, miserable figures, huddled inside their black jackets, crowding round fires built from noxious-smelling trash. Not one admitted to seeing her. Peroni tried every last trick in the book – money, threats, sweet talk – and it was just no good. They knew her. That much was plain. But Laila was an outcast in this bunch for some reason. Too strange, too difficult to fit in.

He hated talking to them too. The way they lived depressed him. It was all such a waste. And it made him think of his own children, warm in a comfy, fatherless home outside Siena, getting ready for Christmas, eyes glittering in anticipation of what was to come.

For the first time ever he wouldn't be there. Not for one minute. He wasn't a reflective man. He hated looking back. There were too many painful memories lurking in the recent past. Time healed, he knew that. One day the hurt would subside and, with that miraculous capacity for self-deception every living being on the planet seemed to possess, the good times would come to be uppermost in his mind once more. Till then he just had to swallow down the awkward mix of emotions that kept gripping him. He'd been a good father but, in the end, a lousy husband. It was just another of life's cruel tricks that one couldn't cancel out the other.

Tired, bored, almost despondent, he took a break and went for a coffee in one of his favourite places, the little café run by the old-fashioned restaurant Checco er Carrettiere behind the Piazza Trilussa in Trastevere. He knew why he went there. He used to take the kids during the summer, watch them wait goggle-eyed as some pretty girl in a smart white waitress uniform piled high some of the best ice cream in Rome.

Today the tiny café was as deserted as the frozen piazza. There was a pretty young girl behind the counter but she looked tired and careworn. He sat on a stool pouring sugar into a double macchiato and knew: those times would never come again. They were locked in the past, untouchable except in his head. A part of him had understood that would happen all along. Kids grew up, invented their own lives, went away in the end. But his own stupidity had hastened the process irreversibly, sent them scattering north to Tuscany, where he'd never be anything but a stranger now.

He finished the coffee and ordered another. On days like this the system needed caffeine. Then he tried to distract himself by focusing on Laila, racking his head again about where she might have gone. Something didn't make sense. He had established a bond with the kid. He wasn't fooling himself there. It just didn't add up that she should flee the house like that, without a word, without any good reason. He was out of options too. Short of pounding the streets aimlessly, hoping for some rare good luck – and surely that *was* a waste of time – he might as well give in, call Leo Falcone, get some sleep then rejoin the team. Maybe even pat the American on the back and say sorry a little more loudly if that was what was needed.

The girl behind the counter came with the second coffee and said, to his dismay, 'I know you from the summer. Where are your kids?'

'It's not ice-cream weather,' was the best he could offer.

'It's not anything weather,' she complained. 'I don't know why I bothered opening the doors. Waste of time.'

'Thanks. I'm flattered.'

'Oh.' She laughed and the sudden burst of amusement brought back the memory of her, not much more than a kid herself, piling up ice cream generously as they waited and watched under the bright, burning July sun. 'Sorry. I was just feeling a bit down.'

Everyone did from time to time, Peroni reminded himself. You just had to stop it slipping into self-pity.

'Gimme an ice cream then,' he said.

Her lively eyes opened wide in amusement. 'What?'

'You heard. A tub. Those cones are too damn difficult for an old guy like me. Coffee. Pistachio. And something else. You choose.'

She looked at him as if he were crazy. 'In this weather?'

'Yeah. In this weather. Me customer, you waitress. Work on the relationship, kid.'

The girl disappeared out back for quite a while. When she returned she'd taken off the white uniform and was now wearing a short red skirt and a black sweater.

She sat down next to him. There were two dishes in her hand, each with a selection of multi-coloured blobs of ice cream.

'It's on the house,' she said. 'I'm calling it a day.'

'Wise move,' he answered and tried the chocolate. It was exquisite, though the cold made his teeth hurt. 'What is it? Boyfriend trouble?'

She eyed him suspiciously. 'Oh, *per-lease.* Is that really the best you can do?'

'It's a start,' he objected. 'You see a pretty young girl. She looks miserable. Nine times out of ten it's boyfriend trouble. Old men like me understand that. We were young men once. We used to cause these problems.'

She licked the pistachio. It gave her a creamy green tongue.

'Well?' he persisted. 'Am I wrong?'

'No . . .' Her voice had that pouty, caustic edge he recognized growing in his own daughter.

'Well?'

'He never calls!' she cried. 'Never! It's always me. I'm always the one who has to phone him. What is it with men? Do they hate phone bills that much?'

He shrugged. 'It's not just men. That happens in relationships. It's how it is. Like old-fashioned dancing. One person leads, the other one follows.'

'It's not like dancing. So why?'

Her face had that frank, questioning intensity you got from teenagers.

'Because.'

'Because of what?'

'Because . . .' He couldn't go on. There was no answer. It was a stupid proposition. He couldn't think of a single good reason to support what he'd just said.

'Do you call your wife?' she asked. 'Or does she call you?'

'My wife calls me. Only rarely and with gleeful updates on how well the divorce is going and what new bills dropped through her mama's door.'

She didn't know whether to believe that or not. 'Really?'

'Really. No need to feel sorry. Crap like this happens.'

'You've got a girlfriend then?'

Peroni was beginning to wish she'd put the uniform back on. It made her easier to handle somehow. 'What is this? I'm the grown-up around here. I ask the questions.'

'So you *have* got a girlfriend?'

He shifted awkwardly on the tiny metal stool. 'Yeah. Sort of. Now. It's not what you think. I didn't have then.'

'Sounds a deep relationship,' she commented. 'This "sort of girlfriend". Does she call you? Or do you call her?'

Peroni swallowed a huge chunk of gorgeous lemon sorbet, which stuck at the back of his throat and made him gag for a moment. Once the coughing stopped he was dismayed to find some of the *gelato* was dribbling down his chin. He never would get the hang of eating this stuff.

The girl handed him a napkin. He dabbed at his face then said, 'Bit of both. What's it to you?'

It was a lie. Teresa always called. He had just never faced the fact till then.

'You're eating my ice cream for free, mister. I can ask any damn thing I like.'

She poked the front of his coat with a long fingernail. 'Men who don't call piss me off.'

'I am getting that message.'

The green eyes narrowed. 'Are you? Are you really?'

He thought about it and wondered how he'd come to develop this habit of having weird, half-jocular arguments with strangers in cafés. It seemed a very Roman routine. Nothing like this ever happened in Tuscany. People were too polite there. The Romans just spoke a thought the moment it entered their head.

'I am hearing what you say, my girl. It doesn't mean I intend to act on it.'

'We'll see about that.'

She took his ice-cream dish, even though it was only half-eaten.

'Hey!' Peroni objected. 'That's mine.'

'No it isn't. I gave it to you.'

'OK.' He threw some notes on the counter. 'How much?'

She threw the money back at him. 'I told you. It's free. I just don't think you phone her. You're a man. Why would you?'

'That's my ice cream,' he repeated. 'I want it back.'

She waved at the door. 'Go outside and call your girlfriend. Now. You can have some more when you come back and say you've done it. And no lying. I'm not as dumb as I look.'

'Jesus Christ . . .' Peroni cursed, and added a few

more epithets under his breath that it was best she didn't hear. 'What is this?'

'Christmas,' she hissed. 'Almost. Hadn't you noticed?'

Damn teenagers, he thought. You never got an ounce of respect from them. Though maybe it wasn't such a bad idea after all. Not that he was letting on.

'I was going to do this anyway,' he objected, heading for the door, trying not to listen to her muttering, 'Yeah, right,' straight into his big back.

It was crazy. Now he thought about it he *never* called Teresa. He had to look up her mobile number in his address book because he hadn't even programmed it into the phone.

Teresa answered on the third ring and was quiet for a moment when she heard his voice.

'Gianni?' she asked eventually. 'Are you OK?'

'Of course I'm OK! Nothing wrong with me phoning you, is there?'

The pause on the line said otherwise. 'Not exactly. Though I have to tell you I am in a very strange apartment right now dealing with a stray head. That lady you met earlier if you remember. I think we have all the pieces at last.'

'Jesus,' he swore quietly. 'Listen, Teresa. There's something I need to know. About Laila. What happened this morning? Why'd she leave like that? Have you any idea?'

She sighed and said something about taking the call outside. The line was quiet for a short while then Peroni heard the unmistakable sound of the night wind roaring behind her.

'I told her you were going to get fired unless she

gave you something about what happened in the Pantheon,' Teresa said over the noise. 'I'm sorry. I thought it might help.'

Peroni made absolutely sure he got the tone of voice right, that there was no edge to his words.

'I wish I'd thought of that,' he said. 'It was really clever. Classic stuff too, Teresa. Good cop, bad cop, huh? Maybe they should pin a badge on you and let me drive the corpse wagon.'

He could almost feel the tension on the other end. 'Don't be so ridiculous, you big goof. Falcone would be lost without you. Gianni?'

'Yeah?'

'You mean that? I did the right thing?'

'Of course I mean that! It should have worked too. If she had anything to tell us . . .'

She sounded so relieved he felt like going back into the café and hugging that mouthy kid.

'Gianni, she does have something. That's what I don't understand.'

'Me neither.' If Laila did have more to tell that ought to have dragged it out of her. 'I just don't get it.'

'Unless . . .'

Teresa Lupo would have made a good cop. Everyone in the Questura understood that implicitly.

'Unless what?'

'She keeps stealing things. What if she stole something from this guy? What if he took his jacket off when he was doing what he did? Do you think Laila could resist a peek? Or rather more?'

It was an idea. He wasn't sure where it got them.

'I don't know. But if she stole something why doesn't she just give it to us? I mean, it's not as if we don't know about her habits. I must have emptied her pockets ten times this morning.'

She didn't say anything. He was glad of that. She was thinking.

'I'm improvising here so don't treat it as any more than that,' she said after a long moment. 'What if she hid it somewhere? What if that's why she ran away? To get what she stole, recover it from somewhere? Then give it to you?'

It just fell into a place in his head, the little compartment that said: *right*.

'God, I wish I could kiss you now,' Gianni Peroni sighed.

The sound of short, tinny laughter flew through the cold night air. 'I'm wearing surgical gloves covered in blood. I'm standing on the roof of some dead woman's apartment freezing my ass off.'

'All the same . . .'

He was an idiot, moping over his kids. They were safe and comfortable and warm. He'd drive up to Tuscany when the weather cleared, take them to one of those little country restaurants they loved, maybe introduce them to Teresa Lupo too. They were just a couple of young people learning to live with damaged parents. It wasn't ideal, but there were a lot worse things the world could throw at you.

'I'm sorry if I've not exactly been normal lately,' he said, his voice choking a touch, doubtless from the aftermath of the lemon gelato.

'If I wanted "normal", Gianni, do you think I'd be dating you?'

'No, I mean . . .'

The words dried up. He was terrible at this. He just hoped she got the message.

'Can I go back to my head now?' she asked. 'This isn't the right way to have a conversation like this.'

'OK.'

'And thanks for phoning by the way.'

He heard her cut the call, looked at the empty Piazza Trilussa and said, 'You're welcome.'

Then Gianni Peroni went back into the café, smiled at the girl, said thanks, and sat over a newly replenished bowl of ice cream thinking about what Teresa Lupo had said.

Laila stole something. *Where?* In the Pantheon, surely. Laila hid that something. *Where?* In the Pantheon. *Where else?*

He looked at his watch and thought about that miserable, florid-faced caretaker and the hours he kept. The place closed at seven thirty. Maybe she'd been there already. But if that was the case why hadn't she tried to get in touch? Wouldn't she wait till the very last when there were hardly any people around? Or – and this thought appalled him – had she left the thing somewhere that meant she had to spend another night there to recover it?

The waitress was reading a magazine. He placed a ten euro note on the counter and got up.

'Hey, kid,' he said. 'You want to know why that boyfriend never calls you?'

The green eyes looked at him with steady, intrigued intent. 'Possibly . . .'

'Because he's a jerk. That's why.'

*

William F. Kaspar sat in the yellow Fiat Punto he'd ripped off from the cavernous underground car park by Porta Pinciana, waiting, thinking, watching the steady, light fall of snow descend on the deserted Via Veneto, listening to nothing but static from the tiny device clipped into his ear. This could go on forever. Not that he was worried about being caught. The weather meant the car park was dark and dead and deserted. He'd been able to swap the Fiat's plates with those of a dusty Lancia that hadn't moved in days. Even when the theft got reported they'd be looking for the wrong car.

That was the kind of thing the old Bill would have done. This recent carelessness wasn't like him. He'd tested his luck in the Net café and, for once, got away with it. Still, this was bad. This was unlike him. He knew who he was: William F. Kaspar. He knew where he came from: Kentucky, a big, old stud farm outside Lexington, where the horses flew like the wind across green fields that stretched forever, where family meant family, a tight, unbreakable bond of love, and you could get good whiskey straight from an illicit still if you knew where to ask.

Kentucky was where he'd grown up, where he'd loved his first woman. After college in Alabama (and the memory alone sent a Dan song, with its refrain about the Crimson Tide spinning through his head), a Kentucky military academy had started him on the long, hard road to becoming a soldier, filled him with a love of the classical world through campaign lessons about Hadrian and Caesar and Hannibal. A Kentucky congressman, no stranger to the covert world himself, had first marked him out as someone whose talents could be used outside a conventional military career.

Memories. Fading ghosts, blurring the line between reality and illusion.

It was a lost world now, a distant sea of faded, two-dimensional mental pictures. He couldn't return there even if he wanted to. He'd assembled his team, the best team, the Babylon Sisters (*shake it*, his head said immediately, right on cue) and he'd screwed up, been betrayed, whatever. There'd been blood on the ground, the holy ground, on the floor of the ziggurat, gore tracing the outlines of the patterns there, a red stain on the filigreed stone tattoo Hadrian himself had once touched. He'd wrapped the corpses of his own men and women in that same pattern, trapped in something as mundane as camouflage webbing. Then, before he'd had the chance to go down with them, bad luck got in the way. Thirteen wasted years that changed forever what he was and what he could be.

A killer.

No, that didn't worry him. Bill Kaspar had killed plenty in his career. Never unnecessarily, never without good reason. It went with the turf. Sometimes it was the only way to stay alive. He'd killed in the jungles of Colombia and on the streets of Managua. He'd taken men down in Afghanistan and Indonesia. And the Middle East. He'd been there a lot, enough to speak good Arabic, Kurdish and Farsi. Enough to help him convince a few people who should have known better, men who, temperamentally, hated everything American, that he really could be on their side, put some weapons their way, provided they had the money and information to share.

He'd read every last book he could find on Hadrian, knew every twist and turn of his career all the way from

Italica to Rome. Long before these new voices came to occupy his head, Bill Kaspar had thought he heard Hadrian talking to him sometimes, a strong, educated voice carrying across almost two millennia. The voice taught him lessons that kept a man like him alive. How it was impossible to fight battles on multiple fronts, which made it necessary, on occasion, to convert an enemy into a friend. How important it was to be a true leader, one everyone could look up to. And how the ambition was, invariably, more important than the achievement because, in the end, everything was dust and death and failure, a shallow, temporary grave in a foreign place far from home.

Hadrian was rash sometimes, too, and arrogant. The mind that could imagine a building like the Pantheon had also seen fit to slaughter those who stood in his way. Kaspar had murdered Monica Sawyer brutally, his head full of screaming voices, feeling his power enter her body, and still he couldn't quite work out why, still he knew that the patterns he'd painted with her blood, the holy frieze of interlocking shapes, was powder over a stupid misdeed, a disguise that failed to hide the enormity of the crime. She wasn't a part of the endgame playing out on the streets of Rome. She hadn't – there was no avoiding the thought – *merited* that particular death.

He was Bill Kaspar. He could have prevented that, locked her in the bedroom with a gag round her overactive mouth and stayed safe and warm in the apartment knowing not a soul could see there was anything wrong. He could have tried to explain to her that he was, in his own frame of reference, an honourable man set upon an honourable mission. He'd been abandoned, cheated, robbed, even here in Rome.

Bill Kaspar didn't kill people because he wanted to. Only because he *had* to. Hadn't he let Emily Deacon live that night partly for the same reason? The bug was a long shot. He was lucky it provided anything. Or was his reluctance a symptom of a greater problem? Had some unconscious part of his head now started to operate on its own, demanding a victim, any victim, just because it hated the idea of being cheated?

Hadrian, the brightest emperor of them all, the man who set limits to the empire, who said this far, no further, was crazy by the end and Bill Kaspar knew he couldn't even hope to stand in the shadow of that colossus.

He wasn't sure about any of this. He wasn't sure it was worth worrying about either. What mattered was finishing the job. For the life of him he couldn't think of any way he could do that without involving Emily Deacon. It was possible she was the key to the whole damn thing anyway, and that Steely Dan Deacon, in spite of appearances, in spite of the way Deacon had protested his innocence just before he died, had been in charge all along. Kaspar knew he was running out of alternatives. He didn't dare hang around Net cafés any more in case they were being watched. Steely Dan's girl had to provide the answers. Somehow.

The headphone came alive just after five, the sound of the thin traffic working its way just far enough up the hill to break through over the embassy's electronic fog. Then a car engine, something like the notching of gears.

She was in a vehicle. He pulled the Fiat forward until its yellow nose edged out into the Via Veneto and watched the big iron gates. A red Ford was coming through them, Emily Deacon behind the wheel.

'Little Em,' he said to himself.

Kids didn't get to pick their parents. It wasn't her fault Steely Dan turned out the way he was. From what he'd seen, what little he'd heard on the hidden mike, she wasn't even part of the current plan. They'd just brought her in for old time's sake, maybe. Or to tease him, to say: *Look, the Deacons just go on and on.*

In that case, he thought, they ought to look after their precious belongings more carefully.

There was scarcely any traffic. A good agent – and he knew she didn't fit into that category just from watching her the night before – should have been alert, should have seen that a little yellow Fiat was dogging her all the way.

Little Em drove and drove, all the way out to the Via Appia Antica, where she took a turn into what looked like a farm drive, barely passable in the drifts. He carried on for a few hundred yards before pulling into a deserted bus stop. He loved this place. In happier times he'd walked miles and miles along the Appian Way, thinking about the tombs, wondering about the dead feet that had trudged this way over the centuries.

He popped in the earphone and turned up the volume on the radio. Two voices: Little Em and the young Italian he now recognized.

Bill Kaspar listened intently, wondering all the time about his options.

Then he realized he couldn't stay here. He heard something he should have figured out long, long before.

You're getting old and careless, white boy, the ghost of

the black sergeant whispered in the back of his head. *Git out there and find what belongs you.*

He reached into his bag and pulled out the digital music player he'd stolen from a backpacker in the Corso a couple of weeks before. It had all his favourite music on there: the Dan, the Doobies, Todd Rundgren and a couple of hundred others, all good hippie listening for a sixties child turned spook.

It had stacks of spare space for more recording too and a full battery charge, enough to store another ten hours of conversation right alongside the holy grooves.

There was a spare mini-jack in the bag. He connected the radio to the player and hit the record button. Then he placed the kit carefully in a dry patch behind the bus shelter, where it was hidden, not that anyone was going to walk along this deserted piece of imperial Roman highway on such a bitter, hostile night.

It was a good twenty or thirty minutes to the centro storico and the more he thought about the journey the more William F. Kaspar realized he was in danger of losing the gift. The voices inside him were getting louder all the time. It was a question of killing them before they killed him.

Nic Costa was nodding off on the sofa when the doorbell rang. Emily Deacon walked straight in, grinning, looking bright and rosy, as if she could go without sleep forever.

She had a briefcase in her hand and a notebook computer bag slung over her shoulder. 'Where is everyone? Gianni? The kid?'

'Short story: she ran away. He's looking for her now.'

'Oh no,' she murmured, genuinely shocked.

'Don't worry. Gianni will find her. He won't stop till he does. I got a call from him half an hour ago. He wanted to check out a theory Laila stole something from our friend then dumped it in the Pantheon. Maybe she's going back to retrieve it.'

She considered the idea. 'I think possessions are important to him. Perhaps that's why he wanted to find her. But the idea she could leave something in the Pantheon. Wouldn't you have found it?'

'Not if it was hidden. I'm starting to come to the conclusion that anything's possible right now. Besides, if you knew my partner better, you'd understand there's not much point in arguing.'

He looked at her, trying to remember what he'd promised to do.

'You forgot, didn't you?' she asked with a smile.

He was trying to drag that morning's conversation back from the depths of his memory. So much had intervened in the meantime.

'I promised I'd check a couple of names for you.'

She held up the laptop case. 'It's OK. I came prepared. I've been following the logs. I know what's been happening. A busy day.'

Costa doubted she knew half of what had really gone on. He led the way to the living room and watched her set up her gear on the coffee table in front of the low sofa.

'You can say that again. Coffee?'

'I'd rather have a real drink,' she said, throwing the

black jacket over the back of the sofa, getting straight down to work. 'You do have wine here?'

'Wine,' he sighed and wondered how long he could keep his eyes open. Then he went to the kitchen, opened a cold bottle of Alto Adige Sauvignon and brought back a couple of glasses. The hard mountain grape had a kick in it. He ought to be able to stay alert for a little while before crashing out completely.

Emily looked animated, a little too much for his liking. She was making a deliberate and obvious effort to throw off the trappings of disguise he'd first seen two days before in the Pantheon. The more Leapman froze her out of the case, the more she seemed determined to find herself. It was an attractive transformation to witness and the distraction was beginning to worry him.

'Are you all right?' she asked. 'You look exhausted.'

'I'll survive. You said you know what happened?'

She shrugged. 'Just from what I've seen in the log. Leapman isn't updating me on anything at all. I heard a woman was killed. You guys managed to find where.'

The memory of the little cabin, and a head rolling crazily off a chair, John Wayne screaming in the background. 'Oh yes.'

The blue eyes blinked at him. 'Are you sure you're OK?'

'I'm sure.' He didn't want to go into detail. She looked unprepared. 'It was different though, somehow. Let me leave it at that.'

She opened the computer, scanned the room for a phone socket, plugged in the machine, then returned to the sofa, motioning for him to join her. 'Different . . . that's interesting. I don't think our man likes different.'

'You think you're starting to know him?'

'I gave you his name this morning. Now I've got a story. A hell of a one. A story that was supposed to end differently I think, with heroes and victory and what we like to call "closure".'

Nic Costa took another sip of the wine and tried to convince himself he wasn't that tired as he sank into the cushions by Emily Deacon's side.

She hit a key and a couple of images popped up on the screen.

'These are photos I took of some documents I found in the embassy. Leapman may be acting as if I don't exist but I got a little help there anyway. It took me to places I couldn't visit before.'

'Photos,' Costa repeated.

'That's right. They'd have my hide if they knew I had them.'

He groaned and went to the kitchen, returning with a dish of peanuts.

Emily Deacon cast a wry glance at them.

'You Italians really know how to treat a woman.'

'Yes and I'll show you sometime. So you're stealing information from the embassy?'

Her narrow, pale eyebrows rose perceptibly. 'I thought that's what you wanted. Besides, it's not the kind of stuff you can photocopy, Nic. Are you turning prissy on me? Do you want to hear about it or not?'

He raised the glass and toasted her. 'Talk away, Agent Deacon. I'll try not to fall asleep on you.'

'That won't be hard,' she replied with visible certainty. 'This is a story that begins in 1990. The Gulf War is about to happen. We were kids then, of course. You do remember the first Gulf War?'

'Sort of. My old man was a Communist Deputy at

the time. I remember him burning the Stars and Stripes outside your embassy.'

She stared at him. 'You're kidding me.'

'Not at all. He took me with him. We're an unusual family.'

'I can believe that,' she conceded. 'So you do remember the war. Better than me but you're a couple of years older. It's like any war. Each side, naturally, wants some intelligence. And they want it before the fighting even starts. So they put people in beforehand. For reconnaissance. To establish links with the Iraqi opposition. Guess your own reasons, it doesn't matter. They're putting together a team, mainly American, maybe a couple of Iraqis for local knowledge. They're putting it together here, in Rome. Don't ask me how I know. I just do. They don't want anyone outside their immediate circle to find out. Does that sound plausible?'

Military affairs weren't Costa's scene. His late father had a favourite rant about the army. Something along the lines that war was a hangover from another era in mankind's development, one they'd soon leave behind. Marco Costa hadn't lived long enough – quite – to see how wrong he was.

'It's a story,' Costa said.

'No, Nic,' she said firmly, 'it's the truth. The man we're looking for now was the leader of that team, on the military side anyway. William F. Kaspar. And somehow what happened to him then is behind what's happening now.'

She paused. 'Do you mind if I smoke?'

It took him by surprise. 'You smoke?'

'Sometimes. I have been known to own a boyfriend

on occasion too. Are you shocked? What is this? A monastery?'

'Not always,' he answered. 'But no one – and I mean no one – smokes in here. If you need a cigarette, do what everyone else does – go outside.'

She looked at the door.

'Later,' he added. 'Please.'

He was thinking about what she said. Every military campaign had to be preceded by some kind of covert activity. It still seemed a long way away from a bizarre streak of killings more than a decade later.

'This is all a long time ago, Emily.'

She shook her head vigorously. 'Oh no. Only for those of us who were young then. For the people who fought there it's like yesterday. That's what wars are like, Nic. Haven't you talked to an old soldier? It's the first thing you notice. It lives with them, day in, day out, often for the rest of their lives. Usually it's the most important thing that ever happens to them.'

'This is Italy. We don't have many old soldiers.'

There was a sharp intake of breath and a cold flash of those blue eyes. 'OK, OK. I represent the great imperial power and we're just brimming over with them. So take my word for it. *When it comes to war, memories don't fade easily.* Especially for him . . .'

She pointed to the name in the middle of the weird, rambling memo that was on the screen. The one that said: SUBJECT: BABYLON SISTERS. STATUS: YOU HAVE TO ASK?

He read it, page by page, stumbling over the odd, colloquial language.

'William F. Kaspar again,' he said when he'd finished. 'OK. I didn't have time to chase the diplomat

I mentioned. But I called the desk about *him*. Honest. There's nothing.'

'I'd be amazed if there was. I don't know much myself. There are no military records. Nothing personal out there. Just this one memo.'

He was onto that point straight away. 'This is all about some big secret or something?'

'I think so.'

'Then why's there still some evidence left? Just this one piece?'

'*I don't know!*' Something about its provenance exasperated her too. 'Maybe it was a mistake,' she suggested, and didn't look him in the eye when she said it. 'They happen. It *was* filed under the wrong keywords.'

Costa was starting to convince himself she knew more than she was revealing at that moment. But before he could pursue the point she was moving on, tapping her forehead, impatient to get over her point.

'Besides. It isn't just this memo, Nic. It's what's in here too. My dad knew this guy. I vaguely remember him coming round to the house. A big, noisy man, all laughter and presents. Loud. And scary too. He was sort of the boss, I think. You can still hear the tone in this memo. He's the guy who's leading this assignment, assembling the teams, taking them into action. My dad with him.'

Cases went bad when they began to bite into your own private life. He knew that only too well from his own experience.

'Are you sure? That your father was a part of this?'

'Absolutely. There's a whole chunk of 1991 when he wasn't around. I remember it clearly. I'm an only child. You notice things like that. He was gone and while he was away you could touch the atmosphere in that apartment the embassy gave us. Everything felt so odd. I've tried to talk to my mom about it and all she says is he was away somewhere, working.'

'Maybe he was.'

'I don't doubt it. Now I know where. And I know it did something to him, too. When he came back he was . . . different. He'd changed. Something had marked him. He wasn't . . .'

She hesitated, trying to be precise about this last point.

'He wasn't the same dad any more. A part of him, the good part, all the life and joy, they'd gone. He was cold and unhappy. It didn't take long and he was gone too. Out of the house, talking to the divorce lawyers. There was just my mom and me and a lot – I mean a *lot* – of bad feeling.'

'I'm sorry.'

Emily Deacon was waving a hand at him in embarrassment.

'OK, OK. I know what you're thinking. This is just a run-of-the-mill family break-up I'm trying to rationalize by blaming it on something else. First point. Bill Kaspar killed my dad. No arguments there. I knew that without a doubt when I looked into his face and watched him trying to decide whether to kill me too. Second point. Yes, I do want to know why, but it's not just for me. It's for all of them. Whatever brought him to kill my dad was the same thing that brought him to kill those others. That's what closes this case for everyone.'

He could see what she'd been through, getting scarred twice over. By the change in her father when she was a kid and by his death a few months before. Nonetheless there was a strong, rational line in her argument. Emily Deacon could tough it through the pain, or so she thought.

'We need proof, Emily,' he said.

She fired up a Web browser, hammering in a flurry of words. 'You don't just get it from hacking embassy computer systems either. Sometimes it's waiting out there on the Net. Take a look at this and see what you think.'

Costa vaguely recognized what he was now looking at. It was a newsgroup, one of those anonymous bulletin boards the surveillance people browsed for raw intelligence. There was a short message starting a thread with the title 'Babylon Sisters'. The first entry, the one opening the discussion, had been posted on 30 September.

Emily Deacon stared at the screen and said without emotion, 'I found this just by looking on the Net. It's public and it's meant to be. Someone put it there for a reason. The memo tells you what Babylon Sisters meant. It was the codename for the operation. My guess is that Babylon was the closest notable location to where they were headed. The name's from an old rock song my dad liked. Maybe Kaspar had the same tastes. And here it is thirteen years later. Think of the timing, Nic. This was posted three days after my dad was murdered.'

He looked at the first message on the screen and hated what he saw, felt tainted by the craziness of the language.

> The Scarlet Beast was a generous beast. Honor his memory. Fuck China. Fuck the ziggurat. Let's

> get together again back in the old places folks. Reunion time for the class of '91. Just one spare place at the table. You coming or not?

'You get this kind of crap everywhere on the Net, Emily.'

'Of course. It's meant to sound like that. Whoever wrote that message doesn't want it to mean anything to anyone but Bill Kaspar. They know what Kaspar's like. They know that, from time to time, he's going to walk up to a PC somewhere in the world, fire up a search engine and type in two words "Babylon Sisters". Sooner or later he's going to hit on this. Sooner or later he's going to respond. Which he does. Read the second message.'

He hit the key for the next window.

> Lying fuckhead, treasonable, cowardly scum. I've waited long enough now. 'Bill Kaspar' my ass. This is the real item, dweeb boy. Fear not. There will be a reunion. And soon. Pray we don't meet.

The reply was dated that morning, signed, simply, 'killthem@killthemall.com'.

'It could be Kaspar sending messages to himself,' Costa suggested. The language sounded like the kind of internal argument that might lurk inside the head of someone who could dismember a woman, park her head in front of the TV to make a room look 'normal', then smear the walls with her blood in a strange, repeating pattern, over and over again. 'He's crazy enough.'

'Why wait more than three months before answering yourself? What's more, consider this. I managed to get a look at some of the rosters. At eleven this morning, just after Kaspar's reply got posted, Leapman ordered a couple of the five security guys I never knew existed out onto the street. Want to bet where they're looking? Net cafés, just to see if he can't resist the bait second time round. You can see what's happening?'

He could and he wondered if they appreciated how futile it was likely to be. The city was full of places, large and small, where you could wander in off the street and buy fifteen minutes online. Five men couldn't cover every last Net café, money changer and bookshop in town in Rome.

'Would Leapman write something like this?'

She shook her head slowly, deliberately, and he couldn't stop himself watching the way her soft blonde hair moved. 'No need to. We've specialists to do that. Someone from profiling maybe, who's got access to files I don't possess. The syntax is very deliberate and direct. Maybe Kaspar is a good ol' boy or something, which could explain the exaggerated accent. Maybe they just copied it from that first memo I showed you. Though I doubt it. If they knew that was still around on the system my guess is they'd have erased it.'

There were so many possibilities here. Costa wished his head were in better working order to consider them, to separate speculation from fact.

'We need to raise this with someone. Your people. Mine. Maybe there's something here. Maybe we're just seeing what we want to see.'

'Oh, Nic.' Her hand brushed his arm. There was a flash of a white smile. 'You really don't understand what we're dealing with, do you? My people *know*. I think a good few of yours do too.'

Not Falcone though, Costa thought. He was sure of that. It just wasn't the inspector's style.

'Finish the thread,' she said quietly. 'Leapman's man came back for a third try.'

He scrolled down and read the third message, posted at noon, again from 'WillFK@whitehouse.gov'.

> Well hang me high and stretch me wide. Just when you think you made somethin' idiot-proof they come along and invent a better idiot. Can't keep those fingers still, can you, Billy Boy? All this cuttin' has turned your mind, brother. Call home. Reel yourself in. Nothin' smells worse than an old soldier gone bad. There's mercy waiting here if only you got the sense to ask for it. Least that way you get to stay alive.
>
> Oh and by the by. What did Laura Lee ever do to you, man? She took a bullet in all that mess back then. So how come she gets dead now and Little Em walks away without a scratch? You turn weakling when there's a WASP around? Or are you just going soft in your old age?

Costa stared at the words on the screen. There couldn't be any other explanation.

'Little Em . . .'

'That's me,' she said.

As Gianni Peroni's luck would have it the same damn caretaker was on duty and sporting the same bad, red-faced mood he'd owned the night Mauro Sandri died.

The grumpy old bastard spent his time alone at the booth by the door of the Pantheon, checking his watch at regular intervals, wandering over to the centre of the building now and then to sweep away the flecks of snow spiralling lightly down through the oculus. Peroni had a seat in the shadows on the opposite side of the chilly circular hall. The place was a wonderful sight, timeless, even with the anachronistic illumination of the dim electric lights. The distant part of him that remembered school history lessons half imagined an ancient Roman emperor coming here, staring up through that open eye, lord of his own realm, wondering what was looking back at him from the greater kingdom of the heavens. Peroni felt more than a little awed by what he saw. It was wrong that a place like this had been sullied by what happened two nights before. That thought depressed him, that and the plain fact he was probably wasting his time. After he'd left the café in Trastevere with such high hopes, Peroni had driven the jeep across the river, parked discreetly in one of the side turnings off Rinascimento and quietly made his way to the monument, taking the caretaker aside for a quiet talk when he arrived. There wasn't a single sign he was in luck. Only a couple of people had walked through the door while he'd been there, and both of them were searching – in vain – for respite from the cold. The place would close in under an hour. It was a dumb idea, but it was the only idea he'd got.

Besides, she'd so much time on him. She could have walked in, picked up anything she'd left behind, and walked back out into the premature wintry darkness hours ago. But then what? Peroni clung to the belief Laila acted the way she did because, after Teresa's invented story, she wanted to help him. She'd have made contact somehow, surely. He tried to draw some encouragement, too, from the fact the caretaker was adamant no lone, black-clad kid had been in. Given how few visitors the place was getting in this extraordinary bout of ice and snow, there ought to be some comfort in that.

His mind was wandering when the caretaker ambled over, picking snowflakes off the sleeve of his tatty uniform.

'Hey, mister,' he moaned, 'seeing as how I seem to be doing you favours day in and day out around here, how about you do one for me?'

'What?'

He nodded at the booth and the small, private office down the same curving side of the building. 'Cover for me. There's supposed to be two of us around but he's sick and, what with the weather . . .'

He licked his bulbous lips and Peroni knew what was coming. 'All you got to do is sit there and look important. You're up to it.'

It wasn't a big favour. The place was empty. Peroni had no intention of sweeping away the snow. Nor had he anything else to do. He'd checked in with Falcone, heard the news about the dead woman's apartment, and received not the slightest reprimand for his behaviour earlier with Leapman. He recognized the resignation in Falcone's voice. The whole case was in stasis, buried under the weather and the search for something – anything – in the trail of places the elusive killer had abandoned along the way. The likelihood was that until the guy did something – something stupid, without spilling blood preferably – they'd just be sitting around twiddling their fingers, waiting, not that Leo Falcone would admit as much for a moment.

'Where are you going exactly, friend?' Peroni demanded.

The man's florid, wrinkled face squinted back at him. 'It's no big deal. I need a drink. I've been freezing my balls off in this place all day long. There should be a rule about working in weather like this. What am I? An Eskimo or something? Just half an hour. That's all I ask. Here . . .'

He led Peroni over to the office by the side entrance, the one with the closed-circuit TVs and security systems that had been so carefully disabled two nights before.

'Everything's working again now. All you need to know is where the circuit-breakers are. If a bulb blows, it'll throw the switch. You just throw it back and I change the bulb later. If I can be bothered. Also, I'm going let you have a special treat for helping me. When I come back I'm gonna let you close the door, all on your own. I don't allow civilians to do that ordinarily. Big privilege.'

Lazy bastard, Peroni thought. It was just a door, one of two, the other closed. A big, very old door.

'Is that so?' he asked.

'You bet,' the caretaker said and was on his way out already, picking up speed with the eagerness of a man in desperate need of alcohol.

Peroni sat down on the hard chair behind the glass front of the booth. Then he thought about what he was doing and pulled himself back into the darkness of the little cubicle. Entry into the place was free. People just walked in and out as they pleased, except for the odd dumb tourist who couldn't believe it was possible to get into a historic monument without a ticket. There was no need to make his presence obvious, none at all.

So he sat on the chair behind the glass and did what came naturally to him in the solitary gloom of the booth. He thought about his kids, wondering what they were doing, whether they were happy, whether they missed him. He thought about Laila, trying to imagine what kind of life she led, what had brought her all the way from Iraq to the streets of a hostile city where no one, as far as he could work out, knew who she was or cared much either.

And he looked at this odd old building, with its spherical interior pointed towards the sky like half an upturned eyeball, the pupil set on the stars. Peroni tried to work out where it lay in the tangle of facts they'd assembled so far. He hadn't listened much to Emily Deacon's lecture about why it was important. Temperamentally he inclined towards Joel Leapman's view. That a man who carved weird geometrical shapes out of the skins of the people he slaughtered was just plain crazy, however you tried to rationalize it. Thinking about the idea again inside the Pantheon itself, he was no longer so sure. The kind of killer they were hunting was, undoubtedly, deranged and dangerous. That didn't make him illogical or erratic. The very opposite, in fact. If they'd thought this through – if events had given them the chance even to begin the process – he'd have suggested to Falcone that they should have left some plain-clothes guy around here all day, just on the off chance. The old saw about people returning to the scene of their crime was part of the argument. That did happen. More to the point, this place obsessed the man somehow. It was part of his story, part of the way he saw the world. In its angles and curves, the shadowy corners of its precise proportions, he found some hidden truth that made sense of what he was trying to achieve.

Several ideas were starting to form in Gianni Peroni's head at that moment, each of them pushing the memory of his kids and a stray Kurdish girl from his mind.

Then he glanced at the long vertical slit of the door, outlined by the lights of the square behind, and saw a slim, recognizable figure slip through, casting a long slender shadow on the geometric floor.

Peroni sat in the booth, trying to work out how to handle the girl. She'd fallen straight into the shade to the right of the altar opposite the entrance, hopping the rope designed to keep out the public, intent on something. Every movement was deliberate, determined. Teresa had been right. She was back here to retrieve something. Then another shape came through the door: the caretaker returning, walking steadily, head down, not the shambling gait Peroni expected of a man who, just half an hour earlier, looked as if his mind was set on downing three quick coffees laced with brandy.

Peroni glanced at his watch.

'You're five minutes late,' he moaned at the uniform now heading for the booth, then he walked towards the altar, straight through the sharp beam of moonlight tumbling through the oculus.

The girl was just visible behind some kind of drape at the side of the altar, half-concealed by the cloth.

'Laila.'

He spoke her name firmly, with warmth and familiarity. All the same it wasn't enough. Her skinny frame stiffened visibly at the sound of a human voice and he began to wonder: if she ran now was there any way a man approaching fifty could possibly stop her reaching the door and disappearing once again into the night?

'It's me,' he said. 'Peroni. You don't need to worry. There's nothing to be scared of. Nothing at all.'

Except . . .

Just a sudden flashback of all those doubts that drifted wordlessly through the back of his head in the booth waiting for the caretaker to get back. All those wonderful little nightmares kids – or, more accurately, their existence – sent scattering through the mind at random times: car crashes and meningitis, the wrong friends, the wrong time to cross the road, rubella, crappy bike helmets, a random falling meteor.

And, Laila being a girl, all those fears about men. In the street. In the home. Men who ought to know better. Men lurking half-hidden under the cover of night, and all of them looking for the same thing: someone weak enough to fill the role of prey.

It was a shitty world sometimes, though he guessed Laila had learned that at a very early age.

There was movement from behind the drape. She walked out. Her dark eyes were glittering, a little moist maybe. But she was smiling, smiling in a way he hadn't seen before. Smiling naturally, a little shy, a little proud too.

She had something in her hands that looked very much like a man's wallet and Gianni Peroni was aware that he didn't give a damn about the thing, however interesting it might prove. The case could wait. There was something more important going on here.

'Hey,' he said and held out his arms, wishing to God she'd just run straight into them.

That was too much to ask. She walked up, holding

the wallet in her right hand, grinning now, wiping tears – of joy, relief, fear, just what? – from her cheeks.

Peroni put his arms round her skinny shoulders and hugged that frail, frightened body to his big chest.

'Don't you go giving your uncle Gianni frights like that,' he whispered into her lank, musky-smelling hair. 'He's an old man, too old for this business.'

And she wasn't going to the Questura either. They could sleep at Teresa's. Or Nic's if she preferred. Anywhere there wasn't a soul in uniform or the dead, disinterested face of a social worker looking at her, shaking a disappointed, middle-class head, thinking, 'Damaged goods, damaged goods, put it down the list and let someone else pick up the problem.'

Uniforms . . .

He hadn't even spoken to the caretaker since the moron got back from his secret drink. It was time to kiss goodbye to this weird, spooky space and re-enter the land of the living.

Soon, too, because when Peroni turned he could see the idiot was now closing the door, that big vertical slab of bronze that had stood in the same archway for almost a couple of millennia, watching generation after generation walk through and gawp at the mysteries within.

Which was odd, given that he was supposed to be handing over that particular privilege as a reward to the dumb cop who'd stood duty while he'd lined his gut with cheap brandy.

'Hey, buster,' Peroni yelled, 'you've still got some customers inside. Remember?'

The door kept moving. It slammed shut and the sudden absence of the electric lights from the square made

Gianni Peroni blink, sent a brisk rush of pain and fear stabbing through the back of his head.

Laila was clinging to him. She was shivering. The caretaker was nowhere to be seen.

Gianni Peroni pushed the girl firmly back into the corner and whispered in her ear, 'There's nothing wrong here. Trust me. Just stay out of the way until your uncle Gianni sorts this out.'

She didn't protest. She went and crushed herself up behind the drape again, so hard against the ancient slabs of the stone wall that it looked as if she were hoping she could somehow creep inside the cracks.

There was a sound from nearby close to the little office the caretaker had shown him. Someone was flipping the circuit breakers. The lights were going off, one by one, in a circular dance. The CCTV cameras too, he guessed. This guy had been here before. Laila knew that, maybe straight away, just from sensing his presence.

Smart kid, Peroni thought, then yelled out into the airy, pregnant darkness, lit now by nothing more than the silvery light tumbling down the oculus.

'Listen, mister, I'm armed. I'm a cop. And you're not going anywhere near this kid, not unless you come straight through me. And that's *not* gonna happen. Understand?'

Then, just for form, 'Best give yourself up now. Or climb out the window and curl up in the cold somewhere. You hear me?'

It was just a laugh. The kind of laugh you got in the movies, hard-edged, nasal, knowing. Foreign too, somehow, because Italians didn't laugh like that, they didn't know how to make such a shapeless, wordless sound become a figure of speech in itself, full of meaning, brimming with malevolence.

All the same a man couldn't scare you just by laughing. Not even this guy with his magic scalpel and his skilful fixation on shapes.

No. Peroni knew why the sound made him shrink inside himself, shivering, wondering which way to look. It was the way it echoed symmetrically around the hidden axes of the building, the way it ran along some hidden geometric path, crossing and recrossing the empty interior, time and time again, almost as if the man who made the noise planned it that way, rolled his own voice into some mystic complex of ley lines until it floated upwards and out of the ancient dead eye, out towards the moon.

Peroni flipped the safety catch on his service pistol and tried to remember the last time the weapon had been fired in anger.

'Laura Lee? Who the hell is Laura Lee?'

She had an answer already. She just wanted to make him earn it.

'Let's take this one step at a time. Decode the first message before anything else. Remember, this is three days after Kaspar has killed my dad in Beijing. Can that be a coincidence?'

Anything could be a coincidence, Costa thought. You could ruin an entire investigation by reading too much into shreds of half-related information like this.

'Maybe.'

'No! Think about it. Kaspar's reached right into the heart of the US diplomatic service here. He's killed a military attaché. He knows, as sure as hell, there'll be all manner of people on his back. So what do these guys chasing him do?'

It could be true. He saw the logic. 'You think *they* sent him this message?'

'Damn right I do. Maybe it's us. Maybe the CIA. I don't know. But this is someone from our side dialling into his private line. And they're saying, "We know who you are, we know where you've been, we know what you've done. Time to call it a day, Bill K, before you get hurt too."'

Costa wondered about the implications of that idea. 'They seem very forgiving in the circumstances.'

'You noticed?' she replied with a brief, icy scowl.

'And Leapman?'

She cast him a sideways glance.

'Have you talked this through with him?'

Costa found himself subjected to a wry and very penetrating look.

'Do you really think that would be wise right now? If he doesn't know already, he'll go ballistic when he discovers how I found out. And if he does . . .'

Leapman knew. At least that's what she suspected. Costa thought about the way the FBI man had acted ever since that first unexpected meeting in the Pantheon. Some unspoken knowledge seemed to underpin everything he did.

'And the ziggurat?'

She keyed up something on the computer: a page full of technical archaeological jargon and three photos of an ancient, mound-like site.

'A ziggurat's a kind of ancient temple in Iraq. My guess is it's what Kaspar used as a base for the mission.

There's nothing in any of the official records, of course. But a UN archaeological inspection team was sent into Iraq last summer to try to assess the damage to historical monuments caused by two wars and the Saddam regime. I found this . . .'

The page was about a temple close to a place called Shiltagh, near the banks of the Euphrates between Al Hillah and Karbala, slap in the middle of ancient Mesopotamia. It was less well known – or, as the report put it, less well documented – than the famous ziggurat at Ur. But it had been damaged during the first Gulf War. What must once have been a low, stepped pyramid was now a crumbling, wrecked mound, its original outline only faintly discernible. Mortar craters pockmarked the broad ceremonial staircase entrance.

'Looks like a hell of a battle,' he murmured.

'Exactly,' she agreed. 'This isn't collateral damage. It's not aerial bombardment either. There was one big, vicious fire fight here and the report dates the damage to 1991.'

'So why's this place special?'

'For two reasons. The allied troops never got this far in 1991. There couldn't have been a pitched battle between conventional soldiers.'

'All the same . . .'

She hit a key and said, interrupting him, 'It's the pattern, Nic. The sacred cut. It's everywhere. This is where he gets it from.'

She keyed up a photo of what he assumed was the subterranean interior of the ziggurat. The walls were peppered with bullet marks. Huge chunks had been carved out of the masonry around the door as if someone had tried to fight off an entering attacker. But the pattern was unmistakable: carved stucco on the walls, repeating itself in every direction. And elsewhere too. There were what looked like spent munitions boxes, wrecked equipment. At the centre was a pile of dark material, clumped together in a heap.

She hit the zoom key on the photo. The material became clearer: bales of ancient camouflage webbing.

'This has the pattern too,' she said. 'They'd probably use it for making some sleeping quarters, getting a little privacy. It's just a coincidence, of course. The webbing's got that shape because that's how it's made. Maybe it makes it strong, I don't know. But, what with the walls and the webbing, I imagine that's all he saw when they came for him, when he watched the rest of his team getting taken, killed, all around him. On the walls. In the quarters they'd made for themselves. Can you imagine what that must have been like?'

The floor, the low, curving ceiling, reminded him of what he'd seen painted in blood in the tiny apartment that stank of meat, just a few hours ago.

'I imagine it wouldn't leave you. Ever.'

'Right,' she agreed. 'So what do you do? You just live that nightmare over and over again until you understand what caused it. You get free. You hunt people down in the same kind of sacred places and see if that same pattern gives you any answers.'

She paused, thinking to herself about where this was going.

Then she looked into his eyes, not flinching. 'Do you think he's found some answers? Do you think he's even close?'

He thought of the single word written in blood in the cabin. 'Not enough. When he killed that woman he wrote something, over and over, underneath the pattern. A question. "Who?"'

It didn't seem to make any sense to her either.

'He's been killing people he knew,' she said. 'Why would he ask that?'

'I don't know. You said they'd all been strangled with a cord?'

'That's right,' she agreed.

'No, it's not. He didn't use cord. At least not in the Pantheon. It was this stuff. Webbing, wrapped up into a ligature. Teresa held it back. Leapman is going wild. It was the same with the woman we found today. Teresa got positive ID back from forensic on the first sample. This is US military issue webbing. You can't buy it retail. And it's not from years ago either. This particular type wasn't manufactured until last year. As far as we can work out, the only place it's been used in the field is Iraq.'

'Whoa,' she sighed. 'Now you're the one who's going too fast.'

He had to ask. 'If this man is that consistent, surely he would have used it on the others? Did he?'

'I don't know.'

Costa said nothing.

She squinted at him, then pointed at the computer. 'You think I'm holding out on you? After this?'

'No.' He laughed. 'Not at all.'

Her fingers flew on the keyboard. 'Let's see. I've got the standard reports on here anyway. The ones we sent round to you.'

Carefully, one by one, they went through each of the case file summaries. They were brief, reduced to just a few pages, but were supposed to contain all of the essential relevant information.

'This is ridiculous,' Emily snapped. 'Why the hell didn't I see this in the first place? Why didn't your people?'

'You're not a detective. And we didn't have the time. Remember?'

'Sorry.'

She'd left the last document on the screen open. It was the report on her own father's death. Now he thought about it, the omission almost screamed at them from the screen. The summary gave a cause of death – strangulation – but contained no forensic data on the material used by the murderer.

Emily pointed at the screen. 'You've worked on murder investigations before?'

He nodded. 'Sure.'

'That can't be normal. Just a cause of death. Nothing about the actual ligature itself. Forensic would have information there, wouldn't they? Something that could be useful?'

'Absolutely. A couple of years ago Teresa Lupo coaxed some skin samples out of forensic when they were about to give up on a domestic we had. When they took a good look again they had proof the husband was responsible. He'd pulled the cord so tightly he'd left material there himself.'

Emily glowered at the screen. 'Watch this. I still have some clearance.'

She hit the keys. The modem inside the machine cracked and whistled. Costa watched her thrash her way through more security screens than he'd ever seen in his life. Finally she got to where she wanted: a report topped by the FBI logo. The full file, of which until then he'd only seen the summary.

'Forensic, forensic, forensic . . .' she whispered. '*Shit*!'

She'd scrolled down until she found the section. It contained just five words: PENDING. REFER TO HIGHER AUTHORITY.

'You could . . .' he began to say.

'. . . try the others? You bet.'

She bent down over the computer, head in hands, furious. Costa gingerly put a hand on her shoulder, then removed it.

'Emily?'

'Say something useful. Say something I want to hear.'

'You just made a discovery. You've just worked out what those people were really killed with. Not just "cord". The same thing we found here. US military webbing. Maybe he brought it with him. Maybe he acquired it here. Either way, we know. Why else?'

She took her head out of her hands and smiled brightly at him. 'Christ, you're right too. It's the dog that didn't bark.'

Costa looked baffled.

'Another time, Nic. Now what do we do?'

The last thing she wanted, he thought. 'We leave this till the morning. We continue this conversation with other people around.'

'Is that what you want?' At least she didn't argue. There weren't many options open to them.

'You mean, am I scared?' he asked.

'Kind of.'

'No.'

'Don't you ever get scared?'

He looked around the living room. It felt good with another person there. The fires were doing their job at last. The place finally seemed warm, human.

'Not here,' he answered. 'Not now. But I have to tell you, another fifteen minutes and I fall fast asleep, Agent Deacon. You'd better have something else to amaze me.'

'Oh I have,' she said with a grin, and went back to stabbing the keys of the machine.

Peroni had never done well on the weapons range, never paid much attention to the smartass firearms monkeys who thought you could run the world through the sights of a gun. He was a vice cop, top rank for years. He didn't mind front-line work. When he was a senior officer he'd made damn sure he didn't let his men take risks he'd never face himself. All the same, vice was nothing like this. It was pimps and hookers, turf wars and stupid, cheated johns. Black and white in the corners sometimes, but more often a difficult, indeterminate shade of grey. Not something shapeless moving through the dark, unknown, unseen, looking to kill for no real reason at all.

He did what seemed natural, put his big arms out and covered the girl with his body. A futile gesture, one designed more for reassurance than anything else. The huge door opposite was completely shut. The side exit was doubtless locked too. This man made no mistakes. They couldn't flee. They couldn't do much but wait and face whatever lay out there.

And think . . .

Even a stupid old vice cop could do that.

'What do you want?' he yelled into the darkness.

Someone moved, feet tapping on the ancient stone floor, a menacing presence shifting around the echoing interior like a ghost. He could be anywhere. The sound of his shoes on the hard floor bounced around the upturned stone eyelid, came at them from every direction.

'*What do you want?*' Peroni yelled again.

The footsteps stopped. The hall was silent except for the faint rumble of a lone car making it through the night in the distant world beyond.

'What's mine.'

It was an American voice. Flat, middle-aged, monotonous. A voice that sounded as if most of the life had been squeezed out of it somewhere along the line. Peroni wondered if he could guess where it came from. If he could just point the service pistol in that direction, loose off a few shots and hope something – good luck, God, the remnants of a benevolent shade still lurking here – would send one piece of metal spinning in the right direction.

But he didn't believe in God or ghosts. You had to make your own way.

Peroni turned, still doing his best to cover the kid behind him, peered into her face and held out his hand. She was clutching the wallet to her, thin fingers tight on the leather, as if it were the most precious thing in the world.

'Laila,' he whispered. 'Please . . .'

Stealing's a bad thing, he wanted to say. Stealing gets you into big trouble, marks you out for life, as visibly as if you were wearing a sign round your neck saying 'evil'. Or a magical symbol carved out of your back.

That was why cops like him spent their working days chasing the little thieves, looking for those telltale marks. It was too hard trying to catch the big, smart guys, the ones who carried scalpels and didn't baulk at using them. And as for the really big fish, well they just got immunity from their paid politicians anyway. None of which helped a dumb cop on the street work out the difference between what was truly good and bad one little bit.

She passed it over to him without a word, eyes glittering, shiny, full of fear.

'Here!' Peroni bellowed into the darkness and sent the wallet spinning out into the heart of the building, hard enough, he hoped, to take it into the shade on the other side where their unseen thug could collect it, say a quick thank you, then disappear into the night leaving everyone safe and sound.

Instead the thing fell with a gentle thud slap bang in the middle of the tiny mound of snow building beneath the oculus, and sat there under the silver light like a beacon, like a bright, shiny trap.

'I didn't mean to do that,' Peroni said, half to himself, half to the figure in the dark. 'I'm not playing any tricks here, friend. Just take the damn wallet and go, will you?'

The gun felt heavy in his hand. Laila was beginning to squirm behind him. If there'd been an easy and obvious exit he'd have sent her flying towards it, screaming at her to get the hell out of this makeshift tomb in the centre of a slumbering, snow-covered city. Instead, all he could think of was how to hide her from whatever was approaching, keep her frail body protected behind his.

And even that wasn't enough. When it came, straight out of the darkness, it came as a storm of pure physical force, furious, relentless. The man was punching and kicking and screaming, pistol-whipping Peroni's skull with what felt like a hammer. The gun flew out of Peroni's hand, clattering across the stonework, spinning into the shadows. He tried to dodge, to find some way of shifting his frame away from the sudden, vicious onslaught of violence, but it was impossible. His hands left Laila and tried to cover his face. He felt his breath flee from his lungs, his mind start to wander off into another place.

. . . death, they called it, somewhere this man knew very well indeed. Somewhere he liked to visit often, in the company of others.

'Just let her go,' Peroni mumbled, aware that the iron taste of his own blood was feeding into his mouth as he spoke, bowing his head now, knowing what was to come. 'What can a kid do to you?'

He saw the butt of the pistol now, racing down towards him through the dark, heard what the figure at the other end of that powerful, sweeping arm was saying, over and over again.

Busy, busy, busy, busy.

He was a busy man, Peroni thought. That was about all they knew of him. Then even that was gone once the pistol butt connected, gone into an agonizing blackness where nothing made sense, not even the words he heard through the rushing bloody haze inside his head.

*

Emily was still thinking about the pattern, the sacred cut. She wanted to get the story straight in her own head first, told in the order she chose.

'This ziggurat is unique, Nic,' she said. 'Read the report. That design is not uncommon, but an entire room, the holiest of holies, was decorated with it throughout. There's nowhere like it in the whole of Iraq. Probably in the world. The place was uncovered back in the 1980s, at which time no one had the money to excavate it properly. It's only now people are starting to see what's really there. The irony is the Romans probably knew about this kind of architecture all along. They borrowed from it for buildings like the Pantheon. The resemblance can't be coincidence. Hell, it even had an oculus. Hadrian could have copied the whole damn thing.'

It was hard to argue with that conclusion.

'So what do you think happened?' he asked.

'Let's start with some facts. He knew my dad. They were in the ziggurat together. My dad and those other people came out. Kaspar didn't. Work it out.'

It wasn't hard.

'Laura Lee?' he asked again.

'I guess she was the woman who died in the Pantheon. It's not her real name. God knows what that is. I tried to look at the files on her this afternoon. All gone. Buried so deep they might as well not exist. Why would anyone want to do that?'

The answer was always the same. 'Because something went wrong.'

'Exactly. Listen to the case I'm making here. *None of this is random. It never has been.* He's had thirteen years in some stinking Iraqi pit to think about this. So, come this year, Iraq's free. He doesn't walk up to the nearest American base and say, "Hey, take me home." For some reason he doesn't want to come in from the cold. He wants to get even. So he begins on the line that led to my dad.'

There was something missing. She knew it too.

'Why?' he asked. 'If you were in jail that long, why'd you want to prolong the pain?'

'I don't have the answer to that yet. Maybe Joel Leapman does, but he isn't telling. You heard him. Publicly he's just sticking to the line that Kaspar's crazy. But listen to the tone of some of their messages. You said it yourself. They're offering him a lifeline. This sounds stupid, but I think in some way they still regard him as a hero. It's the only thing that makes sense. Otherwise, why have an FBI unit and God knows who else here? Why not just leave it to you people to clean up all the crap?'

'He doesn't trust Leapman,' Costa suggested. 'Or anyone.'

'I know. Maybe he really is just plain crazy. Until we get the chance to ask him there's no way of telling. Hell, if I'd known this last night I *would* have asked. Perhaps that's all it needs. You just have to leech the wound.'

Costa didn't like the idea one bit. 'I don't think that's your job.'

'You could be right,' she agreed hesitantly. 'But someone's got to do it. Bill Kaspar has some entire messy chapter of history running round and around in his head, and until we understand that we get nowhere. I went back over the names of his victims again this afternoon. Most of them just don't exist, but those that do have some interesting details. The second guy was an executive with a private oil-distribution service. He'd worked in Iraq before the war. One of the women had been attached to the US embassy in Tehran for a while, civilian contract supposedly. It's obvious, isn't it? They're just the kind of people who could be involved in this kind of covert activity. One way or another they got out and he didn't. Now he's back and he's been killing his old comrades. One by one. And somehow I don't think he's done.'

The doubt must have been obvious in Nic's face.

'You have a problem with that?' she asked.

'Yes. Why the hell did Laura Lee or whoever she was come here in the first place? Surely she must have known. And how did he track down all these people?'

'He's a professional, remember? It's what he does. You've got to see him close up to understand that, Nic. He must have been something. Maybe that's what's eating him up too. Knowing he failed.'

There was still a gap somewhere. 'It doesn't answer the question about her. If she knew, why would she put herself in danger?'

'I can give you one simple reason,' Emily replied with a grim certainty. 'She didn't have a choice. She's still in the service. Leapman made her come to Rome, just as he made me. We were both bait. She got unlucky. Kaspar took her from straight under Leapman's nose, snatched her out of his grip and carved her up like that. Do you wonder Leapman's running around like a bear with a sore head? Imagine what his boss is saying right now.'

Costa could. Men like Leapman attracted their own kind. Someone kicked down on him. He kicked down in return.

'Are you with me so far?' she asked.

'I think so. But what do you want me to do?'

'You've done it. I wanted you to listen. I was sort of half-hoping you'd tell me I was crazy.'

'You are crazy. Just not about this in all probability.'

'Thank you, Mr Costa,' she said primly, then closed her eyes and gently let her head slip down onto the back of the sofa. 'Jesus, I feel as if I could sleep for a million years. And, maybe, when I wake up all of this could be gone, just a bad dream, the kind you get from eating the wrong cheese.'

She was close enough for him to smell her hair. A part of him wanted to reach out and touch a small, golden strand, know what it felt like under his fingers.

'I don't know what the hell to do,' she said in a quiet, half-scared voice. 'Aside from keep away from cheese.'

He looked at the wine bottle. It was just about gone and on empty stomachs.

'I'll skip the cheese,' he said, 'but I am going to find us something to eat. Then . . .'

It was just a glance, he told himself. Just an expression in her eyes.

'. . . we sleep on it.'

She'd moved against him, just enough for him to feel her shoulder against his. He hadn't meant it that way. Not consciously.

The blue eyes fixed him. Nic Costa felt lost in them. She looked grateful. Sharing the burden of doubts had helped her, brought the two of them closer. A brief smile flickered on her face. She was very close. On another occasion, under different circumstances . . .

He stirred uncomfortably on the sofa, looking for something to divert the way the night was moving.

'So what the hell is the Scarlet Beast then?' he asked.

It worked. There was a flash of delight on her face, an expression he was beginning to recognize, beginning to look forward to. She knew something about this too and couldn't wait to tell him.

'First,' she said, pushing aside the bottle, 'no more wine. We need all the concentration we've got. And food, Mr Costa. This odd bachelor pad does run to food and water doesn't it?'

'I'll see what I can do.'

'Good. There's just one more secret. And then –' Emily Deacon made a conscious effort to get the words right – 'I'm through.'

Laila was half-yelling, half pleading, in another language, a musical one quite foreign to him, though he knew somehow what it was. Her own: Kurdish. He'd heard enough of the street immigrants speaking it to be familiar with the odd cadences, half Western, half oriental.

And in his hurting, confused head, Peroni knew what she was saying too.

Please, please, please.

She was a thin, dark figure dancing on her light, light feet in this shadowy hall, begging for her life from an unseen stranger while the big, burly cop who was supposed to be keeping her safe curled into a pained ball on the stone floor like a damaged child.

Please, please, please.

He tried to stand and the hammer blow of the pistol

came down again, dashing him to the stones under a flurry of obscenities.

Laila screamed, louder this time, a noise that might even filter out into the night air through the open eye of the oculus.

No, no, no, no, no.

Then it came to him, with a sudden grim certainty that made him feel more miserable than ever. She wasn't arguing for her life. She was begging for his. Trying to bargain with this unseen monster to keep away the hurt and that final act of silence.

'Don't waste your breath, Laila,' he spluttered through bloody lips. 'Run. Let this jerk have his fun.'

Then the world was moving. A strong, firm hand gripped him by the collar of his coat, pushed him hard against the wall, into a faint stream of moonlight falling through the oculus.

A powerful guy, Gianni Peroni thought. That was a big load he was throwing around like a sack of potatoes. A big . . .

Peroni found himself staring into a face that surprised him. It belonged to a man about his own age, clean-shaven, handsome in a sharp-featured way, keenly alert, devoid of emotion. Not the kind of face you expected of a killer, more an academic or a doctor. He was wearing glasses. Maybe it was the odd silver light of the moon, but his skin seemed to have an unnatural tinge to it. Something in his eyes, the engaged, angular line of his mouth, told Peroni it was worth listening just then. The gun pointing straight at his temple helped too.

'Let her go,' Peroni said once more.

The unfeeling, incisive eyes kept boring into him. 'What's it to you? A Kurd?'

'A kid's a kid,' Peroni answered, tasting the warm trickle in his mouth again.

He didn't say anything. Peroni had no idea whether he was going forward with this or just rushing himself into an early grave. The powerful hands grabbed him again, pushed him hard against the wall.

'Don't struggle,' the man said. 'It just hurts more.'

Then he dangled something familiar in front of Peroni's face as it mushed up against the stonework: a couple of pairs of plastic handcuffs, the sort the cops kept for special occasions.

'Yeah, yeah,' Peroni grumbled and shoved his hands out behind him, bunched up the way they did in training, holding his palms together as the cuffs came on, cutting tight into his skin.

'You,' the American said, jabbing a finger at Laila.

She held out her hands in front of her, looking meek and obedient.

He nodded. 'You're a smart little cookie, huh? You want some advice? Quit stealing. It just leads to trouble.'

The plastic went round her slender wrists with rather more care than he'd allowed before. Then he bounced Peroni round again, pulled him tight to the girl, withdrew another cuff from his pocket, looped it to join the two of them together through the wrist restraints, and tied off the join around the narrow iron support for the altar rail. They couldn't move a metre. Just to ram home the point, the American reached into Peroni's pocket, took out his phone, dropped it on the floor and stomped the thing into pieces.

'I worked with Kurds once,' he said sourly. 'They'd call you brother, they'd give you anything, they'd die for you. Then one night they'd see you'd got money in your baggage, come in and slit your throat, walk out and spend it on a new VCR. You know why?'

Peroni sighed. 'I'm a cop, mister. I walk these streets. I do my best.' It was worth saying anyway. 'I try to put people like you in jail if I can.'

It was as if the other man didn't even hear that last part. 'I'll tell you why. Because we taught them how. You think about that the next time she steals something.'

'Yeah,' Peroni replied sourly, without even thinking. 'Nobody's really responsible for anything these days, are they?'

He wondered if he was going to throw up. Or faint. Or both, possibly in the wrong order. 'I guess,' he added, 'it wasn't really you who carved that woman up in here the other night. Just someone else wearing the same skin.'

The gun came down. 'You know you could just be right.'

The American drew out a small torch and shone the beam briefly in Peroni's face. Then he pulled out the wallet, opened it up and took out a couple of old, battered photographs, held them beneath the beam. Two bunches of people, out in the desert somewhere. They were wearing military fatigues and sunglasses, looking as pleased as punch, posing against a couple of those huge jeep things the Americans loved.

He was in the first photo. Younger, happy, in control. The boss maybe, posing with his team, eight or so men and women, smiling at the camera, lords of their little universe.

'I got all of them inside me,' the American murmured. 'Every one of them. I watched them die and I couldn't do a damn thing because we were just walking straight into some stupid little turkey shoot, not knowing what was waiting there for us.'

'I guess that picture must be important to you, huh,' Peroni said.

'You could say that.'

He pushed the other photo to the front. A different set of people but the same kind of crowd. One of them familiar, Peroni realized. Emily Deacon's dad, looking a whole lot younger and happier than he had in that formal shot from a few months ago that they'd seen in the embassy after she walked out. And a couple of women too. One who just might have been the corpse in this same building two nights before.

The man's mouth came close to Peroni's face. 'Ain't they just the pretty ones?'

The grey, stony face didn't flicker, but something was going on. The man was thinking. He had the time too. There was nothing Gianni Peroni could do that would shape the flow of events just then.

'So you're just a minion?' the American asked. 'A local cop? Those guys from the embassy told you nothing?'

'Yeah, a minion. I just know what they think I need to know.'

Peroni gazed into the icy eyes, wondering what, if anything, could move this man. 'That there's a lunatic out there, carving some pattern out of people's backs, for no reason at all. And he sure loves US military webbing too.'

That struck a nerve somewhere. The guy was laughing. Not the cold, dry laughter Peroni had heard in the dark. This was more human somehow, more scary because it came from a place deep inside him, and it was the kind of laughter that could just go anywhere, from joy to despair in a heartbeat.

'No reason?' he asked, and pushed the gun back into Gianni Peroni's face. 'You believe that?'

Peroni looked down at the dead grey metal barrel and tried to tick off the few remaining options in his hurting head.

'Not really,' he murmured.

He'd found some pasta and a jar of tomato sauce. They sat on the sofa together in front of the empty plates, aware of the clock ticking towards midnight, dog tired. Nic Costa wasn't even sure he wanted any more questions answered. He wasn't sure what he wanted at all.

Emily leaned back in the soft cushions, closed her eyes and asked, 'Do you have a bible?'

He blinked, wide awake all of a sudden. 'Excuse me?'

'A bible. This is a good Italian household, isn't it?'

So many things to explain. So many preconceptions. 'Yes, but that doesn't mean I have a bible. I wouldn't dare bring one through the door. I'd have my old man's ghost haunting me forever. I told you. He was a Communist. Do you really need one?'

She thought about it, retrieved the notebook, turned it on and started looking for something.

'I can't do this from memory. The Deacons aren't

exactly regular churchgoers either. But when I was in training I spent three months researching a bunch of religious fanatics on the Net. Nice people. All white. All armed to the teeth. All as crazy as they come. There is a reason here. Bear with me.'

He leaned over, close to her shoulder and watched the skilful way she worked the Web. After a brief search Emily brought up a page from some bizarre religious site, one covered in woodcut engravings of mythical beasts next to a comic-book colour illustration of a naked woman writhing on a red, many-headed dragon.

'This is just one of their places. You can read about every last damn conspiracy under the sun here. How the Jews run everything. Except for the stuff that's run by the Catholics. While both of them are really under the thumb of the Illuminati. And you know what they keep going back to for inspiration?'

'Ordinarily I'd suggest "drugs and drink", but I rather imagine . . .'

'If only they would, Nic. Parts of Montana would be *so* much improved. They go to Revelation. The last book of the New Testament. Heard of it?'

Costa opened his hands in a gesture of despair.

'You remember,' she continued, 'that Kaspar mentions "the Scarlet Beast" in that original memo from 1990. Leapman, or whoever, is taunting him with the same phrase now. So it's important. The only reference I can find anywhere is in here. I remember it because these fundamentalist guys just can't get it out of their heads. It's meant to explain everything. Listen . . .'

She began reading from the screen. '"So he carried me away in the spirit into the wilderness: and I saw a woman sit upon a scarlet coloured beast, full of names of blasphemy, having seven heads and ten horns."'

Costa's head reeled. 'This is a little rich for me right now.'

'Stay with me. It gets weirder. A couple of sentences later. "And here is the mind which hath wisdom. The seven heads are seven mountains, on which the woman sitteth." Seven mountains, Nic.'

His mind was a blank. This was so far from his normal realm of experience.

'Here's a clue,' she said. 'Think of it as seven hills instead. And another clue. The image of a woman was often used as a cipher meaning "church".'

A small burst of insight defeated the exhaustion. There was only one way to interpret that, surely. 'You mean the Scarlet Beast is Rome?'

She nodded. 'Quite. You have to remember. I read that as someone who'd *lived* in Rome. So I just had to go back and find out what the hell was really going on. Turns out it's simple. These guys are just doing what lunatics have done forever. Rewriting history the way it suits them. Revelation was written at a time when Christianity was being torn apart by oppression from Domitian or whoever. They really did face their own particular apocalypse, but it wasn't a supernatural one. It was real and it came from Rome. Because they were under such threat, they had to refer to it in code. Later, people just started to like the code *because* it's a code. When the Church split off into factions the same message that was supposed to encourage solidarity among Christians was used to make the case against Catholicism. That the pope's just the new Roman emperor, the Antichrist or something. You wouldn't believe some of the stuff you can find out there.'

More blind alleys, more complexity. Costa found himself drifting off. 'So Kaspar's a fanatic?'

'I doubt it.' She was on a roll. There was no stopping her until this particular thread was through. 'This is someone playing a game. You need codenames for projects like this. So they compete to come up with the craziest ones. It started all those years ago when the Babylon Sisters got together. Maybe Kaspar thought of all this terminology. He could have been mocking his own background. He doesn't sound like a city guy. Maybe he comes from some place out in the boondocks where this kind of stuff isn't uncommon. It was appropriate on another front too. Rome was where they met up to begin the mission. Here's another chunk of Revelation. Same chapter. "And upon her forehead was a name written, Mystery, Babylon the great, the mother of harlots and abominations of the earth." You see?'

'Sort of,' he lied.

'It's a joke within a joke. They have to use fake names and IDs. It's that kind of job. Why not have some fun along the way? These guys were just hamming it up among each other. Scarlet Beast. Babylon Sisters. Throw in some backwoods fundamentalism, mix it in with a bunch of old jazz-rockers called Steely Dan . . .'

'Who?' He was wondering how much longer his head could contain all this.

'A band. A very good one, actually. One all these people got off on, I suspect. At least, my dad did. I remember him playing their records when his buddies came round and the beer started to flow. Just bear with me, Nic. These people were having fun, playing spooks, everything NTK like he says.'

'NTK?'

'"Need to know." They're the rules you play when stuff is so secret you don't tell anyone anything – your real name even – unless you absolutely have to. It's a kind of game and my dad used to love games. He was always coming up with crazy ideas.'

She'd been racing ahead until that memory, which made a little of the brightness go out of her eyes.

'At least, he was back then. They were just playing with words. He did it all the time. These guys are still doing it. Your boss asked Leapman. How did we know he'd come to Rome? Remember his answer?'

Costa did. The FBI man flatly refused to deal with the question.

'I remember.' He considered what he'd seen on the screen. 'He couldn't say it, could he?'

She followed him all the way, keying up the message again. 'Kaspar came to Rome because he got invited.'

Costa read it out loud. '"Let's get together again back in the old places folks. Reunion time for the class of '91. Just one spare place at the table. You coming or not?" Which translates to "Come to Rome, we're waiting for you."'

Emily punched his arm lightly. 'See! You can get there.'

'Thanks.'

There was more to the argument, though, and he was surprised she hadn't seen it.

'This all begs a big question.'

She gazed at him, amused, bright and attractive

again. 'I thought it begged several, actually. A couple of dozen right off the top of my head.'

Suddenly there was an expression of surprise on her face, as if she'd seen something unexpected.

'Nic. For a moment then you stopped staring at me as if I'm the cleverest kid in the class. I don't like that. I *am* the cleverest kid in the class. Aren't I?'

'Of course you are, Little Em.'

'Don't call me that,' she said coldly, drawing back from him. 'Don't ever call me that.'

'I'm sorry. It was stupid of me.'

'Yes . . .' It was almost a pout she was making now. She was young and old in the same body. Costa wanted to laugh. More than that, though, he wanted to kiss her. After making the point.

He reached over and messed with the computer, got to the right page.

'What are you doing?' she asked nervously.

'Looking for something. Here: "Honor his memory."'

'I just said that, Nic. Are you sleep-talking on me?'

'And here. In the original memo: "The Scarlet Beast was a generous Beast."'

She blinked. 'So?'

'You're right about the place, Emily. I don't doubt it. But listen to the words. It's more than that, too.'

He read the two sentences out again. She listened carefully. Costa watched her lively intelligent eyes, saw them glitter when she caught the point.

'Christ,' she murmured. 'How could I have been that stupid?'

'It's a riddle. It's meant to be obscure. Besides, there's no saying my interpretation's the right one.'

She waved away his doubts. ‘Of course it is. I was just reading into it what I wanted to see. This is a place *and* a person, isn’t it? The Scarlet Beast’s the paymaster. The man even Kaspar was ultimately beholden to.’

‘I think so.’

The idea stirred so many thoughts in her head. ‘Is he the bad guy then?’ she asked. ‘Does Kaspar blame him for this? He thinks he was betrayed somehow?’

Costa threw up his hands in desperation. ‘It’s just guesswork.’

‘Then who the hell was he? If it wasn’t Kaspar?’

Costa searched for the memo on the computer, found the sentence, highlighted it with the cursor.

‘It’s just a guess. That’s all.’

They looked at the sentence from the document: *Let it be known that I, William F. Kaspar, the Lizard King, the Holy Owl, Grand Master of the Universe, etcetera, etcetera, shall be attending the court of the Scarlet Beast presently.*

She screwed up her face in bewilderment. ‘Someone in Rome? Does that make sense?’

‘What was that you said about “need to know”?’

‘OK. OK. Point taken. Distance *does* makes sense. So maybe even Bill Kaspar doesn’t know who’s really in charge. Maybe he’s guessing right now . . .’

Emily was thinking hard. She looked at him with scared eyes. They both knew where this was going.

‘Or maybe he does,’ Costa said quietly. He scrolled through some of the sentences in the original memo, pointing them out.

The Scarlet Beast – where do they get these names, Danboy? This one of yours or what? . . . We possess a God-given duty to deliver and it is a mighty relief to old Bill K.

this faceless bastard has volunteered you already. Though I cannot help but wonder, dear friend, whether you didn't understand that all along. NTK, huh?

'No, no, no, no, no!' she said with conviction. 'My dad was lots of things but he wasn't a traitor. That just isn't a possibility.'

'Kaspar could be wrong,' Costa suggested without much enthusiasm.

'So what are you saying?' she asked abruptly. 'Kaspar thought my dad was taking part in his own escapade? Funding it and playing along too?'

'Can you rule that out?'

She shook her head. 'I don't know.' Emily was going to stick up for her old man, but not in face of the facts. 'Theoretically I guess so. The way these operations were funded in the past was pretty secretive. Someone just dropped a bag of money out of nowhere and let the team get on with it. You had to have someone running finance, logistics. Dad was big time here in Rome. But . . .'

She leaned back on the sofa and, for a full minute, covered her face with her hands. When she took her fingers away from her cheeks there were tearstains there and plain fury in her eyes.

'I still don't get it. I'm awful at this crap. I can't believe my dad was too, and that's not just family talking. He was so damned organized, Nic. If you knew him you'd know he couldn't just screw it all up in the desert, get away with his own hide then leave that poor bastard to go crazy in some Iraqi cell putting one and one together all the time over the years, working out who to blame. He was a good man. He wouldn't . . .'

She couldn't go on. Costa wondered whether he

could bring himself to say it, then realized he'd be selling her short if he didn't.

'They thought Kaspar was a good man at the time, Emily. Now look . . . You said yourself. Something changed.'

'No,' she insisted. 'You didn't know him. Maybe you can believe that's a possible answer. But listen to me, it isn't. Not for one moment.'

'I can't think straight this late,' he said. 'Let's open this out a little in the morning.'

Her eyes scanned his face, searching for the doubts and prevarication. 'What do you mean by that? You call your boss, I call mine? We tell them what we think then walk away and hope it'll turn out right?'

He shook his head. 'No. I don't think it's that simple. Also, I don't walk away from things, not until they're done. It's a family fault.'

She let out a low, spontaneous burst of laughter. 'You are so not the Roman cop I thought I'd meet.'

'I'll take that as a compliment.'

'It's meant that way.'

'Good. And you . . .' He had to say this because it was true. 'It's odd. You don't know it but you could pass for Italian. Most of the time anyway. When you're not around Agent Leapman. I never did believe that line about people spitting at you on buses.'

'It happened once,' she confessed with a shrug. 'People like preconceptions. They're compartments you can use so that everyone feels safe and comfortable for a while. They mean you don't have to think too hard.'

'One more reason to avoid them.'

'Well, I'm certainly getting lots of preconceptions shaken straight out of me right now,' she said, smiling, looking around the old, airy room, with its dusty corners and faded paintings. 'This is a beautiful place. If I lived here I don't think I'd ever go beyond that front gate. You could just stay here and never get touched by the crap.'

'Or anything,' Costa said quietly. 'I've been there.'

'Really.' Americans had an astonishing, unnerving frankness sometimes. She'd turned to stare straight into his face, trying to work out what to make of that last statement. 'I guess we all get there sometime. When I was a kid I thought we'd never leave Rome, you know. It was how life was supposed to be. Safe. Happy. Secure from all those big, black surprises you never learn about till you're older.'

'You'd rather not know about them?'

'No.' Her smile dropped. 'But I can try to understand why it all fell apart. I can . . . Oh shit.'

Her face was down in her hands again. He wondered if she were crying. But it was exhaustion probably, nothing more.

Emily Deacon slowly rolled herself sideways, over towards his shoulder, let her head fall softly onto him, didn't move as his fingers took on a life of their own, reaching automatically for her long, soft hair.

Eyes closed, in the shy way strangers use when they kiss for the first time, he tasted her damp, supple mouth, felt her lips close on his, slowly working, until that moment of self-realization came and they both broke off, wondering, embarrassed.

She kept her head on his shoulder. He stared at the dying embers of the fire.

'I'm making a hell of a mess of this professional

relationship, Mr Costa,' Emily Deacon murmured into his ear. 'Are you OK with that?'

He closed his eyes and wished to God he didn't feel so exhausted. 'I'll work on it.'

She brushed his cheek briefly with her lips once more then said, 'Give me a moment.'

Nic Costa watched her walk upstairs to the bathroom and wished he wasn't so gauche with women. He'd no idea what the hell she expected of him next. To follow her into one of the big, airy bedrooms? To wait so they could talk some more, not that he felt there were many words left in him after this long, long day?

He hadn't planned any of this. He hadn't wanted it, not now, in the middle of a sprawling black case that involved her more than was safe. Sometimes life just refused to do what it was told. Sometimes . . .

'What's his name? This guy from the embassy who tells you nothing?'

Peroni's head was wandering. The feeling of nausea wouldn't go away. Still, this wasn't a time to lose focus. He glowered at the gun, not saying a word. There was a point to be made here, a kind of relationship to be established.

'Joel Leapman,' he said, once the guy got the message and lowered the barrel. 'You know him?'

The man grimaced. 'If he's in the business I think names don't mean a lot. Besides, I've been away for a while. What does he say he is? CIA? FBI? Something else?'

'Why ask me?'

The barrel of the weapon touched Peroni's cheek. 'Because you're here and you're not dumb either.'

'He *says* he's FBI. He's got people with him who are FBI. One, anyway. You met her. Last night.'

'Yeah. I know.'

'Glad you didn't hurt her, by the way. She's a nice kid.'

He was thinking. Peroni judged it best to let him reach some decisions on his own.

'No accounting for breeding sometimes,' the American said in the end. 'I need someone to run a message. That makes you a lucky man.'

Peroni tried to offer up an ironic smile. 'You could have fooled me. Right now I feel like something just drove over my head.'

'You'll live. You –' he waved the gun at Laila – 'and the thieving little kid. I give you a couple of hours to figure a way out. Don't make it sooner. I might still be around. You can find that idiot who was supposed to be in charge round the corner, peeing himself, I guess. Tell him he's damn lucky. When you're paid to look after a place like this . . .'

He cast his sharp eyes around the interior of the Pantheon.

'. . . you'd best do it properly.'

'And the message?' Peroni mumbled.

The smart, deadpan face came up to his. 'I was coming to that. Tell this Leapman guy I'm running out of patience. I'm bored looking. This time round he delivers. Or the rules change.'

'Delivers what?' Peroni wondered.

He got a grunt of impatience in return. 'He knows.'

'You're *sure*?'

That cold, dry laugh again. 'Yeah. But just in case, you tell him this. I talked to Dan Deacon before he died. He planted some doubts. I want to know if I'm done.'

It was the last thing Peroni was expecting to hear. 'Listen to me,' he said. 'You're done. Is that good enough?'

'*Don't fuck with me!*' The American went from placid to furious in point one of a second. The gun was waving around crazily again.

'OK,' Peroni replied quietly.

'I want proof. Tell them that.'

This was important. 'Done.'

The gun came back to his cheek again. Peroni lifted his neck to get away from the cold, oily metal.

'I hope so,' the American murmured. 'Because if he's not listening it all gets really bad around here. Tell him I'll give him a little present real soon just as a reminder.'

'*Really* bad?' Peroni heard himself saying, without consciously forming the thought, watching the American walk away towards the side office, out towards the night, not listening any more, which was a shame.

Peroni believed him. Every single word. This man had rules. He could have killed them both. Maybe somewhere else, in different circumstances, when the pieces of the puzzle happened to fit, he would have done too. He just needed the right words, written on a piece of paper, all neat and geometrical, lined up in the magical order he sought.

That was all any of them had to do. Find the pattern, show him the runes, and then the city could quit waking up each morning wondering whether there'd be blood swimming around the floor somewhere, and that ancient tattoo cut straight out of someone's back.

Peroni waited till he heard the door close on the outside. Then he did his best to push back the feeling of nausea and the pain in his head, tried to concentrate, to think straight.

'Gianni?' the girl whispered, holding herself close to him, shivering with the growing cold. 'What do we do?'

'We wait, Laila,' he said, with as much assurance and certainty he could muster. 'We wait a while. Just like the man said. Then we get out of these things and go somewhere nice and warm and comfortable. My friend's place maybe. It's not far away. Let's sit down, huh?'

He found his way to the floor, the girl following him. Peroni closed his eyes and wondered how badly he was hurt, wondered too at the American's closing words. Maybe the body in the car was just a taster of what was to come: random, shocking acts, designed to persuade Leapman to do the right thing. Maybe he had something nastier in store overnight just to hammer home the message.

'Gianni,' the girl whispered.

'Just give it a minute,' he groaned. His head was spinning. His face hurt like hell.

Then something intervened, some semblance of sleep.

When he came to, jogged by a push from the kid, the place was different, noticeably colder and darker too. A stream of snow was still circling down through the oculus. Laila had her head down at their wrists, working at something.

'How long was I out?' he asked.

'Long time,' she said and looked up at him, half smiling. 'Doesn't matter now.'

Her mouth and her right wrist were covered in blood. Peroni saw in an instant what she'd done: spent all the time he was unconscious biting and wriggling at the plastic of her cuffs, working the flexible material over and over until she found a way through.

She stood there, half wondering whether just to flee again. That was her natural instinct.

'That's good,' Peroni said confidently, as if he hadn't a clue what she was thinking. 'If you reach into my jacket pocket,' he continued, 'you should find a pen-knife there. It's in a little compartment with a zip on it. You should be able to get at it now.'

There was a moment of hesitation, then her slim hand angled its way into his coat, an easy, familiar motion, and came out, so quickly, with the knife. And his wallet.

'Laila.'

The kid was crying. Real tears, streaming down her cheeks, more than he'd seen when the two of them faced the man, when they both knew they were so close to losing their lives.

'Not now,' he pleaded. 'I need you to help me. I need *you*.'

Then she said something that made his blood run cold. Something straight from the man, said it with the same fervour, the same darting eyes looking everywhere.

'Busy, busy, busy, busy . . .'

A part of him wanted to think you could heal a damaged child with nothing but love and affection and honesty. But Teresa was surely right. It went deeper than that. Laila suffered from an illness, a malady as real as a fever, just more damaging since it lurked inside her, unseen, unfathomable, misinterpreted by a cold, suspicious world.

Peroni turned and raised his painful wrists.

'Get busy with these, huh?' he murmured.

'Then?' she asked.

'Then we get you something to eat. And a comfortable bed. Your uncle Gianni's got work to do. You've saved his skin tonight, you know.'

'I did?' she asked, only half believing him.

'Sure you did.'

He forced his wrists round towards her.

'You're not going to leave me here like this, are you?'

She thought about it, but not for long. Then she opened the knife and started to cut at the plastic.

Ten minutes later Peroni had freed the terrified caretaker, who was locked inside a portable office by the side of the building.

After that he called Leo Falcone.

Upstairs, in the rustic, faded bathroom, Emily Deacon stood before the flaking mirror and peered at herself, trying to find answers for questions she couldn't quite start to frame.

She was never good at relationships and she knew it. Getting close to someone was like a drug. It solved so many problems but it had side effects too. Commitment left the window open for pain to blow in like poison on the breeze. It made the inevitable parting even harder, turned friends into enemies. She'd felt this way, seen this attitude blight her tentative, stumbling efforts at building a relationship, ever since she was a kid.

Ever since Rome.

When her dad came back from his turn with the Babylon Sisters, playing out some bloody vaudeville act deep in the desert in Iraq, damaging himself irreparably for reasons that still eluded her but were now getting closer.

Why him? Why not someone else? Was he really Bill Kaspar's boss pretending to be his best buddy? And, if so, why did Kaspar feel justified in coming back to snuff out his life inside a beautiful wooden temple in a park in Beijing thirteen years later, carving into his back a shape from an ancient temple outside Babylon? Was he that desperate for revenge?

She looked at herself in the mirror and said, 'Except he didn't stop.'

If she was right, every last person who'd escaped Iraq was now dead. So why was Kaspar still killing? What would bring him to a halt?

The answer lay in his obsession. It was incomplete, somehow, and maybe he didn't understand why himself. There were attractions in the belief, however crazy, that you could bring order to a life by placing it in the middle of an intricately symmetrical pattern of shapes and ideas. But it was the kind of process that belonged to the lost, the detached, the fated. It was, ultimately, the easy way out, derogating responsibility to an inanimate, dead simulacrum of perfection, a fake paradise buried inside a tangled whorl of lines and curves. In the real world it was the untidiness, the lack of completeness, the unpredictability of everyday life that made each day human. That random, unforeseeable force lay at the back of a relationship too. If the magnetism of personal attraction could be rationalized, it couldn't, she knew, exist.

Was that why she'd struggled to keep a man until now? Her insistence for some kind of reason, some element of proof? The face that stared back at her had no answers. What she saw was just another part of the riddle. She was still working to shrug off the child Emily, whose earliest memories lay in that different, early Rome, where she'd spent the first ten years of her life thinking the world was a bright, colourful heaven, a place of kindness, grace and beauty where the hard decisions always belonged to someone else.

Innocence, ignorance, two sides of the same coin.

'You've got to grow up sometime,' she said to herself. That was why she'd bitten Nic's head off when he called her 'Little Em'. A part of her recognized how apposite it still was.

She washed her face, cleaned her teeth, sat down on the toilet seat and held her head in her hands, trying to find a strand of logic that would allow her to go forward.

There was still a missing piece and she knew her head couldn't cope with trying to locate it. She was too damn tired.

She got up, checked her face and hair once more in the mirror, wondered what she really saw there: a scared adolescent, a woman trying to identify herself among all the noise of modern life? Or, more likely, someone halfway between the two, a changeling shifting shapes, wondering what she would be in the end.

Emily Deacon was aware that, for the first time in her life, she was about to take the initiative, to tell a man it was time he took her to bed. Even if nothing happened there except the closeness of sleeping next to another human being.

Scared, in the way she felt when she was a kid, embarking on an adventure beyond the bounds of normal life, excited, awake all of a sudden, she went downstairs.

He was asleep on the sofa, spread out, fully dressed. Completely asleep, not moving a muscle except for the faint rise and fall of his chest.

'Nic,' she said softly, so quietly she didn't know herself whether she wanted him to hear.

She closed her eyes and laughed inwardly.

'There's always tomorrow,' she whispered in a voice no louder than a breath.

And there's always a cigarette.

She went to her purse, took out a Marlboro and a lighter, pulled the black jacket around her shoulders and opened the door very quietly, making sure she didn't wake him.

The air was still, the night arctic and exquisitely beautiful. The sky had cleared completely. A too-white moon shone like a miniature cold sun over the rounded, snowy landscape punctuated by the outlines of the tombs on the Appian Way.

She lit the cigarette, took a long drag, watched the smoke curl its way towards the bare writhing muscle of a vine winding its way around a trellis and imagined how beautiful this shaded, grape-laden terrace would be during the summer.

'And I can't even get myself a man,' she murmured, then wished she could laugh out loud.

The voice was cold, American and familiar.

'I wouldn't say that,' it grunted.

A powerful arm came round her neck. A hidden hand forced some kind of cloth into her face, pushing the fabric hard around her nose and mouth. There was the slight sound of glass breaking inside the rag, a smell that made her think of a hospital operating theatre, long, long ago, in the ancient facility on the Lateran where her father took her when she broke her arm trying to make her bike fly like something out of *Power Rangers.*

This won't hurt . . . Steely Dan, where are you now, and what the hell did you do all those years ago? . . . someone said, her dad, a faceless hospital doctor, Kaspar the Unfriendly Ghost, grinning Joel Leapman, Thornton Fielding, all concern and pity, Nic Costa even . . .

Every last one of them said the stupid phrase simultaneously, seeing her feebleness from somewhere beyond her vision, somewhere outside the aching corona of the moon.

This won't hurt one little bit.

SABATO

The weather was changing and not in the way any of them expected. The snow hadn't turned to rain. It had gone away, for a while anyway, leaving the sky to the sun, a sun that was starting to remember how to shed a little warmth on the city. A thaw, perhaps a temporary one, was in progress and a trickle of grey slush and grubby water was beginning to make its way into the gutters as proof. It was still damn cold, though. A bitter, persistent wind was blowing in from the sea, a harsh taint of salt in its blustery folds, warning that the vicious snap of cold had yet to retreat entirely.

Falcone strode along the Via Cavour, thinking. Harder than he'd done in a long time. The previous night, before he got the message about Peroni, he'd made some calls, discreetly posed a few questions that had been bugging him. Now, with a set of considered answers, all legalese, all full of ifs and buts, racing around in his head, he was facing some important decisions. He had fifteen minutes before the meeting he had demanded with Viale, which had been fixed for nine in the SISDE building around the corner. Moretti and Leapman would doubtless come along for the ride at

Viale's invitation. Falcone had yet to decide how to handle himself there. Two of his men had risked their lives the previous day. That gave him the right to throw around a little weight. Peroni's injuries had proved less serious than they looked in the hospital at two that morning, when the doctors had stitched and dabbed at a face that had already taken more than its fair share of punishment. Afterwards Falcone had sat with him, next to Teresa Lupo and the Kurdish girl, and agreed, without hesitation, to his first demand: that Laila be placed temporarily in the care of a social worker Peroni knew who lived at Ostia, that very night. Then the girl got up, kissed Peroni on the side of his cheek that didn't bear a bruise or wound and went off with a plain-clothes female officer, giving the three of them the chance to talk some more, to exchange ideas, and to wonder.

Peroni was looking to him for something. There were limits to being jerked around, even by the grey men. Falcone had spoken to Costa first thing that morning and knew he felt the same way too. The American woman had told Costa a long, interesting and highly speculative narrative that tried to explain what was happening around them now in Rome. Then she'd gone missing, leaving her things in his house. Costa hadn't a clue where.

Falcone had phoned Joel Leapman immediately to report the fact they didn't know where Emily Deacon was. It was the right thing to do. Her car had gone. He also wanted to judge the FBI agent's reactions. Leapman seemed genuinely puzzled. Concerned, even. It was one more weapon Falcone could use.

He'd recognized, too, the worry in Costa's voice that morning. She wasn't a field officer. There were personal reasons why she might step out of line. But there were personal issues everywhere in this case. Peroni and Costa carried them because they – and Falcone – were present when the unfortunate Mauro Sandri fell bleeding in the snow outside the Pantheon three nights before. For most cops that would be bad luck. To them – and Falcone understood this was one reason why he defended the pair constantly – it was a challenge, an outrage, a tear in the fabric of society which demanded correction. This dogged resistance of theirs had led to Falcone trusting them with information and thoughts he was reluctant to share with others on the force. Ineluctably, events over the past eighteen months had made the three of them a team, a worryingly close and private one at times. Costa, in particular, had reminded Falcone why he'd become a cop in the first place: to make things better. Hooked up to Peroni, the pair had shaken Falcone out of his complacency, dared him to throw off the dead lassitude and cynicism that came with two decades in the force. Costa and Peroni asked big and awkward questions about what was right and what was wrong in a world where all the borders seemed to be breaking down. No wonder Viale hated them.

When Falcone turned the corner he saw them, standing together outside the anonymous grey SISDE building next to a Chinese restaurant, an odd couple who looked nothing like plain-clothes cops. Peroni was shuffling backwards and forwards on his big feet, hugging himself in a thick winter coat, scanning the sky, which now bore fresh scratches of white, wispy clouds that could be the presentiment of more snow.

Costa wasn't thinking about the weather. He was

examining the fresh marks on his partner's battered face, looking concerned.

Falcone walked up and peered into Gianni Peroni's face himself. 'I've seen worse. Think of the up side. You weren't that good-looking beforehand.'

'I could sue for that,' Peroni replied. 'I could call you up in front of the board and out you for the bitch of a boss you are.'

'Do that,' Falcone said, almost laughing. 'I'll get there one way or another soon enough.'

'Are you sure you wouldn't rather be at home in bed, Gianni?' Costa asked.

'Don't nanny me, Mr Costa,' Peroni replied curtly. 'Do you think a few cuts and bruises are going to keep me away from all the fun?'

Fun? It wasn't that, not for any of them, Falcone thought. It never had been. Even when Peroni had been an inspector in vice, before the fall, he was a man known for his seriousness.

'The funny thing is,' Falcone observed, 'I've never known anyone get beaten up so often. What's the secret?'

'Working with you,' Peroni responded. 'Until I was bounced down to your team of misfits, I never got beaten up at all. Not once in my adult life.'

Falcone thought about this. 'You want a transfer?'

'You know damn well what I want. I want my old job back. I want position. I want men who drive me around. I want to deal with the admirable world of dope and prostitution because I tell you, Leo – sorry, *sir* – it's much saner than yours.'

'Is that so?' Falcone replied, amused. 'So how are

you now? Did your friendly pathologist tend your wounds well after I left?'

'I'll live,' Peroni said with a smile. 'But I'm getting heartily sick of this weather. And heartily sick of this case too.' He nodded at the sky. 'I know you don't run that crap, which I hate to say doesn't look finished to me. But do you think we can do something with the second?'

Falcone sniffed and looked at Costa. 'One way or another. Emily Deacon. Where is she?'

'I don't know,' Costa said, shaking his head. 'She took the car. But her computer's still in my house, which is odd. I've been calling and calling. Maybe Leapman . . .'

'I asked,' Falcone replied. 'He sounded a little worried for once. You don't imagine, for one moment, that she's gone out and done something stupid, do you?'

'I don't think so,' Costa replied, though he didn't look too sure.

Peroni cast a grizzled glance at Falcone and moaned, 'Families. Leapman should never have brought her in. What kind of an asshole is he?'

'The kind who knows exactly what he's doing,' Falcone said firmly. 'Nic, perhaps it's best if you skip this meeting. It could be a little . . . career damaging I suspect. You've got more ahead of you than us.'

Peroni's jaw dropped. 'What? What the fu . . . ?' He put his hands together, praying. 'Why me, Leo? Why me?'

'Put out a call for her car,' Falcone continued. 'Try some of the obvious places. Did you get me those printouts?'

Costa passed over the manila envelope with the pages Falcone had asked for.

Peroni wasn't looking happy at all. He scowled at the grey SISDE building. 'Career damaging, Leo? I've been there often enough already. And I don't like these spooky people. They're bad company. Let me wet-nurse Nic, here, hold his hand. Or I could go to the Questura and make some calls, clean your desk, press your suits. Anything . . .'

'Or,' Falcone suggested, 'he could drop you off at home and let you get some rest. You're not immortal you know, Peroni. You got a fair beating last night.'

'Yeah!' the big man barked back. 'All the more reason for sticking with this, don't you think?'

Falcone shrugged. 'Your funeral then. If you're in, you're coming into this meeting with me. I'd appreciate a witness. Some back-up. Leapman will be there, I imagine. Commissario Moretti too, since they'll need someone to take notes. Who knows? You might even enjoy yourself.'

Peroni groaned. 'Oh, sweet Jesus . . . enjoy?'

Falcone was smiling again. A big smile. It was warm. It was worrying them and he liked that.

Costa felt moved to ask, 'So what are you going to do, sir? Is there anything the two of us ought to know about in advance?'

Leo Falcone grinned. He felt good for a change. He felt he was about to let something go, kick off the shackles more firmly than ever, straight in their faces, in a way they wouldn't ever forget.

'I thought I might see how far a man can go before he gets himself fired,' he said brightly.

*

Cold, cold, cold.

. . . the old black voice said: *Git off that fat ass, boy, and sort yourself out.*

Bill Kaspar did as he was bidden. At nine a.m. he let himself out of the empty portable office that sat on the roof of the Castel Sant' Angelo, walked past the sheets and scaffolding of the restoration work that had closed the place, then sauntered down the spiral stairs and out through a side door beyond the closed ticket office. The castle had shut up shop for the holidays. The builders had abandoned work because of the weather. There would be a trickle of dumb tourists who didn't know this. They'd turn up puzzled at the front gate of Hadrian's mausoleum, seated majestically on the banks of the Tiber, a position so regal the place had later become a papal palace and refuge joined to the Vatican by a narrow, elevated corridor down which the pope could flee to safety in extremis.

And, Kaspar knew, because he'd checked, that those rubber-neckers would never see a thing. Inside, the mausoleum was a vast, prolix tangle of chambers, tunnels and hallways, largely invisible from the street, where passers-by saw little but the gaunt, exterior walls and the statue of the Archangel Michael triumphant at the summit, sword raised towards the Tiber. Tombs had little use for windows. What mattered, what ran through the building like a central, muscular nerve, was the spiral ramp that rose past the original crypt, where the emperor's ashes once lay, up through grand halls and collections, empty staff quarters, kitchens and galleries, out to the roof.

It was a five-minute walk across the river to a hunting and fishing shop on the Lungotevere. There Kaspar spent most of his remaining money on two of the biggest, thickest winter coats he could find: all-consuming khaki parkas with furred hoods you could pull tight round your face so no one could see a thing except your eyes. He kept his old black woollen jacket and carried his acquisitions back in a bag, working to marshal his thoughts in the way a man of his nature always did before a battle.

It had been a painful night. Talking to Emily Deacon, trying to work out what to do with her, how much faith he could place in what she told him, how easy it was to fill in the gaps. That had gone on for hours. Then, when he couldn't take any more, he'd shut her away and finally fallen asleep, only for the mother of all nightmares to come roaring up from deep inside his psyche, haunting him with all those sounds and memories he knew only too well.

Just the recollection of it now made him sit down on one of the granite stanchions stuck deep into the snow outside the Castel, sweating feverishly inside his black coat. The human mind was a cruel, relentless mechanism. Nothing could expunge those images – the raging squall of gunfire, the screams, the blood. The slaughter as they fought on the geometrical floor of the temple deep in the heart of the ziggurat, surrounded by that magical pattern, the same one he had held in his hands as he'd dragged the webbing around him, stupidly, as if it were some kind of disguise that could fool the vengeful wall of hate and pain closing in on all of them.

Kaspar looked at his watch and checked the date – 23 December. Thirteen years ago to the day. Thirteen long, long years, during which he'd prayed for release constantly to any god he could remember. Time lost itself in that place. Between the beatings and the torture, between the endless, pointless interrogations, he'd fought to contain the memories deep inside himself because they, more than anything, could keep him alive. The baleful, accusing faces of those men and women who had died because he failed spoke to him, demanding justice. Bill Kaspar had little affection for life, even when he got out of the Baghdad jail and learned the harsh reality of what it meant to be 'free'. It was a question of justice. That was all. Of silencing those angry interior voices that rose up to taunt him any time, anywhere.

He thought again about the day ahead, tried to go through all the possibilities, all the ways in which he might fail again. Then he walked around the perimeter of the squat mausoleum, beached like a whale on a winter plain, found the side entrance, went inside and climbed the ramp all the long winding way up to the roof.

Emily Deacon was locked inside the women's toilet belonging to the closed café. Kaspar liked to think of himself as a gentleman, in spite of appearances. He opened the door, stood back, gun in hand in case she got ideas above her station. It was damn cold up there and windy too. She came out, teeth chattering, skinny arms wrapped around herself, blinking at the bright sunlight, staring up briefly at the gleaming bronze statue of Michael, sword in hand, poised to strike, a fearsome, vengeful figure that dominated the skyline of this quarter of Rome.

Kaspar nodded at the winged giant.

'Scary bastard, huh?'

She put a hand up to her eyes to shield out the sun, long blonde hair blowing around her face.

'Depends how you look at it,' she said. 'He's supposed to be sheathing his sword. It's a symbol. The end of the plague or something. I forget.'

She was a smart kid. Not a bad kid at all. He used to be able to see that in people. Maybe a gift like that could come back.

'You listened a lot when you lived here. Was that your dad doing the talking?'

'What's it to you?'

He took hold of her arm, propelled her forcefully to the edge of the parapet, with its dizzying view down to the footbridge crossing the Tiber to the centro storico and beyond. The wind was more blustery here, so cold it hurt.

'Did he teach you opera, Little Em?'

She was struggling. It didn't mean much against his strength. 'Don't call me that.'

'O Scarpia, avanti a Dio!' he yelled, half sang, over the parapet in a loud, theatrical voice.

'Opera's not my thing,' she said quietly.

'Really?' He felt he had the demeanour of a college professor just then. Maybe it was Steely Dan Deacon himself, those WASP New England genes bouncing up and down. 'Informative, Emily. Do you mean to tell me you've never wanted to leap off the edge like that yourself? Never wanted to know what happens?'

'Not for one second. I've got too much to do.'

Kaspar shook the character out of his head. He didn't believe Emily Deacon. There was something in her eyes – he'd seen it two nights before in the Campo. She hadn't really given a damn then whether she lived or died. She was more interested in seeing the thieving little kid, the light-fingered bitch who'd walked off with what memories he had, get away scot-free. The girl didn't get that from her dad.

'Like see me in hell?'

'That among other things. Besides, it wasn't about curiosity. Tosca knew what happened, didn't she?' Emily Deacon asked. 'I thought that was the point.'

'Yeah,' he agreed, relaxing his grip a little. 'I guess that's true. I used to like opera myself. A lot. But if you don't hear it for years and years it kind of loses its touch.'

'It's easy to lose touch, Kaspar,' she said with a quiet, blunt certainty. 'Sometimes there are good reasons. Don't you think it's time to call it a day? I can do it for you. We could go straight to the Italians. You don't need to say a word to the FBI at all. There's enough to hold you here for years, whatever Washington tries in the courts.'

She wasn't going to back down, act timid, play the little kid. In a way he was pleased. She was Steely Dan's daughter, with a twist.

'We've talked this through. No going back now.'

'What if you're wrong?' she asked. 'What if you've screwed this up too? And it really was just my dad and those other people all along?'

'Then they need to give me a little proof.'

Emily Deacon peered into his face. 'Tell me, Kaspar. Was it something my dad told you? What *do* these people say?'

'Nothing,' he grunted. 'How do you talk to a ghost?'

'I don't believe that.'

He didn't like remembering. Dan Deacon had uttered those few words at the end, after Kaspar had tried so hard, with such vicious, constant brutality, to squeeze it out of him some other way. Yet sharing them diminished their power somehow. So he told her then about the Piazza Mattei, how Steely Dan Deacon had mentioned it twice, how he nearly thought the answer might lie there after all, but when he'd gone round, tried to pound some truth out of the man who was living in the house at that moment, it turned out to be just an illusion.

This was important. Emily Deacon understood that too.

'What if it's all an illusion?' she asked. 'Just some crazy voices in your head?'

The line between what was real and what was imaginary was tough to decipher sometimes. He could hang on to some truths, though. An ugly black Marine with half his face shot away. A brutal Ba'ath party torturer reaching for his sticks, taunting Kaspar for his stupidity. They were real. Too real.

The dark side of him, the part that had killed Monica Sawyer, wondered about throwing her over the wall there and then. She had Steely Dan in her veins all right. The incisive part that could look right through you.

'What if it is?'

'You thought they'd go away when you killed that woman in the Pantheon. What did they call her? Laura Lee? She was the last, wasn't she?'

'Names,' he murmured. 'Don't mean a damn thing in this business.'

'But then you killed that other woman. You never

meant to. And still you're hearing those voices. What do they say, Kaspar? *Shake it?* Are they ever going to stop?'

'Kids,' he said quietly and looked out over the river, nailing the pattern inside his head again, because in those lines existed order, sanity, a kind of peace. Trinità dei Monti hung high in the distance, the Piazza del Popolo lay to the left and somewhere behind the bulk of the Palatine hill was the Colosseum, perfect in its place, a monument to martyrs everywhere. Something else too. When Kaspar stared ahead, squinted, remembered, he could see a tiny cabin set on the roof of a block across the river. A part of him changed there. He took a life for no good reason. The journey veered down a turning he'd never expected.

He grabbed Emily's arm firmly again, pushed her down the stairs, over to the portable office and kicked the door open.

The gear was on the floor. What lay in front of them was all he had left now, proof of his diminishing options.

'Did you listen to what I said to you last night?' he barked. 'Or was that dope I gave you still messing with your head?'

'I listened,' she said quietly. 'Did you listen to me?'

'Every last word.' He hesitated. 'So, Agent Deacon, do you want to stay alive or not?'

She laughed right in his face. 'They won't play, Kaspar. Joel Leapman doesn't give a damn about me. Any more than he gave a damn about Laura Lee and the others. All he wants is you. He isn't going to hand over anything in return for my hide.'

'You're wrong.' He looked at her. She seemed very young all of a sudden. And a part of her was really scared.

He took one of the parkas out of the bag and threw it at her. 'This is as warm as I could find. You're going to need it. And those . . .'

He pointed to the two waistcoats, green military vests bought the week before when the idea first came to him, now all prepared, a couple of lines of little yellow canisters running up and down the front.

'I made them myself, Little Em. And I am, as always, a master of these dark arts.'

The Lizard King, the Holy Owl, Grand Master of the Universe . . . All the names came back to mock him.

He smiled. She was right about the voices. That insidious WASP intuition of hers made it easier. He didn't give a fuck how she felt now.

'You think they're gonna fit?' he asked.

Costa looked everywhere. The block in the Via Veneto. The places they'd visited when they were searching for Laila. He even managed to track down the Deacon family's old address, a spacious apartment in Aventino now occupied by a polite Egyptian surgeon who'd no idea what had happened to his predecessors and had seen nothing at all of a young, blonde American woman.

Traffic found the car. The vehicle had been parked illegally on the Lungotevere near the Castel Sant' Angelo, something that rang alarm bells straight away. Emily wouldn't have left it there willingly. It was partly blocking one of the busiest thoroughfares in Rome. The towaway squad had pounced on it at seven that morning and it was still unclaimed. They'd also found a stolen yellow Punto in the Via Appia Antica. Emily could have been taken.

Costa wanted to talk this through with someone. Peroni preferably. Or even Falcone. Perhaps he would later that morning, but he wanted to talk to someone *now*. And it was obvious who. So he swung the jeep back to the Questura, parked clumsily in the last slushy place outside the morgue building and walked in.

It was never still, never without activity there, Costa thought. This was a kind of temple to death, a constantly manned staging post on the final journey for hundreds of unfortunates each year. His own late partner, Luca Rossi, had once lain on a slab here, tended to by Teresa Lupo, who'd had no small amount of affection for him either. Someone else could have done the job. Luca was shot. Nothing special. No forensic needed. They knew all along who was responsible. They got him too. Costa had made sure of that himself, in his own way.

Luca's death hadn't deterred her for a moment. This was what she did.

He glanced around the room. Silvio Di Capua was supervising one of the morgue monkeys cleaning up a dissection table. Teresa was nowhere to be seen.

Costa walked over to her assistant. 'Silvio?'

They got on pretty well considering Di Capua was scared witless of most cops he met. Costa made a point of treating him with respect and, in particular, never using the nickname 'Monkboy'. In return Di Capua could, on occasion, be almost helpful.

'No,' Di Capua said instantly.

'No what?'

'No to whatever it is you want me to do. I'm not

breaking the rules again. I'm not doing this instead of doing that. There's an order to the way we work here, Nic, and I'm determined we stick to it.'

Costa couldn't stop himself laughing. Silvio Di Capua really did sound as if he felt in charge.

'I was just looking for Teresa.'

'What do you want? Ask me.'

'It's personal.'

The little man scowled. 'Personal? Don't you think we have rather too much of the personal around here? We've got work to do. We always have.'

Costa gave him the look he'd been learning from Gianni Peroni. He'd perfected it just enough for it to work on a minor pathologist with ideas above his station.

'She's off duty actually,' Di Capua said, blushing. 'Which means she's in here, of course, getting through some admin. Try the clerk's office. She's kicked him out for the day.'

This was something new. Teresa was famous for her aversion to paperwork. Costa walked round to the tiny cubicle of an office and found her tapping away at the computer. He got a wary glance the moment he walked in.

'Don't tell me there's more on the way, Nic. I have to catch up on a few things once in a while.'

He opened out his hands, slapped the pockets of his coat. 'Search me. No new customers. Honest.'

'Is it important? I've got people screaming for budget figures. Now I've summoned the courage to try to put some together I'd really like to get this done.'

'It's important.'

She pointed to the chair and said, 'In that case, sit.'

'Thanks. So what do you think about Emily Deacon?'

The sudden question surprised her. 'In what way?'

'What's driving her?'

She pulled a face that said: *Isn't it obvious?* 'Family. The fact it was her dad that died. What else? Does she look like an FBI agent to you?'

'Looks can be deceptive. Lots of people think I don't look like a cop.'

She pushed the keyboard away from her. 'That's simple. You're . . . a little shorter than most. You like art, don't eat meat and rarely lose your temper. You could pass for a sane, intelligent human being most of the time. Is it any wonder you stick out like a sore thumb around this zoo?'

'You're too kind.'

'I know. So why the questions about Emily Deacon?'

'She's missing. Or, to put it another way, I don't know where she is.'

'Are you supposed to?' she asked. 'I mean, she's a grown woman. What about that pig of a colleague of hers? Does he know?'

'No. It's just . . .' He didn't want to go into details about the previous night. He wasn't sure what to make of them himself. 'She was at my place yesterday. This morning she was gone. No note. Nothing. Then her car's found double-parked in town, which I don't think is like her.'

'Ooh. "Yesterday. This morning." Interesting.' Teresa Lupo was rubbing her hands with curious glee.

'I could be wrong,' he said, ignoring the invitation to go further. 'She went off on her own yesterday and had a pretty interesting time.'

'Sightseeing?'

'Digging up a few facts we weren't supposed to know.'

A rueful thought said: *Perhaps more than she told you.*

'She's a smart woman, Nic. Maybe she's just out there looking for some more.'

'I thought of that. So why doesn't she answer her phone? Why did she leave her computer at my place?'

'Ah. The arrogance of men. Could it be because she doesn't want to hear from you? After all, the Leapman guy isn't interested. And if you're being honest, do you really want some rookie FBI agent hanging around all day long?'

He didn't answer that.

'Oh,' Teresa said with a heavy sigh which indicated, Costa thought, that she perceived some personal interest on his part. 'In that case let me simply say this. Emily Deacon strikes me as a very intelligent, very honest woman. Which, given the situation she's in, may be part of her problem.' She paused, surprised, perhaps, by the thought that followed, and what prompted it. 'Honesty's a risky trait in this business, don't you think?'

That was about Gianni Peroni. He couldn't miss it.

'No,' he said with some conviction. 'Honesty's all we've got. And Gianni's OK, if that's what you mean. He saved that kid's life last night.'

'I know. He was brave as hell. What else do you expect? But is that what saved them? I don't know. Gianni said something about a message. Busy, busy, busy. Not one he understood, though.'

'All the same—'

She interrupted him. 'All the same he's doing fine

because he's kind of adopted that Kurdish girl. I know what's in his head. He thinks some cousin of his will take her on full-time or something. Then she can get regular visits from Uncle Gianni. But –' this was difficult for her to say – 'he needs to break that habit, Nic. This is a tough world. You can't hope to cure it with just love and honesty and putting away bad guys from time to time.'

He didn't like what he was hearing. This was the kind of sentiment he got too often from Falcone. 'Why the hell not?'

'Because it breaks you in the end. It weakens you. I can see that happening with Gianni already. He's guilty over his family. He's . . . vulnerable. More than you think. He's got to learn to bury some of this deep down inside otherwise it's just going to mess him up. I know. I love the man.'

From the sudden blush on her face it was obvious this had just slipped out. 'By which I mean,' she corrected herself, 'I think he's a wonderful human being. All that caring. All that compassion. I wonder what the hell he's doing in a job like this. Whether he can keep it up.'

She frowned. 'I used to wonder that about you once upon a time. Now . . . You'll make it. That's good.'

'And Emily Deacon?' Costa asked. 'What about her?'

'I just don't know. A part of me says she'd love to walk straight out of that job and sit in the corner of an old building somewhere, sketching away. Have you talked painting with her yet?'

'No,' he replied, a little offended.

'Keep your hair on. You will. And I hadn't finished. A part of me says Emily is deeply, deeply pissed off about what happened to her dad. So hung up over what happened, maybe, that she'd do anything to put it straight. Regardless of the consequences. Regardless of the pain it might cause her or anyone who gets in the way. Do you understand what I mean?'

Costa did. He'd known it all along. He just needed her to confirm the fact.

'What are you going to do?' she asked.

'Get a coffee. Wait for Falcone to call.'

She looked at her watch. 'To hell with budgets. I *hate* numbers. Also I'm supposed to be off duty. Let's make that two coffees.'

They walked out of the gloomy morgue building then round the corner to the little café Teresa Lupo used. It wasn't popular with cops. That was one reason why she liked the place. The ponytailed youth behind the counter looked a little scared when she walked in.

He usually did. That meant the coffee came quickly and was, as usual, wonderful.

As good as the Tazza d'Oro. He recalled Emily Deacon talking about her favourite café, then glanced at his cup and wondered whether he wouldn't be better off going round there and checking it out.

Teresa Lupo's hand fell on his arm. 'Relax for a moment, Nic. You and Gianni aren't the only cops in Rome.'

But it felt that way just then. Falcone had pulled them aside for some reason of his own, one he had yet to explain.

'Talk to me about Christmas,' she said. 'Tell me what it was like in a pagan household.'

Was that really what the house on the Appian Way was? Nic Costa knew he suffered from the same misapprehension as every kid. The childhood you got was the normal one. It was everyone else's that was weird.

And a few memories did come back. Of food and laughter and singing. Of his father drinking too much wine and behaving, for once, as if there was no tomorrow, no great battle to be fought, nothing to do in the world except enjoy the company of the people around you, people who loved and were loved in return.

'It was happy,' he said.

She was already ordering her second macchiato. Teresa drank coffee as if it were water. 'What more can anyone ask?' she wondered.

'Nothing,' he muttered.

His phone was ringing. Falcone had promised to call.

The voice shook him out of his inertia. Emily Deacon sounded distant, tired and scared.

'Nic,' she said.

'Emily. I've been looking—'

She interrupted him briskly. 'Not now. I don't have the time. You must listen really carefully. It's important. You have to trust me. Please.'

'Of course.'

There was a pause on the line. He wondered how convinced she was.

'I'm with Kaspar,' she said finally. 'I can bring him in, Nic. No more killings. No more bloodshed. But you've got to do what I say, however crazy it sounds. Otherwise—'

There was a noise at the other end of the line. Something physical, something like a scuffle.

'Otherwise, *Nic*,' barked a cold, American voice, 'you and Little Em don't ever get to have fun.'

Costa listened. When the call was over, he found Teresa Lupo staring at him with that familiar look of tough, deliberate concern he'd come to recognize and appreciate.

She pushed back the empty coffee cup, looked around the empty café. 'Like I said, Nic, I'm off duty. If there's anything . . .'

Peroni looked at the men behind the desk, ran through the short yet precise brief Falcone had given him in the lift and wondered what a new career would be like. Maybe he could go back home and see if there was an opening for a pig farmer near Siena. Or ask the girl in Trastevere for a job doling out ice-cream cones. Anything would be better than facing up to more time with these three: Filippo Viale, smug as hell, with an expression on his face that said you could sit there forever and still not get the time of day; Joel Leapman, sullen and resentful; and Commissario Moretti, neat in his immaculate uniform, pen poised over a notepad, like a secretary hanging on someone else's orders.

Leapman stared into Peroni's face as Falcone and he walked in and took the two chairs on the opposite side of the table.

'You sure had a good argument there,' the American observed. 'Don't you think it's time you worked on your personal skills?'

Peroni glanced at Falcone, thought what the hell, and said quite calmly, 'I am tired. My head hurts. I'd rather be anywhere else in the world than this place right now. Can I just announce that if I hear one more smartass piece of bullshit the perpetrator goes straight –' he nodded at the grimy office window – 'out there.'

Moretti sighed and glowered at Falcone.

'Sir?' the inspector asked cheerily.

'Keep your ape on a leash, Leo.' Moretti sighed again. 'You asked for this meeting. Would you care to tell us why?'

'To clear the air.'

'And Emily Deacon,' Peroni said. 'We'd like to know some more about her.'

Leapman grimaced. 'I've already told you. I have no idea where she is.'

'Do you think Kaspar's got her?' Peroni asked.

The three men opposite looked at each other.

'Who?' Leapman asked eventually.

'William F. Kaspar,' Falcone answered.

Peroni watched the expression on their faces. Viale blanked them out. Moretti was baffled. Leapman looked as if that rare creature, someone he loved, had just died.

'Who?' the American asked again.

Falcone glanced at Peroni. The big man reached over the desk, grabbed Leapman by the throat, jerked him hard across the metal top, sending pens and a couple of phones scattering. Peroni held Leapman there, close enough to his face to give him a good view of his stitches and bruises. The FBI agent looked scared and shocked in equal measures. Viale still sat in his seat, smirking. Moretti was out of his chair, back against the wall, watching the scene playing out in front of him in horror, lost for what to do.

'Clearly that burger I shoved in your face didn't make the point,' Peroni said quietly to Joel Leapman, who sweated and squirmed now in front of him. 'We've had enough, my American friend. I've been beaten up because of your lies. I've watched a young child afraid for her life. We've got people putting themselves in harm's way. Good people, Leapman. Now it's time to cut the crap. Either we start to hear something resembling the truth from you or this little charade comes to an end this minute. We're done playing dumb cops. Understand?'

Moretti finally found his voice. 'You!' he yelled, pointing at Peroni. 'Back off now! Falcone?'

'What?' the inspector snarled back. 'Look at the state of the guy. Look at your own man, Moretti. It's the least he's owed.'

Then he patted Peroni on the shoulder and said quietly, 'You can let him go, Gianni. Let's listen to what he's got to say.'

Peroni released his huge paw from Leapman's throat and propelled the American back across the table.

'Viale?' Leapman's voice was full of threat. 'Do something.'

The SISDE man opened his hands and smiled. 'Tut, tut. This is my office, Leo. I don't want anything untoward happening here. Let's have a little calm. What's the problem? This is just police work. Take orders. Do as you're told.' He paused and glared at Peroni. 'Get yourself some new minions too. That way you can keep your job.'

Falcone looked him up and down. 'No, it isn't.'

Viale looked puzzled. 'Isn't what?'

'Police work. And I'm not worried about my job, Filippo. Are you?'

'Don't threaten me,' Viale murmured.

'I'm not. I'm just putting things straight. You see this . . .'

He pulled the orders from the Chigi Palace from his jacket pocket and placed them on the table. 'These have your name on them and Moretti's too. That ought to worry both of you. A lot.'

Viale made a conciliatory gesture. 'Leo . . .'

'Shut up and listen,' Falcone barked. 'I took some advice last night. It seemed appropriate in the circumstances. Although you people seem to have forgotten the fact, there is such a thing as a legal system in this country.'

'There's also such a thing as protocol—' Viale began to say.

'Crap,' Falcone interrupted. 'There's right and there's wrong. And this is very, very wrong. I checked. You can't just write out a couple of blanket protection orders like parking tickets. There are rules. They need a judge's signature, for one thing.'

Falcone pushed the papers over towards the SISDE man. 'You don't have that, Filippo. You're just trying to fool me with some fancy letterhead and bluster, and hoping I'd never notice.'

Moretti bristled inside his black uniform and stared at Viale. 'Is that true?' he asked.

'Paperwork,' the SISDE man said to Falcone, ignoring the commissario. 'Bureaucracy. People don't work that way these days, Leo. I don't. I don't have to. Surely you know that?'

'It's the law,' Falcone said quietly. 'You can't pick and choose the parts you want. None of us can. Not even you. You know that too. That's why you just put a few SISDE signatures on there, badgered Moretti to do the same, and never bothered with the judiciary at all. You couldn't handle this case yourself. It's just too damn public. You had to get us on your side and you had to break the rules to get there.'

Viale's phoney friendliness failed him. The dead grey eyes surveyed the two cops on the other side of the desk. 'Is that so?' he asked.

'Oh yes,' Falcone continued. 'The only circumstance when an order like this gets judicial approval is if it's a matter of national security. *Our* national security. Not that of another country. Though I don't believe even that's the case here. You've deliberately railroaded a genuine investigation into a case which involved the murder of an Italian citizen. You've jerked around the police, you've given a *carte blanche* to a foreign security service to work here unimpeded, all outside Italian law. And for what? So Leapman can pursue some kind of personal vendetta against an individual we have every right to arrest on our own account. I could throw you in a cell right now. I could pick up the phone and have you in front of a magistrate by lunchtime.'

Viale sniffed and considered this. 'You're a judge of what is and isn't national security, are you?'

Falcone smiled. It was going their way. 'Until someone proves me wrong I am. So, gentlemen, are you going to do that? Do we get to hear who William F. Kaspar actually is? Or . . .'

He left it there.

'Or what?' Moretti asked.

'Or do we arrest all three of you and haul you up in front of a public court for . . .' Falcone turned to Peroni. 'How many did we have the last time we added them up?'

'Oh.' Peroni frowned, counting them off on his fingers, staring at the ceiling like a simpleton, pretending it was hard to remember. 'Conspiracy. Wasting police time. Forgery of official documents. Illegal possession of weapons. Use of the electronic media to issue criminal threats. Breach of the death registration rules. Withholding information—'

Viale lost it. 'You *dare* threaten me, Falcone! Here! Do you have any idea what you're doing?'

'I think so,' Falcone answered quietly. 'And also we have these.'

He took the sheets of paper out of the envelope and threw them on the table. Leapman snatched them up and stared at them, aghast. They were copies Costa had made that morning of the material Emily Deacon found the day before: the Net conversations and, most damning of all, the memo from 1990. The one marked 'Babylon Sisters'.

'Where the hell did you get this?' Leapman murmured.

'From Emily Deacon,' Falcone replied. 'And now she's missing.'

The FBI man was a picture of bitterness. 'That little bitch sure knows a lot of things she's not supposed to. I thought—'

'What?' Peroni snapped. 'That she was just a dummy? Like the rest of us?'

'Yeah,' Leapman agreed with a sour face.

Peroni pointed a hefty finger in his direction. 'Wrong again, smartass. And here's another thought. What if she's dead too? You don't honestly think you can keep that under wraps, do you?'

It was remarkable. Leapman was thinking then,

exchanging glances with Viale. Something was going on. Peroni risked just the briefest of glances with the man at his side. The twinkle in Falcone's eyes told him he wasn't wrong. The ruse had worked. They were through.

Leapman shook his head and muttered, 'This is a mess. Such a mess.'

Moretti had put down his pen and turned a sickly shade of white. He regarded the men alongside him and scowled. 'You told me none of this would happen, Viale,' the commissario complained. 'You said—'

Peroni took immense pleasure in breaking in. 'Must be a hell of a pension you've built up over the years, Moretti. I was in that position once. Hurts like hell when they take it away from you. Mind you, jail too . . .'

Moretti closed his eyes briefly, then shot Peroni a look of pure hatred. 'You ugly, sanctimonious bastard,' he hissed. 'You don't have to deal with these people, day in, day out. You don't have to listen to them pushing and pushing, threatening, cajoling: "Do this, do that".'

'I thought that was what you got paid for,' Peroni replied, then added a final, 'sir.'

'We don't have time for this, gentlemen,' Falcone reminded them, looking at his watch. 'Where's it going to be? Here, or in the Questura?'

Costa was getting desperate. The picture of the heartless ultimatum Kaspar had set was starting to damage his concentration. Teresa was doing what she loved: cruising the Questura for any titbits of information she could glean by badgering people who, by rights, shouldn't even be talking to her. He'd taken on the obvious task of working the street. No one answered the bell at the address Emily had mentioned. He'd peered through the window, looking at the spare furniture, the kind you got in a rented apartment not a real home, and thought about breaking in. It was difficult to see what it could tell him about what had happened there thirteen years before. Then he'd hammered on six doors to no avail. Struggling to work out what to do next, he watched one of the Jewish bakers lugging flour through the doorway of his tiny store, smelled the fragrance of fresh bread on the cold December air, and, against his own wishes, felt his stomach rumble. He had to approach this with the same cold, deliberate dedication that Kaspar was showing he possessed. Either that or he could panic them all into another bloody disaster.

At the heart of the Piazza Mattei was the little fountain of the tortoises. It was a modest creation by Roman standards, and possessed a comic touch that had amused Costa when he was a boy. Four naked youths, their feet on dolphins, were struggling to push four small tortoises into the basin at the summit of the fountain. It was ludicrous, almost surreal somehow. And today, he noted, the water was flowing.

He walked to the fountain and climbed over the low iron rail protecting the structure from the carelessness of motorists negotiating the narrow alleys of the ghetto. Then he dipped a finger into the snow at the foot, in the central basin. It went through easily. The ice was melting. He looked at the sky. The bitter cold was still around, but a change in the weather was imminent.

It had to be. Something in the human psyche lost sight of facts like these from time to time. When extraordinary events occurred, one adapted, almost came to regard them as normal, forgetting to allot them the perspective they merited. Rome would return to the way it was supposed to be in December. Planes would fly again, buses and trains would run almost to time. One way or another, the killings would cease. Chaos, by its nature, was impermanent.

What mattered was bringing events to a close quietly, with as little damage as possible. He didn't know if he could do that. Falcone was in his meeting, but once he emerged he'd be on the phone, asking questions. Would Costa have any answers? If he did, would he be inclined to share them with his boss?

And . . .

He had to ask himself. How much of the truth was Emily telling him? Ever since the previous night when he'd forced her to confront the idea that her father was the man behind Kaspar's miserable fate in Iraq, he'd felt there was something she was concealing.

Teresa had looked up the report on the attack in the Piazza Mattei the previous October and tried, in vain, to find something new. The facts were plain, baffling and suspiciously thin on the ground. The American academic had been staying temporarily at Number Thirteen as a house guest, while conducting some academic research at the American embassy. He'd been assaulted in the square by the fountain. It was pure luck that a couple of cops were in the vicinity. No one had been apprehended. No motive could be found. It could be a blind alley . . .

Then Teresa had suggested she try to find out something about the property itself. After fifteen minutes – a period of time in which Costa, to his frustration, had got nowhere – she phoned back, ecstatic. The earliest deeds she could track showed Number Thirteen had been owned by the same private company based in Washington as far back as 1975. That, in itself, was unusual. Foreign owners rarely kept properties for that length of time. The firm wasn't listed in the US phone book. It didn't show in any of the financial records which she'd bullied some lowly minion in research into checking. Something stank, Teresa thought. He felt sure her instincts were correct. The tough part was turning them into hard fact. It was all going nowhere unless he could prise something out of the memory of someone who'd lived in the square for some time.

'What you do in circumstances like these,' Costa thought, trying to still those pictures running around his head, 'is get yourself a coffee.'

He walked into the little café on the square, ordered a large macchiato and dumped a couple of extra shots of caffeine inside it from the coffee and sugar sludge parked on the bar in a bowl. Then, as he waited for the sudden caffeine jolt to hit, he tried to remember a few old tricks, tried to think what Falcone would have done in the circumstances.

The inspector had just a few mottos, all of them rarely heard, all of them apposite. One came to Costa at that moment. Curiosity was the basis of detection. Without it, a man learned nothing. Without it, you might as well be an accountant.

He tried to recall the substance of the reports he'd read over the last few days in the Questura and set them against the conversation he'd had with Emily after Kaspar had handed her back the phone. Then he finished his coffee and called over the middle-aged proprietor.

He should have worked this out earlier. The ghetto never changed. Places were handed down from generation to generation. He was just a short stroll from the commercial heart of the modern city, but this was a village, one where everyone knew everyone else. Rome was, in some ways, still a collection of individual communities living noisily cheek by jowl. It was what separated Rome from other capitals he had visited, cities that seemed to be metropolitan sprawls, with ill-defined borders and areas where not a soul lived at night.

'Who's the oldest resident in the square?' Costa asked, flashing his card.

The man kept polishing a glass with a spotless cloth, thinking. 'You mean the oldest who's still got half a brain?'

'Quite.' Costa sighed. 'Listen. I don't have the time . . .'

The cloth came out of the glass and jabbed at a house on the other side of the square. 'Sorvino. Number Twenty-one. Ground floor. Don't say I told you.'

No one liked talking to the police. Not even café owners, who'd be the first to start screaming down the phone if someone walked off with an extra sachet of sugar.

'Thanks,' Costa murmured. He threw a couple of coins on the counter then walked out into the cold morning air.

He went to Number Twenty-one, which, thanks to the vagaries of house numbering in the ghetto, was four doors down from Thirteen, and pushed the bell marked 'Sorvino'. A stiff-limbed little woman in a faded blue floral-pattern dress came to the door and peered at him through round, black-rimmed glasses. She was eighty, maybe more, at an age when it was difficult to tell. Short, but proudly erect, as if to say: to hell with the years. She took one look at the badge and nodded him into the living room. It was immaculate: crammed with polished antique furniture, a selection of small framed photographs, and what seemed like hundreds of pieces of Jewish memorabilia.

'I was hoping to talk to someone with a memory,' he said rapidly. 'Someone who's lived here a long time.'

'Is eighty-seven years long enough for you?'

'More than enough,' he replied, smiling, hoping he didn't look too impatient.

She picked up a delicate porcelain cup, still half full. 'Camomile tea. I recommend it for people of a nervous nature.'

'Thanks. I'll remember that.'

'No you won't. You're young. You think you can live through anything. What are you looking for? It must be something important.'

'Very. Facts. Names.' He hesitated. 'Names mainly. I've been knocking on doors. Getting nowhere.'

'The ghetto's changing. You don't see families the way you used to.'

'I want to know about Number Thirteen.'

'Ah.' She nodded and closed her eyes for a moment, thinking. 'Il Duce had a girl there during the war. German. Ilse I think she was called. Not that he ever visited, you understand. He wouldn't dirty his hands coming to meet the likes of us, now would he?'

Jews of her generation had a mixed attitude towards Mussolini. Until the later stage of his career, Il Duce had taken little interest in anti-semitism. Costa could recall his father telling stories of how some Jews even joined the fascist party. Relatively limited numbers were transported to the concentration camps. It was the old Roman story: nothing was ever quite black and white.

'What happened to the house after the war?'

She looked at him severely. 'I'm not an estate agent.'

'I know that. I just wondered who lived there. You're a kind woman, Signora, I'm sure. You would want to know your neighbours.'

'No more than they want to be known,' she said primly.

'Of course.'

'Soldiers,' she said with a shrug. 'American soldiers, for a while anyway. Nice men. Officers. They had beautiful manners, not like Roman men. They were strangers. I was of assistance to them now and again. I like strangers to go away with fond memories of Rome. As a good citizen should.'

'Of course. And then?'

'You're asking me who's lived there for the last fifty years?'

'That would be useful.'

'Huh.'

It was never easy dealing with this generation. They resented something. That the world had changed. That they were getting older within it, powerless.

'Please try to think. A man was attacked there earlier this year. Do you remember?'

'I heard it! Fighting in the street! Here! Not since the war . . .' She frowned. 'The world gets worse. Why don't you do something about it?'

'I'm trying,' he replied.

'Not hard enough it seems to me.'

It was a reasonable observation. 'Perhaps. But I can't . . .' He corrected himself. 'None of us in the police can do that on our own. We need your help. Your support. Without that . . .'

She was a bright-eyed old bird. She didn't miss a thing. 'Yes?'

'Without that we're just people who enforce the laws made by politicians. Regardless of what anyone thinks. Regardless of what's right sometimes.'

'Oh my,' she said, smiling, revealing small teeth the colour of old porcelain, a little crooked, just enough to show they were natural. 'A policeman with a conscience. How they must love you.'

'I don't do this to be loved, Signora. Please. The house. Whose is it? Who's lived there over the years?'

'Who owns it? Americans, I imagine. They look like government people to me. Government people who don't want to *say* they're government people. Not that I care. They keep it in good repair. What more can I say? They come. They go. Different ones. Not for long, usually. Just a few weeks, as if it were a hotel, I imagine. Not long enough to get to know the likes of me. Pleasant men, mind. Always men, too, on their own.'

She was trying to remember something. Costa waited, knowing he couldn't let this interview run and run, wondering whether there were any other avenues left open to him.

'And?'

'They were solitary creatures,' she said testily. 'Not the kind you could talk to easily in the street.'

'All of them?'

'Most.'

'Do you remember any names? It's possible this man who was attacked was mistaken for someone else.'

'So many,' she said, frowning.

Even the old ones didn't try much these days. Costa took out his card and gave it to her, pointing out the mobile number.

'If you think of anything. I was probably mistaken in any case. If these men were only here for a short time . . .' It was unlikely to be a case of mistaken identity. 'I was hoping there was someone who stayed there longer. Some years ago. A man, perhaps, who regarded it as his home.'

The old, bright eyes sparkled. 'There *was* one. Ten, fifteen years ago. I recall now. I think he stayed there for a year. Possibly more.'

'A name?'

'Even less talkative than most of them, from what I remember. Somewhat abrupt I thought, but perhaps that was just his manner.'

'A name?' he insisted.

She shook her head. 'How could I possibly know that?'

Teresa had checked. If it was a normal rental property there would be residency records. None existed. It was a bolt hole for one of the American agencies, surely. They would have a simple way around all the regulations ordinary citizens had to face.

'I may have a photograph, though,' she said brightly. 'Would that help?' She nodded at the gleaming walnut sideboard next to him. It was covered in small, mounted pictures. She passed him one. 'You know what time of year that is?'

It was winter. Men, women and children, all in heavy

coats, stood in front of the fountain of the tortoises holding lit candles.

'No.'

'Shame on you! Have you never heard of Hanukkah? Why should the Catholics steal all the fun for Christmas?'

'I'm sorry. I'm not a Catholic.'

'How shocking,' she said with a laugh. 'Still, I forgive you. We have a little tradition. Every year we take a photograph of ourselves. Just the people living here. By the fountain. *Every* year. I can show you ones when I was a young girl before the war.' Her eyes twinkled. 'You wouldn't recognize me. I wasn't the old thing I am now.'

Costa's mind was working overtime. 'He was in the photograph?'

'He didn't want to be! The poor man was walking home just as we were lining up out there. We insisted. A little *vino* had been taken, you understand. He didn't have a choice.' She paused to let this point go home. 'We can be very persuasive when we want to be, you know.'

'I can believe that. When?'

She frowned. 'I really couldn't say. I've so many photographs.'

'Possibly ten, fifteen years ago?'

She crossed the room picked up a couple of photos, took off her glasses to peer at them, then returned with one in her frail hand and passed it to him. Costa scanned the faces there. He looked at the back. There was a year, scribbled in pencil: 1990.

*

'You want to know who Bill Kaspar is?'

Joel Leapman looked like a man speaking from personal experience, and there was something in his eyes – impending pleasure, or a hint of a nasty surprise around the corner – that Gianni Peroni really didn't like.

'OK. I'll tell you. Kind of a soldier. Kind of a spy. A mercenary. A go-between running shuttle between men who, like him, didn't really exist either. One of the best. Take it from me. He was the sort of guy you'd follow anywhere, right into hell if that's where he wanted to go. An American hero, we thought. Not that anyone would ever call him that out loud, you understand. And now we're going to hang him out to dry. Life's a bitch sometimes.'

Leapman's tale confirmed just about everything Emily Deacon had discovered. Back in 1990 Kaspar had been called to lead one of two covert teams into Iraq on an intelligence mission well behind hostile lines. The venture was a disaster. The day after they arrived to establish a forward base inside an ancient monument outside Babylon the Republican Guard had attacked in force. Dan Deacon was out on patrol with his own team when it happened. He radioed for assistance and was ordered not to engage in the meantime. Forty-five minutes later two Black Hawks, backed by fighter support, had made it to the scene. The ziggurat was a smoking shell. From what surveillance could see Kaspar and his team were dead. They didn't have the manpower to take on the Iraqis in any case. Deacon's crew managed to escape to a deserted farm two miles away, where a helicopter snatched them from the approaching enemy, though one female member was badly wounded along the way.

The mission didn't exist. The combatants, as far as their relatives were concerned, remained incommunicado on private training exercises in the Gulf until, two months later, an army captain visited their homes with stories of dead heroes in the real conflict, which was now under way. There could be no medals, no public mourning. Not even a private Purple Heart. None of them was officially in the military. Dead spooks wear no honours.

Wars make noise. In the tumult of the conflict the loss of nine unknown, unseen individuals made little impact. Money went around to keep families and others quiet. The men and women who survived went back to their jobs, in the diplomatic and intelligence services, and in civilian life too. They kept their secrets, they got on with their lives. The battle was won. Saddam went home, leaving a trail of corpses in his wake, claiming victory. And Kuwait was free beneath the smoke of burning oil fields.

All in all, Leapman said, the verdict was that the war was half a job well done. There were people who thought they should have gone all the way into Saddam's palaces in Baghdad. But that wasn't part of the UN brief, and military people lived by UN briefs back then. The objective was to recover Kuwait and hope that Saddam learned his lesson. They got part of what they wanted anyway.

He took a swig of the bottle of water he'd brought with him and looked at each of them in turn.

'You get all that for free,' Leapman said. 'It's history now, anyway, and who gives a shit about that? What comes next, though, is different. If this goes public then everything goes way over our heads, gentlemen. It won't be me or Viale here who's screaming blue murder. It'll be service chiefs and army guys or worse and none of us wants that. Understood?'

Peroni found himself nodding automatically, as if he had a choice.

What happened next, Leapman said, was they realized Baghdad had got insight. Post-war, someone somewhere was helping them.

'Helping them how?' Falcone demanded.

'Background,' Leapman answered. 'It was a question of adding things up and working out what didn't make sense. There were sanctions in place by then. Tough sanctions, ones that worked, as well as sanctions can, anyway. All the same, we knew Saddam was getting wind of things he shouldn't. He understood some of our military hardware better than he ought. He took out three Iraqis we'd placed near to him to keep an eye on what was going on. He had intelligence, stuff he wasn't supposed to know. So we had to ask ourselves what was going on.'

'Kaspar?' Peroni wondered. 'I thought you said he was a hero.'

'Yeah. I also said he was dead. Great cover twice over, huh? We went back and talked to people in Deacon's team again. They were awkward about it. I guess, if you go through that kind of experience, you don't want to think ill of your comrades. But a couple of them, Deacon included, had their suspicions. Or so they said after a lot of prompting. You've got to remember. At that stage we thought Kaspar was blown away along with the rest of his team. But maybe that was what we were supposed to believe. And all the while he was living the good life in some quiet palace out in the desert, counting his money, gradually spilling out every last thing he knew, while Saddam lapped it up. What do you do?'

You didn't have much in the way of options, Peroni thought. 'You look for proof.'

'Exactly.'

Leapman nodded at Viale. 'SISDE already had someone secreted inside Iraq. Dan Deacon came back to Rome for a couple of months and worked alongside Viale here to send in a new team, see if anyone was talking about an American on their side. Four officers went in. One came back. The others . . .'

Leapman shook his head. 'I don't even want to think what happened there. One report we got said Uday disposed of the poor bastards personally. You heard the stories about how he used to feed the lions?'

He let them digest that in silence.

'They weren't fairy tales,' Leapman continued. 'They weren't the full story either. Anyways, it was Deacon's place man who did come back and he had some news. There was an American there. He was talking. And he was some big tough guy who seemed to know everything. Fitted Kaspar in every respect. Some hero, huh? And you know something? We couldn't touch him. He was just going to have to sit there gossiping day and night until we came back another time. We were working with kid gloves then. It took all the persuasion we had to get that covert team in just to look for intelligence. We couldn't be seen to be running heavier missions, maybe to capture him or take him out, because that would screw up any chance we had of rebuilding a coalition to finish the job. Not that *that* worked either. What a mess . . .'

'Still,' Peroni said with a smile, 'you got there in the end.'

'Yes we did!' Leapman barked back at him. 'And one day you people might realize what a damn big favour we did you.'

Falcone shook his head. 'You're getting away from the subject, Leapman.'

'Yeah,' he moaned. 'None of you ever like that conversation. OK. So, come last spring, we get back. And we say to some of our intelligence people, look out for this guy called Bill Kaspar. And when you find him throw him in a cell somewhere, call home and leave him alone with us for a little while.'

Peroni had to ask. 'Us being?'

'What's it matter? What's in a name?'

'It matters because you're supposed to be FBI,' Falcone pointed out.

'Sue me,' Leapman grunted. 'The point is this. Ten days into the war we find Bill Kaspar running like hell in some little town outside Baghdad. Our guys do just as they're told. Lock him up and wait for a special team to come and take out the trash. And you know what he does?'

What men like that always did, Peroni thought.

'I can imagine,' he said.

'No.' Leapman shook his head vigorously. 'You can't. The men who picked him up were low-level grunts. They understood he was supposed to be a bad guy. They told him so. I *know* Bill Kaspar. He could've taken them out one by one if he'd wanted. What he did instead was go crazy. I mean angry crazy. Outraged. Some stupid sergeant knocked him around a touch and told him he was a traitor. Kaspar went ballistic, demanded to see the platoon commander, the guy above him, the regional commander, Dubya himself. Why? Because we'd got it all wrong. He wasn't sitting there in some Iraqi palace unloading secrets for dough. The poor bastard had been in jail all along, probably getting tortured daily after a breakfast of dust and shit, doubtless not saying a word because that's what Bill Kaspar is like.'

Leapman took a big deep breath before going on. 'We got fooled good and proper and he knew it long before we did. He listens to this dumb sergeant for a couple of minutes, thinks it through, and then he's out of there. Doesn't even kill one of the grunts on the way, either, though a couple of them won't walk too well for a while. Can you believe that? And all we know is some lowly soldiers have got a report that doesn't add up to much, then let the guy we wanted so badly escape out into the mess that was going on all over the place. We didn't stand a chance of catching up with him after that. For one simple reason. He didn't want to be caught.'

The American shook his head in wonder. Peroni couldn't begin to imagine how this would work.

'He had no money,' he objected. 'No one to help him.'

'*He's Bill Kaspar!*' Leapman yelled. 'I keep telling you. Kaspar wrote the book on every last trick and scam you can pull in circumstances like that. You could parachute him onto Mars, come back six months later and he wouldn't just be alive he'd be sitting in a nice house with lobster on the table, fresh champagne on ice in a bucket and some goddamn hippie CD from the seventies on the hi-fi. He survives. He's the best there is at it.'

'When did you know?' Falcone asked.

Leapman grimaced. 'It took a while. We didn't even realize Kaspar had made it to the US. We thought he'd hide out in Syria or somewhere. These people in Deacon's team . . . most of them were civilians by this time. We didn't put two and two together until those deaths in Virginia. By then there were just too many coincidences. All the same we still couldn't work out what he was doing. As far as we were concerned, Bill Kaspar was a renegade, a wanted criminal. We couldn't figure out what possible reason he'd have for risking his neck by coming home and killing these people. Then . . .'

He mulled over how far to go. 'Then we worked out that the only evidence we had against Kaspar came from Deacon's place man on that covert mission a few years earlier. Nothing else corroborated the story. Certainly not the other three guys who never made it out of there. So we started taking a few peeks at the bank accounts of some of the others, the ones who got out. They'd done their best to keep it hidden in the early years. I guess after a time you get lazy. There's a whole lot we don't know. Was this arranged before they went into Iraq? Did one or two of them know and just face the rest with the choice when they got there? Live and be a rich traitor or die and be an unsung hero? It's just guesswork now. Operations like these don't keep records for good reasons and everyone involved, bar Bill Kaspar, is dead. But we were starting to firm up our suspicions by the time he made it to Dan Deacon in Beijing. We were certain after that. Deacon had half a million dollars stashed away in a bank account in the Philippines. The moron never even spent a penny of it. Can you believe it?'

Leapman was fishing for sympathy. Falcone wasn't amenable.

'The woman who died in the Pantheon?' he asked.

'What about her?' Leapman asked.

'She knew. She must have known. You brought her here.'

'Yeah,' he snarled. 'So we screwed up. I had five men watching her. How Kaspar got round them sure beats me.'

Falcone wasn't letting go. 'And she came here because . . . ?'

'Because, mister, I didn't give her any choice. She was a criminal. I could have snapped my fingers and she'd be gone for good anyway. She had damn all in the way of real intelligence. She got shot by accident after they went in and scarcely knew what happened. So I gave her a chance to make up. Had it worked she could have walked free.'

'Generous,' Peroni observed. 'Why didn't you just try talking to him direct?'

Leapman reached over the table and scattered Costa's papers in front of them.

'*We've been trying!* What do you think all these messages are about? If I could just get him on the phone . . . I'd apologize. Then I'd tell him it's time to end this crap and throw himself on our mercy. Except now . . .'

They waited. It had to come from him.

'Now he's killed someone else,' Leapman muttered. 'Which shouldn't have happened. He had a full pack. The only one still standing is him. There's no reason he should take out someone who's nothing to do with any of this. Unless he thinks it's gone beyond talking. Kaspar always had a pretty old-fashioned view about patriotism. He came out of some Iraqi jail thinking he'd be home and free with someone quietly telling him he was a hero. Instead he walked into all this crap. Us treating him as if he was a turncoat. If he feels his country's abandoned him – written him off as a traitor – I suppose he thinks anything goes these days.'

'I suppose he's right,' Peroni grumbled.

'Finally,' Leapman said, with a long, pained sigh, 'we agree on something.'

Costa met Teresa where they'd arranged by phone, close to Largo Argentina, and briefed her on what he'd discovered. Then the two of them walked the short distance to the café where Emily had said she'd be waiting for them. He didn't recognize her at first. She was standing at the counter of an empty Tazza d'Oro, close by the Pantheon, anonymous inside a too-big khaki winter parka with the hood still up. He nodded at her as they entered, got a couple of coffees and the three of them retreated to a table.

Emily Deacon looked frightened, but a little excited too. Costa reached forward and gently pulled the hood down to her neckline, revealing her face. She managed the ghost of a smile and shook her long blonde hair automatically. It seemed lank and dirty.

Emily glanced at Teresa. 'I thought perhaps it would be you and Gianni.'

'Gianni's tied up,' Teresa said instantly. 'I'm the best you've got.'

'No.' There was a flash of a smile. 'I didn't mean that. Sorry. You've got something?'

Costa nodded at Teresa. 'We think so. But put us in

the picture first, Emily. What the hell happened last night? How did you find Kaspar?'

'I didn't. He found me. You fell asleep.' She felt awkward with Teresa there, Costa guessed. 'I went outside . . . I'm sorry. It's the last thing I wanted, believe me. But maybe . . .'

She bit her lip, wondering whether to say it. 'This could be the one chance we get. It's important you understand the situation. See this.'

She flipped down the collar of the jacket and pointed to a tiny black plastic square. 'It's a mike. Kaspar's listening somewhere. He can hear every word I say. He'll be able to do that all the time until this is over, so don't *anybody* get any smart ideas. And if the mike goes dead so do I. This guy knows his stuff. You've both got to understand that. It's best we don't mess with him.'

Costa scanned the bar without thinking.

Emily put her hand to his chin and pulled his attention back to her. 'He could be anywhere. Don't even think about it. There's a deal on the cards here. Let's just focus on that. We mustn't screw it up.'

He nodded. 'I understand.'

'Good.'

Teresa was staring at a mark on her neck. 'Are you hurt, Emily?' she asked.

'I must have fallen,' she said. 'That's all. Don't worry about me.'

Then Costa gently pulled down the first few inches of the zip on the front of the parka.

'No, Nic,' Emily ordered. She took his hand, pulled it away from her, then jerked the zip back up. 'Not here. Not now. That's not what matters. Don't think about that part. We don't even get that far.'

Teresa said quietly, 'That's what we all want, Emily. But can we stop him?'

'Yes!'

'You're sure?' Teresa reiterated.

'I'm sure!' she snapped. Then, more quietly, 'And I'm not in a position to argue. OK?'

Costa found it hard to work out whether she was saying what she did for Kaspar's benefit or because she really believed it.

'He killed your father, Emily,' Teresa pointed out. 'He killed all those other people. How can we trust him?'

She frowned. 'I know that. But he talked to me last night. We went over a lot of things. He had his reasons. He feels he had some justification. That there was no other way. I don't agree with that for one moment. I don't imagine he'd expect me to. But . . .'

Nic took out a pen from his jacket pocket, slipped it onto the table next to a napkin.

'He just wants to know justice – his definition of justice – has been done,' she said, looking at the pen, thinking.

Then she scribbled two words on the paper.

You know?

Costa nodded and wrote a name next to the question.

She closed her eyes. She looked a little faint. Then she picked up the napkin, stared at the writing there, fixed him with those sharp, incisive blue eyes and mouthed, 'Sure?'

Costa cupped his hand over the mike, leaned close into her left hair, smelled the trace of shampoo on her hair, a familiar scent, one from his own home, and murmured, 'I'm sure he lived in an American-owned house in the Piazza Mattei in 1990. He was the only one there. Is that enough?'

Her cheek pressed into his, her lips briefly kissed his neck.

'Oh yes,' Emily whispered into his ear.

She took his hand off the mike, brushed her lips against his fingers and smiled broadly, just for a moment.

'If Kaspar wants justice,' he said. 'All he's got to do is walk into any Questura. That's why we're there.'

'He will. I promise.'

She scribbled out an address and a time, then gave it to Teresa.

'That's where he wants the evidence delivered and when. No one but you two know that. He might want to test you. I'd be surprised if he didn't. And –' she paused, making sure they understood this last point – 'make it good evidence. Please.'

Nic Costa wanted a magic wand at that moment. Something that could just spirit them out of there, take away all the trappings of death and violence, put them back into a world that was whole and warm and human.

'What if something goes wrong?' he asked. 'If there's a delay . . . how do we get in touch with him?'

'No!' Her eyes were pleading with him. 'He won't buy that, Nic. He's too smart. You do things his way. Or . . .'

Kaspar would be utterly inflexible, Costa understood this. He was offering to surrender. The terms would surely be his.

'I'll call Falcone when I can get through,' he said. 'I'll make the arrangements.'

'And me?' Teresa asked.

Emily reached into her jacket, took out a plastic security swipe card then scribbled an incomprehensible jumble of letters and numbers and an email address on the napkin. 'If you can talk your way into Leapman's office, this will get you on the system. After that . . . You and Nic need to try and find some way to work this out together. I can't . . .'

Maybe it was some kind of delayed shock. She let go and rocked back on her chair. Her face was white at that point. She was on the verge of breaking. Costa could see it and he didn't have the words to help.

Teresa Lupo intervened. She bent forward and put her arms around Emily's slight shoulders, clutching the huge coat to her, which was a statement in itself. 'Emily,' she whispered, 'keep going. We can do this.'

Then Teresa was gone, not looking back, not wanting to see what Costa knew would be a difficult moment of intimacy.

Her hands felt his again, just the briefest touch. She was cold now, she was sweating.

'Make it work, Nic,' Emily Deacon said softly. 'This isn't just for me.'

She leaned forward, kissed his cheek, her lips cold, not quite real somehow. Then she shuffled the hood around her head, disappeared into its bulk, and, eyes firmly on the floor, walked away, out into the bright, biting morning, out towards the hulking presence of the ancient shape around the corner.

Peroni listened with a growing sense of unease as Falcone forced them to focus on the message Kaspar had given him the previous night: proof.

Leapman was adamant, in a confident way that worried Peroni no end. 'It was Dan Deacon. This was his show all along. Kaspar'd surely know if he had half a mind left.'

That wasn't the point, Peroni thought, and surely they knew it. 'Can you prove it?' he asked. 'I looked into this man's face last night and he's going to take some convincing. I told you. He spoke with Deacon. I don't think . . .'

'Deacon! Deacon!' Leapman yelled. 'The bastard was a traitor through and through! How the hell can anyone rely on a word he said?'

Peroni tried to work out what game Leapman was playing because it was certainly deeper than it appeared to be. 'The man was trying to save his life at the time. I don't think people are very adept at lying in those situations.'

Leapman glowered at the SISDE man. 'Tell him.'

Viale made that slight, amused gesture he used to put people down. 'We lie any time we damn well feel like. Welcome to our world. Best accept it.'

'What we accept,' Falcone said curtly, 'is that Kaspar is making a direct threat, one he is doubtless determined to carry out, *in this city*. We're under a duty to understand and respond to that. It's important we know what we can offer him to back down. Can you prove it was Deacon?'

'No,' Leapman replied. 'If you want a straight answer.'

Peroni felt like grabbing the guy by the throat again. He seemed so detached from the problem. He looked as if he were turning down an expense claim. 'Why not?

These things must cost millions of dollars. You've got to have accounts, records, something.'

The American actually laughed. Gianni Peroni found he had to make a conscious effort to stay in his seat.

'What planet are you people living on?' Leapman asked. 'That's the last thing any of us would want. These operations are specifically designed so that, if they go wrong, the shit stays on the ground and doesn't seep anywhere near the rest of us. Those are the only circumstances under which they can function. Kaspar knows that as well as anyone. He invented half the rules. Asking for an audit trail now shows how deranged the guy is. He might as well ask us to go out in public and hang ourselves.'

'You've got—' Peroni continued.

'No!' Leapman insisted. 'Listen. These were the rules Kaspar played by. He can't buck them now. Deniability's everything. No papers. No bank transactions. Nothing. Just a bunch of money going missing in some accounts in Washington, in ways no one's ever going to notice.'

Commissario Moretti finally found his voice. 'You heard what they said, Viale. I'll go along with this so far, but I don't want trouble here on the streets of Rome. That wasn't part of the deal.'

'It's a tough world out there,' Viale said softly, staring at the table. 'We'll cope.'

'Dammit!' Moretti screeched. 'We do cope. We're the police. We're here for a reason.'

'You're here because you're convenient,' Viale yelled. 'I've never had a cop who rolled over as easily as you did. Jesus. Leo here wouldn't have fallen for a trick like that. He'd have checked. He did in the end. You . . .'

He didn't even attempt to disguise his contempt for the man in the uniform two seats away. 'You're just a stuffed-up buffoon with a pen and a few shiny buttons on your jacket. You're useful to me, Bruno, but don't overestimate your value. And don't get in the habit of talking back.'

The commissario went silent and stared at the desk, shaking his head. Shock, Peroni thought. And maybe even a little well-deserved shame. Or so Peroni hoped.

'He's going to contact us somehow,' Falcone insisted. 'He's going to want something.'

Viale reached over, took Moretti's pen and notepad and made a couple of indecipherable scribbles. 'Then we'll give him it. I'm not having another innocent death here either. I can put some documents together. Keep him occupied until we find him.'

Peroni wanted to scream. 'Don't you understand? This guy's no fool. You can't just slip him some phoney letters and hope he'll swallow it. He's wise to tricks like that already.'

Leapman nodded. 'He's right. If you give him fake stuff it'll only make him madder. Then what?'

Viale looked immensely pleased with himself. 'Who said it was going to be fake, Joel?'

'What?' the American snarled.

'You heard.'

The SISDE man got up from the desk and walked over to the far side of the office, where there was a set of heavy-duty, old-fashioned filing cabinets secured by combination locks. He flicked through some numbers on the nearest, slid open a drawer and rapidly retrieved a blue file.

Leapman uttered a low, bitter curse.

'Oh please!' Viale was loving this. 'This was your show. We were just housekeeping. And –' he waved the file at the American – 'housekeepers keep records. I was just rereading them last night, Joel. To refresh my memory. We have a habit around here. We note down conversations afterwards. We like to make sure we remember what we can. You may have had lots of reasons to cut off everything at source. We had just as many to keep a few reminders of what really happened. Just in case someone started pointing fingers in our direction later. We're your allies. We're not your lackeys. Or your fall guys. You didn't really think we'd be willing to go down with the ship, if it came to that, did you?'

'Well, well, well,' Leapman spat back at him. 'It's the people on your own side who fuck you up the most.'

Viale came back to the desk, withdrew a photo from the file and threw it on the desk. It was of a group of men and women in casual, semi-military uniform, working on a jeep. The shot looked snatched. None of them knew they were being photographed. The location was wild countryside, maybe Italy, maybe not.

Leapman glowered at the image in front of them. 'What the hell were you doing taking that?'

Viale scattered some more photos on the desk, all of the same scene.

'Being prudent,' Viale continued, pointing at the picture. 'Look at the date.'

It was printed on the bottom of the photo: 12 October 1990.

'This is before Kaspar even knew about the project. And there's Dan Deacon.'

Peroni couldn't believe they'd get away this lightly. 'That just means he was in on the deal. Doesn't mean he was running it.'

'Details, details,' Viale replied, dismissing the idea with a wave of his hand. He patted the file. 'Kaspar just needs something new to interest him and here it is. Some documents. Some photos. Something that points the finger straight at Deacon, too. While he's looking at that . . .'

He waited to make sure they all got the point.

'Joel?' Viale asked. 'Can't you see what I'm offering you?' He opened his arms, a gesture of generosity. 'These men you have here? They're good, aren't they?'

'They're good,' Leapman agreed.

'Then what more can you want?'

Peroni shook his head. It wasn't supposed to work out this way. He looked at Falcone, who was following the conversation, watching Viale, idly stroking his silver goatee, not an iota of expression on his face.

'Am I really hearing this?' Peroni demanded. 'Do you think we're just going to stand to one side while you people run up a little assassination squad under our noses?'

Viale pulled a puzzled face. 'What's the alternative? He can't go into a courtroom in Italy. That would be much too embarrassing all round. And I don't just mean for present company either. You don't think we're our own masters in all this, do you? We're just following orders too, from people who want results without having to bear the consequences. It's an invidious position. It always is. The people who were involved in this are still around too, mostly. You don't honestly think you'd be allowed to bring down a minister? Or an entire government?'

Falcone looked at Leapman. 'You can prosecute him. We could arrange extradition.'

'I wish,' the American replied.

'I thought he was a hero!' Peroni yelled. 'He's in this situation because you people screwed up!'

'True,' Leapman said with the merest expression of regret. 'But the operative word there is "was". Before he went really crazy I thought maybe we could just put him in a cabin in the woods someplace. Let him spend the day reading his books and taking potshots at the bears. But this latest killing . . . That woman was nothing to do with him or us. That changes the game for me. He's an animal. A liability. It's for the best.'

Falcone stood up and said, simply, 'No. This has gone far enough.'

'Sit down, Leo,' Viale sighed. 'Let's not be overhasty.'

'This is not—'

'*Sit down and hear me out*,' the SISDE man bellowed. 'Or I will, I swear, destroy every last vestige of your career this instant. And his too.'

Peroni leaned forward and gave him the scowl. 'It's rude to point,' he said.

Viale looked hard at him across the table then lowered his extended finger. Falcone returned to his seat. The SISDE man nodded in gratitude.

'You will both do what I say,' he ordered. 'This . . . creature will surely get in touch with us before long. We will deal with that as we should. Two of Leapman's men—'

'No, no, no!' Leapman objected. 'Not enough. You haven't been listening to what I said. You can't deal with Bill Kaspar as if he were some kind of street hood.'

Viale wouldn't budge. 'Two's all you get. This gets done discreetly or it doesn't get done at all. I've seen the heavy-handed way your people work, Leapman, and I'm not going down because they're trigger happy. Take it or leave it. I will deal with the logistics. Falcone will deal with the practical side of things. He can use this goon here. And the other one. Costa. Best keep this between the three of you, Leo. No point in taking chances. Kaspar has to be made to meet someone to take delivery. Once that's taken care of, then . . .'

Viale didn't say any more.

Peroni undid his jacket, pulled his gun from the holster, rolled it onto the table, then flung his police ID on top. 'I won't be a part of this. Not for you, not for anyone.'

'You already are a part of it,' Viale spat back at him. 'If you drag me or anyone else into a court, Peroni, I'll just tell them you knew all along. Same goes for you, Leo. Don't threaten me. Ever.'

'Now that,' Leo Falcone said thoughtfully, 'is an interesting exercise in inter-agency liaison.'

Viale's stony gaze was full of pure hatred. 'You stuck-up prick. You think you're so much better than the rest of us. Use your head, Leo. Did you never ask yourself why I took such a close interest in you in Al Pompiere the other night? You don't really think you're still in line for a job here, do you? You blew that years ago. I was just covering base. We met. We talked privately. We were seen.'

He nodded at Moretti. 'It all happened with his permission.'

The commissario stared at his fingertips and was silent.

'I seem to recall,' Viale continued, head cocked to one side as if he were remembering something real, 'we discussed the ramifications of this case in full then. Don't you? And I'd certainly have to mention that if I got asked in a courtroom.' He beamed at them. 'A man can't lie on oath after all.'

Falcone thought about this for what seemed to Gianni Peroni an eternity. Finally, he turned to Moretti. 'They'll throw you to the dogs when this is over. You know that, don't you? The moment it's convenient. They can't use you again, not after this. You're spent material. Tainted.'

'Don't worry about me,' the commissario muttered. 'Worry about yourself. And –' Peroni was smiling very hard at him – 'your ape.'

Peroni could feel the doubt and the tension rising inside the man next to him. Falcone had been through civil wars inside the Questura many a time and usually came off best. This was altogether different.

'Leo . . .' Peroni began to say.

Falcone put a hand on his arm and said, 'Not now.'

Filippo Viale smiled. Then he pushed Peroni's gun and card back over the table.

'You two can wait downstairs,' he said. 'Call when you hear something.'

*

Around midday the caretaker looked up, saw Nic Costa walking towards the booth inside the great bronze doors of the Pantheon and emitted a long, low howl of grief.

Costa stopped in front of him and took out his ID card.

The florid, cracked face pulled an expression of intense distaste. 'No. Why me? Why don't you bastards turn up on someone else's shift? I've been shot at. I've been beaten up and locked in a closet. Stay away. Please. I just do the menial stuff around here. I want a quiet life for a day or two.'

Nic Costa surveyed the vast, airy interior of the building. There were just five other people there. Four of them, two men, two women, were walking around the walls, idly staring up at the oculus, now letting a bright, blinding stream of white, winter sunlight into the shadowy hall. The men seemed too young to be Bill Kaspar. Leapman had officers on the street, though. It was possible they'd got wind of the situation and decided to get into position.

The fifth person, Emily Deacon, had, he presumed, done exactly as she was told. She'd pulled a light metal chair out of the congregation area and placed it on the circle that represented the epicentre of the building, the spot directly beneath the opening above. Now she sat there, hugging herself in the over-large parka, hunched over, allowing him the occasional glance.

'We need to empty the building,' Costa said.

'Oh! Really?' the caretaker snarled. 'What is it this time? Alien invasion? The plague?'

Costa was walking over towards Emily, the man

following in his footsteps, emitting a stream of sarcastic bile.

He stopped and turned to face the caretaker. 'It's a bomb scare.'

'Oh yeah?' The man was furious. 'Well, let me tell you, mister. We have procedures for bomb scares. I've done training. I know the rules. Someone calls me. Police cars turn up outside big time making a lot of noise. Not one scrawny little cop who hasn't got his ugly uncle in tow this time . . .' He remembered something of the night before. 'Not that I'm complaining on that front, you understand.'

Costa knelt down in front of Emily. She sat underneath the bright white eye, hands on her lap, calm, expectant, the focus of the building's powerful, living presence. He took her fingers in his and looked into her face.

'How are you?' he asked quietly.

'Ready.'

'Emily . . .'

She reached up, flicked open the collar, letting him see the mike. A reminder: somewhere close by Bill Kaspar was listening.

Besides, she knew what he was going to say. There could be other ways. They could try and sneak in a disposal expert. Or track down Kaspar before he had the chance to hit the trigger.

'I want to go through with this, Nic. I want to know.'

'Understood,' he said, stood up, reached forward, took her face in his hands, kissed her forehead, just for a moment.

The caretaker was standing beside them, tapping the

stone floor with his right foot. The sound echoed round and round the hemisphere, bouncing back from every angle of its curves.

'So?' the man said petulantly. 'Procedures? Where's the rest of you, huh?'

Costa ran his hand to Emily's neck, found the zip, pulled it gently down, carefully, carefully. She was taking short breaths, looking at him, not what he was revealing.

He'd got the zip halfway down when the attendant saw. Strapped to Emily Deacon's slight young chest was a military green vest loaded with bright yellow canisters, familiar shapes, joined to one another by a writhing loom of multi-coloured wires.

'It's a bomb,' Costa said again, hearing the man retreat in a flurry of hurried footsteps behind him. 'Several, actually. I'll clear the building myself. When it's empty, lock the doors, go to your office and await my instructions.'

The other four visitors were French, two couples. Not Joel Leapman's team, not unless they were unusually good at hiding who they were.

Nic Costa let them out of the building, took a good look around, and wondered where and how William F. Kaspar had hidden himself in the tangled warren of alleys that made up this ancient quarter of Rome. Then he took a second flimsy seat out of the seating area, placed it next to Emily Deacon and began a long, long phone conversation with Leo Falcone.

Back in the grey building off the Via Cavour Commissario Moretti squared the closure of the Pantheon on unspecified security grounds, then fled to the Questura pleading other appointments. Viale and Leapman went into a huddle on their own. No one seemed much surprised by the news Costa had imparted through Falcone. No one saw it as anything other than an opportunity to snatch Kaspar either. Peroni was genuinely appalled that the idea of Emily Deacon sitting with explosives strapped to her body, a deadline ticking over her head, one that expired in precisely ninety minutes, seemed peripheral somehow, an inconsequential fact in a larger, darker drama. Even to Leo Falcone, in a way. The game had moved on. It was now about closure and survival. A part of Peroni – not a part he liked – almost envied the way Moretti was able to duck out of the door, hide in his office and try to pretend this was just another ordinary day.

When Viale gave the order, they left the SISDE building in two cars. Falcone sat in the passenger seat of an unmarked police Fiat as Peroni drove through the slushy, empty streets. The others came in a plain grey van with a couple of small antennae sprouting from its roof, a vehicle that to Gianni Peroni screamed 'spook' to anyone with half a mind and a small measure of imagination.

Two of Leapman's henchmen – Viale stood by his decision – had materialized outside the building as they left, unbidden as far as Peroni could work out. They were anonymous-looking creatures, youngish, short hair, long dark winter coats, hands stuffed deep in their pockets.

Peroni thought about them as he drove. These men were trained in firearms and covert operations. It was what they did and, in spite of Viale's doubts, Peroni was in no doubt they were efficient at it. Whereas he was a cop, one who hated guns, hated the use of violence as a means of resolving an issue, saw it as the ultimate failure. As did Costa. And, Peroni hoped, Leo Falcone.

The dour inspector made another call, to Costa from what Peroni could make out. It wasn't easy. Falcone had spent most of the time listening, then asking brief, cryptic questions.

When Falcone was done, Peroni navigated a couple of patches of grubby snow still staining the Piazza Venezia and decided he couldn't keep quiet any longer. 'You mind if I ask you something, Leo?'

'Is there an answer I can give that will stop you?' Falcone replied.

'No. What are we doing here? I mean, even if that SISDE bastard does have us trussed up like a Christmas turkey, what's the point in making it all worse? If we're screwed, we're screwed. Why do it twice over? Why not make ourselves a few friends by throwing up our hands and letting someone else sort out this crapfest?'

Falcone rubbed his chin and stared at a couple of tourists wandering idly across the road, oblivious to the presence of traffic.

'Very good question,' he conceded after a while.

'Do I get a very good answer?'

'Maybe. Maybe not.'

The grey van was a couple of hundred metres in front, disappearing towards the main drag of Vittorio Emanuele and the side turning down to the Pantheon.

'They're right in one respect,' Falcone said quietly. 'Kaspar has to come off the street. You know that as well as I do.'

'Of course I know that!' It was as if Falcone was

trying to be exasperating. And succeeding too. 'It doesn't meant we just rub him out. I mean . . . what kind of a world are we living in? I don't want to act like I'm judge, jury and executioner. If I wanted that I'd move to South America or somewhere.'

'Pragmatism—'

'Bullshit!'

Falcone pointed to the grey van disappearing ahead of them. 'Keep up. So what do you suggest we do?'

'OK! Here's an idea. We go back to the Questura. We find some nice, powerful uniform one office above Moretti. There has to be someone there who will listen.'

'In the end,' Falcone agreed. 'But then we don't get Kaspar. Or they get him anyway and disappear off the face of the planet, leaving us to answer all the awkward questions. Plus, there's the small matter of Agent Deacon. Who's looking out for her now, do you think? Leapman?'

Peroni turned that one over in his head. Bombs were terrorism. Terrorism, inevitably, fell outside the Questura's remit. Everything got handed on, to SISDE and some specialist guys, probably in the Carabinieri. It all took time, resources, intelligence. Everything they didn't have.

Falcone observed, 'You've gone uncharacteristically quiet all of a sudden.'

'Oh for Christ's sake!' Peroni bellowed. 'Stop kicking me in the teeth every time I come up with a suggestion. There's no wonder you never stayed married. Always the fucking smartass, Leo. No one likes those.'

It was an uncalled-for outburst. Falcone now sat in the passenger seat giving him that glacial stare Peroni knew so well.

'Sorry, sorry, sorry. I apologize. I'm a little tense. What do you think we should do? Short of rolling over and let these bastards screw us any which way they feel like?'

Falcone let out a brief laugh. 'It's obvious, isn't it? Your own partner gets it. Judging by the conversation we just had he got it straight away.'

Peroni thought his head might explode. He took one hand off the steering wheel and waved a fist towards Falcone's face. 'Yeah. That's because you and Nic come out of the same mould, except neither of you recognizes it. The one marked "sneaky bastard, handle with care, will bite when you least expect it". Whereas *I*—'

'You're just an old vice cop who got busted down to the ranks for one transgression of a minor and personal nature.'

'Quite,' Peroni replied and wondered why there was such a wheedling tone in his voice. 'Enlighten me, Leo. My head hurts.'

Falcone glanced at him. Just for a second something in his expression bore a slight resemblance to sympathy. 'It's simple,' he said. 'People like Leapman and Viale. They just get their power from one thing.'

'Which is?'

'They play outside the rules. They think they're immune from them. They do that for a good reason too. The people they deal with – terrorists, others doing the same job – take the same view. They're all willing to do things most human beings, through matters of breeding and responsibility and taste, would find repugnant.'

Peroni thought about this, wondering if he understood

already the direction the conversation was going. ‘So . . . ?’

‘So if we want to win, Gianni, we have to do the same. Let’s face it. Given the squeeze they’ve got on us, what’s the alternative?’

‘I wish I hadn’t asked that,’ Peroni grumbled. ‘I wish I’d just stayed ignorant instead. Me and my big mouth.’

‘You and your big mouth. There’s just one problem.’

Peroni blinked. ‘Just the one? Are you sure?’

‘We don’t have the people. I’m in. You and Costa too.’

‘Wait—’

‘Shush, Gianni. Let’s not play games now. There isn’t time. I couldn’t call anyone else even if I wanted to. Moretti would know and then it really would be over.’

‘Yeah . . .’ Peroni found himself uttering a brief, mirthless guffaw. ‘And who’d be crazy enough to dump their career alongside ours anyway? Tell me that. Who?’

Falcone had leaned back in his seat now, eyes closed, calm and cool as they come.

‘Just a crazy person, I guess,’ he said and flicked a sideways glance in Gianni Peroni’s direction, one that, to Peroni’s astonishment made him feel more miserable than ever.

The taller of Joel Leapman’s spooks was called Friedricksen. He had the face of a blond-haired naive teenager and a mature, muscle-bound body that spoke of long painful workouts in the gym. Costa stood next to Peroni and Falcone and watched him step around the seated figure of Emily Deacon, poking at parts of her zipped-up parka with a pencil, bending down, sniffing, moving carefully on. Peroni wished they'd had one of the old guard from the city bomb-disposal squad there. They looked like professionals. This guy had all the conviction of someone who'd done the course and then moved on to aerobics.

Then Emily herself got sick of matters, muttered a low curse and pulled down the front of the jacket, exposing the two lines of yellow metallic shapes there and the nest of brightly coloured wires running between them.

'Holy fucking shit!' Friedricksen barked and leapt back a couple of feet in shock. 'Do you know what they are? Do you have any idea what this crazy bastard's messing with?'

Emily let out a long, bored sigh and stared at her boss. 'My, Joel, I am *so* disappointed you didn't introduce me to your goons. They fill one with such confidence.'

Leapman glowered at the man. 'You're supposed to know munitions, Friedricksen. Talk.'

'I do,' the spook complained.

'What is it?' Peroni asked. 'Dynamite or something?'

The young American pulled one of those sarcastic faces that always improved Peroni's mood. 'Yeah. Sure. The sort you get in the cartoons. Bang. Bang. This stuff's like nothing on earth. You wouldn't get it on a Palestinian. The wiring, maybe. Though that looks a hell of a lot more professional. More complicated too. It's these . . .'

Gingerly, he pointed to the metal canisters.

'Unbelievable,' he groaned, shaking his head all the time. '*I* couldn't get hold of them. No way, man.'

'So give us a clue,' Costa suggested.

'They're BLU-97s. Bomblets. You read all that stuff about unexploded munitions in Iraq and Afghanistan blowing up little kids who pick them up because they're bright, shiny and yellow? These are the babies. Jesus . . .'

He worked up the courage to get a little closer and take a more detailed look. 'They come with a parachute cap that lets them down slowly from the main container. Looks like the guy's taken them off and put in some kind of electronic detonator stub instead. What a lunatic. That thing's got PBXN-107 inside, which makes dynamite look like play putty. You got three hundred or so preformed fragments built into the case. They're made for piercing armour, not anti-personnel stuff.'

Friedricksen counted the bombs strapped to the khaki vest. Now Peroni thought about it, they looked remarkably like soft-drink cans. No wonder kids picked them up.

'Eight,' the American said. 'If he detonates them now, we're all ground beef. Probably enough force in the blast to bring down this creepy hole too.'

Filippo Viale, who had been staying a safe distance behind everyone throughout, came further to the front. He stared at the woman in the chair and asked, 'Disposal?'

'Yeah! Right!' The idiot actually laughed. 'Get some guy with an X-ray machine, a week to spare and a death wish and you might just stand an outside chance.'

Viale bent down in front of Emily Deacon, peering

into her face like a teacher staring at a recalcitrant child. 'What did he say to you, exactly?'

'Who the hell are you?' she asked.

Viale didn't even blink. 'Someone who might be able to save your life. What did he say?'

'Exactly? He said he was giving me precisely ninety minutes from midday. Then he'd push the button. He's got this mike thing . . .'

She flipped the collar and showed them the mike.

'He's got plenty of range,' Costa said. 'He could be listening to us from as far away as the Campo or the Corso. Somewhere –' he thought about what she'd told him – 'busy.'

'Why do you say that?' Falcone asked.

Emily took the question. 'He's got another one of these vests. I saw it. He's not fooling. He's wearing the damn thing himself. He said he planned to go somewhere there are lots of other people. Perhaps a department store. A café, I don't know. The idea is that if you're dumb enough to try to track him down he can take out dozens of people. He just presses a couple of buttons and I'm gone, so's he and anyone near either of us.'

Leapman emitted a short, dry laugh. 'Jesus. I said he was the best.'

'Comforting,' Costa observed, then he looked at his watch. 'We've got just over an hour to deal with this. So what are we supposed to do?'

Viale nodded at the mike on her collar. 'He's listening to this? Every word?'

'That,' Emily said with an icy sarcasm, 'is the whole point.'

Joel Leapman pushed in front of Viale and announced, 'Let me deal with him.'

The American leaned down gingerly over her, conscious of the bright yellow canisters on her chest, conscious too he wanted to make a statement. It seemed somewhat ridiculous. Kaspar had set the timeframe they had to work to. It was too tight to contain any room for manoeuvre. He knew precisely what he was doing.

'Listen to me, Kaspar,' Leapman said in a loud, clear voice. 'This shit has to come to an end. We've got some documents you can look at. We can prove you've got the people you wanted.'

Viale reached into his leather briefcase, pulled out the blue folder and waved it at Leapman as a reminder.

'We've got it with us right now,' Leapman continued. 'All you've got to do is come and collect. Then you can take off this jacket of yours, put your hands up and come catch a plane home, because I am *not* wasting any more time on you, man. Maybe we do owe you an apology. Maybe you'll get one and we can keep you sweet somewhere nice and private, in spite of everything. You've got to see these things we have for you here and put an end to all this. It doesn't leave any room for doubt. But you have to pick it up yourself. This is all deep, deep stuff and I am not letting it out of my sight, not for one moment.'

'Won't work,' Emily Deacon said quietly. 'What kind of idiot do you think he is? He won't walk straight in here just on a promise.'

'He has to!' Leapman insisted. 'I can't have a bunch of secret files going walkabout in a foreign city just because he says so.'

'Kaspar gave you his word!' Emily yelled. 'Give him some proof and this is all over!'

Leapman threw his arms up in the air and started yelling, so loudly his cold, metallic voice rang around the circular hall, rebounded from his shady corners. 'His word? His *word*? Fuck his word. The guy's a loon. A loose, out-of-control maniac. I don't give a damn . . .'

Costa walked over and grabbed him loosely by the collar, ordering him to be quiet.

Then Emily Deacon was screaming, writhing on the chair, not knowing whether to move or stay still. A noise was coming from her jacket, a noise that was making her stiffen with shock and anticipation. There were seven men in the hall at that moment. Leapman and his team scurried for their lives, disappearing into the shadows, Viale trying to keep up with them. Nic Costa looked at his two colleagues. Then he walked over to Emily Deacon, found the hidden pocket on the front. Something was vibrating beneath the fabric, making a wild, electronic noise, a butchered kind of music, a short refrain that rang a bell somewhere in his head.

'The Ride of the Valkyries'. All reduced to a series of beeps on a piece of silicon.

Costa ran down the zip and removed the phone.

'Jesus, Nic,' she whispered. 'I never knew that was there.'

He touched her blonde hair, just for a moment, and murmured, 'He's improvising. So should we.'

Then he looked at the handset, working out the buttons, hit the one for speakerphone and placed it on the chair Filippo Viale had so quickly vacated moments before.

'Mr Kaspar,' Costa said, 'it's now a little under

twenty minutes to one. By the timetable you set we have just forty minutes or so to resolve this matter. Best we make this a conference call, don't you think?'

Twenty-five minutes before, after briefly calling in at the morgue to pick up some props, Teresa Lupo had taken a taxi to the Via Veneto, then used her police ID to talk herself into the US embassy. She'd checked her notes. She remembered the officer who'd been sent round to clean up after the death in the Pantheon, the one who forgot to take the clothes. Dumb acts denoted dumb people in her book. So she looked up his name from her scribbles and told the security officer at the desk in reception she needed an urgent audience with Cy Morrison that very moment. The uniforms on the door had scarcely looked at the box she was carrying. A bunch of clothes in plastic evidence bags didn't seem to make much impact on their security scanners.

Morrison, a weary man in his mid-thirties, came out straight away. He looked overworked and more than a little grumpy. 'What can I do for you?'

She held out the box, placed it on the counter, and smiled. 'Your nice Agent Leapman needs these. He wants them in his office. Now.'

He really didn't look the brightest of buttons. Or the kind to argue too much. 'I tried to call him earlier,' he said. 'Agent Leapman's not here at the moment. I don't think Agent Deacon's in the office either. I'll make sure Leapman gets them.'

'You don't remember me, do you?'

'Should I?'

'The Pantheon. Two days ago. You came to pick up the body.'

He swore under his breath. 'Oh. *That.*'

'You forgot something.'

He was starting to rise to her attitude. 'Miss—'

She flashed the police ID at him. '*Doctor.*'

'*Doctor* Lupo. I will take these things and make sure they go to the proper place.'

'Yes, well you won't mind if I make sure.'

'What?'

She sighed, as if she were trying to keep her patience. 'You left them in the Pantheon, Morrison. I had Joel Leapman screaming down the phone at me this morning as if it were my fault or something.'

'What?' he asked again.

'You came to pick up the body, didn't you?'

'Yeah! Which we did. And it's not like normal or anything. Hell, I'm not running some damn funeral-home service here. We shouldn't be doing this kind of stuff anyway.'

She tapped her shoe on the shiny reception floor. 'You took the body. You left her stuff. You wouldn't be *fit* to run a funeral home. If it wasn't for me, these things could have been lost for good. Not that I'm getting any credit for it. Do you wonder Joel Leapman's going berserk over this?'

The woman behind the counter was starting to stare now. She had a little 'serve you right' smile on her face. Joel Leapman couldn't be that popular around here, Teresa thought. But maybe Cy Morrison wasn't either.

Morrison walked a little way away from the desk to get a touch of privacy. 'Listen,' he said in a low, furious voice; 'I'm not interested in what Joel Leapman thinks.

I don't work for him. I'm damned if I'm supposed to clean up whatever mess he leaves behind either. Just give me the things and it's done.'

'No,' she snapped. 'I'm not having him screaming at me because you fouled up again. I want to see them in there. If they turn up missing again he's going to go ballistic and I don't want that coming in my direction.'

'Dammit!' Morrison yelled. 'Since when did you get the right to give orders here?'

She took out Emily's security card and waved it in his face, keeping the photo side away from him, hoping, hoping. 'Since Joel Leapman told me to go see "that moron Morrison", gave me this and told me not to let go of this stuff until I saw it safely on his desk with my own eyes. Now, do you want to accompany me there? Or should I just find my own way? God knows,' she lied, 'I've seen enough of that place and that man these past few days.'

Cy Morrison peered at the security card. Someone like Joel Leapman wouldn't give these things out lightly, she guessed. It had to mean something. Still, Morrison ought to check the photo, and some inner reminder of that was just beginning to work its way into his consciousness.

'Plus,' she added, wondering if she was going to foul up here, and what trying to talk your way into a secure office in the US embassy meant for your career, 'he needs these *urgently*.'

Teresa Lupo dug deep into the bottom of the box and retrieved one of the bags she'd taken from the apartment the previous day.

'This was yesterday's woman,' she said. 'You heard

about that? Turns out she was American too. Maybe I'll be calling you to pick up *her* corpse before long.'

Morrison looked the squeamish sort. 'Oh no. Not again. He called me a "moron"? That bastard had the nerve to do that? After all I did for him?'

'Does that sound out of character to you?'

He didn't answer.

'She was decapitated,' Teresa said, getting his attention back on the bag. 'While wearing this nightdress.'

The scarlet garment lay in a large evidence bag, the bloodstains going black and stiff beneath the plastic. Morrison eyed the bag sideways. He looked a little queasy.

'Of course if you want to take responsibility yourself –' he didn't have that in mind at all – 'I'd just have to tell Leapman you'd done that, you understand. So if it went missing, if anything got tampered with, damaged, lost, altered in any way which meant it couldn't be used in a court of law . . .'

Scaring men was fun sometimes, she thought. A skill to be cultivated.

'You do know about rules of evidence, don't you?' she asked. 'You do understand what happens if this doesn't get handled in exactly the right way? If one thumbprint goes in the wrong place?'

'Frankly,' Morrison muttered briskly, 'I don't give a shit. If the guy gave you his card, go play in that pit of his. And find your own damn way out too.'

With that he stormed off, back in the opposite direction, away from the office she wanted, just round the corner and down the hall.

Teresa Lupo whistled a little tune as she walked there. Then she ran Emily Deacon's ID through the security slot, waited for the lock to retreat and walked in.

She'd been thinking this through all the way, phrasing the right message, tweaking the nuances. She'd had an uncle who took her hunting once, when she was a kid. Hated the entire experience. All except for the dog. The wonderful dog, who was as lovable as they came but could flush out a single pheasant in a field of corn just by scenting where the bird lived and emitting a single bark in its direction.

A minute. That was all it would take to type a simple email, swiped with Emily's ID card to authenticate it as genuine, mark the message as urgent as hell, hit send, and stand back to see what happened.

She hammered the keyboard with her fat, clumsy fingers.

'Now run, you bastard,' Teresa Lupo said to herself and hoped to God this made a difference. Those hard canisters she felt as she hugged Emily Deacon's scared, skinny body kept popping pictures into her head of what they could deliver on her cold, shining table if anything went wrong.

'That was a piece of cake,' Teresa Lupo whispered to herself. 'You should do this more often.'

The box lay on Leapman's desk now. Rightfully most of the contents belonged to him. But not the nightdress from the apartment. She had just brought that along as a last resort, for effect. And that was evidence of her own, something she could need for a crime that remained in the jurisdiction of the state police.

'Wasted on these people,' she sniffed. 'All of it.'

They'll know, too, she thought. When the dust settled, Leapman would be able to look at that odd box on his desk, retrace her steps, work out how this was done.

'What the hell?' Teresa Lupo murmured, then picked up the evidence packet with the blackened, stained silk shift, placed it in her bag, went out and called a cab for the centro storico.

'Look around you, gentlemen. Enjoy the view.'

Costa had placed the phone on the empty chair next to Emily. Now they crowded close to it, listening to Bill Kaspar's voice crackling out of the speaker, clear and determined.

'Can you imagine being in a place like that, watching your buddies going down one by one, clinging to a piece of webbing as if it could keep out the fire? All because some asshole you thought you could trust wants a cut of the action?'

'We get the point,' Leapman grumbled.

There was a pause. 'OK. I hear you. The man from the Agency. Or wherever. Right?'

Viale made a gesture to Leapman: *Pursue this.*

'Listen, Kaspar,' Leapman continued. 'It doesn't matter who I am. All I want to do is make sure you understand something. We know what happened. Washington's got no doubts. Not any more.'

'You think you know—' the tinny voice interrupted.

'You got screwed! Live with it! You're not the first. So you and your people went down there. In some place like this. It's tough. In war you get casualties.'

Kaspar waited before answering. It was a scary moment. 'We were "casualties"?'

'You and lots of others. Except they let it go. I don't know. I don't get . . .'

He was struggling. Viale sat down and stared at him, disappointed.

'You don't get the symmetry,' Kaspar said. 'Understandable. I guess you needed to be there.'

Leapman fought to get a grip on himself, glanced at Emily and said, 'Look, Dan Deacon fooled us all. You, me, Washington, everyone. We never even began to guess until a good way through all this. I'm sorry. Is that what you want to hear?'

The voice on the phone – hidden somewhere they could only guess at – sighed. 'Ignorance – such a poor excuse. Being smart's not about when or where you're born, you know. It's about who you are. That's history, man. The guy who built that place you're in – he was called Hadrian, a little history for you there. He could fight battles. Run empires. Think about life. Sit right where you are now and imagine a whole cosmos in his head.'

Leapman blinked hard, looked at Viale and made the 'crazy' sign with his right index finger.

'I slept above his mausoleum last night,' Kaspar continued. 'I thought I'd dream about him. I didn't. It was just the same damn shit I always get. Which doesn't make sense, since they're all supposed to be dead now. You follow?'

'So we're going through all this because of your dreams, Kaspar?' Leapman asked. 'Are you listening to yourself? That's how crazy people sound. That's what—'

The voice from the tinny speaker cranked up several decibels. 'Crazy! *CRAZY! This seem crazy to you?*'

There was a sudden, unexpected noise behind them. Something coming out of Emily Deacon's jacket and not a phone this time, a pop, like the report of a small gun, and she was screaming again, afraid to move, afraid to stay still. A bright spark, alive and fiery, was worming its way out of the uppermost yellow canister on the vest.

The men were scattering again. Costa took a good look at the jacket, walked over, tried to hold her still, wrapped a handkerchief around his fist and jabbed at the burning object. It came out, stinging his fingers. He threw it to the floor, where it fizzled ominously.

'Don't play games,' Costa barked at the phone. 'She didn't deserve that.'

'You don't know what you deserve!' Kaspar yelled back. 'You don't have a clue.'

Costa wasn't even listening. He was back with Emily, hand to her head, noting the tears in her eyes, the look of terror there.

'I'm sorry,' she gasped when she'd calmed down a little. 'I'm sorry.'

Kaspar's laugh rattled out of the phone. 'Good! Are you people learning something here? Improvisation's everything. A man needs tricks up his sleeve. What you got there was the demo. Just a detonator going into sand, folks. A little firecracker to keep you on your toes. Still leaves me with seven real ones, though. Plus the set I got here, somewhere you'd never guess, full of lots of people who surely wouldn't want to die without knowing what Christmas presents they've got. Ask your munitions moron to stick his nose round Little Em's vest there. This is real, people. Don't ever forget that.'

'This is real,' Emily Deacon murmured to no one, head down.

Viale, Leapman and the two Americans were slinking back to the centre of the hall now, looking somewhat ashamed.

Costa scowled at them, picked up the phone, turned off the speaker, and held the handset to his ear, ignoring Leapman's protests. 'My name's Nic Costa. Rome police. Tell me what you want, Kaspar, and I'll tell you if they can give it to you.'

A pause on the end of the line. A wry, amused laugh, and Costa knew somehow: he was dealing with someone very smart. 'Finally. Mr Costa. This call sounds different now. Are we talking privately, son?'

The voice in his ear had changed. The person behind it sounded closer. More human. And just a little apprehensive too.

'Yes,' Costa replied and listened, very carefully, as he watched Gianni Peroni restrain the furious Leapman from grabbing the phone.

'I like that. So you think you can convince them to let you out of that place with something?'

'Yes,' Costa said, and tried to sound convincing.

'Good. I'm impressed.'

'Meaning?'

That laugh again. 'Meaning we're halfway there already. 'Cos I got something for you.'

Then the line went dead. Nothing, not a single background noise, a half-heard word from a third party, gave Costa a clue about where Kaspar was really located.

Leapman was shaking with fury. Peroni let him go. The American pointed at Falcone and spat, 'That was not part of the deal.'

'You were losing it,' Falcone said coldly. 'If you'd

gone much further she'd be dead, and the rest of us too probably. Save your thanks for later.'

'You—'

'Shut up! *Shut up!*' Emily Deacon looked ready to break. She was hugging herself inside the deadly parka, gently rocking backwards and forwards, tears streaming down her cheeks.

'For God's sake,' she pleaded, 'either give him what he wants. or just get the hell out of here so he doesn't take the rest of you too.'

To Costa's amazement, that did, at least, give the FBI man pause for thought.

'What *does* he want?' Leapman demanded.

'Just what he asked for last night,' Costa explained quietly. 'Proof.'

'Great,' Leapman grunted. 'And in return?'

Costa phrased this very carefully. 'In return, he swears he'll give himself up. He'll take off the vests, disarm them both—'

'What?' Viale looked livid. 'We're supposed to take that on trust? I want him in my sight before he gets a damn thing. I'm not waiting on a promise.'

Costa caught Emily's eye. He wanted her to know there was still hope, still room to make things right. 'I guess he's thinking much the same way. He wants me to take him the evidence you've got. He'll check it out. If it's real. Then—'

'Where's the delivery?' Falcone asked.

'I don't know,' Costa lied. 'He said he'd phone along the way. And don't try to follow me. If he sees that, sees anything that suggests we're trying to trick him, it's all over.'

Costa watched them turn this over in their heads. He knew what defeat looked like.

'He's set this up so we don't have a lot of choices,' he went on. 'He's not stupid enough to walk in here to collect. I don't think we're in a position to get round him either. Do you?'

Leapman stared at the stone floor in despair. 'Jesus,' he moaned. 'The bastard's still running rings around us now.'

Costa risked a hopeful glance in Emily's direction. 'Let me do it. What's there to lose? He's adamant. If he gets the documents you promised, he comes back with me and he's all yours. He said he'd "surrender". That was the word he used.'

A military word, Costa thought. One that would strike a chord with a man like Joel Leapman.

'Do we have any other options?' Falcone wondered. 'Is any part of this negotiable?'

Costa shook his head. 'Absolutely not. I wouldn't even know how to phone him back. He blocked the number.'

'Bill Kaspar,' Leapman sighed. 'What a guy.' He looked Costa straight in the face. 'This place is a church or something, right?'

'Among other things.'

'Really.'

Leapman walked over to Viale, held out his hand, then, when the SISDE officer didn't move an inch, took the blue folder from under his arm.

'This is mine by rights,' Leapman said, handing him the thing. 'I read it on the way here. There's no one in there but Dan Deacon. If that doesn't convince him

Deacon was to blame then nothing will. You go act the errand boy. We can just stay here and pray.'

The sky was having second thoughts. It was still bright, but there was a hint of hazy ice seeping into the blue. More snow, Costa thought. Not for a few hours, but it was on the way, a final random throw of the dice for this extraordinary Christmas.

He walked out of the shadow of the Pantheon doors, waited as Peroni closed the vast bronze slab behind him, then strode down the steps into the piazza, close to where Mauro Sandri had fallen three nights before. So much in such a short space of time. This must have been what it was like for Kaspar in Iraq. Constant movement, constant threats. That experience informed the man now, made him what he was. Obsessed with detail and planning, tied to the symmetry of the complex web he'd spun around all of them, weaving his way through its intricacies with an extraordinary dexterity.

Teresa Lupo sat outside a café. She looked at him and tugged her thick coat around her, then sipped at a cup of something that steamed in the cold, dry air.

Costa stopped by her table and scanned the square. It was almost deserted.

'Did it work?' she asked.

'I believe it did,' he answered. 'And one day you're going to have to tell me how.'

'Just some predictable pleas and threats.' She sighed. 'I'm not really cut out for this.'

Just for a moment he smiled. 'You could have fooled me. Here.'

He threw the file on the table. 'Keep it safe.'

She looked at the folder, opened it, flicked through the sheaf of papers, each with the SISDE logo on top, each marked 'secret'.

'Oh my,' she said softly. 'Are we in deep now?'

'Keep the faith,' Costa said and walked on, to the far side of the square, and waited a good two minutes.

Then the phone rang and he heard Kaspar's now familiar voice.

'You got good people, Costa. I like this. So where are you going?'

'Piazza Sant' Ignazio,' Costa said.

'Good. I guess you really are who you say you are. But just to be safe I'll send you someplace else—'

'Time!' Costa yelled.

'Walk fast, brother. Via Metastasio. You know it?'

'Of course!'

'Just as well. Look for someone dressed just like Little Em there. Big winter parka, hood tight up to the face. I'm not taking any chances.'

'Sure.'

The line didn't go dead. 'You didn't ask.'

'Ask what?' Costa wondered.

'Whether I'd really stick to the deal.'

'What's the point?' Costa asked. 'You're going to do what you're going to do, aren't you?'

'Of course, Mr Costa,' Kaspar said, laughing.

It was just a sound on the cold, thin wind. But Nic Costa could have sworn that Kaspar had let his guard down at that moment. Some real snatch of his voice had carried into the square from nearby. If only . . .

He pushed the idea from his head. He wasn't up to taking on William F. Kaspar. None of them were.

'I'm sorry I interrupted you last night,' the voice

said. 'She's an interesting kid. Much more so than her dad, if you want to know.'

'If she dies, Kaspar . . .'

The man seemed offended. 'If she dies, I guess you've really fouled up. Now go.'

Nic Costa strode rapidly through the narrow back streets, hands thrust deep into his pockets, thrashing through the slush.

He looked at his watch. There were twenty minutes left now before the deadline ran out. Fifteen by the time he got back. Hopefully accompanied.

Trying to kick the doubts out of his head, to convince himself there really was no other way, Costa looked ahead.

He was there, just as promised. Wrapped tightly in a parka that was identical to Emily's, bulky underneath with the same kind of deadly gear.

Nic Costa walked up and said, 'Let's go.'

There wasn't an answer. He hadn't expected one. There wasn't even an expression Costa could read. The hood was pulled tightly over his head, so that all the world could see was a couple of bright, intense slits for eyes, so narrow it was hard to gauge whether there was any expression there at all.

The two of them set off down the street in silence, walked into the square and ascended the low steps in front of the Pantheon, where Costa called Leo Falcone and waited for the bronze gates to open.

Twenty metres away, shivering from the increasing cold, Teresa Lupo gulped down the last of her cappuccino, watched them go inside and pulled out a phone. She had to think about the number. It wasn't one an employee of the state police was used to dialling.

They took an age to answer.

'Typical,' Teresa whispered to herself.

Then a jaded male voice came on the line. 'Carabinieri.'

Even on the phone they sounded like pricks. 'I don't know if I'm calling the right number, Officer,' she said, trying to act as stupid as possible.

'What do you want?' the bored voice sighed.

'You see the problem is, I could be imagining this. But I swear I just saw a policeman – a state policeman – getting frogmarched into the Pantheon by some man with a gun in his hand. And the place is closed too. All shut up. When it should be open. That's not right, now is it?'

'You saw what?'

She couldn't believe she had to repeat herself. At least the idiot went quiet when she did, adding a very few details for verisimilitude along the way.

'The thing is,' she added, 'it *was* a police officer. I suppose I shouldn't be calling you really. I suppose I ought to call them.'

Some slow-burning spark of intelligence began to glow on the other end of the line.

'We'll deal with it,' the man said. 'The Pantheon?'

'Exactly.'

'And your name?'

She took a good look around her, pulled the phone away from her face, made a bunch of the most disgusting noises she could think of straight down into the mouthpiece.

'Sorry,' she shrieked, holding the thing away from her face, 'you're breaking up on me now . . .'

And hit the off button. They had ways of tracing you, even when you withheld your number. Besides, Teresa reasoned, she didn't need the phone any more. She just had to wait until those big bronze doors opened.

'Hate waiting,' she murmured, then dashed back into the café for another cappuccino before returning to her cold and solitary chair by the cheery stone dolphins.

It was Leapman by the doors, trying not to look triumphant. Costa came in behind the figure in the huge parka, watched him shuffle to the centre of the room, heard the huge door close behind them.

'Nice work,' the American murmured, patting Costa on the back then striding to catch up with the parka.

'You're welcome,' Costa said and stealthily slipped his hand into his pocket, retrieved the pistol, holding it low and hidden by his waist.

The figure came to a halt in front of the group in the centre of the building: Viale and the two Americans, now joined on either side by Falcone and Peroni.

'Bill Kaspar,' Leapman murmured, no mean measure of respect in his voice. 'What a man. You just walk right in here, bold as brass, like you promised. You read that stuff, huh? You happy now? I hope so, Kaspar. Because we've been waiting for this moment a long, long time.'

Leapman's hand came up to the parka hood, a big service revolver in it.

'So you just unwire yourself and the infant here. No tricks. Nothing. We've kept to our part of the deal.

Indulge us in a discussion and then we'll be taking you home.'

The only part of the man that was moving was his head, swaying from side to side, as if he were trying to shake something away.

'It's not as simple as that.'

Leapman blinked, lowered the gun for a moment, turned and glowered at Emily Deacon as if her words were some impudent intrusion into his day. 'What?'

'She said,' Costa muttered into his ear, letting the barrel of his own weapon slide with some deliberate menace onto Leapman's cheek, 'it's not as simple as that. I'm taking the weapon, Agent Leapman.' He glanced at the others. 'And the rest of you.'

'What the—?' Leapman yelled, letting the pistol fall into Costa's grip all the same. 'Jesus, Falcone—'

To the American's fury Falcone and Peroni were relieving his agents of their guns too, with a careful, professional attention that didn't brook any resistance.

Falcone pocketed Friedricksen's piece and watched Peroni do the same for his partner. 'You're making too much noise, Leapman,' Falcone replied. 'Stop yelling and start listening.'

Then he looked at Viale. 'You?'

The SISDE man was flushed with outrage, even under the grey afternoon light. His gloved hands waved at them in anger. 'This is insane. What on earth do you think you're doing?'

He pulled out his phone and started stabbing at the keys.

'Peroni!' Falcone ordered.

The big man was over in two strides, relieving Viale of the phone.

'Check him,' Falcone barked. 'He probably thinks he's too far up the damn ladder to carry a gun but I'd like to know.'

Viale held his arms loose at his side as Peroni gave him a none-too-delicate frisk. 'You three are really at the end of the road, you know. You can't fuck with people like me, Falcone. I'll crucify you, I swear.'

'Yeah, yeah, yeah,' Peroni grumbled. 'Clean,' he announced. 'I guess he expects others to do his dirty work for him. Sharp tongue, though. If I hear much more, I'll have to do something about that.'

'As good as dead!' Viale yelled. 'All of you!'

Peroni stood very close in front of him, looked down into the SISDE man's apoplectic face and said, very slowly, in that tone Costa recognized, the one that could silence the meanest street hood. 'Now be a good boy and shut the fuck up.'

'Later,' Viale spat and turned quiet. Peroni pushed him up to the silent, resentful Americans.

'So, Miss Deacon?' Falcone said. 'Where do we go from here?'

'Straight to the point.' She got up, faced the figure in the parka and pulled down the hood, exposing the shaking head, then ripped the fat slice of shiny metallic duct tape straight from the man's lower face.

Thornton Fielding screamed with pain, shot his fingers to his mouth, pulled them away, astonished, then stared at the small assembly of people in front of him as if he'd just woken up from a bad dream, only to find himself slap bang in the middle of another one.

'Is this some kind of a joke?' Fielding yelled. He was looking in horror at the vest strapped to his chest, with its yellow canisters and loom of wires. 'Are you serious, Leapman? What the hell is this? Get it off of me. Now.'

Nic Costa was watching the expression on Leapman's face all along, wondering. There was nothing there but shock and surprise. Leapman screwed up his eyes and turned to Falcone. 'What is *he* doing here?'

'Talking,' Costa said, intervening. 'If he wants to stay alive.'

Emily came up to close to Fielding, looked at his jacket, then at hers. 'These are BLU-97s bomblets, Thornton. Adapted for the task, specially for the two of us. I watched Kaspar do it this morning. A cap detonator in each. Wired to a remote only he controls. He knows what he's doing. Also –' she flipped the mike on her collar – 'he can hear everything we say.' She nodded at Leapman. 'If he doesn't like what they do, I get to be the martyr. If he doesn't like what he's hearing from you – bang, it's you. Or maybe both of us. Who knows?'

There was a cast of stark terror in the man's eyes. 'Sweet Jesus, what does that lunatic want from me?'

Emily stayed close to him, not letting Fielding escape her eyes. 'The same thing I want, Thornton. Some answers. About what happened here in Rome, back in 1990. You do remember that, don't you?'

He shook his grey head in astonishment. 'What? What are you talking about? Listen . . .'

He looked at Leapman, then at Falcone, appealing to them. 'This is the truth. I swear. One hour ago I'm at my desk in the embassy. I get some crazy email from Emily here saying she was in big trouble with you guys somehow and I *had* to go to some place near the Corso right then.'

Leapman scowled at him, then at Costa. 'She was here an hour ago. She couldn't possibly have sent that.'

'It was internal!' Fielding screamed. 'Came from her PC, goddammit! Made it sound like the world was falling in or something. Like it involved me too.'

'That's because it does, Thornton,' Emily said quietly.

'This is *ridiculous*,' he shouted.

Leapman walked up to Fielding, interested. 'What happened?'

'I get there and some hulking great lunatic in a uniform jumps me, drags me into an alley, puts this *stuff* on me, and says if I don't wait where he says until some guy comes to fetch me I'm dead. And sticks that stinking tape over my mouth too. And that's exactly where I stay until *he* –' Fielding pointed at Costa – 'turns up.'

Costa got a withering glance from Leapman and smiled wanly in return.

'So what the hell is going on here, Joel?' Fielding demanded. 'If this is one of those damn training exercises of yours—'

'It's no exercise,' Leapman responded. 'You were here? In Rome? In 1990?'

'Sure!' Fielding yelled. 'It's no great secret. It's no great secret why I'm *still* here either. I'm the resident queer, remember? I didn't get moved around back then because I was a security risk. I don't get moved around now because I'm part of the furniture. Big deal.'

'I didn't know that,' Leapman said quietly.

'*Get this crap off of me!*' Fielding yelled.

Costa walked up, took a good look at him. 'Can't do that. Kaspar put it on you. He's the only one who can take it off.'

Fielding's face screwed up in disbelief. 'You bastards sent me out to meet that lunatic?'

'Looks like it,' Leapman observed. 'So where the hell is he now, Mr Costa?'

'Search me,' Costa shrugged. 'I just took the phone call. Could be anywhere in the vicinity from what we understand. He said that, unless he got some answers, he'd start setting those things off in –' Costa looked at the watch again – 'a little under ten minutes. If you believe him, that is. What do you think, Mr Fielding? Do you think he's really capable of that?'

Fielding wasn't playing this game. 'I never met the man! Not till you tell me he just leapt out and put me in this crap.' He looked at Leapman and muttered, 'Joel – this isn't going to look good on anyone's record.'

Emily Deacon reached forward and touched some of the wires on Fielding's vest. He jumped back like a man who'd had a sudden shock.

'He'll do it, Thornton,' she insisted, 'unless you talk. Now's the time. We're good listeners.'

'About what?'

'About the Babylon Sisters. About who was behind—'

Fielding wasn't taking any of it. 'Jesus, Emily! I told you. I did everything I could. Didn't you read what was there? Didn't you get the message? Do I have to spell it out for you?'

'Yes,' she said quietly. 'You do.'

'Fine! All that crazy private army stuff was down to Kaspar and your old man. Dan was boss class. Kaspar was the soldier. Just a couple of old hippies with guns and a blank cheque from the security services or someone. You wonder it all got screwed up?'

'*No!*' She was adamant. 'You showed me what you wanted to, Thornton, and for a reason. It was nothing to do with me. It all was about protecting yourself.'

'This is insane. What the hell are you talking about?'

'You!' she yelled. 'You were pulling the strings then, you're still pulling them now. I couldn't work out why there was just one document left on the system when you let me in. Was that an accident? Of course not. It was the document that pointed to my dad, not you. That was why you put it there. For me to find.'

'Joel? We need your men in here.' Fielding wasn't budging. Costa thought of the minutes, ticking away, and wondered how long the unseen Kaspar would wait.

Emily Deacon stood directly beneath the oculus and allowed herself a glance through the eye above. 'It's about places, Thornton. That's what he's been trying to work out for himself all along. Places like this. He and my dad used to meet here, talk things through. He told me so. But my dad was discussing that mission with someone else too. Someone in the Piazza Mattei, someone Kaspar never did get to know.'

That scared him. Just a little. 'What of it?'

'That's what my dad said to Kaspar. Before he died. The one thing. That he wished he'd never gone to see the man in the Piazza Mattei. Kaspar thought he'd found that man, too. He went back there a couple of months ago. He'd worked out there was a property in the square the spooks had been using for years and years. He attacked the guy living there, trying to get some information out of him. He didn't kill him, though. This wasn't his man. He was just after intelligence and the man had none. Kaspar didn't kill just anyone. Not then.'

'So?'

'So he didn't get his information. But we did. We *know.*'

Fielding looked at her, astonished. 'You're taking the word of that lunatic? I'm here because of that?'

'Yes,' she said quietly. 'I am.'

Then she put a hand to the front of her own vest, took hold of the tangle of coloured wires.

Costa watched in horror. 'Emily—'

'I can show you why, Thornton,' she said, ripping at the wires on her chest, tearing them from the canisters in one rapid, bold movement.

Fielding cowered, half crouching down on the floor. Nothing happened. She just stood there, making the point. Then she threw off the parka, let if fall to the floor, and ripped down the zip on the vest, got rid of that too.

Friedricksen was fleeing for the shadows in an instant.

'Get back here!' Leapman yelled at the man, then picked up the vest to look at it. He pulled out the detonator from one of the canisters, upending the contents so they fell onto the floor in a steady stream. Cocking his head to one side, he took a closer look, scratched at the metal with his finger.

'Fake,' Leapman said.

'It's a Coke can,' Emily said. 'Painted yellow, reshaped with putty. Plus a little white spirit to give it the right smell and a detonator that's as a real as they come. Kaspar's broke. He didn't have enough for two sets.'

'Neat,' Leapman conceded. Then he pointed at Fielding's vest. 'And this?'

'Oh,' she said brightly, reaching down for the parka, taking something out of the pocket. 'That's the real thing. Absolutely.'

She grabbed Fielding by the scruff of his jacket. 'That can blow us all to pieces, Thornton. And you know something?'

Emily now held a small, plastic device up in her hand, thumb on a button. 'It's not Bill Kaspar who gets to make that choice. It's me. He trusted me with that. He trusted me with a dummy jacket. Who do you think I believe, Thornton?'

Costa was aware that Falcone was glaring at him. 'Emily,' he murmured, 'this wasn't part of the—'

'It is now,' she said, circling her man, holding the remote in front of his face. 'Talk to me, Thornton. Or don't. Because I really don't care either way. Not any more. You screwed my dad. He was a good man. You just sold him and his people down the river, let them get there, and hoped – what?'

He was nervous, Costa thought. Just not nervous enough.

'You've got to do something here, Leapman,' Fielding pleaded. 'This kid's as crazy as her old man was.'

'I guess,' she went on, ignoring his remark, 'you hoped that, once they got there, knew it was a case of give in or die, they'd all think the way you did. That this wasn't their war, not really. All they had to do was put up their hands, go quietly. That was part of the deal. And when it was over. What? Some quiet, secret negotiation with Baghdad. A handover at the Syrian border. Everyone comes home. You disappear and get rich. No awkward questions.'

She was jabbing a finger into the dark and Fielding knew that. He was growing more confident. She was starting to realize it too.

'But Bill Kaspar didn't go quietly, did he?'

'Sand?' he sneered. 'And Coke cans? That's what the big man's up to these days?'

'Proof,' she murmured. 'That's all anyone wants.'

Thornton Fielding's forehead glistened, shiny with sweat, shaking from side to side. 'No, Emily. What they want is an end to this shit. That lunatic put away where he belongs. He killed your dad. You're supposed to want that too.'

Emily Deacon's delicate fingers worked their way onto Fielding's vest, found the topmost canister in the middle row beneath his chin.

'Don't move, Thornton,' she ordered. 'I wouldn't want to choose the wrong one. The rest are wired in parallel and will blow if I tamper with them. Kaspar only showed me this once.'

He was rigid, uncertain whether this was a bluff or not. She flicked off a set of wires, delicately removed the canister from its webbing holster.

'He thought you might need convincing,' she said, then flipped the detonator, starting a small, livid spark at its head, and launched it into the darkness near the doors.

Fielding blinked at her. Leapman and Viale were already on the floor. Emily Deacon placed her arms around Fielding, held him tightly.

'Remember when you danced with me?' she asked. 'When I was just a kid? We'd go round and round, circles and circles, like a couple of human compasses describing pretty patterns on the floor. People like shapes, Thornton. They make you feel comfortable. They make you think the world's more than just a mess of chaos.'

A hot, fiery blast roared from somewhere close to the bronze slabs, began to occupy the interior of the building sending a deafening, screaming roar echoing around the hemisphere. From somewhere outside came the wailing sound of a siren. She clung to him tightly, keeping the two of them upright, struggling against the heat and force of the explosion.

'That's what Kaspar's been looking for,' she said, holding the remote to his cheek, finger on the button, the two of them describing a slow, lazy circle on the stone floor. 'Something that restores some order. And maybe it's not there at all. Maybe I should I press this and make us nothing. No memories. No guilt. No hate. Does that sound appealing to you?'

Fielding was silent, eyes screwed tight, fighting to control himself.

'He was my dad, Thornton. He thought you were his friend. I remember you in our house. Eating with us. I remember . . .'

This recollection had some force, it was obvious in her eyes. 'You hated that music of his. You used to bring round those big band tunes, dance tunes, little me, big you, all those years ago. And you killed him. Long before Kaspar got there. Somehow I knew he had died back then. I just never wanted to see it.'

He put his hands on her shoulders, stared into her face, shook her, hard. 'Dan took the money too, Emily! No one made him. No one made any of them, not on his team. If that fool Kaspar hadn't started shooting, they'd all have been in and out of there and no one the wiser. One team rich, smart and in on the deal. The other poor and heroes and still with their consciences. It's a dirty world. You're telling me you never noticed?'

Costa saw the sudden grief in her face. The way her finger tightened on the button.

'I don't believe you,' Emily Deacon insisted.

Fielding pushed her away. She didn't protest.

'Then why did he come back and say nothing?' he asked. 'Why didn't he come back and start asking some questions about what went wrong?'

'He didn't know!' she screeched.

Fielding broke, gripped her shoulders again, peered into her face with glistening eyes. 'You're too smart to believe that,' he said after a while. 'Aren't you?'

Emily said nothing. She just stood there, shaking her head, staring at him, furious.

'Think about it,' Fielding continued. 'He did nothing because he was on the payroll, Emily. Everyone on his team was. Before they even went in. Not that it was the money. In the beginning anyway. The others, yes. Not him. Not me.'

'Then what, Fielding?' she wondered. 'You're telling me this was all some moral decision too?'

Thornton Fielding looked, for a moment, as if he'd forgotten the deadly armament strapped to his body. He was mad with her, furious she didn't get it.

'You're so young,' he spat at her. 'You really have no idea.'

'Tell me.'

He closed his eyes for a moment, shook his head, clutched the deadly vest to him. 'Dan and I had been working together off and on for years. Since Nicaragua. We'd spent all that time throwing all manner of dirty shit at dirty situations. And you know what? It never cured a damn thing. We were just so *sick* of being part of that machine, deciding who was right, who was wrong. Sick of the fact that so many of yesterday's friends turned out to be tomorrow's bad guys. Your dad had this huge sense of duty, but duty has to be earned somehow by the people above you or you start to question it. His got used up in the end. We both felt that way. And that's the killer.'

He looked at Leapman, and there was disgust in his face. 'In that kind of situation either you become like him, some automaton who does what he's told and doesn't think twice. Or you become the enemy. There is no in between. We'd taken the money, but the truth is we'd have done it for free. We didn't want the war to spread. There were all these lunatics saying it had to go on, all the way to Baghdad. Mission creep, deliberate from the outset. As if we were a liberating colonial army, bringing peace and joy and freedom to the world. Babylon Sisters wasn't about Kuwait. It was about being there as a forward base once the hawks back home persuaded Bush to go all the way. You get me?'

She was listening, trying to take all this in.

'Emily,' he pleaded, 'you have to understand. Dan and I had agreed this in advance. No one need have got hurt. He'd arranged for us to get our guys taken, along with him. They'd all be freed, unharmed, later and no one would be the wiser. A straightforward deal. Except . . .' He sighed, hung his head, stared at the stone floor. 'We didn't bring Bill Kaspar in. Dan and I talked about it but, in the end we just didn't have the guts. We thought he and the rest of them would lie down once they saw what they were up against. We didn't think he'd feel the urge to make nine people dead heroes all of a sudden. So Dan and his crew had to watch a bloodbath, knowing they couldn't do a damn thing to stop what was going on. And then—'

He didn't want to continue.

'Then what?' Emily asked, livid.

'Then you find yourself facing painful choices. It wasn't his fault. Not mine. Not Kaspar's really. It was just a stupid idea that began as a good one. A couple of tired spooks dragging out some peacenik idealism we thought might stop the world from tilting even further out of balance. Stupid. Dumb as they come, and when those Iraqis came back to each and every one us after the war, kept calling, kept asking for more, threatening to expose us if we didn't go along with them, we found out exactly how dumb.'

She was shaking her head. 'He wouldn't—'

'He did!' Fielding cried. 'We all did. There wasn't any alternative. It was either go along with what they wanted or see every last one of us in jail or worse. Until Kaspar got out, of course. And you know the funny thing?'

There was a sudden look of bitter hatred on his face. 'By then it didn't matter. If Bill Kaspar hadn't come ahunting all of this would have slipped out of sight. Except,' he added sourly, 'when you got to waking up in the middle of the night sweating from the memories.'

There was activity beyond the big doors. Loud-hailers, brisk, bossy Carabinieri voices.

Fielding nodded at the button and took several steps back. 'So you want to press that, Little Em? If it makes you feel good, go ahead.'

'Oh, Thornton,' she said immediately. 'It will make me feel so very, very good.'

Emily Deacon hit the button and Thornton Fielding's vest lit up like a string of firecrackers. Costa was over to her in a flash, trying to drag her down to the cold, hard floor.

She fought him, watching Fielding all the time. 'Don't worry,' she murmured. 'Kaspar's broke. It's just Coke cans, sand and a few detonators. And a little fertilizer for the one I got to throw. You'd be amazed what I've learned over the last couple of hours.'

Thornton Fielding did a fiery little jig around the heart of the building then, when the detonators burned out, fell to the ground in a crumpled, sobbing heap.

Nic Costa looked into Emily's face and a part of him was convinced he knew what she saw at that moment. An image from a different time. A young girl dancing with her father's good friend, not knowing what darkness lay beyond the bright, white room in which every happy memory seemed to exist, and how difficult it was to see into the mind of another human being, even one you thought you knew and loved.

'Nic,' she said with a sudden, bright efficiency. 'Inspector Falcone. Gianni. Are you ready?'

There was an expression on Falcone's face Costa didn't recognize. Finally, he put a name to it: astonishment.

'Of course,' Falcone replied, then grimaced at the dejected figure of Thornton Fielding crawling underneath the grey eye of the oculus. 'I think,' he said to Leapman, 'that belongs to you.'

They followed her to the bronze slab doors, helped her pull the right one back on its ancient hinges. A flood of Carabinieri poured into the hall, asking questions, waving guns, playing out the Weaver stance, shrinking back somewhat as Falcone barked at them about this being a state police show.

'Come with me,' she said.

Costa and Peroni walked behind her over to the office. She took out a key, opened the door and let them in.

There was a well-built, craggy-faced man there, in a caretaker's uniform that was one size too small for him. He was leaning back in a chair, feet on the desk next to a mobile phone and a small radio, laid out in a precise line parallel with the edge of the surface. An old and dusty copy of Dante's *Inferno* lay in front of him, open at the page.

William F. Kaspar took out the radio earpiece, looked at the three of them, nodded to Emily and said, 'As I always say, improvisation is the key to everything, Agent Deacon. Nice job. I'm proud of you.'

He waved the book at them. 'Mind if I keep this? I found it in here and, to be honest, I don't think it's one of his.'

He pointed to a figure bundled into the corner, gagged, hands tied behind his back, wearing a grubby vest and underpants. Peroni recognized the florid-faced caretaker and stifled a laugh.

'Let me tell you,' Kaspar continued, 'this guy is a world-class moaner. Plus he has potty mouth beyond repair. Beats me how they let him look after a place like this at all.'

Falcone pushed open the door of the side entrance. There were no Carabinieri there. Only a fresh, light scattering of snow coming down through the growing darkness.

Costa waved a pair of handcuffs in the air. Emily Deacon forced her way in front of him and peered at Kaspar.

'How are things?' she asked.

He stared through the open interior door, back into the great circular hall, looking as if he were saying goodbye. Then he peered closely at the objects on the table. The book. The radio. The phone. All set in a line.

'Quiet,' Bill Kaspar said, and shuffled the items in front of him, making a random pattern, like three dominoes rattling aimlessly around a board. 'Quieter than they've been in a long time.'

NATALE

Teresa Lupo stood at the kitchen window, working her way through the mountain of dishes Peroni had left in his wake. He'd retreated now to the living room with Nic and Emily, clutching a bottle of grappa, and begun to talk in that low, concerned way she'd come to recognize. Leo Falcone was outside with Laila, working to put a little life back into the disintegrating snowman before better weather came along and melted it into the hard earth.

She had been astonished when Falcone accepted the invitation to Christmas lunch. She was a little surprised she'd gone along with the idea too, but the expression on Peroni's face when Nic Costa floated the idea meant there really was no other option. Peroni wanted to cook. He wanted to sit down at a table with other people. A kid, more than anything.

And Falcone . . . He was a lonely man. He had nothing else to do. So now it made sense for him to be wearing a heavy office coat, parading around the diminishing white figure, wondering where best to place an old, limp carrot. Laila, who'd been ferried to the farm from the social worker that morning and would be ferried back in the evening, watched with an equal amount of seriousness. The two of them were driving her crazy.

'Lighten up, for God's sake,' Teresa muttered. Falcone drove her crazy a lot. But never quite like this. She'd always known he was an intense, solitary man. She'd never realized this was as much a puzzle to him as it was to everyone else. Watching him walk slowly around the snowman, carrot in hand, looking as if he were about to enter into the most important decision he'd faced in his entire life, made Teresa Lupo feel uncomfortably sympathetic towards a man she didn't, in truth, much like.

Unable to contain herself any longer, she threw open the window and yelled at him, 'The face, Leo. Try putting it on the face.'

Falcone gazed back at her in despair, sighed, then nodded at Laila.

'The carrot's not the problem,' the girl said. 'The face is.'

Teresa looked at the blasted thing. The face was wrong.

'Well, just *do* something,' she snapped.

'But . . .' Falcone protested.

She slammed the window shut, not wanting to hear any more or see it either. There were people on this planet for whom time was a stranger. People who took no notice of the passing years, never stopped once to add them up and work out the sums: what was now possible, what would soon disappear from your grasp once that hand ticked past midnight on another New Year's Eve.

Peroni said he'd found the last turkey in town. She stared at its carcass, a bundle of fleshy bones that resembled a small, stripped dinosaur. God, they could eat. The girl in particular. Peroni's cousin outside Verona, who'd offered to take Laila in, just for a few months to see if it could work, was going to have to buy a new freezer. Even Nic Costa had tried a tiny taste of the turkey, which Peroni had cooked to perfection, slathered in oil and garlic and rosemary. That was something she'd never thought she would see.

She turned back to the window again. The girl was remaking the face, shifting the stark gaze of the creature's coal eyes straight at the house. Falcone was watching her, finger to his cheek, thinking. About more than a snowman too, she guessed. There'd been a storm hanging over all of them since the events in the Pantheon two days before. The media hadn't gone to town on the story beyond the plain details: that a killer had been apprehended by the state police. Then their interest seemed to wane. The papers and the TV people liked stories with beginnings, middles and ends. Bill Kaspar didn't really fit that profile, not without the blue file of SISDE documents, which Falcone had now taken into his care. And done what with? She half knew. She'd asked him out straight when they were alone together briefly and got that mute, secret stare in return. Falcone had presumably put them in a safe place known only to him, in case any of them needed insurance in the future. All the same, some kind of internal investigation was going on in the Questura at that very moment. Falcone knew a damn sight more about it than he'd let on over lunch. The same was probably happening round at the SISDE offices. And the Americans? She didn't have the heart to ask Emily Deacon whether she'd still got a job or not. It didn't seem right. She and Nic were, if not yet an item, sure to be one soon, Teresa thought. They had that glint in their eyes.

Great, she thought. Nic finally gets a girl and she lives in America, a different world, across a distant ocean. Probably jobless too, though with that beautiful blonde hair and a pretty, magnetic face that went from cool to angry to childlike in the space of a couple of seconds it wouldn't take long. God, she thought. Can't men pick them?

After all, Gianni Peroni had picked her and that made no sense at all.

'Who am I kidding?' she murmured, suddenly mad at herself. 'I'm the catch of a lifetime.'

She watched Laila place the carrot in the centre of the snowman's face, turn to Falcone and smile. Such an open, untainted smile, one she'd not managed to get out of the girl however hard she tried. One that, to her alarm, Falcone returned with just as much sudden, unbridled warmth. Then his phone went and the old Leo climbed back on board. An urgent desire for a glass of grappa rose in Teresa. She walked into the living room, saw Gianni Peroni there, now alone on the sofa, head back on a cushion, mouth open.

'Move over you big lunk,' she grumbled, then shuffled down beside him and poured herself a big glass of the clear stuff.

Those smart, piggy eyes opened and looked at her. 'Yes?'

'Yes what?'

'You look like you want to get something off your chest.'

'No I don't!'

He shrugged. She was going to have her say anyway and he knew it.

'I wish you were right, Gianni. I wish you could talk someone out of being ill. And Laila is ill, you know. All that stealing. It's just a part of something else. Being sick. Not quite able to work out what's real and what's not.'

'I know.'

He was being infuriating. It was deliberate.

'There isn't a pill. This cousin of yours. They're farmers or something? It's not enough. You can't just explain the situation and watch the child's eyes light up listening and then suddenly she goes, "Aahhh".'

He thought about it. 'This is true. But I think she's a country girl, really. You can see the city harms her. A move might help. Just a step in the right direction. Maybe. I don't know. It's Christmas. Can't we leave all the worrying to one side for a day?'

He was right. It was another of his infuriating habits. No one could cure Laila in a day. But getting her out of Rome, with its vicious round of traps waiting to ensnare even the most street-smart of kids, was surely a good idea.

'OK,' she conceded. 'But will you kindly disagree with me when I want an argument? I hate punching thin air.'

She wanted to pummel her fists on his big chest. She wanted to take him home, throw him in her bed, ignore all the precautions and see what happened when you stopped thinking about the future for once.

'No,' Gianni Peroni replied and kissed her a couple of times on each cheek.

'What's going to happen?' she said quietly.

'Why ask me?' he shrugged. 'I'm the last person to know about anything around here.'

To her amazement, Peroni hadn't sulked – not seriously – when he discovered what she, Nic and, to an extent, Falcone had cooked up between them to try to persuade Thornton Fielding to give himself away. He was, she now understood very clearly, as straight a cop as anyone could find in Rome. The idea of trusting someone like Kaspar – even for what seemed to be the best of reasons: that there simply was no choice – was one he found deeply uncomfortable.

'I said I was sorry, Gianni. There really wasn't time. Or an alternative.'

And also, she thought, you're just too damn honest to get away with deceptions like that.

'I know. I just felt awkward that you put your job on the line. Going into the embassy. Calling the Carabinieri, for God's sake. I mean . . . That's just downright rude!'

'Sorry,' she said meekly. 'Won't happen again, honest.' Then, more seriously, 'So what happens to us?'

The shadow of a grimace flickered on his face. 'Between Leo, Nic and me we seem to have pissed off plenty of people. Not for the first time either. You should be OK, though. Leapman's got bigger things to worry about. Besides, you're a civilian. You can keep me. That was a good meal, huh? Bet you didn't know I could cook too. I could have a meal waiting for you on the table when you come home. Be a house husband.'

That wasn't funny. 'Sure, sure! You can cook. Is there anything you can't do?'

'Still looking.' He hesitated. 'I'm not too good at being handsome. Or . . . *talking* from time to time.'

She put a hand to his cheek, just lightly, because it was still bruised from the beating Kaspar had given him, and there were black scabs hardening over the marks he'd been carrying for years.

'You'll do just fine,' she said. 'I meant what's going to happen about you and me, actually.'

'Ah,' he said softly. 'You mean will I walk away once this is over? Will I run back to my wife? Or decide it's just better being single after all?'

'That and a few other things.'

'As everyone seems to have been saying these past few days, it's a new world, girl. Who the hell knows what will happen tomorrow?'

'Who the hell wants to know any more?'

Peroni put his slab of a hand on the side of her face, tousled her hair with his fat fingers, then threw his arms around her and instigated a bone-breaking, bear-like hug.

'Season's greetings, Teresa,' he whispered. 'Let's go home soon, huh? Laila gets picked up in an hour or so anyway.'

'I've got that spare bedroom. If you like, she could . . .'

He smiled. 'You don't have to do that.'

No, she thought. It was unnecessary. But she wanted to ask. She felt the need to please him, still, and there hadn't been many men who'd prompted that urge in her.

'It's a deal,' she said, and watched Leo Falcone come in through the back door, Laila behind him, the tall bony inspector looking pleased as punch.

He stood there, smirking.

'Leo . . . ?' Peroni asked hesitantly.

*

The studio was a mess. Cobwebs hung down from the ceiling in thick, extended clumps. Canvases stood on easels, half-hidden by old sacking. There were suitcases on the floor, brimming with dust. Scarcely a soul had been in the room since his sister Giulia moved out to Milan almost five years before. The beauty of the place was obvious all the same. Floor-length French windows ran down the southern side of the house, allowing in so much light it could be dazzling in summer. For a painter, anyone who dealt in the visual, Costa thought, this would be the perfect home. Giulia even slept in it sometimes, falling asleep on the little couch, covered in spatters of colour, exhausted.

Emily Deacon worked her way around each canvas, peeking under the coverings.

'She's good.'

'I know. She's also dedicated, which means she's broke most of the time and chasing commissions from ad agencies in Milan the other half. The artist's life.'

'That was one reason I studied architecture. The good old Deacon breeding. Make sure you've got a career. Even if it's one we'll never let you pursue.'

That morning, when she had arrived at the house, he hadn't asked her about the meeting she'd had at the embassy the day before.

All she said was that she'd spent the whole of Christmas Eve in debriefing with a security team and had then been shunted into human resources. He knew what that meant. Disciplinary procedures. Or worse.

It was impossible to avoid the question forever.

'What are you going to do?' he asked.

Her bright eyes locked on his face. She was happy, unworried by any of this.

'You mean do I quit before they fire me?'

'If it comes to that.'

'It already has, Nic. I've handed in my resignation. I'm done. I don't even have to clear my desk. They'll send the stuff round to me. They hate me that much. Great, huh?'

'I'm sorry.'

'*Why?*' she laughed. 'I'm delighted. I may not know exactly who or what I am but I'm damn sure I know what I'm not. That job was for someone else. Besides . . .'

A hint of inward anger crossed her face.

'Think about it,' she said with a shrug. 'I just did what my dad did thirteen years ago. I got to the point where I wasn't prepared to take any more of their bull-shit and I broke. I threw out all the rules. I acted as if rules didn't matter. I knew better.'

'Emily . . .' He came close and grasped her shoulders lightly. She didn't move away. 'You did what was right. We all did.'

'I know that! But if I carry that badge I do what I'm supposed to. I don't make it all up to suit me. To match my own personal hang-ups. That's selfish, and they deserve someone better. Someone who's more profes-sional than me. More professional than Joel Leapman too. Even if I stayed I'd foul up again before long. It's just not me. I have a renegade gene, Nic. Got it handed down to me. Should have known as much all along. And so have you. And Gianni. Maybe even Falcone, I think. How you get away with that amazes me.'

There was something in what she said. Costa recog-nized it, feared it a little too.

'Nic,' she asked, 'would you really have tried to

arrest them all? If you hadn't managed to find out about Thornton Fielding? And Kaspar had just walked in there?'

'Would he have walked in?' Costa had been asking himself that a lot.

'If he'd got that folder instead of Thornton Fielding? I think so. He was tired. He was sick of being broke and on the street. He was scared too, of himself, and for a man like that I doubt there's anything scarier. The fact he couldn't control what he was doing any more. That was the last roll of the dice. All the same –' she glanced at him, a forthright expression on her face – 'the idea of you taking those guys on. You didn't have the numbers. They had the authority.'

'Authority's not the same as being right.'

'True,' she agreed. 'And being right's not the same as being the one who wins.'

Costa had avoided thinking about the alternative too much. The odds would have been stacked against them. Even so, Falcone had been adamant. Whatever the consequences, there would have been no way they would have allowed Leapman and Viale a free hand.

'So what happens to you guys?' she asked. 'Are they throwing the book in your direction yet?'

He shrugged. Costa had been there before. In worse circumstances sometimes. He could live with it.

'Maybe,' he said quietly. 'Emily, I wish I'd known. That it was all some kind of game. That you had Coke cans round your neck, not real bombs. You scared the life out of me, out of all of us.'

She waved a finger at him, an expression so Italian he had to remind himself she was a foreigner. 'Oh no. I'm not taking flak on that. I guess you don't do Gilbert and

Sullivan in Italy. "Corroborative detail intended to give artistic verisimilitude to an otherwise bald and unconvincing narrative." As long as you guys thought they were real bombs, your minds stayed focused. You didn't go near the detail trying to pick holes in it. This was a one-shot deal. I couldn't take any risks.'

'We were running errands for the man we were trying to take.' He didn't want to push it. He didn't want to leave it unsaid either. 'That was a little unusual.'

She wanted to clear the air too. 'You were running errands for me too, Nic. I sent you running round to the Piazza Mattei, remember? Kaspar was just going along with my hunch that you'd find something there he couldn't. Besides, do you think we could have won it on our own?'

He didn't have a ready answer there.

'I know,' she went on. 'You feel deceived. With some justification. I'm sorry. Only I'd do the same thing again. Convincing you everything was for real was the only way. All anyone had to do was look at your face and they knew they had to go along with you. Besides, it was real too. Just not in the way you all expected.'

He laughed a little. She looked relieved this wasn't going to turn into an inquisition.

'Also,' she added, 'Kaspar was going to use me one way or another. I had a choice. Be a reluctant hostage. Or go along with him, try to steer things a little and see where they led.'

'Legally . . .' He didn't want to push the point. They could have picked her up themselves if they wanted. Wasting police time. Running a bomb hoax. Falcone had ruled out the idea immediately. Another officer could have thought differently.

'I don't think anyone would dare throw the law at me,' she answered. 'Or at any of us. That would be too embarrassing all round, surely. I'm sorry, Nic. I imagine you thought you knew me. But how could you? We only met a few days ago.'

'True.'

She lifted the lid on a box folder that stood on a table, the only thing in the room that didn't seem covered in dust. It was new. Without asking, she lifted the lid and stared at the prints inside.

'What's this?' she asked. 'It's recent.'

He stood by her and flicked through the professional-sized black and white photographs.

'I picked them up in the office when I went in yesterday. There's a filing cabinet for photos in here somewhere. I wanted to keep them.'

'What are they?'

No one wanted Mauro Sandri's last few rolls of film. Not his parents, who didn't even want to see them, scared of the associations they had. Or forensic, who'd closed the case.

'This was the night it all began. The photographer we had with us. The one who died.'

'Oh.' She stopped on a single print. Costa hadn't had time to go through them all. This one surprised him.

'I don't remember him taking that one,' he said.

It was in the briefing room before they'd gone out that evening. Mauro must have snatched it from the door. Costa was there, showing some report, probably on the weather, to Gianni Peroni. Falcone stood in the background, observing them. The photo was remarkable. Somehow Sandri had captured such life, such expression in their faces: Costa's seriousness, the way it was received with a touch of jocularity by the grinning Peroni. And Leo Falcone peering at the pair of them, just the trace of a thin smile on his normally expressionless face.

'He must have been a good photographer,' Emily said. 'To take a candid shot like that and you never even knew.'

What was it Mauro said that night in the deserted café? If you asked, people would just say no in any case.

'It's about stealing moments,' Costa reflected.

'Sorry?'

'That's what Mauro said. About the kind of photography he did.'

She looked at the picture, thinking. 'Smart man. And you know what makes him extra smart?' Emily held the photo in front of him. 'He's just recording something there everyone else sees but you three. You're a gang, really, aren't you? A close one too, which is dangerous. If you were in the FBI and someone saw this they'd be breaking you up tomorrow. Can I keep this?'

He picked up the roll of negatives. 'I'll get you a copy.'

'OK. That's not to say there won't be the opportunity, by the way,' she added.

'The opportunity for what?'

'For us to get to know each other. I've made a decision. I'm going to go back to college. Get a master's. Here. There's a good school. Why not?'

He shook his head. 'To do what?'

'Finish learning how to draw buildings. Then learn how to create them. It's called being an architect. It's what I should have done all along.'

This was all so sudden. 'When?'

'As soon as I can get in,' she said with a shrug. 'There's nothing keeping me in the States, really. I need the change too. Now. I keep thinking about what happened. Not the details, the reasons. All those people breaking their backs over some stupid convictions. My dad and Thornton Fielding. Joel Leapman in his own way too. They all thought – no, they *knew* – they were doing the right thing. And look where it got us. I'm sick of certainties, for a while anyway. I want to get a few doubts back in my life. Besides . . .'

She paused, trying to make sure this was clear to herself too, he thought.

'My dad's dead and buried now,' she went on calmly. 'He wasn't before, and I just didn't want to face that fact. I'm not proud of what I found out about him. But he was still my dad. There was still a part of him that always loved me. I've got this relationship with him right now. I . . .'

Her voice did falter then.

'Last night, I cried and cried and cried. I lay in bed in that soulless little apartment and let it all out. Just me, a very wet pillow, a resignation letter and some memories. Everything ended then, Nic. All this fake existence I've been trying to lead on someone else's behalf. You know something?'

This puzzled her. The doubt, not something he was accustomed to seeing in her face, was obvious.

'In my head I kind of talked to him. I felt he understood. Your dad's gone. Tell me, is that crazy?'

Emily was always astonishing him. She just came straight to the point, never minced words. He'd grown up in this farmhouse. He'd watched his father turn from youth to middle age, to a sick, frail, prematurely elderly cripple. He knew what she was talking about.

'What did you say?'

'All the things you never got round to when he was alive. About how you never appreciated the good times as much as you should have. How the bad always seemed worse than they really were. And how the time came when you weren't a kid any more. You had to cut the cord, however painful that would be on both sides.'

Costa didn't know what to say. He didn't have conversations like this. Not with anyone.

'You didn't answer me, Nic.'

'Did you feel better? After?'

She grinned. 'Much. And the really crazy thing is it almost felt as if he did too.'

He put Mauro's photo back into the folder, the little photographer's words ringing in his ears.

'I know that feeling,' he said.

She leaned into him, face just inches from his, bright eyes glittering and curious.

'My,' she murmured, 'that *was* hard.'

'Where will you stay?' he asked, desperate to change the subject.

'That's the first on my list of doubts. I've no idea.'

Nic Costa was aware he was blushing and wondered how much it showed. 'This is not . . . something you need answer quickly. It's nothing more than a thought. No strings. Take it or leave it.'

'OK,' she said, listening.

'As you've noticed . . . I have this huge house. You can use the studio. Use one of the rooms if you like. No strings. It's up to you.'

She thought about it. 'No strings. That means rent.'

He waved a nervous hand. 'Of course. Rent. And there's no rush. Just think about it.'

'OK.'

'And . . .' He was stuttering. His cheeks felt as if they were on fire.

She screwed up her face, looked into his eyes and asked, 'Are you sure you're Italian?'

'Just . . . no strings. No need for a quick decision. Tell me whenever you feel like it.'

'Nic!' Her voice had gone up a decibel or two. It bounced around the dusty room, echoing from the corners. 'I have thought about it. I said OK. OK means yes. I would love to stay here for a while. Do a little dusting. See how everything works out. It would be a . . . pleasure.'

The blue eyes bore into him, amused, mischievous.

'Just one thing,' she added.

It took a little while to get the word out. 'Yes?'

She walked up to him, spread the fingers of her right hand across the base of his neck and reached round, gently stroking the nape, sending electric shivers up and down his spine.

'Can we please sleep together before I start paying rent? Because if it happened after I would find it very freaky indeed.'

'Purdah? Where the fu—'

Peroni's eye caught Laila, who was looking shocked at the suddenness of the outburst.

'Where the hell is purdah?' he demanded. 'It's in the north, isn't it? They're trying to get me to quit. They know I hate those miserable bastards up there.'

'Gianni . . .' Teresa Lupo stood opposite him, her arms folded, a look of tried patience on her face. 'It's not a place. It's a, a, a . . .'

'A figure of speech,' Emily Deacon interjected.

'Quite,' Teresa agreed.

Peroni waved a big, angry arm at Leo Falcone. 'So where's this figure of speech when it's at home? Will someone tell me that?'

Nic Costa didn't like the expression Falcone was wearing. It was sly. Amused. And he wasn't saying a damn thing.

'Just a minute,' Costa said, pointing a finger at the lean inspector. 'This is off duty. You've eaten my food. You've drunk my wine. Today, of all days, I have the right to call you Leo. Understood?'

Nothing but a frown on the long, intelligent face.

'So what's going on?' Costa asked.

Falcone took a deep breath. 'As I was attempting to explain before the volcano exploded, there is news. I have spoken with the Questura. And others.'

He fell silent, pointed to a bottle on the coffee table, smiled with approval, motioned for the others to pick up the glasses he'd brought in from the kitchen, filling them as they did.

'This is champagne,' Falcone announced. 'Not prosecco, thank God. I had it in the boot of the car. Just in case.'

'We don't want to talk about the wine, Leo,' Teresa Lupo growled, snatching a mouthful of liquid bubbles. 'Facts, if you please.'

'Facts,' Falcone agreed. 'The news is that Moretti will retire immediately. Filippo Viale the same. There will be no criminal prosecutions, no further investigations. The matter will drop, which is for the best. Kaspar will be tried in Italy, naturally, and plead guilty, which should diminish the publicity somewhat. And . . .'

He eyed Costa and Peroni in turn. 'We three are going into purdah.'

'Will you stop saying that?' Peroni roared. 'For how long?'

'A little while.'

Costa knew these games. 'Is that a short little while or a long little while?'

Falcone considered this. 'Probably nearer to long. We have to let things blow over a bit.'

'*Shit!*' Peroni had his eyes screwed shut and was chanting a little refrain that ran, 'Please don't make it in the north, please don't make it in the north, please . . .'

Falcone listened, cool and detached, in silence.

'*Where*, Leo?' the big man bellowed, unable to contain himself any more.

'Venice,' Falcone said with no emotion whatsoever.

Nic Costa blinked. Emily had slipped her arm through his. She was coming to Rome. She was going to live under his roof. And he'd be on the other side of Italy, watching the grey lagoon ebb and flow, alone.

'I love Venice,' Emily said, and squeezed his arm. 'It's not so far.'

Teresa Lupo asked, 'Am I going?'

'No,' Falcone replied, shocked at the idea. 'This is a police matter. What's it to do with you?'

'Oh, nothing. Venice?' She was trying to remember something. 'I've only been there once. Since school anyway. Got drunk after a rugby match in Padua. I don't recall a lot to be honest. But . . .'

She looked at Laila. The poor kid didn't know what was going on.

'It's not far from Verona, Gianni. You can visit Laila as much as you want. I could come over too from time to time. If you like.'

She tousled the girl's hair. Laila smiled back at her. A real smile. Teresa Lupo stifled an urge to hug her.

'I hate Venice,' Peroni moaned. 'It's cold and damp and horrible. The food stinks. The people are cheating, miserable good-for-nothings . . .'

Falcone looked at his watch. 'We start Monday week. It would be best to avoid the Questura in the meantime. Take a vacation. Enjoy yourselves.'

He was different somehow. Costa worked out what it was. For once, Leo Falcone seemed genuinely content, free of all those invisible burdens he was used to carrying around on his stiff shoulders. He was looking forward to the change. He needed it. Perhaps they all did.

'We did the right thing,' Falcone declared. He smiled at Emily, curious, as always. 'Particularly you. If Nic hadn't gone to the Piazza Mattei . . .'

'I was guessing, Leo,' she answered. 'Really. It was just a stab in the dark.'

Falcone looked dubious. '*Really*?'

She sighed. 'It's such a long time ago. Maybe it was just my memory playing tricks. I remember . . . sitting on that fountain, underneath the tortoises, finishing an ice cream. It was summer. Very hot. And my dad had left me there to go and do some business in one of the houses. This happened more than once, I think. I never did see who he was visiting, but I understood something. It was someone he knew. Not a stranger.'

Emily glanced at Laila, who was bored by this conversation, engrossed instead in a teenage magazine Peroni had brought her.

'I remembered the name of the place. Because of the tortoises. I remembered being so happy I thought that world would never disappear.' Then, a little ruefully, 'I was a child.'

Falcone nodded, acknowledging her point. 'What you did was very brave. You risked everything.'

He looked at each of them.

'All of you. I'm grateful.'

'Don't hug me,' Peroni growled. 'Don't even think of it. Venice. *Venice?* What is happening to my life?'

'We're taking a little detour,' Falcone said. 'Let's try to enjoy the ride. And now . . .'

He downed the champagne and looked at his watch.

'I must be going. Ciao!'

Falcone moved so quickly. He had his coat back on and was about to leave before any of them could object, stopping only at the threshold as a final thought struck him.

'Oh,' he said, 'one more thing.'

Peroni and Costa watched him with a mute foreboding.

'Uniforms,' Falcone said. 'You will be needing them. Best get measured after the holiday. When you've lost some weight.'

Then Leo Falcone was through the door, with what, in another, might pass for a skip, leaving the growing storm behind him.

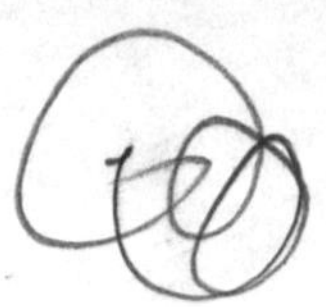